81/- o

T   friends and
hard workers
Enjoy & God bless

Pete O.

Grey Wolves Howling

A Novel of Chechnya

by
Peter O'Neill

Robert D. Reed Publishers
San Francisco

Robert D. Reed Publishers
750 LaPlaya, Suite 647
San Francisco, CA 94121
Phone: 650-994-6570 • Fax: -6579
E-mail: 4bobreed@msn.com
http://www.rdrpublishers.com

Typesetter: **Barbara Kruger**
Editor: **Barbara Kruger**
Cover design: **Irene Taylor, it grafx**

ISBN 1-885003-58-7

Library of Congress Catalog Card Number 00-102831

Manufactured, typeset and printed in the United States of America

European Russia

Autonomous Regions of Chechnya and Ingushetia

"We Should Not Forget!
We Should Not Forgive!"

Memorial to the victims
of the Russian Repression
Groznyy, Chechnya

Garyk

1

Garyk Ivramovich Gadayev sat amid a pile of debris. His back was propped up against the tumbled remains of a wall. This was all that was left of the stone cottage that had served as a home for the Gadayev family for more than seven generations. It was fitting that the home was in ruins, for Gadayev's life was also completely unraveled and lay in ruin as well. A heavy five-day growth of dark whiskers was beginning to cover his square jawline. He was a big man, a few inches over six feet tall, broad at the shoulders, but still not too broad in the middle. In fact, he was relatively fit for a man recently turned forty, all things considered.

As a child he ran freely about the low mountains which rose before him. The rocks and trees formed a magical kingdom in which he and his twin brother Viktor reigned with unbounded merriment. The goats and sheep were their subjects. Birds sang for their entertainment alone. And, of course, there were the wolves. They moved silently through the mountains by day, seemingly oblivious to the human events taking place around them. Years ago, Garyk's father told them that the grey wolf was the guardian of this land, never to be harmed intentionally, unless one's very life depended upon it. "They watch us from the mountains and tell the Almighty One about us. That is what we hear at night, my sons, when their howling is caught by the wind."

Life had been good then. Simple, yes; hard, yes, but it had been good. The cottage lay in a small valley where the family had been farmers for more than three centuries. It was an angular valley, with the mountains rising sharply on either side. Verdant and filled with rocky crags and outcrops which formed a patchwork of colors and contours. Over the years a few small fields had been cleared away, the rocks used to build several cottages and the tower that rose majestically from the side of the hill. Those other structures had been destroyed years earlier during the Great Repression. Many of the fields had been reclaimed by nature and served primarily as a pasture for a small herd of goats. Potatoes, carrots and cabbage were their cash crops, although it seemed that rocks were always the most plentiful harvest.

Their valley was not really noted for its agricultural bounty, lying, as it did, in transition between the more fertile Sunzha Valley to the north and the Caucasus Mountains to the South. Its relatively poor fertility had actually been a boon to the Gadayev clan over the centuries, as the periodic swarm of invading Mongols, Georgians and Russians tended to overlook the familial territory. The family was never really political, but they were proud Nokhchii, as the natives of Chechnya called themselves, and over the years, much Gadayev blood had fertilized this soil. In 1937, the Soviets had forced most of the family out of this valley and onto the collectives to the North. The homes of several of Garyk's great-uncles had been burned down at that time to keep the families from returning.

In the fifties, things changed. Petroleum and natural gas were found in abundance throughout these hills. The Gadayev family was allowed to return to work the oil fields. Garyk and Viktor were tested early in their schooling and both were found to have an aptitude for things mechanical. They were sent to technical school in Groznyy, some thirty kilometers from home, returning only for weekends and holidays.

While Viktor had a natural talent for taking things apart and putting them back together in perhaps not the same, but usually better fashion, Garyk was more into numbers. He loved math and took to physics like the veritable duck to water. Viktor returned to the oil fields as a mechanic's apprentice third class. Garyk was enrolled in the Chechen-Ingush State University in 1973. Computers were just starting to make an impact in this part of the Soviet Union. Garyk soon knew more than his instructors. His grasp of all things electronic led to his being noticed by those persons whose job it was to take note of such things in the Soviet Union.

Colonel Vladamir Illianovich Pushkin appeared one afternoon and Garyk was summoned to the First Prorektor's office to discuss what role young Garyk might play in service to the motherland. The Colonel was tall and trim, features accentuated by the neatly tailored cut of his uniform. The red stripe that ran down the outside of his trousers disappeared sharply beneath the top of his gleaming black knee-high boots. On his chest was a sea of campaign ribbons, testament to his many years of distinguished service. He kept his hair short, not quite a crew cut, but still acceptable by military standards and wore thin wire-framed glasses. He stood in the center of the

Prorektor's office, his hand extended in greeting to the young man as he entered the room.

Garyk had only been in this office once before, since it was rare for a student to be summoned to meet with the head of the university. It was an erudite room, lined on three sides with floor to ceiling bookshelves, neatly stacked with the tomes of education. Two functional leather armchairs faced away from the door and toward a large mahogany desk with several piles of papers neatly arranged upon it. An oversized leather chair was framed by two windows that looked out on the common area. The walls on either side of the windows displayed a host of diplomas, certifications and awards.

Garyk thought it strange that the Prorektor was not present. Instead, a third man sat on a metal folding chair in the corner of the room as a silent observer. He had on a brown tweed jacket and a pair of dark gray corduroy pants that had seen better days. His hair was brushed back over the top of his head and fell almost to collar length. Anyone growing up in the Soviet Union realized the significance of his presence; he represented the omnipresent Committee for State Security (KGB).

The Colonel began speaking as soon as the door had been closed behind Garyk. "Comrade Gadayev, how good to meet you. I hear many good things are spoken about you here at the University."

"Comrade Colonel," Garyk replied, giving an instinctive nod of the head. He was not sure why he had been called away from his communications lecture, and was on guard now, facing this unknown military figure. One thing was certain, he sensed that this meeting was going to have a significant impact on the course of his life.

"Yes, my young Gadayev, many very good things. It seems that you are quite the expert when it comes to this new computer technology, is that not so?"

Garyk couldn't help but smile, even under these circumstances. He took great pride in his ability to program computers. "I enjoy working with computers; yes, that is true, Comrade Colonel."

"Ah, this is good! The computer is the future of modern Russia. Don't you agree?"

"Very much so, yes, I do."

The man in the corner had not stirred throughout this opening repartee. Unlike the Colonel, whose white hair lent an air of distinction, this fellow's mottled gray-black hair just made him look old, older even than his fifty-some-odd years. He looked through Garyk, rather than at him, as if there was no one else in the room. It made the young man ill at ease, but he wasn't sure just why.

"Let me introduce myself," the Colonel continued. He clasped his hands behind his back as he spoke. "I am Colonel Pushkin. I have been put in charge, you might say, directed by the highest possible leaders, to see to it that we are prepared to meet that future. Do you understand?" Garyk said nothing and the Colonel went on, "The Soviet Army has need of technically skilled engineers, especially ones well versed in computer programming, electronics and nuclear physics. Our scientists, unfortunately so it seems, have fallen behind the Americans. We are, shall I say, at a temporary disadvantage. Quite frankly, Comrade Gadayev, the Soviet Army needs young men just like you."

Garyk felt the bottom of his stomach drop away. He was momentarily unable to breathe. Yes, he had thought about the possibility that a military career might provide him with an opportunity to pursue his love of techtronics, but not right away. Not RIGHT NOW! However, in 1976, one did not refuse such an offer. Offer, no, make that order.

Garyk reached out to grab the back of one of the armchairs, which was positioned just in front of him. Steadied, he found the ability to speak. "Comrade Colonel, it is," he paused briefly, trying to find the word, "an *honor,* yes, quite an honor for you to think of me in this way. Actually, I never really thought that I would make such a good soldier."

"Ah, not a soldier, young Gadayev. No, not a soldier, but an officer." The Colonel extended both his arms in a gesture of affirmation. He would have reminded Garyk of one of his professors responding to a foolish answer, had it not been for the uniform he was wearing. "Comrade Garyk Ivramovich, we wish to make you an officer in the Soviet Army."

The man in the corner still did not move. Garyk could feel his eyes penetrating him as he studied his reaction to this proposal very carefully.

"I am even more honored, Comrade Colonel, but I still have considerable time left here at the University. Perhaps when I have completed..."

"Nonsense," Pushkin waved him off with a quick stroke of the hand. "You have learned all that this small institution is capable of teaching you. Why, I hear that even now it is you who are teaching them, is that not so?"

"There are many fine instructors here." Garyk said this rather flatly. Yes, he had hoped to move on to a larger university, but not in the Army. How far from home would they send him? Would he ever come back?

"That may be, but still, there is little more for you to learn here, my son." Colonel Pushkin moved behind the desk which the Prorektor had been urged to give up for this conference. He sat down, and motioned for Garyk to assume his place in the chair, which was still giving him moral support. "No, no, there is no benefit, either to you or our great mother country, for you to continue on here. We have already made certain arrangements, if you are willing to accept, of course, for you to move on to the Moscow University. They have, I am sure you already know, the most advanced computers in all of Russia. That is, outside of the Army, of course." An expansive grin broke across Pushkin's face for the first time, exposing a row of teeth slightly yellowed by age.

"When do you expect me to start? The semester must already be well under way there, too."

"That is true," answered the Colonel, "but of course we still must make you an officer, is that not so?" He shrugged in a friendly manner to soften what was clearly a monumental statement.

"Yes, Comrade Colonel, I suppose that is so. When did you want me to join you?"

The Colonel rose. "Why, you already have my young Gadayev, you already have! You will leave tonight for officer training at a camp just outside of Novgorod. My friend here, Comrade Lemchenko, will assist you in getting those things together that you might need. All else will be provided for you. The rest of your belongings can be forwarded to you once you are settled in Moscow."

And that had been it. Colonel Pushkin moved back around the desk, shook his hand, retrieved his great coat and fur cap from the back of the other chair, and left the room. No answer was really expected. The Soviet Union had need of his special talents and it knew best how, when and where to deploy them.

Lemchenko walked with him down Klara Zetkin Street to his apartment. Garyk had walked this route many times before. There was a row of small shops situated in buildings built during the time of the tsars. They passed a small café where he and his friends spent many an evening in idle chatter, and then crossed over to a row of modern four story apartment buildings whose austere concrete façades stood in marked contrast to the quaint row of shops.

No words were spoken between Garyk and this strange fellow Lemchenko. Garyk knew that he was there not so much to assist as to insure. The apartment was on the third floor, just one room but with a private bath. His bed and a small sofa that could open out to serve as a second bed were the primary furnishings, along with a desk that contained a typewriter and a makeshift computer he was assembling himself. Books, papers and clothing were scattered all over.

He had chosen to live alone. Not only did that afford him more time to work on his computer, but it also accommodated Viktor's periodic visits. Once in the room, Garyk began to pack a few personal items. Lemchenko nodded occasionally; signaling an affirmative or rejecting certain items as the young man assembled his belongings on the bed. At one point Garyk threw his hands up in despair. "Just what am I supposed to wear?" he shouted, after the man had given another negative response to a pair of Americanized jeans and sweater.

"You will be given all of the new clothes you are going to need in Novgorod," he finally spoke, "Military clothes. I will have someone come in tomorrow and box up all the rest of this." Lemchenko swept his hand in a gesture across the room. "We will hold it for you. Don't worry, it won't be lost. You better take that overcoat there, it will be much colder where you are going."

2

The trip to Novgorod seemed interminable and yet it was filled with wonder and amazement. The young man had spent his entire life in the confines of the Caucasus. Groznyy was the center of the known universe. The world began to unfold before his eyes. To be sure, he had seen these things before, in films and on the television. But now they were real, unconfined by screen or tube. They traveled by train, from Groznyy to Astrakhan where the Volga River flows into the Caspian Sea. There they transferred to the main line that followed the river up to Volgograd and then through the Don Valley up to Moscow. The final leg would bring him all the way north to Leningrad.

Lemchenko saw to it that they arrived at the Groznyy terminal within fifteen minutes of their scheduled departure. At first, they traveled in a coach. Lemchenko arranged for seating in the reserved car. First class, of course, was not an official Soviet designation, being out of step with the "people's revolution." There were, however, cars reserved for ranking members of the government, their families and associates. Heroes of the State who served their mother country well. Once it became available, they transferred to a car with private compartments and traveled together in this fashion for several days.

As a traveling companion, Lemchenko was, to say the least, stoic. He could go for hours without uttering a sound. He purchased the Moscow paper at the Groznyy station just before boarding and buried himself in it even before the train began to move. Garyk's occasional questions or remarks were either answered with a grunt or simply ignored. So it was with a bit of a start that Garyk was roused from gazing out the window into the darkness by Lemchenko's first full sentence in nearly two hours. "So, my young friend, it seems that you have quite a future ahead of you now." He had apparently completed the entire paper and placed it, neatly folded, on the empty seat across the aisle.

"I think that you know much more about that than I do," the young man replied.

"Perhaps, but not much more. I, too, am a servant of the state. I know only that you have been selected to be part of a new program, which will train officers for a more modern Soviet Army. I am merely to escort you to the training camp."

"Escort," Garyk said with an air of skepticism. "Am I your prisoner?"

"Ah, my young Gadayev, so much distrust. It was the same when Comrade Colonel Pushkin told you of your selection. So much distrust." Lemchenko was actually smiling; the first sign of any human compassion Garyk had detected in this man since he first entered the Prorektor's office earlier that afternoon.

"And how should I react, then?" Garyk turned his head to face the man seated next to him for the first time during this encounter. "This morning I was in class with my friends. Now I've been swept away. Could I have really told the Colonel, 'No, thank you, sir, I prefer to stay here?' No, I have been grabbed out of my life. No one knows where I am or why I have gone."

"Comrade Gadayev, let me tell you this." Lemchenko's voice grew somewhat sterner and he turned in the coach seat to face his ward squarely. "For many years I have watched young men who have been chosen for certain duties to the Motherland. My job, you might say, is to evaluate them; to insure that there have been no mistakes made. Do you see? Many young men, with futures far less promising than yours, have been much more receptive to their call to service. Is it not an honor to serve Mother Russia?"

"I am not a Russian. I am Chechen. My people have been murdered and others have been sent off to who knows where by Russians. She is no mother to me."

"I would advise you not to speak so rashly." Lemchenko's voice dropped to a whisper, even though the seats around them were all empty and most of those in the car had already nodded off to sleep. "The Soviet Union knows of no ethnic distinctions. Today, you are a Russian. Soon you will be an officer in the Soviet Army. That is where your allegiance must lie, Comrade Gadayev, please be certain of that. Absolutely certain."

Garyk made no reply. Lemchenko picked a piece of thread off the sleeve of his jacket and continued. "Please understand what lies ahead for you. They will give you the most advanced education available. You will become an expert in these new technologies. You will be asked to use that expertise to insure the very survival of the Soviet Union in a modern age that goes well beyond my understanding. You have been chosen for leadership and that leadership will give you a very comfortable life, there is certainly no question about that, my young friend." He turned his back to the young man and settled himself in. "Now it is time for me to get some sleep. As for your friends and family, there will be much time available during our trip for you to write to them. I am sure they will be glad to hear of your new situation."

They arrived in Volgograd in mid-afternoon. This city of nearly one million people was alive with all the activities one could image of a thriving metropolis. Groznyy was less than half the size of this city. Garyk had truly entered the new world. Gone were the Islamic trappings of his Moslem background. Having withstood the German offensive and Soviet counter-offensive bombardments during the war and been completely rebuilt over the past three decades, Volgograd was modern Russia. Even its name was new.

Garyk, of course, was just a child of five when this tribute city to Joseph Stalin was renamed, a move that was meant to erase for all time the memory of that wartime dictator. Yet the minds of people are sometimes harder to erase than the pages of history textbooks. So it was that Garyk heard stories about Stalingrad as he grew up.

A vast industrial complex spread out before him as he watched in amazement from the train. The lifeline for all of this was the railroad. They progressed slowly through the maze of interlocking switches, with more freight cars than Garyk ever imagined could exist. Volgograd marked the end of the second leg of this journey. They needed to change trains for Moscow. A two-hour layover permitted him the luxury of moving about. Lemchenko remained at his side, of course. They ate in a small restaurant across from the station. A simple meal, even by Russian standards, but a gourmet's treat in comparison to what he was accustomed to as a struggling student. Lemchenko kept an everwatchful eye on the clock, mindful not to miss their connection.

At a stall back inside the station Lemchenko purchased a loaf of dark brown bread, some cheese and a sausage. "This will be better than anything that they may have aboard," he said with a wry smile. "Ah, let us not forget this, my young comrade," he said, reaching for a half-liter bottle of vodka. "Tonight we shall dine in elegance, eh!"

The mood had changed from the day before. Garyk knew that Lemchenko, he never did learn this man's first name, was responsible for getting him to Novgorod as expeditiously as possible. This position required that he remain aloof, but human necessities also dictated that he could be polite, if not engaging to his new ward.

They boarded a modern train with sleek new cars for the trip to Moscow. They were on the main line, a route that linked the industrial complexes of the Soviet Union and was more frequently traveled by those with whom the Party found favor. Their compartment featured a small sink and private bath, as well as fold-down bunks to sleep in. Garyk was beginning to accept that fate had, in fact, dealt him a strong hand this time.

The train traveled up the Don River Valley, the river visible for much of the afternoon. Lemchenko was again lost in his Moscow paper. Garyk had picked up a few books to read, as well, so the day sped by. He was thankful for the space that this compartment afforded, as it allowed him to stretch out his long legs from time to time. Frequently he would look up and marvel at the wonderful world passing by his window.

That evening they shared sandwiches made from Lemchenko's purchases. The sausage was richly spiced and the aroma combined with the pungent odor of the cheese engulfed the compartment. There were glasses by the sink, but Lemchenko opted for the more traditional mode of consumption, straight from the bottle. After taking a healthy swig, he passed it to his companion, who declined. "I may now be a Russian," Garyk said with a touch of sarcasm, "but I am still a Moslem at heart."

Lemchenko took back the bottle and raised it in salute. "Ah, my very young comrade, you have so much to learn."

As the evening passed, Garyk finished writing a letter. Lemchenko took another swig from his bottle and nudged him in the arm. "So, you have advised your girlfriend where you have gone? Did you tell her she will have a fine young officer to admire when you return?"

"No, I don't have any girlfriends right now. It's to my brother actually."

"Oh, yes, the twin brother, Viktor, I believe."

"Why, yes, that's right. I didn't think I'd mentioned him before."

"Probably not, but you see, it is my job to know these things. He's an oil field worker, is he not?

"You do your job well." Somehow, Garyk was not happy that this man knew so much about his family. "What else do you know?"

"No other siblings, not living anyway. Your father is dead also. You live with your mother and grandmother, that is, when you're not at the university."

"Right again. I don't know if I should be impressed or angry."

"What is there to be angry about, my young Ivramovich? You seem to possess some special talents that may be of value to your country. Your country has a right, therefore, to insure that you are the proper person to receive the new training and privileges, that is all."

"But you were wrong if you thought I had a girlfriend."

Lemchenko chuckled at this. "Perhaps. The report said no. I was just checking to be sure."

The two engaged in further casual conversation. Lemchenko held his vodka well and made a point of not being as open about his own life. Garyk did learn that he was married, lived somewhere in or near Moscow and had three children. However, it was never exactly clear what Lemchenko's specific duties might be, other than as an "observer" of people.

3

If Volgograd had been exhilarating, then Moscow was an inspiration. All of what was the Soviet Union was embodied in this city. From the legacy of the tsars to the communist industrial state, it was there in the spires, the flags, the billboards and the men and women on the streets in their various uniforms and work clothes. This was Russia. This was The Soviet Union. This, now, was a part of him, too.

At the station, an army officer, Captain Valariev, met them. He appeared a bit roly-poly for an army officer, a function more of height—he was about five foot seven—than of excessive girth. He picked them out amidst the crowd, also having had the opportunity to study the young man's file ahead of time. After greeting them both, the captain motioned for Garyk to follow him.

"We have been waiting for you, Comrade Gadayev. Come, meet some of your new associates."

Garyk followed him into a private room, off the main terminal complex. Inside were seven young men. They were about the same age as he, perhaps a bit younger. They had been standing in a group, drinking coffee and chatting about some upcoming athletic competition. Captain Valeriev made the introductions all around. Most of these young men came from areas around Moscow. One was from the Ukraine.

Then the captain turned to two young women who were also in the room, standing off by themselves. Clearly, they had separated themselves from this group of men, boys actually. "Comrades Natashia Tretiak and Katryn Moldatin, allow me to introduce Garyk Gadayev. He has just joined us from Groznyy."

Garyk had not noticed these two young women before. Comrade Tretiak nodded absently to the new arrival. She was a typical Muscovite, medium height, slightly plump but not really fat by any means. Her blonde hair fell to her shoulders and was pinned back on each side with tiny barrettes, revealing a round Russian face. Katryn

Moldatin had glanced over to check out the latest arrival when Garyk first entered the room, but remained engaged in her conversation with Natashia. Now, her eyes met Garyk's as they were being introduced. His were deep and dark. His dark hair fell haphazardly over his rough-hewn face. "Welcome to the club." She smiled broadly and extended a dainty hand in his direction.

Garyk, too, was caught up in the depths of her eyes. They were the bluest he had ever seen, even from across the room. Her hair was blonde too, but almost white and cropped just where her neck met her head. She was shorter than the other girl by a few inches. Petite, but well proportioned. Very well proportioned, Garyk thought. He fumbled to take the hand that was offered. "Nice to meet you both," he said, without ever looking at Natashia.

And so it was that Garyk and Katryn met. Those were the only words spoken at that first encounter and the two quickly separated. Yet, a bond had been established. Garyk joined with his male colleagues in casual conversation and glanced occasionally off to the corner of the room, catching her eye once or twice more. Even from a distance, he was aware of the scent of jasmine that she wore.

A rather stocky young man with a pockmarked complexion pressed his hand into Garyk's and said, "Boris Bubka's the name and computer's the game"

"Oh, hi," responded Garyk, a bit taken back by this young man's brashness.

"Her name's Natashia," Boris went on, assuming it was she that Garyk kept looking at "Nice enough, I guess, but she can be a real pain in the ass at times. Thinks she knows everything, isn't that right, Ivan?

"Yes," another of the young men answered with a snort. "Ivan and I, and those two over there, we all grew up together. Natashia too. Anything you want to know about her, ask any of us."

"Oh, no," Garyk finally responded. He realized now the gist of Boris' remarks. "No, I'm not interested, really."

"Uh huh, I can see that." Boris slapped him on the back. "So, did old Pushkin come and visit you too?"

"Why, yes, he did. Did you meet him?"

"We all did. The five of us together. Most of the others got one to one chats."

"That's right," another young man named Alexandr chimed in. "Showed up in my apartment one afternoon. Scared the shit out of my mother. Well, not him so much as this KGB guy named Boranski who came with him. He actually escorted me here to the station."

Garyk suddenly realized that Lemchenko was gone. He had not

followed them into the room. His mission was over, having delivered his charge to the good captain. No good-byes were required. He had simply dropped out of Garyk's life as suddenly and as quietly as he had entered it.

Captain Valeriev was standing by the door speaking to two other occupants of the room to whom Garyk had not been formally introduced. Both were young corporals, taller than the captain was and ill at ease with being drawn into conversation with their superior officer. They both looked relieved when the door opened and an older man entered. He was also in uniform, one festooned with ribbons, service stripes and braid. He was a sergeant major, but he carried himself in a fashion far less rigid than the captain. He walked up to the Captain and rendered an almost casual salute.

"Everything is ready, Captain." He spoke in a polite but informal manner, handing over a package of tickets bound together with an elastic band. "The train is scheduled to depart in ten minutes. I suggest we leave immediately."

"Thank you, Sergeant Major," the captain replied, with a curt nod of his head. Turning to the young people gathered there, he spoke in a commanding voice, "Come, comrades, it is time for you to pick up your bags and follow me. There is little time to waste. Stay close together."

The Sergeant Major opened the door and the Captain led the small entourage out. He walked quickly across the main concourse of the station, heading directly towards the gate that would lead them to the Leningrad train. The young men and women had to nearly break into a run to keep pace. Each had one or two small bags to carry, which hindered their ability to keep up. The two soldiers and the Sergeant Major brought up the rear. Once on the platform, Valeriev paused to check the car assignment. That allowed the Sergeant Major enough time to catch up and move to the head of the small column.

"This way, Captain," he said, pleased to take charge. "We are in car number 917. We will have that car to ourselves."

The car had been made especially for the Soviet Army. It was a half coach, with four private compartments and a small kitchen. In between was an area that had a few tables. The car could hold an entire platoon, up to fifty officers and men, if necessary. Captain Valeriev, of course, had the commander's compartment. In addition to a bed, it had a couch, desk, chair and a private toilet. Once his party settled in, he took up residence in his compartment and was not seen by Garyk for the duration of the trip.

The Sergeant Major, whose name Garyk learned was Dimetri Kosygyn, also had a private compartment. However, he spent most of the time out in the open area, seated at one of the tables. That way he could be a silent observer or, on occasion, engage in some of the casual conversations.

The young people generally took advantage of the extra space and spread out. Boris and his three companions from the same Moscow academy sat together in two rows. Alexandr had begun a conversation with another boy back in the room and they sat together to continue their talk. Katryn and Natashia also chose to sit together, but remained close enough to the others to be able to join in to the conversation when it suited them. The seventh chose a seat by himself, as did Garyk. It was behind and to the right of Katryn, allowing him to watch her and smell that perfume. The corporals sat together in the last row. This allowed them easy access to the kitchen, as they were responsible for feeding this group and tending to their basic needs. Their activities were closely monitored by the Sergeant Major.

At first Garyk distanced himself from the others. He was, after all, well into his third day of travel. Most of the others had started from home that day. He also felt like an outsider with this group. Their Muscovite dialect was much different than his. He was very much the provincial; still encountering a whole new world as the train made its way ever northward. How far from home was he now, he wondered.

As the evening wore on, he was drawn into more of the banter. Once in a while Katryn would turn back towards him if he were part of the group conversation. It amused her to think that he was keeping an eye on her. They were all into computers, and conversations that dealt with new programming techniques or the latest in electronic breakthroughs were easy for him to join. Talk about families and friends was harder at first, but soon he was part of the group experience. They were all part of some great adventure and anxious about what tomorrow might bring.

Their talks went well into the night. They gathered around the tables for a late supper, then gradually started to doze off, one by one. Garyk sat with his back propped against the car wall, both legs stretched out across the seat. His denim jeans were less fashionable than some of the others and tattered around the cuffs. From time to time he nodded off, waking with a start whenever the train made a sudden lurch. Each time he woke, he refocused his gaze on the back of her neck. She was sleeping now, leaning against the opposite wall of the car, two rows ahead of him. She had taken a pillow from the overhead and had that propped against the window. The lights had been dimmed, but her platinum hair glistened. He felt himself becoming erect and turned away.

The light of the sun woke them early. The two women were accorded the courtesy of using one of the private compartments to freshen up. "Don't get used to this sort of favoritism," the Sergeant Major said with a sly look. The ten men took turns in the two small toilet sections at the head of the car. Garyk tried to remember when he had last showered.

Breakfast was simple, some breads and meat. The coffee was strong and bitter. One of the corporals took a tray with something more substantial on it back to the Captain's compartment. Garyk sat with the two boys who had joined forces the day before. They were Sergi and Alexandr. Both were two years younger than he was. Sergi was broad shouldered and had dark hair, brown, not black like Garyk's. In contrast, Alex was a rail, tall and slender, with short dirty blonde hair. Katryn came out of the compartment still shaking water from her hair. It formed a bowl around her head, then fell back naturally into place. Natashia was talking with her friends. The seat next to Garyk was empty. She sat down.

"So, Mr. Gadayev, is it? Tell me, where did you get those deep dark eyes?"

Garyk looked at her fresh, smiling face. She smelled good sitting there next to him, having just reapplied a dab of jasmine. He could feel the stirring again. He couldn't speak. Sergi and Alexander looked at each other and laughed.

"What's the matter, Garyk," Sergi said with mock concern, "did you lose your tongue during the night?"

"I'm sorry," Katryn said. "If you prefer that I sit somewhere else, I can..."

"No, not at all!" all three young men blurted out almost in unison. Katryn laughed and some of the others turned to see what was up.

"No, please do stay," Garyk was finally able to say. "I'm sorry, you just caught me by surprise."

The four of them talked for about an hour. Sergi went to the head and then went back to his seat. Alexandr also excused himself, moving to join the others up front as well. The two of them talked for another half-hour or so. Actually, it was Katryn who did most of the talking. Garyk was pleased just to hear the sound of her voice. It was deep and mellow, not what one might expect from someone so small.

The Sergeant Major decided that perhaps this had gone on long enough. No trainboard romances on this trip. Not on his watch, anyway. He strolled over to their table and said casually, "Can I interest either of you in a magazine?"

"Thank you, yes," she said, taking one of those Paris imitations that Pravda put out. The Party frowned on such things officially, but recognized the need to supply its own watered down proletarian version for the masses. The West was already beginning to make inroads. She took the offered magazine, rose and said, "Well, I guess I'll talk to you again later."

Garyk thanked the Sergeant Major also, but declined his offer of *Engineering, Building a Stronger Nation*. "I have a book I bought for the trip," he said, rising also and returning to his appointed seat. They didn't talk again for the rest of that trip, except as part of various group conversations. He had dealt with girls before, back home and at school in Groznyy. He was no virgin, that was sure. Yet he had never had such a strange feeling before. Perhaps it was just the effects of this long trip. What he really needed, he told himself, was a good night's sleep in a real bed.

4

They arrived in Leningrad in the early evening. It was much darker then Garyk would have expected for that hour. Then he remembered his geography lessons. He had traveled over twenty-four hundred kilometers the past few days. Most of that travel had been due north. The days would be shorter at this time of year. Shorter and much colder!

He recalled Lemchenko's remarks back in his room. He grabbed his overcoat and put it on before deboarding. Underneath he had on a flannel shirt and a light brown sweater. It was not particularly heavy, but proved serviceable enough in the mountains around his home in Shali. Still, he was not prepared for it. This was like no cold he had ever experienced. He felt it in his lungs; his eyes began to tear; it penetrated his denim jeans; he could feel it in his groin. You could actually feel the air. There was a crispness to it. Of course he had brought no gloves, scarf or hat with him.

Fortunately, a military bus was waiting for them, just outside of the station. He had been outside for what, all of five minutes. Yet he was literally chilled to the bone. Inside the bus he could feel his ears begin to ache. He started to shiver uncontrollably. Katryn noticed his distress as she passed by in the aisle. She sat down beside him. She had on a heavy down filled parka with a large fur rimmed hood. Under that she wore a ski cap. She pulled off heavy red mittens and handed them to him. "These may be a bit small for you, but they will help to keep in the body heat." She had a look of genuine concern, which gradually gave way to a broad grin. "So, the mountain boy isn't used to our cold Russian nights. Wait until it gets really cold!"

He looked at her and tried to say something witty, but for the second time he found himself speechless in her presence. It was the chills this time that had driven away his ability to talk. Could it actually get colder than this, he wondered. He held the mittens up to his ears. How did people live here? He couldn't begin to imagine. Finally, he stammered, "Th... Thank you. I... I just didn't... didn't expect it...

to be like this. He would o... only let me pack... a few things."

She laughed a sweet, polite little laugh. "Well, I hope they fit you out for winter gear as soon as we get to the camp. Here, you may want to use this later," she said, pulling off her ski cap. "It's supposed to be one size fits all, but it may be a little tight. Just pull it all the way down over those ears of yours. I'm afraid I'll need the mittens back though." He'd actually forgotten he was holding them up to his ears. Sheepishly, he pulled his arms down and handed them back to her. "Oh, that's okay, you can keep them for a while if you like."

"No, that is all right. I am better now. Thank you." He pulled himself up in the seat, trying to salvage some dignity out of the situation. The bus began to move through the streets of Leningrad. Outside, a winter wonderland unfolded. Snow covered everything, reflecting the lights from street lamps. Buildings glistened against the dark night sky. "What a beautiful city," he said.

"Yes, it is very beautiful," she said. "I remember coming here once with my parents. I felt like I was going to a grand ball at the Winter Palace."

"Oh, so there is really an imperialist under those proletarian eyes," he said with a broad grin. "Do you think that they know this?" He gave a little nod in the direction of the Captain and Sergeant Major, who were seated together in the front row of the bus.

"Don't be ridiculous," she said, her appearance suddenly became stern. "That is not something to joke about, Comrade Gadayev. I have worked too hard to get this appointment."

Garyk felt his heart sink. He was only trying to enjoy this moment with her and now he had put her on the defensive. "I'm sorry, I..."

She laughed a gleeful little laugh. Her eyes sparkled. "No, don't be. But if you could have seen your own face just then." She gave his hand a little squeeze. "Yes, it is a beautiful city. I'd like to show it to you someday. Do you think they'll ever let us get away?"

"I don't know. Probably not right away. In a few weeks, maybe. It should be a bit warmer then, I hope."

That made her laugh again and he enjoyed the sound. He didn't say anything for a while, just watching the city pass by before him. He imagined the two of them walking along the rows of shops and running through the park. Then they were in the country. It was completely dark out there. Occasional lights from farmhouses shown out like bright stars. From time to time there was a glare from a town or small industrial complex. Most of the others were asleep by now. Katryn had nodded off beside him as well. Her presence there beside him was enough to keep him awake.

The bus turned off the main road before reaching Novgorod. Garyk could see a halo of light in the distance, which marked the presence of a city. As they moved through the darkness, fewer lights appeared outside the coach. The camp, obviously, was well away from any population center. They had been on the bus for several hours now. How many days had it been since he was whisked away from school. He'd lost track. What day was it, anyway?

Suddenly they were in a glare of bright lights. The bus stopped at a security gate. Others began to rouse from their sleep. The Sergeant Major disembarked with an official packet of documents, returning in a few moments. The door of the bus was opened only long enough to allow him to exit and reenter; yet a bitter chill swept up the aisle. Katryn stirred next to him, her arm falling across him as she turned back towards him to peer out the window. He was embarrassed by the response this triggered in his loins.

"Well, I guess we're here, wherever here might happen to be," she uttered in a sleepy monotone. Then she sat up straight, shook the sleep off and stretched, extending her arms straight up over her head. Her parka had been placed up in the overhead, so this motion caused her breasts to be fully defined beneath the tight blue sweater. Garyk couldn't help but notice. "Boy, do I have to pee!" she said, breaking the spell.

Once again she'd caught him off guard. The young Chechen women he was used to weren't quite so casual. "Yes," he said, "it will be nice to stop traveling."

The bus started up again, moving down several well-lit streets. On either side were functional, military looking buildings. Soldiers, garbed in heavy winter clothing, their fur lined hoods pulled down over their heads to protect against the night cold, walked their posts. Automatic rifles were slung over their shoulders. The bus turned down a side alley passing several dormitory structures, three story cinder block buildings. It stopped at the third building in this row of six. Spotlights mounted along the roof line illuminated the area in front of the building and lit up the façade. There was an ominous feeling about this place and it made Garyk uneasy.

Captain Valariev stood up at the front of the bus. His army great coat was buttoned high to his neck, the red shoulder boards and collar tabs reflected the dim overhead light. He pulled on heavy mittens and a fur cap with its red star pin. "Comrades, let me welcome you to your new home. You are now all members of the 114th Officer Training Section, Special Unit C. Corporals Popkin and Slemenko will escort you to your billets on the second floor. Tomorrow, your day will begin at 0530 hours."

"Tell me that doesn't mean what I think it does," someone said to a seatmate up front.

The Captain left, followed by the Sergeant Major. They walked quickly into the building. The two corporals assumed command. Up until now they kept their distance. If they had needed to speak to any of these young officer candidates, it had been in polite, casual tones. Now, Popkin stood by the door and barked "ON YOUR FEET!"

Slemenko had taken up a position at the rear of the bus. "MOVE IT, MOVE, MOVE, MOVE!" he bellowed and began herding people down the aisle.

Garyk shot up, forgetting the overhead rack above him. Clearly, he was not the only casualty. He barely remembered to pull on his new hat and button up his coat.

"GRAB YOUR BAGS AND MOVE YOUR BUTTS!" Again, it was Popkin.

They were off the bus and up the stairs. The second floor of the billet was divided into eleven small cells, five on one side of a central corridor and six on the other. Each cell contained two bunk beds, two desks, two wall lockers and two foot lockers. The floors were tiled and gleamed as though they were wet. The walls were gray, the furnishings and blankets brown. A Soviet flag had been painted at the end of the corridor. The first few rooms were occupied, their respective owners standing at the doorways to check out these late arrivals. They laughed and clapped as the newest additions to Special Unit C stumbled passed them in the hallway.

Corporal Slemenko stopped in front of the first empty cell, reached in and flipped on a light switch. "Moldatin! Tretiak!" he called out and motioned the two young women in. Similarly, he assigned each of the others. Garyk wound up at the end of the corridor with Alexandr.

"Top or bottom?" Alexandr asked him.

"Bottom, it's closer," he said, dropping onto the bed and falling almost immediately off to sleep.

5

The lights came on at exactly 5:30 AM the next day. Popkin was walking up and down the corridor banging on the doorpost of each cell. Clearly, he was enjoying the task of wrenching these would-be officers from their sleep. Garyk woke with a start. At first he could not remember where he was. Alexandr's feet hit the floor beside him.

"And so the fun begins," he said to the room in general. Turning down to Garyk, he said, "Boy, did you crash last night. I don't think I've ever seen anyone go out like that."

"What day is it?"

"Tuesday, why?"

"Well, if it's Tuesday then I've spent the past five days on trains and buses."

Just then Popkin appeared in the doorway. "WHAT ARE YOU DOING STILL IN BED?" he barked. "GET MOVING, GADAYEV, you're in the Army now!"

"Where's the head?" he asked, as Alexandr was about to head out the door, obviously heading for that general destination himself.

"Right down the hall," he replied. "You'll love it—four sinks, four toilets, four showers stalls—not bad for twenty-two people. Hey, the best part is we get to share it with six broads."

Clearly the concept of personal hygiene was a matter of secondary importance to the Soviet Army. Popkin was down there now, still barking away. "GET IN, GET DONE, GET OUT!" he was shouting, relishing the moment. These young people were destined to be his superior officers one day. For now, however, he was the boss. "MOVE IT, PEOPLE, THIS ISN'T MAMA'S HOUSE ANYMORE!"

Garyk was wearing only his shorts, revealing a thick mat of curly black chest hairs. Most of the others were clad only in shorts as well. Katryn stepped out of one of the shower stalls as he entered the head. She was wrapped in a towel. "Oh, Mama," someone called out, "come to Papa and let me be your man."

"In your dreams," she responded, moving past Garyk with no acknowledgment of any sort.

He did the three "S's" (Shit, Shower, Shave) in less then five minutes. Back in his room, he found that they had handed out a change of clothing while he was asleep. Later they would stand in line at the clothing center and pick up a full complement of uniforms and work clothes. This contingent distribution was meant to insure some form of uniformity when they first fell out. The new pants were about one size too big at the waist, but an inch or so too short. "Don't worry about that," Alexandr counseled, "you're just going to tuck them into your boots anyway!" The underwear seemed okay, and so did the field jacket. It was made of brown cotton twill and had a fresh new smell. The boots were all right as well, just new and stiff. It would take a while to break them in and get accustomed to having them come up almost to his knees.

Popkin was yelling again, something about falling out to the Day Room. Garyk and Alexandr followed the others down the corridor, downstairs to the first floor and down another hallway. They filed into a large gray room. There were four rows of wooden chairs, six on each side of a center aisle. A large Soviet flag was hung across the rear wall. Two large pictures of Leonid Breznev and Alexey Kosygin adorned the wall to his right. Smaller pictures of other Soviet military notables were hung on either side. A row of windows, up too high to permit any interfering outward glances, but sufficient to let in the daylight, graced the other wall, to his left. A green slateboard occupied most of the front wall. It displayed a few military posters. In front of that was a wooden podium and a small table and chair.

"PICK A SEAT, STAY ON YOUR FEET!" Popkin again.

The room was filled now. The third floor housed another 22 people, bringing their Special Unit to 44. They stood there at semi-attention. It was, of course, only their first day in the Army. Corporal Slemenko entered the room also wearing his field uniform this morning, although his was neatly starched and crisp. He slapped the palm of his hand against the open door, and called out "ATTENTION!"

Captain Valeriev strode into the room accompanied by a senior sergeant who walked two paces behind him and closed the door after they entered. He remained by the door, joined by Popkin and Slemenko, while the captain assumed his position at the podium. Unlike the two corporals, both Captain Valeriev and the sergeant were wearing the brown serge dress uniforms. The insignia on their collars identified both as members of the elite airborne infantry. After getting a nod from the captain, the senior sergeant, in a commanding monotone said. "You may take your seats."

"For those of you who did not meet me before, I am Captain Alexey Valeriev," he began. "I am pleased to welcome you to Special Unit C. You are here because you have all demonstrated certain technical abilities, abilities which our government believes would be beneficial to the Army of the Soviet Socialist Republics. That, of course, remains to be seen. They want me to turn you into officers. Well, before I can do that, we must first make soldiers out of you. That job will be the responsibility of Senior Sergeant Gorki here."

At the mention of his name, the sergeant snapped to attention, the click of his heels sounding across the room. All heads turned his way. "YES SIR!" he said.

The Captain continued, "I think that you have your work cut out for you sergeant."

"YES SIR!"

You will be here, ladies and gentlemen, for the next twelve weeks. During that time you will learn what it is to be a soldier in the finest army ever assembled. You will be required to undergo the same physical training that any soldier in the Soviet Army would be expected to receive. As future officers, you should expect nothing less. The Soviet Union expects, no, it demands nothing less of you. Once you have been proven qualified to serve, then you shall be taught how to lead. Those who cannot meet our standards will be purged from the program. I look forward to following your progress here. Now, I will let Senior Sergeant Gorki get to work."

There was another resounding bang against the door. "ON YOUR FEET!" commanded Slemenko. As they struggled to their feet, the sergeant and captain exchanged salutes and the captain strode out. Senior Sergeant Gorki now assumed the podium position.

Senior Sergeant Boris Dimitryvitch Gorki was a veritable poster child for the Soviet Army. He was tall. Lean, yet muscular. His blond hair was close cropped in a military flat-top. His uniform was perfectly tailored. It sported an array of service ribbons and marksmanship awards that denoted a veteran of close to twenty years experience. His pants were bloused to the top of his boots. The boots had a gleam that outshone even Valeriev's and reflected back images of the room. His face was tanned and square-jawed. He stood at the podium and looked around the room at these young children, babies really, that they had given him to turn into officers in his precious army.

Finally, he spoke. "So, you think that you can be officers in the Soviet Army?"

There was no reply.

"I don't hear you," he said.

A few scattered "Yes, sergeant's" were heard.

"I can't hear you," he said a little louder.

"Yes, sergeant," they all replied, more or less together.

"What"

"YES, SERGEANT!" now more forcefully.

"I STILL CAN'T HEAR YOU," he said loudly.

"YES, SERGEANT!" together, at last and with spirit.

"Well, we shall see about that. This is the poorest excuse for a training company that I have ever been forced to lay eyes on. We shall certainly have to see about that."

They were still standing at more or less attention. Gorki turned and headed for the door.

"Corporal Slemenko, I suppose that these people think that they should be given something to eat this morning. Well, let's see how well they can run first, then take them on to the mess hall."

"Yes, Sergeant!" Slemenko shot back.

Garyk felt a knot in the pit of his stomach. He recalled that brief encounter with Colonel Pushkin only five days ago. "Not a soldier, young Gadayev. No, not a soldier but an officer," the colonel had said. Well it sure looked like soldiering to him. Yes it surely did.

Pushkin, of course, had not been lying. They did intend to make these young people into officers. "Wunderkind" they were called. They had been placed on the fast track. Twelve weeks was certainly not enough time to turn these raw young men and women into officers suitable for service in the most modern and efficient army in the world. But the colonel had been handed a hot potato. The politicos were demanding results. The hard liners in the military insisted on maintaining standards. He had been given a timetable.

The Soviet Union had been sitting pretty for a number of years. Their missile program had launched the space race. During the sixties, they had been clearly ahead. They possessed the capability to launch multiple warheads at the Americans, or anyone else for that matter, with impunity. The West was scrambling to keep up. Best of all, the Americans had embroiled themselves in Southeast Asia. Vietnam was eating up the Americans with little actual assistance required from Mother Russia. It was only a matter of time before the decadent West would collapse.

In 1969, that all began to change. The early successes achieved by the Soviet Union in putting men and equipment in Earth orbit had roused the Americans. The full force of its vast technological empire had been thrown into gear. The Americans not only got to the moon first, they kept going back. Huge strides in computer technologies and rocketry had been made. Fortunately for the Russians, the Japanese were stealing much of the computer technology as rapidly as the Americans could develop it. But the Soviet Union could not rely upon purchasing second hand technology from Japan.

The top brass in the Soviet Army had become too complacent. There was a mood shift in the air. Those in powerful places could sense it. They needed to redouble the effort to put new leadership in place in those strategic areas that would establish the ground rules for future military confrontations. Computers were the key. Find the people who knew how to speak this new techno-language, train them and get them into the field as quickly as possible.

Two Special Sections had already begun the program. They were merely six and twelve weeks ahead. Those cadets had been selected from the more traditional profiles used to screen prospective military leaders. Brighter, to be sure, with IQ scores ten to twenty points above the norm. But still they fit well into the military's parameters and took well to the physical aspects of the regimen.

Special Unit C was the first group of purely scientific types. Normally these young people would have been slotted into research, engineering and industrial positions. Many may have remained at their universities as instructors. Now they were being asked to turn these young geniuses into soldiers. And as if that weren't enough, they had been given all of twelve weeks to do it. The program anticipated that, upon their commissioning, they would be returned to universities to gain advanced degrees. So armed, they would be sent into battle.

Garyk and the others spent the first six weeks in rigorous physical training. They ran, frequently through the snow and, of course, they marched. They did calisthenics. They learned martial arts. They were qualified on automatic rifles and machine pistols. Garyk surprised everyone by scoring highest in marksmanship. He received a special AK-47 training pin, a red star mounted above crossed rifles, which he got to wear on his uniform. Their appearance changed dramatically, too. Their heads were shaved that first day. The young women were accorded the luxury of keeping theirs at four centimeters. In spite of this loss of hair, they appeared taller, partially due to the fact that they were all somewhat leaner. More to the point, they carried themselves in a more erect fashion. The combination of diet and exercise had worked its magic. They were stronger.

To the surprise of both Captain Valeriev and Senior Sergeant Gorki, their numbers had only gone down by seven. Four of those were for physical injuries incurred during training. A broken arm, two broken ankles and a broken leg. Those trainees would be recycled to

Section D. Only three did not make the grade, at least to this point in the program. Gorki, of course, felt that he had not pressed them hard enough. The Colonel seemed pleased, however, and what pleased the Colonel certainly pleased Captain Valeriev.

6

The sixth week of training ended with a four day, three night overland trek. It was April, but still cold, especially at night. The snow had given over to mud. Deep, thick, clinging mud that invaded everything. They arrived back at the billet area late on a Friday evening. Forty indistinguishable bodies, including Sergeant Gorki and the two corporals, clamored out of four army trucks. They all blended together, caked with mud, weary from their four days of war games.

Captain Valeriev stood at the window watching as they disembarked the vehicles. When they had assembled in front of the building, he came out of his office and walked outside to greet them. His clean, crisply starched, eight pocket field uniform was a marked contrast to the wet and grimy troop assembled before him. Their waterlogged backpacks forced them to lean forward as they stood there. AK-47s were held limply at their sides. A few actually leaned on them for support.

"What a sorry looking lot we have here." His tone was more congenial than usual, Garyk taught. "From the look of you, it would seem we lost the war!" He laughed, causing Garyk and the others to join in. "However, I have had nothing but the best of reports about you, not only from Sergeant Gorki, but from your field instructors as well."

Garyk felt a sense of pride swell within him. They had done well, he knew that, but to hear it from the Captain was especially rewarding. He sensed the others were feeling this way too. They made an effort to stand more erect.

"Yes, you have all done very well," continued Valeriev, "so well that I can now with confidence say that you are soldiers. Next week we shall begin to make you officers. For this you have earned a small reward. As of now, you are all on pass. Report back no later than 2200 hours on Sunday. Sergeant, you may dismiss your men."

The Captain disappeared back inside. An electric charge passed through the ranks. Someone had whispered "What did he say?" It was more in disbelief than for the lack of hearing. Since their arrival they had not had a single moment of free time. Now they were being given two whole days!

Gorki stood before them. "Settle down comrades, you heard the man, 2200 hours Sunday! One second later than that and you can kiss your ass good-bye, is that clear?"

"YES, SERGEANT!" came the replied.

"Very well, dismissed!"

They let out a great shout, then raced to get to the showers. Somewhere, they had heard, there were buses to whisk them off to the wonders of Novgorod. The hot water felt wonderful as Garyk stood in the shower and washed away the mud that had seemingly found its way into every one of his pores. Funny, he thought, a few hours ago he had longed just to stand in a hot shower for hours. Now he couldn't wait to get finished and be on his way.

Novgorod was a modest city in a rural setting. It was smaller, actually, than Groznyy, but it was rich in charm. They were dropped off at a bus depot downtown at ten that evening, thrilled by their newfound freedom, but at a complete loss as to what to do next.

"I don't know about you guys," Katryn said, "but I'm famished. I haven't had real food for six weeks and I think that I'll just hole up in the first restaurant I can find and eat the whole weekend!" The others all laughed. The thought of this tiny little thing gorging herself with food was almost beyond their imagination.

"Food is good," it was Sergi this time, "so long as there is plenty of beer and vodka to go along with it!" Again they all laughed.

Alexandr punched at his friend and said, "Yes, the big drinking man. One vodka and we will have to carry him home!"

The group included five others—Garyk, of course, Natashia and two of the young men from her home area, Boris Bubka and Nikolay Rostoy. Anna Bykova, a farm girl from the Steppes region with a quick wit and hot temper, rounded out the band. Fate had brought them all together and over the past few weeks they had formed a bond. They all wore the cadet service uniform, a short brown waistcoat, pants and dress shoes, rather than their boots. Blue shoulder boards with narrow gold bands down each edge and a large gold K proclaimed their cadet status.

For no particular reason, Sergi turned right and started off down the street in quest of food and drink. The others followed. The hour was late and all of the shops and many of the restaurants were closed. They found an establishment that looked promising. A boisterous crowd had already assembled inside. They were, however, able to get a table that accommodated the group and settled in.

It was a soldier's night out. They ate, drank and told stories about their training experiences. Boris was particularly good at impersonating Corporal Popkin. They roared with laughter as he aped the strutting assistant trainer, "YOU PEOPLE ARE PATHETIC! TRETIAK, MY MOTHER CAN RUN THIS COURSE FASTER THAN THIS! HEY, GADAYEV, WOULD YOU CARE TO JOIN US TODAY?" This outburst caused many of the revelers seated at other tables to turn to see what was going on. Since a large contingent in the place were also part of Special Unit C, a chant went up. "Popkin, Popkin, Popkin!"

Anna added her own version of the good Sergeant Gorki and Sergi made a passable attempt at doing a Captain Valeriev knock-off. Boris, again imitating the corporal, looked at Alexandr and said. "Duchek, were you born with two left feet or was that a going away present from your mother?" Alex blushed, remembering a particularly trying day trying to master the art of drill and ceremony.

Sergi looked across the table and said, "Well, Boris, at least old Alex here didn't single-handedly take out a tractor on the rifle range!" Anna howled and slapped Bubka on the back. "Yes, Boris, I nearly wet my pants that day!" She was laughing so hard that tears welled in her eyes. "Oh God, I need another drink," she was finally able to say.

"I swear to God I thought it was a tank. Didn't the instructor say "Commence fire on the tank to the right of marker 'C'?" Anna roared again and the others all joined in.

"Target, Boris, the man clearly said target." Sergi responded after he caught his breath. "You know, they're those green and brown silhouettes."

Boris held his hands up. "Okay, I surrender. Jeez, what a tough crowd."

Garyk was seated across from Katryn, who was flanked by Sergi and Natashia. Occasionally their eyes met and she would give him a coquettish smile. Over the past few weeks they had been accorded only rare opportunities for idle conversation in the busy training routine. For the most part, she had remained somewhat aloof, politely charming, always cordial, but not really chummy, certainly not affectionate. Tonight she engaged him directly only once or twice and made some little joke at his expense, but it was no more or less attention than she accorded to any of the others. Still, she captivated him. The shorter hair accentuated her pixie nature.

He began the evening drinking coffee while the others had opted for stronger stuff. He warmed to the conversation and became caught up in the camaraderie, without experiencing the effects of alcoholic consumption. They were well into the early morning hours and it was time for the inevitable round of toasts that marked a sort of closing ceremony for the evening. Boris stood, a bottle of Vodka held aloft, and proclaimed, "Here's to the men and women of Special Unit C, may we live long in the service of our glorious country!"

The bottle was passed round the table and they each took their obligatory swig. When it came to Garyk he, too, held it up, allowing the smallest of sips to wet his lips then passed it along. Each, in turn, raised up the bottle and made a toast, and sent it off on another circumnavigation of the table. By the third pass, Garyk allowed more than a sip to pass through his lips and he felt the tingling sensation all the way down to his shoes.

When it came to her, Katryn raised the bottle and declared: "To all of us here, my true and good friends, I would give my life for any one of you!"

Nikolay sat next to Garyk. When it came to him, he rose and said, "To the Soviet Army and the Union of Soviet Socialist Republics, which she serves!"

Now Garyk was standing. With absolute spontaneity he said, "To Mother Russia!" He pressed the bottle to his lips and took several full deep swallows. Yes, he was a Russian now.

7

Sergi called their waitress over. She was an older woman, fifty perhaps, who had survived many a night of joyous camaraderie. This particular group of young soldiers had been generally well behaved, not like some. "Excuse me, but we were all so eager to celebrate tonight that none of us thought to get any rooms. Do you know where we might be able to find a place to stay?"

The woman ran her hand across the top of her head. "Oh dear, it is so late. That was not a wise decision, let me think. My cousin runs a small hotel down by the river. It is just a few blocks from here, not very far. Let me try to call him and see if he has any rooms left this evening. It really is quite late, you know."

"That would be very kind of you, ma'am," Sergi told her as she headed off to the back office.

Several minutes went by before she returned. She looked at these youngsters sternly and said, "He was not very pleased to be wakened at this hour of the morning, let me tell you. Still, one can always use a little extra in the pocketbook, if you know what I mean. He has only three rooms left, but you are welcome to share them if you like." She cast a disapproving eye at Natashia, unfairly suspecting that she might be more inclined to share her bed with one of the young men, rather than the other women in the party.

Natashia sensed this and spoke up. "Oh, that would be wonderful, thanks ever so much. Katryn and I have shared a room for six weeks now. Anna, you'll join us, okay?"

Katryn looked up and said, "Oh, you two go on ahead. I couldn't sleep tonight. I think I'll take a walk and find that river. Just save me some water for a shower in the morning."

Garyk overheard this and said, "Is it safe for you to walk alone at this hour? Perhaps I should join you, if you wouldn't mind."

She laughed a little, responding "Oh, and I'm supposed to be safe with you."

As always, she had caught him off guard. "Well, if you'd rather I not..."

"Don't be silly," she said, grabbing his arm. "Come, let us discover the glorious city of Novgorod together!"

They walked and talked for several hours, oblivious to the fatigue that should have set in after their four days of field training and a night on the town. They made an interesting pair, he being a good twelve inches taller. At some point their hands met. He held hers in his; it was so small, almost childlike, and very soft compared to his. She was vibrant and animated as she told him stories about her family.

"My father can be very stern. Well, he tries to be anyway," she said with a gleeful giggle. "One day Papa was preparing for some big meeting. He is always having important people over. Anyway, there he is telling my brothers that they must be on their best behavior when I walk in, I must have been six at the time. I was wearing his best shirt, Mama had just pressed it for the occasion, and my feet were pushed into his big shoes. I think I must have put his shaving soap all over my body, it had something to do with my being an angel or something, I can't remember." She began to bounce as she retold the story. She threw her whole body into the conversation, waving her arms and twisting and turning to demonstrate this point or another. It was a side of her that Garyk had never seen before. He was drawn in to her very being.

They walked along the Volkhov River. The fact that they were both in uniform was enough to fend off any questioning night watch. After some time they headed back toward the center of the city. The streets were deserted at that hour. "Oh look, Garyk, what a charming church, don't you think."

"Actually, I think it might be a cathedral, the Cathedral of Saint Sofia."

"Oh." She cocked her head and looked up at him. "I didn't realize that you were an expert on the city of Novgorod." She poked his arm and laughed.

"I'm no expert, but they did give us a packet of information when we first got to the base. Didn't you read it?

"No, but it seems you did. What else did it say?"

"It's one of the oldest cities in Russia, did you know that? Fifth or sixth century. In fact, it was the first capital. That was way back around 800 and something. I can't remember exactly. The cathedral dates to the eleventh century."

"Well. Comrade Gadayev, I am impressed. Computers aren't your only interest after all. Promise you'll tell me more tomorrow, when it's light enough to see what you're talking about."

"I think it's tomorrow already." The sky was beginning to lighten. Orange streaks began to appear as heralds to the morning sunrise. "I'll promise if that means you'll be walking around with me again."

"Well, I don't know about that." She was bouncing again. "I was rather hoping to spend some time with Sergi." Garyk sighed noticeably and mumbled that was understandable. "No, silly, of course I'll go with you." She threw her arms in the air and jumped up, grabbing him around the shoulders. He caught her in his arms and she kissed him lightly on the cheek. He pulled her close in, their eyes locked and he kissed her full on the lips.

Katryn pulled her head back for a moment, debating with herself, and then she let out one of those gleeful little laughs. Her arms were locked around his neck and he was holding her several inches off the ground. She pressed her lips against his another time. It was a long, lingering kiss. She searched his lips with her tongue, pressed herself to him. He opened his mouth to receive her; their tongues met and caressed each other. He was fully aroused, lost completely in her. Then he pulled his head away.

"What is it?" she asked, concerned that she had somehow offended him or done something wrong.

"Nothing, I... I just needed to breathe."

They both laughed and embraced again.

Garyk lowered her down to the ground, took her hand and headed back toward the river. She neither protested nor questioned where he was taking her. They had passed a boathouse on their walk and found their way back there. It was dank and dark inside. The smell of rotting timbers and gasoline combined with fish. There was some canvas piled in one corner. They collapsed onto it, locked in yet another deep, long embrace. It was April and at this early hour there was still a chill in the air. They were both breathing heavily and little clouds hung over their heads. She began to unbutton his waist coat. He did the same to hers and then pushed up her tee shirt and bra. He held her firm round breasts in the palms of both his hands, groping her mouth deeply with his tongue.

She sat up and pulled off her shoes, undid the buttons on her pants and pulled them off. This was clearly not an exercise for which this training uniform had been designed. He took her upper legs in his hands, massaging the inside of her thighs with his thumbs. She arched back and his mouth found one of her beasts. With his tongue he drew circles around the nipple. He could feel it stiffen at his touch. She groped for the front of his trousers, desperate to get them open. There, she had him in her hands; his full manhood throbbed in her grasp. He sighed deeply as she played him with her fingers. His thumbs were inside her now, moist and warm. They probed her gently, then his fingers combed through the thickness of hairs above.

His index finger found the little mound of her clitoris. He twirled it gently. She moaned, pulling him in closer to her, his head between her breasts. Spreading herself over him, she came down on top of him, taking him fully inside of her. She rode him in slow moving circles. His hands moved around and were on her buttocks, kneading them with force and urgency.

She brought her face down to his. Their mouths pressed together, tongues probing deeply, he caught hers and sucked hard on it. His hands pulled her down unto him as he exploded into her and she let out a cry of ecstasy, riding him even harder. She began to shudder from the thrill of it.

Pulling her head up, she looked at him for a long time. That beautiful smile of hers was back. In her most coquettish tone yet, she asked, "Was that as good for you as it was for me?"

Garyk never knew what to expect from her. After a brief pause, he laughed and said, "No, it wasn't good at all."

She pulled herself up, still straddled across his midsection. Now it was her turn to be surprised by him. The glow on her face faded and the twinkle in her eyes dimmed. "I'm sorry," she whispered.

"Don't be. It wasn't good, it was fantastic! Better than I'd ever imagined."

"Oh, I hate you." She leaned down again and bit hard on his ear.

"Really, you have a funny way of showing it."

She sat up again and looked into his eyes. Even in the dimness of the boathouse she could see the deep dark pools. "And just what did you mean by that remark, better than you'd imagined? Have you been wetting your sheets at night over me, Mr. Gadayev?" Another impish grin crossed her face.

"And just what would you know about such things," he asked.

"I have two brothers, remember!"

He pulled her back to him and held her for a long kiss. They made love again, slower this time and with him on top. She ran her fingers through the dark hairs that covered his chest and moaned as he pressed inside of her. When they had finally finished, she reached up and grabbed the identification tag that was hanging down from his neck. "Yours is different than mine, why is that?"

He rolled onto his side, still gently caressing one of her breasts, and looked to see what she was talking about. "Oh, that, it's an Islamic emblem."

"I didn't realize you were so religious."

"I'm not really. I guess when we were filling out all of those forms at the start I just naturally checked off the box marked Moslem. It's no big deal."

"Oh." She said it in the same way she might have responded if an instructor had corrected her about something she thought she gotten right.

As the heat of passion subsided, they both became aware of the chill and dressed quickly. This time she grabbed his hand and led him back outside. "Come, it's time to find the others."

8

The city was starting to awaken. Shopkeepers and civil servants on the early shift passed by them as they headed off to start their day. Trucks making early agricultural deliveries made their way down the larger thoroughfares. Katryn and Garyk headed back in the general direction of the hotel where the others had planned to hole up for the night. They found a three story tall red brick building with a ginger-bread facade that had not seen paint for several years. A small sign proclaimed it to be the *Hotel Rurik*. A tall gangly young man behind the front desk confirmed that their friends had indeed registered earlier. A small café was located just off the lobby. "There's no sense waking everyone," Garyk told her. "Besides, I'm hungry."

Katryn chuckled. "I think you're always hungry. It's a wonder you stay so thin. Still, you're right, we shouldn't rouse them just yet. Besides, I think we need to talk." They ordered coffee, sausages and eggs. When the coffee came, Katryn held the cup in her hands seeking to absorb all of its warmth. Garyk put his hands over hers and stared intently into her eyes. He was in love. He hoped that she was too.

Looking down at the table, she said quietly, "Well, where do we go from here?"

"What do you mean?"

Katryn directed her gaze away from him and pulled her hands out of his. "We can't ignore what just happened."

"Ignore it, why would I ever want to do that?" he asked, incredulously.

"Look at us," she said, "we're soldiers, cadets actually, but, you know, still soldiers. Six weeks from now they will send us off to where ever. You and I have no control over that. We can't get serious, not now. Maybe not ever."

He felt a knot develop deep in the pit of his stomach. "You can't mean that." He looked at her as though she had just cut out his heart. Maybe she had.

"I mean it more than I want it," she said. "They must have rules about this. They have rules about everything else. I really like you, Garyk. However, I really want to finish this program. I didn't pick this life, it picked me. But I know it's what I was meant to do. Don't you see that?"

Garyk was quiet for a long while. He sat there, both elbows on the table, his hands pressed together as if he were praying. This couldn't be. He had longed for her since that first casual introduction back in Moscow. Everything inside him told him she was right for him. They had confirmed it this morning. "I think that I've been serious about you for much longer than you know," he finally admitted to her.

"I knew that," she said softly. "But this just isn't our time. Not now."

She took his hands in hers this time. Just then Sergi and Alexandr walked into the café. Two opposites, the first broad shouldered and of medium height. The latter taller, leaner and with much lighter hair. This morning, however, they shared one characteristic—bloodshot eyes. "Well, what do we have here, two star-crossed lovers, no doubt!" Sergi was always the one to understate the obvious. She dropped his hands and turned to greet them.

"Oh, don't let us break up this little tête-à-tête," Sergi continued. It looks like we've had a pleasant evening."

She was blushing. Garyk, too. "We've just ordered," he was able to blurt out, "but you're welcome to join us."

"Thanks anyway," Alexandr said. "We'd love to but you know what they say, 'four's a crowd' or is it three, I keep forgetting."

Sergi added, "Yes thanks, but Anna is on her way down to join us and I think Nikolay may have wakened from the dead just as we were leaving. We'll leave you two to yourselves."

"No, really, please join us." Katryn reached up and pulled on Alexandr's arm, dragging him into the booth next to her. "After all, it's all for one and all that crap." She chortled, not quite so convincingly, but she was regaining her poise.

"Well, if you insist," Sergi said, joining Garyk in the other bench seat. Anna came in a few minutes later, pulling up a chair to the end of the table. She was a large woman. The past six weeks had served only to bulk her up more, converting whatever excess fat she had into additional muscle. Nikolay never did make a morning appearance.

They ate heartily. The conversation was much as it had been the night before. Sergi and Alex talked about their plans for the day. Alex volunteered, "I understand that there are some very interesting buildings here that are nearly a thousand years old."

"Yes," Katryn said, "there's a really interesting cathedral about three blocks from here. We saw it last night."

"Oh, really," Sergi said rather dramatically. He turned his head back and forth between the two of them. Katryn was blushing again.

"Am I missing something here?" Anna asked in a deep-throated voice. Everyone else burst out laughing. "What IS going on here?" she asked again.

"It's nothing really" Garyk offered. Sergi laughed so hard he started to cough.

When they finished eating Katryn asked Anna if there was a shower in her room.

"No, I'm afraid it's a communal project here too," she replied, "but you can use the room to change in if you'd like." She held up a room key for her to take. "Just don't wake Natashia."

"Yes, Garyk, don't wake Natashia." Alexandr put in.

"What is that supposed to mean?" Anna seemed to be a little miffed at being out of the loop somehow.

Earlier, Garyk had asked Sergi for a key so he could use his room to get some sleep. He and Katryn both started to head upstairs. As they left, Alexandr confided the big secret to Anna.

"OH, YOU'RE KIDDING!' they heard her boom out as they left. Her deep hearty laugh followed them out the door.

They both slept late into the afternoon. Separate beds. Separate rooms. When Garyk entered the room for which Sergi had given him a key, he found it contained two double beds. Each was occupied. Nikolay lay across the one closest to the door. Boris was curled up on the edge of the other. Garyk pulled off his waistcoat and pants, kicked off his shoes and lay down across from Boris. He fell asleep almost immediately.

Katryn had really planned on just taking a shower and then rejoining her comrades. The hot water felt good. When had she last had the luxury of remaining in the shower for more than sixty seconds? The stall was filled with steamy vapors by the time she finished. Back in the room shared by the other two girls, she toweled off and started to redress. "No," she thought, "better wash these out first." She walked back down the hall and rinsed off her panties, came back to the room and laid them across the radiator to dry. Again she told herself, "I'll just lay here for a bit while they're drying."

Six hours later she woke with a start. It was nearly half-past three. The room was empty. Natashia had gotten dressed and left hours before without waking her. She dressed quickly and hurried out. None of the group was downstairs either. Just as well. She needed some time alone to think.

Around four-thirty Alex and Sergi returned to their room. Anna was with them. Their unrestrained voices echoed as they came down the hall. The three of them had "done the sights" all day. When they noticed that Garyk was still sleeping in the room, they hushed up immediately. Sergi, not one to let anything pass, held open the door to let Anna see inside and gestured grandly towards the bed. "Behold, Prince Vladimir sleeps!" Anna started to laugh heartily.

"And where is the princess?" she added. They all laughed.

Whether it was the sound of them coming down the hall, or just this final repartee', Garyk was now awake. "What time is it?" he mumbled to the wall.

"It's 1635, Comrade Gadayev. ON YOUR FEET, SOLDIER!" commanded Sergi, doing his best to sound like Corporal Popkin.

Garyk rolled over, looked up and threw a pillow at him. "Is it Sunday already?"

Alexandr answered "No, we still have a full day and a half."

"Good, wake me when it's over!" Garyk rolled back to face the wall.

Sergi bounced down on the bed next to him. "Enough of this malingering, young man. The pleasures of Novgorod beckon us to attend."

It was no use to try to sleep and he was fully awake now anyway. He sat up in the bed as Anna came back from her room and stood by the open door. She asked, "Where's Katryn?"

"I have no idea. I haven't seen her since breakfast."

"Uh huh," Anna replied with a smirk. She exaggerated a wink in Sergi's direction and all three of them started to laugh again.

"Honestly, I've been asleep ever since I came up here." He looked at them all very seriously. "Please come in and close the door." Anna did. "I know that you guys think you saw something this morning, but I have to ask you to please keep this here between us. You haven't said anything to the others have you?"

"No" they all responded. Then Anna, as always the wit, asked. "What's the matter, you got a wife back home we don't know anything about?" More chuckles from the group.

Garyk stood up. He was wearing just his shorts, but after six weeks of communal living it made little difference. "No, look I'm serious. Katryn is concerned that if they find out, you know, we may be in trouble. She's sure that they have rules against fraternization within the ranks. She doesn't want to be kicked out of the program. Neither do I, for that matter."

They all agreed. Nothing else was said all weekend.

Garyk went to shower. The others needed to freshen up a bit as well. When he got back to the room Nikolay and Boris were there too. They each had broad round faces, accentuated by the close cropped military haircuts. Boris was the bigger of the two, a good match for Anna. He said, "Natashia told us that she was planning on spending at least thirty minutes in the shower. Let's go down some beers while the ladies get themselves ready for another night on the town."

They all agreed that this was a good plan. The café was closed at this time of day, so they found a new place across the street. Boris told the waitress to bring them two pitchers of beer and glasses all around. Garyk was about to decline and ask for black coffee instead. Then he thought, "What the hell, I'm a Russian now!" and went with the crowd.

They were doing what friends do in such places and he was enjoying himself. Across the room, he noticed a man sitting alone in a booth. He held the Moscow paper up, making it impossible to see who he was. However, Garyk felt he had seen him before. There was something about the clothes he was wearing; rumpled and mismatched, a brown tweed jacket and gray flannel trousers.

They had been there about an hour when the girls came in to join them. All of the girls. Katryn avoided the seat next to Garyk, which was empty. Instead she pulled up another chair and sat across from him, next to Boris. Anna plopped herself down by him. Several more pitchers were ordered and the festivities continued.

From time to time Garyk looked over to see if the man in the corner was still there. He was reading his paper, seemingly oblivious to their conversations. Then, he caught a brief glimpse of him as he folded over another page. He had speckled gray hair and glasses, with ruddy cheeks. Garyk was shocked. It was Lemchenko! Was he spying on him? If so, for how long? Did he know about Katryn?

After another hour Boris announced, "Enough of this drinking. It's time to eat!"

"Yes, that's a good idea," Sergi agreed, "let's see what they have to offer here."

"Oh no, not here." Natashia chimed in. "I'm sure it's quite good, but I'm in the mood for something a little more elegant tonight. Don't you agree ladies?" she said looking at Katryn. They found a charming place. Afterward, they patronized the local cinema. It was a Russian remake of some American love story. Clearly, it had lost a lot in the translation. An uneasy feeling stayed with Garyk all that evening. Every where they went he searched for Lemchenko. Was he still following them? Was someone else following them? Did it matter in any case?

The next day they met around nine. It was difficult to sleep much later when you are used to rising at 0530 every day. They stayed together as a group, visiting the city's citadel, or Kremlin. They bought some bread, meat, cheese and some local vegetables, there really wasn't much available in the stores, and picnicked on the banks of the Volkhov. It was a glorious spring day! For the most part, Katryn stayed with Natashia. Garyk longed for her to be at his side. He understood and respected her position, even admitted that she was actually right. Still, the sound of her voice, the very smell of her jasmine, stirred him deep inside.

They all agreed that it would be best not to incur the wrath of Sergeant Gorki, or worse yet, Corporal Popkin, by coming in at or close to the designated curfew. Besides, they were nearly out of money and dead tired. They boarded a bus back to camp at 1800 hours. They were in their billet by 1900 hours. Garyk was asleep well before the 2200 hour deadline.

9

The next six weeks sped by. Much of the time was spent in the classroom, either in the unit's own day room or over at the tactical training center. They still rose at 0530 hours, ran five to ten kilometers and had physical training classes three times a week. The emphasis was now clearly on making them officers—tactics, military history, problems and procedures of command. They were awash in technical training manuals. Because of their background in science and technology, they absorbed these with greater ease than a normal cadet might have.

Time was precious. Little could be wasted, so they did not get another free weekend again. At best they had a few hours here and there. The weekends were reserved for more field training.

For the most part, Katryn and Garyk kept their distance. They would, from time to time, run together in the morning. Other duties also brought them together during the day. When possible, the group, which included the two of them, Anna, Alex and Sergi would find a table together at mealtime. Sergi did his best to position Garyk and Katryn together. Sometimes Katryn obliged him, at other times she avoided Garyk completely. To most observers they were simply friends, part of an inner group of friends. Katryn became more distant the closer it got to their graduation day.

Garyk at least was able to talk to someone else about his feelings. Alex was like a brother now. The lights had gone out fifteen minutes ago, but Garyk was still awake, lying on his back and staring at the bottom of Alex' bunk above him. "Are you awake?"

"Not really, but I suppose that you want me to be."

"I'm sorry, Alex. It's just that she drives me crazy at times."

"Hey, she's a woman. That's what they're trained to do from birth. Didn't you know that?"

"I guess not. I didn't have the advantage of growing up with sisters."

"Believe me, that was no advantage."

"Why does she do this, Alex? She goes for days, weeks sometimes, without acknowledging that I exist. Just when I've convinced myself that it's over, she plops herself down and reaches for my hand under the table. Her eyes sparkle as she talks to me and she's laughing and joking again."

"Have you ever gone fishing?" Alex rolled over on his side, facing into the room. He propped his head up on his forearm. "If you feel the fish bite the hook, you can't just reel it in. You'll lose him that way. You have to play with him, let him take the line and run with it, just giving it a little tug every now and then. Then you slowly reel him in. That's what she's doing Garyk, she's playing the line, getting ready to reel you in."

Garyk was silent for a while. Alex was a little annoyed, thinking he had fallen asleep after having roused him from his. "No, there's something else," Garyk said softly. "She's afraid that we'll be split up after this. There's less than a week of training left, Alex. None of us really knows what will happen next. They could send us anywhere."

"Well, they did promise to send us back to school, to get advanced degrees and all that."

"Yes, but not to the same school. Those guys from A and B Sections all went to different universities and training centers."

"Well, Garyk, we'll know soon enough, won't we. There's no sense losing any more sleep over it tonight." With that, Alex rolled back towards the wall and fell off to sleep. Garyk remained awake, staring up at Alex' bunk without really seeing it and tried to imagine life without her.

Then it was Thursday afternoon. The unit had been in class over at the Tac Center all day. Tomorrow would be the final day of training. On Saturday morning there was to be a formal commissioning ceremony during which they would all be sworn in as second lieutenants in the Soviet Army. Colonel Pushkin would present them with their insignia of rank, gold shoulder boards with a single red stripe down the center and one tiny bronze star. It would be a grand day. In fact, for most of them it would be the first time in over twelve weeks that they would be seeing their families and friends. This was a public event to be celebrated for the glory of Mother Russia. Viktor Gadayev was flying up from Groznyy. Garyk's mother had refused to get into one of those flying machines, so Viktor was given the honor of representing the family.

It was unusual for them to get back so early in the day. Still, there was much to do. They needed to be packed and ready to depart as soon as the official ceremonies were over. Garyk and Alexandr were just starting a conversation back in their cell when the all too familiar voice of Corporal Popkin resounded one more time down the corridor.

"ANDROPOV, BUBKA, BYKOVA, CHERNENCKO, DIMIRTIEV, DANILOV, DUCHEK, GADAYEV, GORSKY..." he was calling out the roster, name by name. As each name was called and the respective bearer of that name presented him or herself, Popkin tossed them a large, official looking packet. The packet bore the official seal of the Soviet Army. On the front of Garyk's was printed in large red letters:

2LT GARYK IVRAMOVICH GADAYEV

CONFIDENTIAL—

He looked at the package for a few seconds, trying to take in the fact that he was an officer now. Well, technically speaking they still had to wait another day and a half, but there it was, in big bold Soviet red letters 2LT! Alexandr had gotten his first and was already ripping open the seal. "MOSCOW!" he shouted with great joy, "I'm going to the University at Moscow!"

Garyk hadn't even realized the significance of this packet until that moment. These were the Official Orders. The first day of the rest of his life was hidden inside this envelope. He pulled at the seal and tore his open. There were quite a few pages inside. But right there on top was a single sheet of white paper. It, too, bore the official seal, and was stamped in red at the bottom. It read"

"By order of the Supreme Soviet and on behalf of the people of the Union of Soviet Socialist Republics, Second Lieutenant Garyk Ivramovich Gadayev is hereby ordered to report, no later than 0830 hours, Monday June 7, 1976, to the Soviet Army Training Detachment, Moscow University, Moscow, RSSR, to complete the course of studies as set forth on the attached."

Garyk felt that he, too, should be elated. Moscow had the best computer science program in the Soviet Union. It was, in fact, exactly what Colonel Pushkin had told him would happen. Still, he wondered what her orders said. Where were they sending her?

Alexandr was watching him, waiting for a response. Finally, he could wait no longer. "Well, what is it? Where are you going?"

Garyk tried to maintain a grim expression. "I'm afraid," he began, his voice crescendoing as he spoke "that we shall have to remain roommates for a little while longer!" When he completed it he embraced his friend and roommate.

"Moscow, here we come!" Alex said as they hugged.

The corridor had turned into a cacophony of noise uncustomary for the military billet. People were going about from cell to cell to see what fate had bestowed upon each of their colleagues. Garyk didn't notice her arrive, but Katryn was standing in his doorway. The young women had been given permission to allow their hair to grow back over the past month. Hers formed a platinum bowl that accented those blue eyes. She held her official orders in one hand and looked at him with barely any expression at all. "Well," she said softly, "where is it?"

He turned at the sound of her voice. God, she is so lovely, he thought. He was almost afraid to say it. This was the moment they had both been dreading for six weeks. He practically whispered it. "Moscow University."

She didn't say anything. Instead she rushed into the room and jumped up into his arms as she had so many weeks before. She locked him in one long kiss, then she broke it off thrust her arms up in the air and shouted, "YES! YES! YES!"

10

Alex, Garyk and Katryn each took five classes that first summer semester. They had three of them together. As it turned out, they formed a great team. In particular, Katryn and Garyk were a perfect compliment. It was as if they knew each other's thoughts. His strengths lay in those areas where she needed some help and vice-versa. By working together they grasped each new concept quickly. Once again he outstripped his professors' ability to keep up. It was a perfect arrangement. They were students again, except that they were required to attend class in uniform most of the time. They reported in once a week to the training detachment headquarters. Other than that they were essentially on their own, with military pay and housing allotments to boot.

Garyk and Alexandr found an apartment together. It had two small bedrooms off a common room that featured a small kitchen unit, dining and sitting area replete with a settee and two matching armchairs. Best of all, it had a private toilet and shower stall! Katryn was able to live at home. However, the proximity of the apartment to the university made it more practical for her to spend most of her time there when not in the classroom.

Her family, father, mother and both brothers, had all traveled to the commissioning ceremony. There they had been introduced to Garyk. Katryn practically dragged this tall, dark-haired young man over to them and simply said, "Poppa, Mama, this is Garyk, Garyk Ivramovich Gadayev. His family is from Shali, near Groznyy. We're going to Moscow University together." Somehow, they sensed that this had not been a casual introduction. Their suspicions were confirmed once classes began and the young man became a frequent dinner guest. Alex also joined them on many occasions, but clearly there was a special bond between their daughter and this charming young Chechen. Yuri Ivanovich Moldatin was not quite sure of the young man's political motivation, but he found him likable enough. The family was resigned to the inevitable.

After the first six months, Katryn moved into the apartment and shared one of the bedrooms with Garyk. Alexandr was like a brother to both of them. It was a good-sized accommodation which, with three junior officer salaries, they could easily maintain with some style. Their colleagues at the university began to refer to them as The Three Musketeers and they embellished the metaphor.

By the end of May that first year all three were once again seated around the Moldatin's table for dinner. As usual, Garyk allowed Alexandr and Mr. Moldatin to do most of the talking, as the conversation invariably centered on the Communist Party, in which the senior Moldatin was a ranking member. Katryn finally broke in. "Poppa, enough talk about politics for this evening. Garyk has something he would like to say."

Garyk's complexion paled considerably as all eyes were suddenly turned in his direction. He ran a hand through his hair to compose himself. Over the past year he had allowed it to grow in, although it was still considerably shorter than it had been back home in Groznyy. He moved his hand down, forming a fist in front of his mouth to cover a forced cough. "Well, yes, I did wish to speak with you, Mr. Moldatin." He fumbled for the words, self-conscious at having been thrust into the limelight. "I just thought it might be a little more private."

"Nonsense, we are all family here." Alex was seated next to Mr. Moldatin and he received a pat on the shoulder to accentuate this remark. Her brothers were seated across from Alex and Garyk. "What you have to say to me certainly can be said to the whole family."

Katryn was beaming. She was also seated across from Garyk, the two of them on either side of her mother. "Go on, Garyk, it's no different than when we met with Col. Pushkin this afternoon."

"Well, sir," Garyk coughed again. "Kat and I, that is, I would like to ask your permission, you know, to marry Katryn. We've already cleared it with the Army, that is, if it's okay with you."

All heads quickly turned to Poppa. Mrs. Moldatin was a small woman, much like her daughter. She reached out and grabbed hold of both their hands and was squeezing them firmly as she awaited her husband's response. "Well, this is certainly something," he said. He looked squarely at Garyk, wondering what kind of man this was who was taking away the pride of his life. "If the Soviet Army has already given its consent, who am I to stand in the way!"

Mrs. Moldatin let out a cry of joy. She jumped up, knocking over her chair in the process, and embraced her daughter firmly. Alex also rose and grabbed hold of Garyk's hand. "It's about time!" he told him.

The following month they were married. It was June 29, 1977.

Other than becoming Lt. Katryn Y. M. Gadayev, little else changed. Alex remained in the room next to theirs and all three attended classes together. Actually, there was very little class work involved. It was mostly independent study.

The Americans had been making enormous strides in computer technology. Alex was able to disassemble virtually any new piece of micro, macro or mini computer equipment and reconstruct the process of its creation. Companies such as IBM and its upstart new rival, Apple Computer, were more than anxious to sell their new products to any eager buyer. Between them, Katryn and Garyk could decode and reprogram any software package that came their way. Copyrights and patent infringements were not their concern. The Soviet government had no intention of reselling any of this pirated technology. It just planned on using it for free.

Another semester was ending. The Three Musketeers made their way into the Army liaison office that served as a headquarters for the training detachment at the university. It had become a weekly routine, filling out attendance forms and progress reports in exchange for receiving their monthly allotment checks. Once in a while the officer in charge might ask to see them in his office to review their schedules. Mostly they just checked in at the desk where a matronly Sergeant Topkievski would look up from her paperwork, smile politely and hand them the forms that needed to be completed.

This morning she looked up without offering the customary smile. "The General is here today. He wishes to speak with all three of you. Please have a seat." She motioned for them to sit on the long bench that ran the length of the wall between the door and OIC's office. Near the door was a coat rack. On it this morning hung an officer's great coat. The gold shoulder boards with a single star signified that it belonged to a major general.

In a hushed tone Garyk asked the others, "What general is she talking about?"

"I have no idea," Alexandr answered. He tugged on his tie, trying to straighten the knot. "I knew I should have polished these damned shoes last night." Katryn, too, was primping herself for this unexpected encounter with a senior military officer. The door to the OIC's office opened and Sergeant Topkievski stood there holding it for them. "This way, please," she said in a most official manner. As they entered she closed the door behind them and resumed her position behind the desk.

It was a scene reminiscent of the Prorektor's office several years before. Col. Pushkin, no, it was Gen. Pushkin now, sat behind the desk normally occupied by Captain Dimitriev. "Ah, my three prodigies. I must thank you all. I believe that these stars on my epaulettes may be due more to your efforts than to mine. Yes, my little troop of 'wunderkind' has performed very well so far. That is why I am here today."

Garyk tried to look at Alex and Katryn standing on either side of him. He realized that once again a meeting with Pushkin was about to change his life. Did they realize this too?

"My friends," the General continued, "you have completed your studies ahead of schedule. Once again there is nothing else that they can teach you. It is time to put all of this training to good use. Don't you agree?" There was no answer expected. "All three of you have been assigned to work together on a new, top-secret project. As you may know, the Soviet government has been engaged in disarmament negotiations with the United States for some time. A treaty, known as SALT II, is being hammered out as we speak. This will ultimately call for drastic reductions in the Soviet missile arsenal. Many believe that while this is inevitable, it is also foolhardy. What we need to be able to do is to get greater delivery power from the remaining arsenal of weapons. Our entire nuclear delivery system needs to be upgraded. That entails computerized control capability and a satellite relay communications system. That's where the three of you come in. You are to be part of the team that is being assembled to do this."

This meant that they returned to a military environment again. While it was more regimented than the past twenty-four months, they were moving in an elite circle and special privileges were accorded to them. This included a preferential selection when it came to their new quarters. The headquarters was located just outside of Moscow, so Katryn opted for a large apartment not too far away from her parents. Alexandr felt that the time had come to give them some privacy, so he moved into the officer's quarters on base.

They had been settled into their new quarters for about six months when Katryn began to experience a sudden lack of energy. Usually the one to bounce out of bed each morning while Garyk fought for a few precious moments of extra sleep; she barely made it into the kitchen this morning. It was long after Garyk had found were she hid the coffee and figured out how to work the percolator. "Is everything all right, Kat?"

"Oh, I don't know, I'm just so tired this morning." She sounded listless and her complexion was nearly as pale as her hair. Instead of her uniform she still had on one of his old training sweatshirts that came down to her knees.

Garyk was concerned. Vitality was such a significant component of her being. "You really haven't been yourself for a couple of days. Do you think you should see a doctor?"

"I was thinking about staying home and trying to get some..." She turned quickly and rushed into the bathroom. Garyk could hear the sounds of her retching. "Damn, that's all I need." He heard her say.

"Kat, can I get you something? Are you all right?"

"I'll survive." She retched again. "You just go on without me. It's nothing."

Garyk came home early and expected to find her in bed. Instead, he found her almost as bubbly as ever. She ran to great him in her customary manner, by leaping up and wrapping her legs around him. She kissed him. He was amazed.

"It looks like someone is feeling a lot better this afternoon," he said.

"Yes," she answered, "someone is. She's going to have a baby!"

Garyk was bowled over by the news. Once again she had caught him off guard and left him speechless. He held her close, kissing her again and again.

11

They had a boy. Garyk was ecstatic as he came into her room. "Kat, he's beautiful! So are you, I might add."

"Oh God, Garyk, you must be blind, or just horny from not getting any the past few months. I look terrible."

"Not to me you don't. I've just called Viktor to tell him the news about Ivram Garykovich."

"About who? Oh, Garyk, no. You can't seriously think I'd want to name him that."

"Certainly." Garyk was baffled. They had never discussed names. He'd just always assumed. "This is the first male child born in the family. He should be named after my father. It's tradition."

"People will think that he is a Jew." It was the first time he had ever heard her express any bias toward anyone.

"Not a Jew," was his reply, "It's a Sunni name that has been in my family for generations."

"Well, you can let Viktor name his son that. I don't like it. I won't have it."

He had never experienced her like this, even back when she had told him that they needed to put their romance on hold. At least then he understood the concern. This was irrational. She won out, of course. Their son was named Georgi Garykovich Gadayev. They both laughed at the sound of it. Still, a wound had been opened which would fester over time.

They threw a party in the new child's honor. Alexandr was there and Sergi came from off in the east somewhere. He was being very secretive about just exactly what his new duties were. Natashia flew down from her post in Leningrad. Since she was not in uniform, she took the opportunity to let down her hair. It was golden brown and hung over her shoulders. Katryn's older brother seemed to be taking a special interest in her presence. Unfortunately, Anna couldn't make it; they had stationed her out in Vladivostok.

This time Garyk's mother did consent to make the trip with Viktor and his family. After all, this was a grandson! "Mama Gadayev, I'm so pleased to welcome you into my house," Katryn said as she greeted her at the door. She kissed her on both cheeks and bowed politely in acknowledgment of the older woman's status in the family.

"Thank you for that formal greeting, child. Come, now give your Mama a proper hug!"

"Save some of her for the rest of us, Mama!" Katryn was startled a bit to hear that voice, it sounded so much like her husband. Except for his longer hair and rakish beard, Viktor was the spitting image of his twin.

Garyk grabbed his mother and gave her a big hug. "I wasn't really sure you'd actually come. I'm so pleased."

"Don't flatter yourself, Garyk. You know it's not you I came to see. Where is my little grandson?" She spied the bassinet in the corner of the room and pushed past him to pick up the child. "Oh my, such an adorable little one we have here. Garyk, such a pity not to have named him after your father."

"Mama, please, let's not get into that just now."

With all the guests accounted for, Katryn was mildly surprised to hear yet another knock on their door. When she answered it, she found herself facing an older gentleman with speckled gray hair whom she had never met before. "Ah, good evening Lieutenant Gadayev, your husband is in, I trust? I have brought a small gift for young Georgi and would like to present it to him, if you don't mind."

"Garyk," she called over to where he was involved in some deep debate with his brother and her father, "Garyk, dear, there is a gentleman here to see you."

Garyk looked up. It couldn't be. Yes, it was! It was Lemchenko! Garyk elbowed his way over to the door, deeply surprised and confused by the appearance of this man from out of the blue. "Comrade Lemchenko, what a surprise this is!" He said that in all sincerity. Katryn was still standing by the door, looking bewildered. Garyk had never told her about this mysterious visitor. "Kat, dear, this is Comrade Lemchenko. I think I can safely say that if it weren't for him we might not have ever met!"

Even more perplexed by this remark, Katryn took Lemchenko's hand. "Well, it seems that you are an honored and welcome guest in my house."

"To what can I attribute the honor of this visit?" Garyk asked.

"Why, to your new son, of course!"

"But how did you know?"

"Lemchenko knows everything, Lieutenant Gadayev, Lemchenko knows everything!"

Garyk knew that this was the truth and that fact made him very uneasy. He offered Lemchenko a drink and was not surprised when he accepted. "You know," he said with a toothy grin, "that I have a passion for good Russian vodka."

The man presented his gift to Katryn, a red baby outfit, then quietly went and stood alone in the corner sipping his drink. Garyk wondered if he was spying on them even now. After a while, Garyk had an opportunity to drift back over in his direction. "Tell me," Garyk asked, "did I ever see you in Novgorod?"

"Now, why would you think that?" he replied slyly.

"Yes, it was you. You've been spying on me all this time. Why?"

"Spying is such a dramatic word, Lieutenant. As I explained, I think, to you many years ago, it is my job to keep *track* of certain people. You are merely one of those in whom I have, shall we say, taken an interest."

"Just exactly how much did you see back then?" Garyk wondered if he had actually followed them into the boathouse that night.

"What I saw was two people who seemed to be quite capable of handling themselves very well."

"Then you did not report us?"

"What I do or do not report is not a matter for your concern, Lieutenant Gadayev."

"But if you had, they most certainly would have tried to keep us apart."

"Don't be so sure, my young friend. As I said, I saw two people who handled themselves well. From your backgrounds it was plain to me that the two of you should work well together. That you have, in fact, done so is no surprise. I am, however, pleased that the experiment has exceeded everyone's expectations."

"Then you actually arranged for us to stay together?" Garyk was skeptical.

"That, too, my young comrade, is of no real consequence to you." Having said that, Lemchenko chugged down the remaining two fingers of vodka in his glass, handed it back to his host and made his exit as abruptly as he had appeared.

12

The next two years passed by quickly. They were both captains, promoted at the very top of their peer group. Clearly they were on the fast track. They were happy with their work. Happy with their life together.

As good as things were for them, they were not good for the country. Supplies of basic necessities were becoming harder to find. The constant food shortages were unnerving. Even with their connections, and with those that her father could bring to sway, there were times when they had to do without. Sometimes they made jokes about it. At other times she was just plain scared.

Unrest was widespread. Even the newspapers, those dogmatic propaganda mills, were raising harsh objections to the government's policies and practices. This was compounded by the influx of outside influences. There was a time, not that long ago, when the Russian people had been shut off from the world. What they knew about life outside of the Soviet Union was what the Party wanted them to know.

But now people were leaving the country for business, artistic and athletic reasons. They were exposed to Western culture, they saw the opulence and they came back and actually talked about it. American cinema and television shows were actually being seen inside the Soviet Union. In contrast to all the wealth which people saw displayed, there were the empty shelves and long lines, right in the heart of Moscow.

Then there was the other issue. After watching the Americans nearly drown in the tempestuous quagmire known as Viet Nam, the Soviet leadership decided to leap headlong into one of their very own. It was called Afghanistan. They say history repeats itself, but this smacked of instant replay! In December of 1979, Soviet forces were sent in to quell an anti-Communist uprising. People were told that this would be a temporary police action. The military leadership questioned the strategic imbalances that this presented; yet embraced the possibility of earning their own combat ribbons. There is nothing in the world more ornery than a warrior without a war.

Work had progressed well for Garyk and his team. Things were starting to wind down. Several of the junior members had already been reassigned to other projects and there were daily rumors about pending transfers. Therefore, Garyk was not altogether surprised when another white packet with the red Soviet Army seal and his name emblazoned in red letters appeared on his desk one morning.

Garyk took a deep breath before he opened it. I hope they're going to keep us together, he thought. Kat will go crazy if we're separated. He took his letter opener and slit the envelope lengthwise, then pulled out the official orders. "Oh God," he exclaimed, "they're sending me to Afghanistan!"

Alex also received a packet in his office. His orders were essentially the same. He rushed down the hall and into Garyk's office and found him just sitting at his desk, staring at the sheet of paper in his hand. "Oh, you're going too," he said sullenly.

Garyk looked up, not comprehending what Alex had said. "I'm sorry, Alex, what did you say. I was kind of lost in space for a moment I guess."

"Your orders, I got them too. Am I correct in assuming that we're both heading to Afghanistan together?"

Garyk held up his orders. "The 14th Communications Detachment, special assignment. You too?"

"Hey, they wouldn't dare break up the team." Alex sounded less than enthusiastic.

"You're right. Unfortunately, you and I are not the team I was worried about. I don't know how Katryn is going to take this."

"Well, good luck. I guess I better go break the news myself." Alexandr walked slowly back to his own office, shut the door and called home to his new bride of six months. She cried when he told her.

Katryn's reaction was not as calm. "NO! You CAN'T go!" she cried out. It sounded more like an order than a protest. "It's not fair. I won't let them send you!"

"We knew that this might happen someday Kat. Actually, I'm surprised I wasn't called sooner." He said this hoping to calm her, but it had the exact opposite effect.

"NO! NO! NO!" She was shaking. He held her close to him but she beat on his chest, causing the pins that held his service ribbons in place to press into his skin.

"Hey, stop this, you're actually hurting me now."

"Good!" she replied.

"What is it, Katryn, what is the matter. They're just sending me down there for six months. Less if we can get these satellite dishes operational sooner. It's a tactical support group. We'll be working strictly out of the main base camps."

"I don't care. You simply can't go. Not now!"

"Why not, Katryn? God, you're scaring me.

"Well then that makes two of us." She wiped away some of the tears that had streamed down onto her cheeks and took a deep breath, exhaling upward to blow the hair out of her face. "Garyk, I'm pregnant!"

He tried to hold her close to him, but she pulled away. "DAMN YOU!" she screamed and ran into their bedroom, slamming the door behind her. He could hear her sobbing again. He had no idea what to do and found himself pouring vodka into a glass. He chugged down a full three fingers, then poured himself another drink. This will be a long night, he thought.

13

Afghanistan was hot. It was a dry heat that pulled the moisture right out off the pores of your body so that you didn't sweat. And it was dusty. Gritty, actually. The grit got into everything and that was playing havoc with much of their computer equipment. Alex spent a good portion of his time cleaning out the consoles and trying to find ways to seal out the grit.

Garyk and Alexandr had spent the past four months in and around Kabul. Their unit had gotten most of the satellite up-links in place and running on schedule. Once in a while it had been necessary for one or both of them to go into the field for a day or two. Garyk never mentioned that in his letters to Katryn. On one such trip they heard the sound of gunfire, like the steady crackling noise of a string of firecrackers. Actually, it was more like several strings going off one right after the other. The sound swelled and seemed to be getting nearer. Then the big guns at the base camp opened fire. Sudden booms that pierced the eardrums. They were working some 250 meters away from the artillery unit, but they could feel the rush of wind against their legs from the concussion sent out after each discharge. Several seconds elapsed and then the distant thuds were heard, the shells exploding on or near their targets. The gunfire became random and then it ceased.

"Well, that was exciting," Garyk said to Alexandr when the last of the artillery barrage had been fired.

"You can keep your excitement. That's the closest I've heard any gunfire in four months. It was too damned close as far as I'm concerned."

"Yes, I agree. Not something to write home about, that's for sure."

Alex had been working on a computer board, gently brushing away some dust particles. He snapped it back in place and looked over at Garyk. "How are things at home?"

"About the same." Garyk stopped fiddling with a wayward monitor. "Her letters have become very impersonal. All she does is complain about the discomfort she's having with the baby. She never did that with Georgi. Not that I can remember anyway. She makes it seem like it's all my fault."

"It was a bad time to have to leave her, that's for sure. I'm glad my Tashia isn't pregnant now."

There was one major installation that remained to be set up. It was up north, near the border with Uzbekistan. They were to be part of a convoy of trucks bringing supplies of food and ammunition to the headquarters complex near Sharïf. Alex had been going over some schematics with one of the young technicians. Finished, he ambled over to where Garyk was overseeing the loading of their equipment into a truck. "Is it just me or are these soldiers getting younger?"

Garyk looked around at the young soldiers in their brown and tan camouflaged field uniforms waiting to board the escort vehicles. There was a time when he thought that eight pockets was a bit excessive. Now each one held the essentials of war, ammo magazines, first aid kits, food and, most important of all, cigarettes. He nodded in their direction and said, "They're just kids, aren't they?"

Alex shook his head in sad agreement. "Well, I guess after nearly five years in this hell hole, they've run out of adults. Of course, it could be that we've just gotten a lot older the past few months."

"That's true."

Alex removed his glasses and tried to wipe away the ever-present dust. "Well, everything is fine on my end, how about you?"

"Ready to rock and roll. Literally, that is. I understand that the road is deeply rutted and pockmarked with holes, some more than 30 centimeters deep. I think I'll stay with the equipment, you can go with the team."

It was a rough ride. The road wound its way through rugged mountain terrain, with large boulders and rocky crags jutting up on either side. It was a slow, dusty journey. The cab of the truck was hot. The smell of diesel fuel from the exhausts permeated the air. They had been on the road for about two hours. During that time, he had exchanged perhaps a half-dozen words with his driver. His name was Duchek or Checkov, whatever, it was of no consequence. He was assigned to the transportation unit, not a part of their communications team. Another youngster, barely nineteen years old, Garyk surmised.

Attempting to break the monotony, Garyk turned to him and asked, "Have you been down here long?"

"Two months, sir. I guess that's long enough. Seen enough of these fuckin' Moslem monkeys to last a lifetime that's for sure."

Garyk bit hard on his lip. He felt like screaming at this young man

'I'M A MOSLEM TOO, YOU KNOW!' It had happened before. Too often. Alex sometimes caught himself making a remark about the Afghanis, realizing that his ethnic slurs applied as equally to his best friend as they did to the Afghan rebels they were fighting.

The team was in the truck behind his. When they made turns to the right, Garyk could see Alexandr riding shotgun. On occasion they exchanged a little wave to acknowledge that they were both a part of this seemingly endless trek. The trucks were coming down a long grade, laboring in low gear. The outcroppings towered over the trucks on both sides. Out of the corner of his eye, something caught Garyk's attention. A whitish blur. Was it a bird streaking low across the ground?

He turned his head just in time to see the truck ahead burst into a ball of flames. The sound of the explosion followed almost immediately. He lurched forward as the truck came to an abrupt stop. "Shit!" he heard his driver shout. The soldier threw open his door and jumped out, grabbing his AK- 47 before he left. Pieces of metal and other debris crashed against the windscreen. Was that part of an arm on the hood? There was gunfire everywhere and a lot of shouting. He reached for the doorknob and looked about for his own weapon.

Another explosion, this one so loud that it occupied the totality of his senses. It caused a deep, hollow ringing in his ears. For a moment all was blackness. He sensed that his world was slowly rotating in a forward roll. "I am dead," was his first conscious thought. It's funny how the mind works. He recalled a course in western philosophy he had taken years before. Was it Descartes who said "I think, therefore I exist?" I *am* thinking, therefore I must *exist*. Then the pain thrust upon him and he passed out.

The rocket had struck the rear of Garyk's truck, which was fortunate for him. The explosion threw the cab ten feet in the air. It came down, roof first, some fifteen meters ahead. The cab collapsed about him, smashing against his head, breaking his shoulder.

Alexandr jumped out of his truck at the sound of first explosion. He shouted to his men, urging them to get out. The sound of gunfire filled the air as the soldiers, scrambling from their vehicles, fired wildly in all direction. He looked up into the rock canyon walls for any signs of their attackers. At the sound of the second blast he turned and watched as the truck cab arced forward and crashed to the ground. He knew Garyk was dead, but he had to make sure.

The cab was fully compressed on the driver's side. A gas tank mounted to the side wall had split open and fuel was splashing down onto the ground. Alex knew it would be only moments before it ignited, setting the whole cab aflame. He looked through the passenger window and could see Garyk's crumpled body. Blood streamed down from his head. The door was jammed shut but, with some effort, he was able to pull his friend out through the window opening. The gasoline caught fire and the cab was starting to burn furiously.

Garyk moaned and cried out in pain as he struggled to free him, so he knew that he was still alive. Once his friend had been extricated, he threw him over his shoulder and began to look for cover. During this whole time the gunfire had continued. Bullets rained down from the rocks above and the Russian soldiers continued to return fire with their automatic weapons, hoping to find one or more of the unseen assailants.

Alex found a spot that afforded them partial cover. There was a deep gash in Garyk's forehead. He used his own shirt to make a compression bandage and was able to control the bleeding. Frantically, he tried to recall the five step checklist from their first aid training classes. He pushed a stone under his friend's legs to prevent shock and made sure his airway was clear. "It's okay, buddy. Don't you dare leave me, do you hear me, Garyk?" The gunfire became sporadic. The attack seemed to have ended. Alexandr looked around for some assistance. "Medic, I need a medic here. An officer has been wounded."

He saw several soldiers running a few meters ahead. He rose up and waved for them to come over. "Over here, I need some assistance!" The bullet entered the left side of his head, just above the ear, exploding out the right. Alex's lifeless body crumpled down on top of Garyk.

14

She collapsed when they told her. Before they told her, actually. Colonel Sakharov was her commanding officer. A fatherly figure with balding hair that formed a light brown wreath around his head. He wore steel rimmed glasses and clenched the ever-present stub of a cigar in his mouth. He walked into her office and in voice much more subdued than usual said "Captain Gadayev—Katryna." No one called her Katryna. It was a term of endearment her mother had used when she was a little girl. At the age of twelve she had politely but firmly informed her mother, "I am not a child, Mama. My name is Katryn." Garyk and a few close friends called her Kat, but never Katryna.

Two other officers were with the Colonel. They were unfamiliar to her. She knew, then, that he was dead. She had felt it the day before. The baby inside her let forth two powerful kicks. Much stronger than any she'd felt up till now. Stronger, it seemed than any Georgi had delivered. She sensed that he would never hold her stomach the way he had with Georgi, sharing the joy of the life within her. He would never hold this child. He had gone off to war and left her alone to raise two young children. Everything drained from her and she collapsed.

They moved her to a couch in Sakharov's office. Her feet were propped up on one of its arms. She came to in a daze. Barely aware of those concerned friends, co-workers, and fellow officers who hovered over her. "Katryn, Katryn, are you all right?" For a moment she thought she was back at the Novgorod Training Center with her roommate attempting to rouse her. "Katryn, it will be all right." It was Natashia. She was down for a few days of training courses and rushed over when she heard the news.

"What?" Katryn said with a barely audible whisper. She attempted to sit up, but Natashia was holding her down.

"No, stay put for a bit longer. You still look as white as a ghost."

She was back in the present now. "Garyk," she said his name softly, then she cried out, "Oh my God, Garyk!"

"He's all right, Katryn." Natashia held her hand, patting a cold cloth against her forehead with the other. "Well, not quite okay, I suppose, but he is alive!"

"He's alive?" she said, not believing it to be true.

"Yes. Katryn, he's alive. Badly wounded they tell me, but he should recover fully."

Katryn sat up and reached out for her companion. "I knew this was going to happen, I just knew it. I've been feeling something dreadful hanging over me for days." Natashia held her close and Katryn cried. Then she became aware of the others in the room. It was not dignified to carry on this way, not professional at all. She pulled herself up and stood in front of the Colonel, tugging at her blouse. It was a special maternity shirt and it responded poorly to her attempts to straighten it.

"I am sorry sir," she said in the most militaristic manner she could muster. "Please forgive me for acting like a child. Now tell me, how did this happen?"

The colonel placed both of his hands on her shoulders and looked her firmly in the eyes. "There is no need to make apologies Captain. Your husband has been gravely wounded, it is only natural..."

"Natural perhaps, but certainly not professional."

Alexandr had saved his life by stopping the bleeding and getting him away from the burning truck. That afforded the medical team sufficient time to get him to a field hospital and begin the reconstructive process. He remained in the field hospital near Kabul for several weeks. When he was considered ambulatory, he was flown back to a military medical center outside of Moscow.

Katryn walked slowly into his room. He laughed at the sight of her. Barely five two and into her seventh month, she was nearly as wide as she was tall. She blew back the hair from her face and said sternly, "How can you laugh? Do you have any idea what you've put me through?"

Garyk wasn't sure whether she was really serious or just playing one of her little tricks on him. He hoped it was the latter, but sensed otherwise. "I'm sorry, Kat, but you know I've been through a lot myself lately. It's just so good to see you again. You look beautiful."

"I'm a tank."

"Yes, but a beautiful one!" He laughed again and grabbed hold of her hand. He tried to pull her towards him for a kiss. She resisted and he dropped her hand. "I was rather hoping for a warm welcome home."

"I'm sorry, Garyk. I haven't been myself lately. I suppose it's the baby. It's been a lot harder on me this time." For some reason Garyk couldn't fathom, this was all his fault.

The loss of Alexandr weighed heavily upon him. Katryn remained cold toward him, which did nothing to improve his spirits nor speed his recovery. He was still in the hospital when their daughter was born. A nurse came and wheeled him down to the maternity ward. This time there was no discussion or argument over the naming of the child. They were both agreed that she was Alexandra.

Captain Garyk Ivramovich Gadayev was awarded several medals for distinguished service in Afghanistan, including the Order of the Red Star. Alexandr's young bride attended the ceremonies to receive his posthumously. Alex was also awarded the Order of Courage for risking his life to aid a fellow soldier. Katryn attended the ceremony and gave Garyk a big hug and kiss afterwards. Perhaps the pregnancy had been the cause of her melancholia. Things seemed to get better at home. Better, but not quite the same as before. Katryn had changed.

The experience in Afghanistan also changed Garyk. It went beyond the brush with death or the loss of a friend. During his time there he began to question the purpose of the mission. Not the communications mission, the whole Afghan occupation. He had identified more closely with the rebels they were fighting than with the Soviet troops with whom he served. The Afghanis reminded him of his native Chechnya. He took offense to the casual remarks made by those about him that disparaged the Moslem freedom fighters. He also found himself more vocal in his support of the dissident movement growing throughout the country.

More or less recovered, he tried to bury himself in his computers but was more than happy to allow his new daughter to divert his attention. She was a delight and he hurried home early each evening to spend time with her. Poppa Moldatin was a frequent visitor of his new granddaughter as well. He was sitting at the dining table, holding Alexandra when Garyk came in. The conversation soon turned political. Garyk had always avoided such chats with his father-in-law, but not anymore. "Garyk, this is a new side of you. I have never known you to be so opinionated in political matters before."

"I suppose that's because it never really mattered to me before. It was a shock to see Russian soldiers deriding those people just because of their faith. Mr. Moldatin, it's my faith too. My family is Moslem. Will the government turn such scorn on us someday too?"

"But those people are revolutionaries, Garyk. They seek to upset the Union."

"Those people are hungry, Poppa Moldatin. They seek to feed their children! These idiots in the government that you're so fond of can't even provide enough food for us here in Moscow. Do you know how many times Katryn and I have gone without food so Georgi might have something to eat?"

"Yes, it is true that we have all had to endure certain temporary..."

"Temporary? My God, Mr. Moldatin, open your eyes! There's a national crisis developing right here and you don't want to admit it."

Mr. Moldatin rose from his chair at the table and handed the baby over to her mother.

"Garyk, I think I liked you much better when you showed no interest in politics whatsoever. Be careful, my young friend, be very careful." He kissed Katryn, grabbed up his coat and hat and made a hasty exit.

Katryn glared at Garyk. "How can you upset him like that?"

"Oh sure, go ahead and blame me. You always do. Kat, you know I'm right on this. You've complained about the same things, just not in front of your father."

"He's a very proud man, Garyk and he is very much involved with the government you're so anxious to criticize. When you attack the Party, you attack him. When you attack him, you hurt me."

Viktor

15

Viktor Ivramovich Gadayev loved to laugh. He possessed a zest for life, enjoying everything that was about him to its fullest. He was also a quick study and a diligent worker.

He spent two years as a rigger in the oil fields north of Groznyy outside of Chervlënnaya. Though young in years, he impressed both those with whom and for whom he worked and was promoted quickly. One asset, in particular, was his ability to serve as a liaison between the primarily Russian senior staff and the predominantly Chechen and Ingush work gangs. The latter groups tended to converse solely in Nakh, a regional tongue with several ethnic variations. This was a matter of ethnic pride, more to exasperate their Russian overseers than from a lack of formal education.

It was May 1, 1975, and a national holiday. Back in Moscow, the military would be parading the latest advances in modern warfare, not to mention the oldest - shear manpower, down the Novy Arbat and into Red Square past the movers and shakers of the state. But they were far from Moscow, in the very shadow of the Caucuses, free to celebrate the day for what it was, May Day. Yes, they had assembled earlier to hear speeches made by the local Communist Party leadership. They had sung the songs of nationalism. But that was over. The games had begun!

Viktor was taking part in a series of soccer matches. The games were friendly, well mostly friendly, pitting the various work crews against each other. The day was warming fast and he had removed his shirt, baring a manly chest, thick with dark hair. He presented quite a figure, tall and muscular from laboring in the fields. He wore his hair longer than Garyk, his older brother by twelve minutes. It hung in dark ringlets. His jaw was outlined by a narrow beard, which he kept short cropped. His hearty laugh rang out across the playing field whenever a player on either team executed a particularly good maneuver.

Tatyana Dzasokhov found it hard not to notice him. Both her father and brother worked the oil fields. The elder Dzasokhov had done so for twenty-five years. She had a sister who was also married to the oil, as her mother would say. Her family was gathered under a grove of trees by the banks of the Terek River, which bordered the field. She had come over to check on the progress of her brother Borz's game.

At first, she thought him ostentatious. He lacked certain of the skills required to be a truly effective player, yet seemed to have delegated to himself the role of captain. Many of the players, her brother included, were older than he was, yet they deferred to his leadership. It was the laugh that held her attention. She found herself laughing along with him, even if at times she was unsure what might have initiated it. If she turned her interest away from the field for a time to engage in some conversation with friends or casual acquaintances, that laugh would pull her back.

"Hey, Tatyana," her cousin taunted, "has that big brute caught your eye?"

"Certainly not!" She turned her head quickly and her long brown ponytail swished from side to side. The cousin just laughed.

"My, he is a hairy one!" another of her friends put in. "He will surely keep some woman very warm indeed."

"Yes, Tatyana, perhaps you'd do better not to pick such a hairy beast for your bed," her cousin rejoined.

"I have not chosen anyone for my bed!" she protested, but her cheeks had a certain redness to them. "You are terrible," she said to the small band of girls, all about her age, that were enjoying this repartee and started to make her way to the family enclave. Seventeen, she was developing nicely into womanhood, but her body still possessed many of the characteristics of late adolescence. Another of his laughs rolled across the field and she fought the temptation to look that way again.

The game came to its conclusion and the small crowd that had assembled along the sidelines moved back toward the picnic grounds for a noon time repast. She was helping her mother lay out the food, kneeling to take things out of a basket, and hadn't bothered to look up when she heard Borz return. Her father said, "Borz, you played magnificently!"

Borz responded, "Oh, I'm afraid that I didn't help our side very much."

"Nonsense, Borz," she heard a strange voice respond, "you are far too modest about the way you played. Why, your defense was brilliant!"

Tatyana looked up to see who this visitor might be. He was standing directly in line with the sun. She had to hold a hand up over her eyes to make him out. Silhouetted like that, against the sun, she could make out only a dark face with long curling black tresses. Borz said something else and the visitor laughed. My God, she thought, it was him!

"Everyone," Borz called to the group, "I would like to introduce my good friend Viktor Gadayev. I taught him so well that now they have made him my supervisor! Viktor, this is everyone."

She stood up, brushing away the crushed leaves and little twigs that adhered to her skirt. Somehow she felt a bit embarrassed that he should have come upon her on her knees. Viktor was shaking hands with all of the men folk and then was introduced to Mama directly. Almost as an afterthought, Borz turned her way and said, "Oh yes, and this is my little sister, Tatyana." He smiled at her, gave a little nod of his head and moved on with Borz to the table where he gratefully accepted a cold drink that was offered.

"Viktor has no family," Borz was telling Mama, "so I have asked him to join us today, Is that all right with you?"

Mama answered, "What is ours is yours. Such a pity to have no family."

"Actually, I do, but they are not here. My mother and Gran live about twenty-five kilometers from here, out past Shali. I have a brother, too, at the State University. He was too busy with his school chums to join me today."

It was Tatyana's duty as the youngest daughter to serve the others and she busied herself with the task. She made a point of not looking at him when she had to pass the food his way. Still, she caught herself looking in his direction more frequently than she would have wanted to admit. It was his eyes. They were deep set and dark, mysterious yet inviting at the same time.

Her cousin passed by and in a not so subdued whisper said, "I see we have begun to lure the hairy one to our bed after all."

She let out a little shriek, scared that he may have overheard, then threw a towel after the cousin, who pranced off giggling merrily.

16

In the months that followed Tatyana saw Viktor several more times. He would stop by with Borz on the way to some manly adventure. Once he had stayed on for an evening supper with the family. She was never the focus of his attention, yet he always greeted her with a friendly "Hello" and that little nod of the head. Those deep dark eyes twinkled when she had occasion to look into them.

So it was not exceptional or unusual for him to have stopped by on this particular January morning. She answered his rap on their door and greeted him with a mildly surprised "Oh, hello, it is you. Let me get Borz." Her ponytail swayed from side to side as she pranced away. Viktor noticed that she was wearing blue jeans and that they nicely accentuated certain parts of her body as she moved away.

She popped into the kitchen where her father and brother were finishing their morning breakfast. "Borz, it's that Mr. Gadayev here to see you. He seems a bit agitated this morning." Both Borz and Papa came into the front room to greet their guest. Borz was not quite as tall as Viktor, but much broader across the chest. His arms were big and powerful, the result of lifting heavy pipe for five years. Papa was shorter than his son, but sturdy of build. In his day he could take on the best of them. Age had mellowed his temper, but not softened his body.

"Good, thank God you are home!" Viktor blurted out as soon as he saw his friend. Then, turning to the father, "Excuse me, Mr. Dzasokhov, I apologize for intruding upon your family like this."

"It is no problem, Viktor, but please tell us what is the matter."

"Yes, Viktor," added Borz, "I don't think I've ever seen you so uneasy. Is something wrong?"

Viktor pulled a letter out from his coat pocket. "It's Garyk, my brother," he said. "They just came and took him away from the university. He's going to be in the Army now!"

Garyk had written him a letter while he was on the train to

Volgograd. He explained about Colonel Pushkin's visit and the strange Lemchenko. It said all that he knew about this sudden twist of his life, that he was enroute to some sort of training center outside of Novgorod and that he was going to become an officer in the Soviet Army, working on computer programs. There was a second envelope with "Mama" written on the outside.

Borz read through the letter, handing it to Papa when he had finished. As they read, Viktor paced the floor in obvious distress. Tatyana was still standing by the door. She watched the scene unfolding before her and felt concern for this young man, without really understanding what was going on.

Borz had met Garyk once or twice on visits to Groznyy with Viktor. "Garyk a soldier—no, an officer! I would not have thought that."

"Nor I," admitted Viktor. Viktor seemed to calm down and he forced a chuckle. It was not the hearty laugh Tatyana loved to hear. "It's just so sudden, Borz," Viktor continued. "They just walked into his life and grabbed him away. I may never see him again!"

Papa Dzasokhov had finished reading the letter now. "To be sure," he said, "this is an unusual situation. However, I do not think it is cause for alarm at this point. They clearly intend your brother no harm or else why would he be allowed to write this letter to you. There is much to be said about life as an officer in the Soviet Army."

"Yes, of course you are right," said Viktor. "It was just such a surprise. And there's Mama!" The letter had mentioned that Garyk wanted Viktor to personally deliver his letter to their mother. There was no way to reach her by telephone and he thought she needed to have Viktor there when she learned this news.

"Borz, my good friend," Viktor turned to his friend and placed both of his hands on Borz's arms, "I was hoping that you could drive me down to the farm today. I can get away today, but they need me to work all next week."

Borz looked down at his friend's feet, not wanting to see his disappointment. Viktor was not just a good friend, he was also his supervisor. "I only wish that I could do as you ask. Last night I committed to work an extra shift today. In fact, I was just getting ready to leave when you came in."

"That's all right. It was too much for me to ask of you, I know. I can still go by bus. I only looked to shorten the trip. It is no matter."

"Papa" Tatyana broke in. "Perhaps if Borz would not mind lending me his car, you might let me drive Mr. Gadayev to see his mother."

To be honest, the three men had been completely oblivious to the fact that the young woman had been standing there all this time. Now they turned to her, each with some expression of surprise. Papa started "Tatyana, I really don't think..."

"What a splendid idea!" interrupted Borz. "However, I would not be much of a friend if I were to entrust dear Viktor here to the perils of your driving."

"I am as good a driver as you are, Borz, better perhaps." There was an impertinent lilt to her voice and she nodded her head to give emphasis, setting the ponytail in motion yet again.

"Thank you for your kind offer, Miss Dzasokhov, but I am afraid I have already over-extended my friendship with Borz. I wouldn't want to be the one to put him in debt to his little sister."

She took umbrage at being termed the little sister. Is that all he thought of her? "Nonsense," she quickly added, "you are as much my friend as you are his. Besides, I had nothing in particular to do today and a drive in the country would just suit me, that is all." Having salvaged a bit of her pride, she began to leave them.

Mr. Dzasokhov sensed that there was some under current he was missing here. Still, he had taken a liking to this young man and he also recognized that he was, in all likelihood, someone the family would want to count as a friend in the future. He had already surpassed Borz on the work gangs.

"No, Mr. Gadayev, I think perhaps my daughter is right." Tatyana stopped to hear the rest of this. "Borz let her take your friend to see his mother. Just remember, Tatyana, the roads can be very dangerous this time of year." With that, the senior member of the family left the room, leaving no opportunity for further discussion about this matter.

Mrs. Dzasokhov had been listening to this conversation from the kitchen. She turned away from the door as a husband walked in. She looked very pleased, suspecting that her daughter had some ulterior motive for her largesse and wondered to herself what the eventual outcome of it all might be.

Other than a few words to express his deep gratitude, both to his friend for letting him have use of the car and to the sister, for her willingness to be his driver, Viktor said little for the first part of the trip. They had to head south into Groznyy first, and then make their way back out a series of rutted country roads to the farm. As they drove through the city, Viktor asked, "Do you mind if we make a stop. I think maybe I should check Garyk's apartment."

"Sure thing," she replied, "just show me the way!"

Garyk had given Viktor a key, in case he ever needed a place to stay on his rare visits into town. The letter had only been written a week earlier. When they walked into the apartment, Viktor was stunned. Everything Garyk owned had been packed into seven large boxes that were piled, three high, in the center of the room. On each had been affixed a large shipping label which read:

G A D A Y E V, G. I.
694 7765 3569
Hold for Disposition

"Well, they sure are an efficient crew. Garyk would never believe how clean this place could be. There's no sense in rummaging through this stuff now. Everything's all sealed up. It's obviously going to be sent to storage somewhere, just like Garyk mentioned in the letter." It left him with an eerie feeling. It was so easy to just make someone disappear.

"What about the furniture?"

"Most of this stuff came with the apartment. Oh, I guess that lamp belongs to Mama." Viktor walked over to a small lamp with a wooden base that had obviously been made by a young boy. He unplugged it and absently handed it to Tatyana to carry. "There's not much here, is there? Funny, this place always seemed so crowded, what with all of Garyk's clothes, books and computer print-outs scattered everywhere."

Back in the car, she sensed his uneasiness. To break the mood she said, "I suppose if I were to visit your apartment I'd find things just as neat and orderly as Garyk's back there." He laughed. It was that hearty laugh that she first heard last spring. It filled the car. She couldn't help but laugh too.

For his part, he was glad, now, that Borz could not make the trip. He certainly had not planned it this way. Still, he enjoyed the company. Strange, he thought, that she had always seemed to ignore him in the past. "I apologize for asking, I'm sure you've told me in the past, are you still in school?"

She bit down on her lip. Does he think I'm still a schoolgirl? "No, I've finished with technical school. This spring I start training to become a nurse."

"A nurse, why that's a very challenging profession. It takes quite a lot of study, I'm sure."

"Two years."

Tatyana talked softly. Her deep tones fell pleasingly on his ear. He was conscious of just how heavy his own voice must seem to her. For the most part she kept her eyes fixed on the road ahead, turning only occasionally in his direction as she spoke. When she did, and their eyes met, she smiled coyly, then turn back to the road ahead. She had just turned eighteen. He remembered Borz saying something about her birthday. Her dark brown hair was pulled back and tucked under her cap. Dark eyebrows and long lashes highlighted her brown eyes. She was wearing a bulky coat, but underneath he remembered she possessed a supple, well-proportioned body.

17

The car came over a hillock, revealing a small rock-strewn valley. The mountains rose at sharp angles on both sides. There was a solitary structure below them. It was a two story stone house, an expanded cottage really, with a shed attached to one side. It was surrounded by a series of small fields. Although a coating of snow covered everything, Tatyana could tell that the land had not been worked for some years. A handful of goats were gathered in one corner of a winter holding pen where their tiny hooves had trampled the snow into a dark muddy patch. They were nibbling on a mixture of cabbage leaves and straw.

As the car pulled up, a lone figure of a woman appeared around the corner. She was dressed in a long black woolen dress, a heavy black sweater was thrown over her shoulders and she held it closed at the top with one hand. She pulled the other hand up over her eyes to shield them from the sun as she attempted to discern who was coming to visit. A black and gray scarf covered her head in the customary fashion of the Chechen women. She did not recognize this car and was surprised to see that there was a woman behind its wheel. An arm extended out of the passenger window and waved at her. However, it was not until Viktor emerged that she finally recognized who he was.

"Mama, it is too cold for you to come out without your coat."

"I was just feeding my little ones out back." She waved her hand in the direction of the goats. "For that I do not need to put on my overcoat. Now tell me, just why have I been honored with a rare visit from my son today?"

In his defense, Viktor's visits were infrequent, but not rare. In season, he would come to work the garden for her. Enough to plant the few vegetables she would need for herself and the Gran, not to mention the needs of the few goats the two women still managed to keep. He would spend a day or two at a time, tending to those other emergency repairs that required his attention. Several cousins lived just over the hill and they could also help out in an emergency. She was right, though, that at this time of the year his visits were less frequent.

Tatyana stepped out of the car and was stretching her arms after the trip. Mrs. Gadayev surveyed the young woman, then cocked her head in Viktor's direction. "Praise be to the Almighty One!" she said, somewhat derisively, clasping her hands together in mock prayer. "My son has finally brought a young woman home for his mother's blessing!" She spoke to her son in a native dialect that was a little different than what Tatyana was used to hearing at home. Still, she understood enough to blush at the thought.

"Not so hasty, Mama," Viktor chided. This is Tatyana, sister of my good friend Borz Dzasokhov whom I have told you about before. Borz was not able to give me a ride today, so Miss Dzasokhov graciously volunteered to fill in."

Tatyana felt a bit deflated. She was still the little sister.

The Gran was inside, sitting by the fireplace. A small, frail woman dressed much the same as her daughter-in-law, only her clothing had turned gray with age, just like her hair. The elder woman was a few years shy of 80, but looked as though she might have exceeded 100. Her face was gnarled from years of outdoor living on the farm. A red and green shawl was draped over her, which also bore the look of many seasons.

"Will you look who has come to see us now!" Mama said loudly upon entering the cottage. She came through the door, which opened into the main room. It combined the features of kitchen, dining room and sitting room. "It is Viktor, come to present his young lady friend to us!"

Viktor went over to the old woman, bent down and kissed her forehead. "Hello, Gran." He spoke loudly as well, knowing that the old woman was hard of hearing. Pulling himself erect again, he turned toward his mother and said, loud enough for them both to hear, "I have come with strange news from Garyk." Without further word, he handed the envelope to his mother.

"Viktor, what does this mean?" Mama asked, holding up the letter that she had just finished reading. "What have they done with my son?"

"I don't honestly know, Mama."

"Where is this Novgorod that they are taking him to?"

Viktor just shook his head this time, acknowledging that he still had no answer for her.

"Excuse me for intruding, but I seem to recall that it is in the North, perhaps near Leningrad," Tatyana volunteered.

"So far!" was all Mama could say.

"Garyk used to keep a map of the Soviet Union in our room. Let me see if I can find it up there." Viktor headed up to the loft that he once shared with his brother. After a few moments searching, he came back with it in his hands. "Why yes," he observed, spreading the map out on the table for all to see, "It seems that Miss Dzasokhov is quite correct. Here it is, Mama!"

"It is so far to the north," she said with concern. "Garyk will surely freeze to death in such a place."

She talked about Garyk for some time. Tatyana laughed at her stories about the twins growing up. Once or twice the Gran would interject a tale of her own, surprising them that she had been taking in all of the conversation, not merely dozing as they had supposed.

Viktor looked at the old clock on the mantle and said, "Mama, we really need to head back. It won't be fair to Miss Dzasokhov to make her be on the road in the dark."

Tatyana was about to say that she didn't mind at all but Mama quickly replied, "I must insist that you eat something first. See, I have a broth already simmering." There was a large kettle over the fireplace and Tatyana noticed the wonderful aroma emanating from it for the first time. Suddenly she was famished. Mama went to the cupboard and brought out black bread and fresh goat cheese. It was a simple country meal, but it made Tatyana wish that she, too, could have grown up in such a place.

They made their good-byes, with Mama telling Viktor, "Now you be sure to bring this charming young lady friend of yours back to see me again!" She gave him a hug, then turned and embraced the young woman too. That sent a shiver though Tatyana's entire body and a small tear welled in her eye.

In the car, Viktor looked chagrined. "You must forgive me. I hope Mama didn't embarrass you too much."

"Nonsense, she was wonderful. What would make you think that I would be embarrassed?"

"Well, she practically has us engaged to be married!" he blurted out.

She responded with a hearty laugh. "Well, yes, I could see that as quite the embarrassment."

She used the trip home to learn more about his family. "Tell me more about your grandmother. She was such a delightful old woman."

"The Gran, her name is Nadezcha Gadayev. She was married to Zelimzhda, my grandfather, in 1917. She raised seven children in that cottage. All the while the revolution provided a cruel backdrop to their early years and three of her children were dead before the age of ten. My father, Ivram, was the youngest. He was born in 1927."

"Oh," Tatyana put in, I would have thought your mother was her daughter."

"No, when Ivram was ten the Stalin regime began a mass depopulation of the region."

"The Great Repression, yes I know all about that."

"Fortunately for my family, Zelimzhda's mother was a widow and she was allowed to remain on their farm. The others were all transported to Kirovohrad, in the central Ukraine. There they were assigned to work as laborers on several collective farms along the Dnieper River. During the war, Zelimzhda and his older sons were sent as laborers to assist in the defense of Stalingrad. None returned!

"Myriana Namitok, that's my Mama, had similarly been transported with her family during the 1944 purge, which had essentially swept all remaining Chechens and Ingush out of the Caucuses. She was seventeen when she was married to Ivram. Of course it was an arranged union. He was eight years her senior. She lost her first child to a miscarriage. Garyk and I were born in 1954."

She did the math quickly in her head. He was only 22. He looked and acted so much older, no that wasn't the word, mature, yes more mature. So, there is a four year difference in our ages, a respectable difference she thought. "And when did you come back to Chechnya?"

"Well, shortly after our first birthday, Ivram was given the opportunity to return home to work the oil fields. He had his wife, two children and mother to look after. They moved back into the family cottage. His grandmother had managed to preserve it during their seventeen years of exile. Unfortunately, she died shortly after he returned. It was the will of the Almighty that she lasted as long as she did. My mother lost two other children at childbirth. Garyk and I grew up on that mountain valley farm. We were inseparable."

"And what became of your father?"

"He divided his time between the farming chores and working on the petroleum pipeline. He was killed in a construction accident in 1966."

"Oh. I'm sorry. That must have been hard on you."

"I guess, but my brother and I had pretty much learned to fend for ourselves by then. We were what, twelve I guess. Two years later we were sent to technical school in Groznyy. And that, my young friend, is the complete story of my life."

As he said this, she pulled up in front of his housing complex. It was nondescript concrete block structure four stories high. It housed the single oil field workers or those married men who lived away from their families. "Well, here we are. It seems that Borz had no reason to fear for my safety after all! I must thank you for being such a charming chauffeur." With that, he leaned across the seat, and kissed her lightly on the cheek and was out the door.

Shortly thereafter she began her nursing classes. These occupied most of her time, keeping her away from home for long hours each day. If Viktor had occasion to stop by, she missed him. So it was that she did not see him again until after he had traveled to Novgorod for Garyk's commissioning ceremony.

18

Mrs. Dzasokhov impressed upon her daughter that it was important that she be home on time that evening. "We are having guests for supper, Tatyana. Your place is at the table with the family, not off in some smelly laboratory."

"Yes, Mama," she replied dutifully, rushing out to catch the bus that would bring her to the nursing school.

No guests had arrived as yet when she got home later that evening. Mama was in the kitchen and Papa was reading his paper. She could hear Borz in the shower. "Save some of that hot water for me, big brother!" she hollered in at him. "Mama, how do I need to be dressed for this occasion?" she called back.

"Your white dress, I think, should do it," came the reply from the kitchen.

She was still dressing when she heard the knock on the door. Borz must have gone to greet the visitor, because she could here him say, "Well, if it isn't the long distance traveler. So, how was the journey to the great Northlands?"

"Very good I think, but I am thankful to be back home again." She heard the voice and it made her heart leap. It was Viktor. "Mama," she said to the image in the mirror, "you have some plot here I suspect." She found herself thrilled at the prospect of being with him again and hurried to finish and get down to greet him. Knowing that it was Viktor, however, she took the time to double check herself in the mirror. She undid the bow that tied her hair in back and shook her head to let it fall free. It fell over her shoulders and she quickly brushed it out. Satisfied that it was perfect, she opened the door to head down stairs, then stopped to take one last look in the mirror. Her hand moved to her chest and she undid the second button on her dress, pushing back the material on either side. She nodded to the image reflected back at her and whispered "Go get him" and was out the door.

"Ah, it's the little sister," Viktor said jokingly as she came into the room. "My, don't we look splendid tonight!" She could feel herself blush and hated herself for it.

At supper, Viktor told them of his recent trip to the training center at Novgorod. "If he were not my own twin brother, I would swear that I did not know the man." he responded when asked about seeing Garyk again. "Why he looks like a Russian, talks like a Russian, even drinks like a Russian now!"

"I suppose that is the purpose of a military training center," Papa said. Everything must come out uniformly."

"Tatyana," Mama interrupted, "pass our guest some more potatoes."

"Thank you." Viktor took the bowl she offered him and continued talking while he spooned out more of its contents. "Such a change in only three months was really a shock. You had to have known him before. He was my alter ego: very quiet, very shy."

"Yes, that's true," put in Borz. "I was always astounded by that fact that the two of you could look so much alike, yet be so very different. I would like to see this new Garyk for myself."

"Well, you may get your chance. He has three weeks leave before he needs to report for school. They're sending him to the University in Moscow. At first he said he wasn't sure if he wanted to come home. I told him he owed it to our Mama. He will be at the farm next week. I should go over there and see him again before he moves on to Moscow. Who knows if I'll ever see him again after that."

"Yes, I would like to go with you, if you'll have me." Borz said. He turned to his sister with a grin and said, "Unless, of course, Tatyana insists on being your chauffeur again!" Tatyana glared at Borz from across the table. There was a time, when she was younger, that she would have kicked him in the shins for such a condescending remark. Even now she fought the urge to flick a spoonful of potatoes at him. What would Viktor think about that?

"We should all go," Viktor agreed. "I think that my Mama would be delighted to see Miss Dzasokhov again. She seemed quite taken by her on our last visit."

"Really," Mama said. She looked at her daughter quizzically. "Tatyana, you did not tell us about that."

Borz's car was an old one. That it ran at all was a tribute to his ability as a mechanic. It was also a bit small. Tatyana was relegated to the tiny rear seat for the entire trip. She did not mind, delighting to be in his company. Spring was changing into summer. If the countryside had been stark on her first visit, it was alive now with flowers. The first crops were already rising high in the fields that they passed by. When they approached the cottage this time it was surround with young sunflower stalks. In a few months the cottage would be ablaze with them.

She caught her breath when Garyk came out to greet them. Save for the shorter hair and absence of the thin beard, it was Viktor standing before her. He was not in uniform, having found it more prudent to wear his brother's work clothes. That gave the similarity all the more emphasis. He exchanged manly hugs with Viktor, kissing him on both cheeks.

"It is good to see you again, my twin. I'm glad you convinced me to come down here." Garyk walked around to the other side of the car and gave Borz a hug also. "Borz, it has been a long time! Now, who do we have here?" he asked, watching Tatyana attempt to extricate herself from the cramped rear seat. She wore blue jeans and a pink sweater today, with her hair pulled back in its customary ponytail.

Borz made the introduction. "Allow me to introduce my sister, Tatyana."

"Welcome to our home." Garyk greeted her with a little bow of his head, "Or am I mistaken. You have, perhaps, been here before?" Before she could answer Myriana Gadayev joined them and Garyk turned to her and said, "Viktor has come with his friend Borz and Borz's charming sister Tatyana!"

Mama took Borz's hand in greeting then turned and gave a big hug to the girl. "You see this, Garyk, your brother brings this pretty young thing back a second time to meet his Mama." Garyk cast a sly look at his brother as they walked towards the cottage.

They were inside now. The Gran was still seated in her chair by the fireplace. Tatyana wondered if she ever moved from that spot. She wore a heavy sweater, even at this time of year, with the same colorful shawl draped over her. Viktor bent down to kiss her forehead, then introduced his friends to her, assuming she most likely did not remember Tatyana. However, she reached out for the girl and pulled her down to her. In a weak voice she said, "From this one too I should be getting a kiss, I think. So nice that you have come back to see an old woman."

Tatyana was flustered and relieved when the attention turned quickly back to Garyk. Mama asked him, "And when will you do your mother the honor of bring such a charming woman for her to meet?" Then he surprised them all by saying, "Well, Mama, if you had accompanied Viktor to see me commissioned, you would have had the honor of meeting the woman whom I will someday marry."

"And just who may this lucky young woman be that is soon to become my new daughter?"

"I don't know for sure how soon that may be, if ever, Mama. I just know that she is the only woman I would ever wish to marry."

Mama looked to her other son. "Viktor, did you meet this girl?"

"Yes, Mama, I think perhaps I did. However, she was not introduced to me in quite that manner."

"You're right Viktor, you did meet her in Novgorod. You remember Lieutenant Moldatin—Katryn Moldatin."

"Ah yes, the little one with ash blonde hair. I thought there was some bonding between you. You spent more time with her family, I recall, than you did with me,"

Mama had many questions now. Garyk explained about the young woman who had snared his heart. He left out the boathouse, of course. Mama would never approve. He told them that they had both been assigned to attend the Moscow University next month and that she would, most likely be living with her parents there.

"They are Muscovites, then!" Mama said somewhat emphatically. "I take it she is not a Moslem."

"No, Mama, she is not. I don't see where that really matters anymore."

"It is your faith, Garyk." Myriana Gadayev could not have been more emphatic as she spoke these words. "The faith of your father and his father before that. It is much more than that. For centuries Gadayev blood has stained the hands of these Russians. I would not be so quick to turn your back on all of that for some young woman."

There was an uncomfortable chill in the room. Tatyana felt it, but did not know what to say or do. Say nothing she supposed was the best. Garyk was clearly hurt by this but he had expected that this might be her reaction. Still, hearing her say the words cut deeply. He also knew that to continue to debate the issue now would only bring rancor to what was to be a happy gathering. He thought it best to change the subject quickly; direct the attention somewhere else. He cast a hard glance in Tatyana's direction and said,

"Well, it looks as if at least one of us had found a prospective mate that meets with Mama's favor."

Her knees nearly give way as he spoke these words. She inhaled deeply, hoping no one heard, and bit down on her lower lip. Borz turned to her and said, " My little brother has been keeping secrets it would seem!"

"No," Viktor said emphatically. "I am afraid that Mama has let her imagination get the best of her." He looked at the young woman standing there and said to her, "Once again I must make apologies. Please forgive me for putting you in such a situation." As he said that, he detected a hint of disappointment as she reacted to his denial. Could she really have an interest in him, he wondered. Just in case, he quickly added, "Besides, Miss Dzasokhov is studying to become a nurse. She is far too busy to even consider taking a husband for herself right now."

Tatyana was really in a state of confusion. She had been caught off guard by Garyk's remark. She had, in fact, been stabbed by Viktor's quick denial. But was there a deeper meaning to his little addendum. What if I weren't going to nursing school right now she wondered? They were all looking at her. She had to say something. "Yes, I really am much too busy for a husband just now." She tried to add a little nonchalant laugh.

Then the Gran spoke up from her corner position by the fireplace. Her presence there had almost been forgotten. "Time is something we all take for granted. It is best not to put off to the future. The future can hold so many surprises. We often learn, too late, that there was no time left after all."

19

The plan was for them to stay the night, departing sometime in the early afternoon the next day. So after a light lunch, Garyk, Viktor and Borz left to tend to some maintenance chores around the farm. Tatyana was left to fend for herself with Mrs. Gadayev and the Gran. The two older women seemed content to let her clear the table and wash the dishes. Was she already being assigned the duties of a daughter-in-law? She realized that the thought pleased her. "Would you like to feed the goats with me?" Myriana Gadayev asked when she finished that task.

"Oh, yes!" was her enthusiastic reply.

The goats had not been in the pen this morning when they drove up. Now, as the two women came around the side of the house she could hear the clinking of their neck bells. They had been up in the hills feeding on pasture grasses but, being creatures of habit, they knew that the woman would be coming out to give them something special at this time of day. Tatyana was delighted to see them scampering back to the cottage to greet them. While her family never lived in a truly urban setting, neither had she ever been this close to farm animals. They nuzzled up to her, eating carrots right out of her hands. She loved it and laughed like a child.

Working to repair some fencing not too far from the house, Viktor heard her laughing. He couldn't help but stop what was doing and just stand there watching her. Garyk noticed this and he nudged Borz. "What do you say Borz, is it your sister who has caught my brother's eye, or perhaps he is just admiring the goats!"

"I'm sure it's the goats."

Viktor turned back to the two of them and said, "Yes, that little grey one, Binji I think its name is, has quite an attractive hoof, don't you agree." Borz and Garyk both started to laugh and Garyk slapped his twin on the arm. Down below, Tatyana heard the laughing. Garyk's laugh was not as deep as his brother's and it did not rouse her the way Viktor's did. Looking at her brother, she sensed somehow that she was the brunt of this banality. She dropped the rest of the food for the creatures to finish on their own and started back into the house with Mrs. Gadayev.

Once back inside, Mama began questioning her. "Your brother works in the oil fields with Viktor. I know that. What about the rest of your family, child?"

"My Papa works there too. He has since 1955. That's when his family returned from the exile in Kazakhstan. Viktor tells me that you and your husband had been exiled in Kirovohrad and returned about the same time."

"Why, yes, you know about that?"

"Yes, and all about Zelimzhda and Nadezcha too. It must have been hard on all of you, being separated from your families like that."

Myriana turned to the old woman and said loud enough for her to hear, "Do you hear this Gran, the young child knows all about your travels to the Ukraine with Zelimzhda." The old woman nodded and Myriana seemed quite pleased to think that Tatyana had taken the time to learn so much of their history. Turning back to her she asked, "And how are things going for you at nursing school?"

"The studies are difficult, but I enjoy the challenge I think. Mama says that I spend far too much time in the laboratories. I really can't wait to put all this training to good use."

"And how do you plan to do that?"

"I hope to be able to work at a hospital somewhere. Hopefully in a children's ward." Myriana nodded this time and Tatyana wondered if she was passing the test. Thinking it wise to move the conversation away from herself she remarked, "I see you have sunflowers growing outside the door. It should be marvelous here next month. I really do think that they are a remarkable flower."

"Here they are flowers," the Gran said weakly. "But when I was a young woman we worked for five years on a farm that grew them as a cash crop. Zelimzhda, he was my husband, would lift me up onto his shoulders, such strong arms he had then, and all you could see, from horizon to horizon, in all directions, were sunflowers. Such a lovely sight, my child. I think that when I am finally dead I should like to awaken in such a field for all eternity."

The rest of the day was uneventful. She helped with the dinner preparation, of course. After dinner Garyk told stories about his training school experiences. It was manly chatter and she sat in a straight-backed wooden chair, her legs folded beneath her, and just listened. Viktor was correct, she thought, Garyk does seem to be in love with this new life in the Army.

They retired early, so Tatyana awoke early the next day. She went out to watch the sun come up over the hills. It was beautiful. The sun caught the very top line of trees and the valley was rimed in gold. Slowly, the light crept downward, changing black formless objects into dazzling green hues and glistening rock formations. Suddenly she was aware that someone was standing behind her. Turning, she saw it was Viktor. "Do you always come sneaking up on people?"

"Forgive me," he said, concerned that he had alarmed her. "It was just so beautiful, the sunrise, and you standing there watching it, that I didn't want to disturb the moment."

"Yes, it is beautiful," she admitted. "I must say I envy you for having grown up in a place like this." They began to walk together. He pointed out certain places of interest, relating stories about his childhood that each place called back to his mind. In the distance the mournful howl of a wolf echoed through the valley and it caused Tatyana to shudder.

"Don't mind that," Viktor told her. "Those wolves are the protectors of this valley. My father used to tell us they that were sent here by the Almighty One to report on our worthiness. That's what he's doing, reporting in." His hand found hers and she clasped onto it naturally.

The sun's rays were moving lower into the valley and fell upon the ruins of an old stone tower. It seemed to rise up out of the rock outcropping on which it stood. "Oh look," Tatyana exclaimed, "I didn't notice that before."

"Yes, it tends to blend into the mountain unless the light hits it just right. It's over two hundred years old, you know. It was built at a time when the whole valley was populated by the Gadayev clan. They had their own usman who called out the ritual prayers from that tower. Of course, it was destroyed during the Great Repression." He stopped walking and looked directly at her. "It seems that Mama feels I should be calling on your Papa to ask permission to begin the courting process."

"Actually," she said with a nervous laugh, "I think that perhaps my father has been waiting for you to do just that."

"Oh really! And where do you stand in all of this?"

"I think, perhaps, that I have been waiting for you to do just that." He pulled her to him and for the first time they kissed, really kissed. After what she hoped would be forever, he pulled away. Bending down, she tore off a clump of tall grass. "I was serious yesterday," she said to him. "Until I finish my training and am certified to be a nurse, I shall have no time for a husband. You shall just have to wait!" With that, she threw the grass at him, shrieked with gleeful laughter, and raced back toward the cottage.

Most of the others were still sleeping, but Mama was up making breakfast. She grinned broadly when the two rushed in. "Oh, good morning, Mrs. Gadayev," Tatyana said with a start. What would this woman think about the two of them having been out alone together?

"Come, child, don't you think it is time you started to call me Mama?"

20

In 1977, word came down from Moscow that Garyk and Katryn planned to be married that June. Myriana was torn between a desire to see her son married, to meet this woman of his dreams and by her displeasure over his decision to marry outside of the faith. Worst, to marry a Muscovite! In the end, the Gran came down with influenza, giving her an excuse not to make the trip. Once again, Viktor was the sole representative of the Gadayev family.

Viktor was enthusiastic upon his return. "Mama, she is a wonderful person. You must go and see them. Garyk is so happy, Mama."

Viktor had hoped that a year in the university environment would have tempered Garyk's newfound zeal for his new Mother Russia. On the day of the wedding, however, Garyk wore his dress uniform, as did Alexandr, the best man. The formality of the uniform permeated his persona. Then there were the Moldatins. It was never made very clear to Viktor just what Katryn's father did. Whatever it was, he appeared to be well connected within the Communist Party. The number of high-ranking dignitaries that made an appearance at the reception surprised Viktor. Myriana Gadayev would not have been happy there.

As 1978 began, Viktor was offered a new position. Now he would be working at the main refinery in Groznyy. This meant that he could not see Tatyana as frequently in the months proceeding their wedding day. At the same time, her final semester was going to be a hectic one. She would be working many night shifts and attending classes during the day. The good news was that the new position entitled Viktor to a family apartment. Nursing positions would also be much easier to come by in Groznyy.

Viktor convinced the authorities that since he was getting married in May anyway, he should be allowed to move into the family housing unit right away. Tatyana came into Groznyy to help him settle in. After all, this was going to be HER apartment soon and it was best not to let him gain too much influence on how it was to be arranged.

"This is wonderful, Viktor!" They were standing in the middle of their common room. A table and two chairs, a small sofa, armchair and reading lamp were its only furnishings at this point. There was a very small kitchen area in the back and two bedrooms off to one side. The apartment complex was in the southwestern corner of the city and you could see the Sunzha flowing past them out the window. "I only wish we were further from the city, not so close to that smelly refinery. Viktor, promise me we will spend as much time as possible at the farm."

"So, it's a country girl that I am marrying!" He said this with mock derision.

"Maybe, but I can still see us raising many children right here."

"Many children," he echoed. "Just how many did you have in mind?"

"Oh, I don't know. Five, maybe six. Yes, I think six would be a good number."

"Well, if that's the case, we had better get started!" The past two years had worked magic on her body. The fleshy traces of adolescence were gone and her facial features were sharply defined. Her hips had a mature curve and the breasts that swelled beneath her sweater were fully rounded. It was a light blue pullover sweater with a tee shirt underneath. In one motion, he pulled them both up and over her head, revealing those ample breasts. She unbuttoned his shirt and saw the mat of heavy dark hair that adorned his chest. She had to chuckle, remembering their very first encounter.

"What's so funny?" he asked.

"Nothing, really, but if my cousin could only see me now."

He carried her into the bedroom. It contained a double bed and single chest of drawers. He laid her gently on the bed, unbuttoned and unzipped her jeans, and they made love. It was only the second time, in their pre-nuptial arrangement, that they had done so. To Tatyana, however, this was the true beginning. She was in her home now. This would soon be her bed and her husband. Thrill, pleasure, ecstasy ñ they were all mere words, unfit to describe her emotions at this time.

The day finally arrived. Viktor wasn't sure when she looked more radiant. Was it last week when she was presented with her nursing certificate and they had pinned the insignia on her uniform, or now, as she stood before him to become his bride. Then she had held her certificate up in personal triumph. Her hair was neatly rolled up and pinned beneath her little white cap. She smiled and laughed with those about her. Today she was solemn, almost regal, he thought. He could feel her love when she looked at him. Her hair fell gracefully over her shoulders. A lace shawl covered her head. It had been in the family for three generations. The intricacy of its patterns added elegance, but it could not compete with her beauty.

It was a brief ceremony, conducted both by the local magistrate and her family's own usman. Viktor had to attend regular Morning Prayer sessions at the mosque for three weeks before the holy man would agree to bless their union. Garyk and Katryn flew down for the occasion. Katryn did not join the other women in laying out the bridal feast. She was, after all, an officer in the Soviet Army.

Marianna Gadayev's first reaction, upon seeing her daughter-in-law for the first time, was tempered by the uniforms that both Katryn and Garyk were wearing. He had on those terribly high Russian boots that brought back images of her life in the Ukraine. Katryn wore a skirt cut a demure five inches below her knees and sensible black shoes with a one-inch heel. In spite of all that, she could not help but like this young woman. She was charmed as soon as Garyk first introduced her.

"Mama Gadayev, I am so glad to finally meet you. Garyk has told me so many wonderful stories about you." Katryn held both of her hands and raised herself on her toes to kiss both cheeks. "I must apologize for the fact that the Army has kept us much too busy to make the trip down before this."

"Well I'm delighted that you are here now, my dear."

"No thanks to Garyk. He thought that we shouldn't come this time, but I insisted."

As the senior member of the family, the Gran was there to give the new bride her blessing. After doing so, she turned to Katryn and said, "You come to me now. You also should have the blessing of this old woman, even if it comes a bit late." Katryn came to her and the Gran gave her a gentle hug. Then she gently pushed back the platinum hair that rimmed her face and kissed her on the cheeks. "May you walk in his light, my child, and bear many children." As an afterthought she added, "And may we not have to wait so long for them either!"

Katryn blushed. She walked back to Garyk and held onto his arm, resting her head on his chest. "What a strange and wonderful family," she whispered. "We should have come down before this."

The festivities over, Viktor and Tatyana retired to their new home. She threw herself into his arms as soon as the door closed behind them. "Oh my love, promise me that we shall always be this happy," she said and began to kiss him. Once again he picked her up and carried her to their bed. They made love several times. He rolled off of her, breathing heavily and stared up at the ceiling.

"Is something wrong?" she asked with mild concern.

"Not at all," he answered her. "It's just that you've worn me out. I think I may need a nurse."

"Well, you've got one!" she said with a giggle and pounced back on top of him.

In spite of all their efforts, the first child did not come for eighteen months. In fact, she was still in her eighth month when they traveled up to see their new nephew in Moscow. Their first child was a girl. They named her Petruska. It was another two years before she bore them a son. He was called Ivram, after his grandfather. Another two years passed by before Nadezcha, a girl, was born. Like her sister, she also arrived a month after her new cousin up in Moscow.

The coming of this third child had kept Viktor from traveling up to see his brother after the incident in Afghanistan. So Garyk was fully recovered from his wounds when Viktor finally made his way up to Moscow. Fully recovered from his physical wounds, anyway. He had brought the whole family up and the presence of Tatyana, the nieces and nephew seemed to brighten Katryn's spirits. Garyk, however, seemed distant. For the second time in his life, Viktor saw a different man claiming to be his brother.

The two brothers talked about politics. That was something Garyk had never done with him before. Viktor's passion for his beloved Chechnya fueled the emotions that were building inside his brother. "What does Katryn think about all of this?" Viktor asked him.

"To tell you the truth," Garyk surprised him by saying, "we have hardly talked at all since my return."

Viktor was not sure whether he liked this new persona any more than the last. As they drove back down to Groznyy, he asked his wife, "What do you make of Garyk?"

She looked over at him with a very serious expression and said only "He's a changed man."

21

Viktor continued to impress both the people for whom he worked and those who worked under him. He had a reputation for getting the job done. At the same time, he was deemed to be a fair arbiter of issues that affected the workers. The men felt at ease coming to him with problems.

And there were many problems. The Soviet economy was coming to a standstill. Food supplies were erratic in the best of times, nonexistent at others. It was difficult to keep the refinery operating as scheduled for lack of critical supplies. This meant that work gangs had to stand down. He had to tell men, whose families already had little to eat, that there would be less pay or no pay at all. This was not a regional problem. The economic crisis gave rise to political intrigues and dissension. For anyone under the age of fifty-five or sixty, it was the first time in their lives that neither the government nor the Communist Party was in complete control.

At 34 Viktor was an imposing figure. A few inches over six feet tall and broad at the shoulders, his body kept trim by less frequent but occasional athletic activity. He wore his hair shorter these days. It fell to mid-neck when not pulled back in a queue. The beard that outlined his jaw was thicker, strengthening the solid line of his face. He became more active in support of the welfare of his kinsmen and spoke openly about these things. He attended meetings and was involved in political groups. Spurred on by the actions taken by Mikhail Gorbachev to rebuild and restructure both the Soviet economy and its social structure, the National Congress of the Chechen People grew in opposition to the firmly entrenched Communist Party.

Tatyana was proud of her husband. Still, she was concerned about the welfare of her family. "Viktor, are you sure that attending this meeting will not jeopardize your position at the refinery. They can't look kindly on having one of their mangers speaking out against the Party."

"Tatyana, you worry too much. Times have changed."

"Maybe so, but they can change back just as quickly. Even with both of our incomes, it is difficult to feed the children. It's not the cost so much as the availability of food. You may not be aware of this, Viktor, but I have been accorded certain privileges because of your position. That's why I'm deeply concerned that opposition to the Party could lead to reprisals."

"You see, that's exactly why I must go. It is time to put an end to all this favoritism and to put food back on the shelves for all of the people. The times really are changing, Tatyana, this I can see. Chechens have fought and died for self-government, independence and freedom in this region for centuries. Now it was within our grasp. We must take the risks or lose the opportunity forever."

"Yes, but it is the risks that I worry about." She kissed him on the cheek and he was off to yet another political meeting.

To allay her concerns, he sent the children to summer with his mother. Tatyana did not object. There would be fresh vegetables there for them to eat and all of that space to run free in. She took what time she could get from the hospital and stayed there with them for several days at a time. Viktor's newfound political influence and his continued advancement on the job did lead to one major development during the summer of 1990. Tatyana had been away for two days on the farm. Arriving home late, she was surprised to find her husband waiting up for her. He looked at her very somberly and said, "I am afraid, my dearest, that we will no longer be able to keep this apartment."

She was stunned. "Viktor, what has happened? You lost your position because of that stupid National Congress! Didn't I warn you that this would happen? What are we going to do now?"

He had let her rant on a bit, but was careful not to let it get too far out of hand. Tears formed in her eyes and one rolled slowly down her cheek. Even like this she was a joy to behold. As usual, she had her hair pulled back to reveal the fullness of her face. The white kerchief she wore remained high on her forehead and was tied under her chin. He placed his hand under her chin and raised it slightly, kissing her lips. Then he said rather drolly, "Well, I suppose that we will just have to move into our new house. Unless, of course, you would prefer to stay here in the city next to the smelly refinery."

"What new house?" she asked.

"The one they have offered to let us rent in keeping with my new position as Section Manager."

"Oh, Viktor!" She threw her arms around him and gave him a huge hug, and then she pulled back and began to pound him gently on the shoulders. "Why did you scare me like that. I was nearly in tears. Look,

see, I am anyway," she said, wiping away the tears of joy that now
filled her eyes. She was hugging him again, giving him great big kisses. The children were gone, so he took advantage of this time alone
with her. As he had done in the past, he took her up and carried her
to their bed.

After twelve years together, they each knew what it took to please
the other. What was more important was that they each wanted to
please the other. Each found pleasure in feeling their partner's
responses to their giving. They said little, if anything. There was no
need for words now. Each was totally involved in the other, one common spirit.

When they had finally finished, she lay on her side next to him, her
head resting on his shoulder. He lay on his back, head upon hands.
She ran her fingers through the hair on his chest. "Do you think that
we can always be this happy?" she asked softly. He made no reply.

That fall they held elections for the National Assembly of the
Chechen–Ingush Autonomous Republic. At Gorbachev's insistence,
the Soviet constitution now permitted non-communist parties to be
registered. The National Congress asked Viktor to stand for a seat in
the Assembly, to which he had agreed. He was elected. This was a
whole new experience, not only for Viktor, but also for all of the
Chechens, Ingush, Alans and Russians living in the Republic. The various ethnic groups each had an agenda, some centuries old. These
were debated publicly for the first time in memory. The economic
woes remained their primary concern. However, as the efforts of a
fragile central government coalition in Moscow failed to bring the
economy under control, members of the Assembly stood and openly
espoused secession.

While Gorbachev came under direct, personal attack from Boris
Yeltsin, the newly elected president of the Russian Republic, a former
Air Force general, Dzhokhar Dudayev was assuming the leadership of
the National Congress in Groznyy. Viktor was summoned to a clandestine meeting with the Major General in August of 1991. He was not a
large man, but his dark mustache and equally dark eyebrows gave his
face a certain aura. Dudayev sat behind a small table that served as a
desk. It was in a functional office room. A few folding chairs and some
file cabinets were the only other furnishing. The wall behind the
General sported several maps, one of the entire Soviet Union, one of
the Caucasus Region and one large street map of Groznyy. Other maps
appeared to be folded on the table before the General.

"Gadayev," the General spoke in a commanding tone, "you are a
valuable member of our organization. In just these past few months

you have gained everyone's respect for your leadership in the Assembly."

"Thank you, General. I try only to do what I think is best for our country."

"Yes, that is why you are here. Chechnya is now in a position to move forward, do you understand?" He did not wait for a response. "It is important that I know where you will stand in this matter. I must know who are my friends and who is to become my enemy."

Viktor realized the significance of this meeting. There had been rumors circulating to the effect that Dudayev was plotting a coup of some sort. Clearly, Viktor was now on the inside. He wondered if he would be allowed to leave this place alive, should he fail to support their program. "I stand for the Chechen people," he said. "I am Nokhchii!"

"Well said, Mr. Gadayev." The General smiled, amused by his clever choice of words. "But are you to be with us or against us?"

"Perhaps, if I knew what your plan was, I could give you an answer," Viktor responded cautiously.

"Forgive me, but I must be careful in these matters. You understand that it would not be good for you to know too much if, in fact, you are not going to be with us."

"I think I do, General. You can be sure that in such matters I can be relied upon to be *discreet.*"

"Yes, of course." The General rose and came around in front of the table to where Viktor was standing with the two aides who had brought him in. They were both dressed in field uniforms with mottled brown and green camouflage patterns. Dudayev was in civilian attire, a dark gray suit with a checkered tie. He reached up to place his hand on Viktor's shoulder. "Come, let me show you." The General walked him to the map of Groznyy. "We have assembled forces loyal to our movement in Urus-Martan. Tonight we have relocated them here, here and here." As he said this, Dudayev pointed out several areas around the city: the rail yards near the refinery, the military park, and the university.

"In a few hours we will strike a blow for freedom! Here, let me show you this." The General turned back to the table and picked up a sheet of rolled acrylic. One of the aides moved over to assist him in placing this over the map of the city. All of the strategic centers were clearly indicated: the television station and radio transmitters, police and fire stations, hospitals, schools and government offices were each marked and color coded. Viktor was unsure of the significance of some of the small dots, but noted that the residence of the current president bore a red dot and the location of his home was marked in green.

The General continued, "We expect to be in control of the city before midnight. Once we have taken control of these key resources," he said, sweeping his hand across the city, "we shall begin to round up those in opposition. I will personally send that puppet back to Moscow!" Emphatically, the general's hand slapped down on the map of the Soviet Union, right over the location of Moscow.

"I had no idea that you were ready to move this quickly." Viktor was in awe of the possibilities. Childhood fantasies, the idle chatter of his young manhood and even the recent political discussions had all had that 'wouldn't it be wonderful if, but it will never happen' aspect about them. This was real. It was going to happen tonight! He looked the General squarely in the eye, shook his hand and said, "General Dudayev, I am with you!"

The next morning Groznyy awoke to the news that the communist government had been deposed. As usual, Tatyana rose early to get the children ready for school before she had to leave for the hospital. She was a bit annoyed, but not surprised, to find Viktor's side of the bed empty. He had two jobs now, one at the refinery and this new position in the government and she was seeing less and less of him. She could use his help in the mornings getting the children ready.

She was busy in the kitchen when Petruska called excitedly from the main room where she had just turned on the television. "Mother, come quickly, Father is on the television!"

Tatyana rushed in to the room. She couldn't imagine why this would be and feared some calamity must have befallen him. Victor was seated at a desk normally occupied by the morning news commentator. He was wearing his good suit and a tie she had never seen before. His hair was neatly brushed back. My, you are still a handsome one, she thought. A large green, white and red flag was hung behind him. Superimposed on the screen below him were the words *"Viktor I. Gadayev—Acting Deputy President of the National Assembly."*

Her mouth fell open. Petruska was yelling for her brother and sister to "Come and see Papa!"

"Hush, Petruska, I am trying to hear what he is saying."

"...HAVE COMPLETED THE SUCCESSFUL TAKEOVER OF THE CITY GOVERNMENT. WE ARE HAPPY TO REPORT THAT THERE HAVE BEEN NO INCIDENTS OF VIOLENCE DURING THE COURSE OF THIS TRANSFER OF POWER. HOWEVER, ALL CITIZENS HAVE BEEN ASKED TO REMAIN IN THEIR HOMES AT THIS TIME UNTIL WE CAN ASSURE THEIR COMPLETE SAFETY. AS THE ACTING DEPUTY, I WISH TO ASSURE YOU ALL THAT THIS ACTION HAS BEEN TAKEN IN THE

BEST INTERESTS OF THE PEOPLE OF THE CHECHEN-INGUSH REPUBLIC. GENERAL DUDAYEV HAS PERSONALLY ASSURED ME THAT THERE ARE NO PLANS FOR REPRISALS AGAINST ANY FORMER MEMBERS OF THE GOVERNMENT AND THAT PLANS WILL BE ANNOUNCED SHORTLY CONCERNING A NEW, DEMOCRATIC ELEC-TION THIS FALL. WE WILL CONTINUE TO KEEP YOU AWARE OF NEW DEVELOPMENTS AS THE DAY PROGRESSES. THANK YOU AND GOOD MORNING."

"Oh, Viktor'" she said softly to the television, "what have you gotten yourself into now?"

22

True to his word, Dudayev announced a general election in October of 1991. He was elected President and Viktor became the First Deputy of the National Assembly and its primary spokesman. Papa Dzasokhov was elated. He was fond of telling almost anyone who would listen; "Didn't I tell you that this young man was going to be a leader someday! Yes, I was wise to encourage such a match for my daughter, I tell you."

With the chill of winter settling in, Viktor was again summoned to a meeting. The General had a much grander office now, one befitting the president of a Soviet Socialist Republic. Viktor was part of the elite group, one of the movers and shakers. Assembled with him were the Vice President and the men in charge of the Chechen–Ingush paramilitary forces.

"Gorbachev and Yeltsin are both fools!" Dudayev paced back and forth before the large mahogany state desk as he addressed them. Today he wore his tan military uniform. "It is like Nero who played his fiddle while Rome burned about him. They are playing their games of political intrigue while Russia burns about them. It is only a matter of weeks, perhaps even days, I tell you, before it all comes crashing down. I am absolutely certain that the Union of Soviet Socialist Republics will end before the year is out. Does anyone here disagree?"

The General looked at each of those in the room, open to any counter suggestion that might change what he felt he had to do. They were seated in a semi-circle of high-backed chairs upholstered in green, red and white, the republic's colors. There were no dissenters. "No, I did not think so," he continued. "What then, my friends, must we do to protect ourselves from the inevitable?" Again he paused, but no one felt the urge to speak. Each knew that the General already had made some decision and they were anxious to learn what that might be. "I would like to call a special meeting of the Assembly for tomorrow morning. I will address them and wish that arrangements be made to broadcast this live to the people, is that understood?" All nodded that it was. "Good! At that time I shall formally declare the Chechen–Ingush Republic to be a free and sovereign state, independent of the Russian Republic and secede from the Union of Soviet Socialist Republics. Now, gentlemen, your comments."

They all began to talk at once. The General held up his hand for them to be silent again. "Well, I see that you have all been listening," he said. "Viktor, you speak for the people, what do you say"

"Can we hope to succeed in this, General?"

"Actually, I think we can. We may be among the first, but I can assure you that we will not be the last of the republics to do this. The Soviet Union is almost leaderless at the moment. In fact, we have one of our own as Chairman of the Supreme Soviet. Khasbulatov will not sanction any action against his own countrymen. As for the Soviet Army, it is falling apart as we meet. Georgians, Ukrainians, Belarusks are returning to their own homelands to see what may develop. The time will never be better for us to undertake such a move."

The military men discussed plans to mobilize their forces in the event that there was either an uprising internally, or intervention on the part of the Russians. Other strategic options were reviewed and contingency plans discussed. Viktor could feel his heart pounding. He was exhilarated and also scared to death. They were stepping off a precipice and he hoped that there was a large enough ledge below to catch them.

As the meeting drew to a close, the General grabbed him by the arm. In his customary manner he walked him aside and said to him earnestly, "Viktor, you must begin to call upon your fellow deputies in the other republics. Here, I have prepared a list of names. We cannot succeed without the support of the other republics. They must be asked to grant us formal recognition."

The next day was a solemn occasion. Viktor was seated behind the podium with the other ranking officials and dignitaries. He had arranged for special visitor passes for Tatyana, the three children, his mother and her parents to be present on this day of national independence. When the speech was over, the Chechen delegates to the Assembly all stood and cheered enthusiastically. Viktor noted that the Ingush and Alans seemed less enthusiastic. Many of the ethnic Russians walked out. They adjourned outside of the Assembly Hall. As a military band played their national anthem, they watched with pride as the red flags with the yellow hammer and sickle were slowly lowered. In their place were raised the green, white and red stripped flags of the Chechen Republic, each bore the emblem which was the symbol of their homeland, the grey wolf.

Life for the Gadayev family continued, although the circumstances changed dramatically. Viktor had become a statesman, conversing with lesser foreign dignitaries and officials of the Russian Federation. In spite of his efforts to win support for the fledgling state, none had been offered. In fact, their "country" had been reduced in size by the almost immediate break away of the Ingush. Ingushetia was also declared a separate republic, but did not seek to sever its ties with Russia. Hence, they had been granted the formal recognition that was being denied to the Chechens.

Viktor found that he actually had more time to spend with his family now. Being formally involved with government affairs meant he no longer attended after-hours political group meetings. He also resigned his position at the refinery. There were, of course, obligatory social functions that required both he and Tatyana to be in attendance. For the most part, however, his evenings and weekends were free.

He enjoyed the luxury of having a private house. It was a squat, two storied, red brick structure. Large windows that stretched nearly from floor to ceiling made the rooms bright and airy. The ground floor windows had wooden frameworks that arched at the top. A center portico divided the building in two. Best of all, it was surrounded by a small lawn which allowed him the luxury of an evening stroll with his wife, something that apartment living had not permitted.

Viktor's sudden elevation to the third highest ranking official in the government had an immediate impact on Tatyana as well. For the past thirteen years she had continued her nursing duties at the Forth Hospital in Groznyy. She had taken obligatory maternity leaves, of course, but had placed the children in collective day care as soon as she was able to return to work. She loved her job, especially when it afforded her the opportunity to work with children. Her seniority permitted her some preference in the selection of duty rotations and she had turned down one offer of a supervisory position in order to remain "in the trenches."

As the wife of the First Deputy, however, the administrators urged her to take a position that was more in keeping with her current social status. Besides, it wouldn't hurt them or the hospital to be so closely related to the First Deputy's office. She was named Assistant Director of Nursing Care. It was a new position, created solely for her benefit (and theirs), so she was pretty much able to decide for herself exactly what her duties would be. She opted to oversee the training of the young student nurses, making sure that their would still be ample time for her to spend on the floor and not behind a desk.

Viktor was delighted for her. He was still too naïve in the affairs of government to realize that this was not so much a promotion of merit as it was of position. He knew that she had turned down promotions before and was proud of her achievement. The family celebrated with a dinner at the most exclusive restaurant in the city. Her family had all been invited to join the festivities. Papa and Mama Dzasokhov were ecstatic. Papa preened and strutted about the house as they readied themselves for the occasion. "Not only a son-in-law of distinction, but also now a daughter who was an Assistant Director! Didn't I tell you that good things would happen with this young man!" He kept this up until Mama finally said "Enough!"

There was little family similarity between Tatyana and her sister Marika, who was six years older and many pounds heavier. Her husband, Grigor, was well suited to work in the oil fields. He was of stocky build, with muscular arms and huge hands roughened by the toil of over twenty years handling pipe and machinery. He seemed ill at ease in these surroundings, wearing a suit reserved for those rare special occasions such as weddings or funerals. Marika was the primary spokesperson for their family.

Viktor had seen little of Borz in recent years, ever since he married and began to raise a family of his own. When they met at family gatherings he was always cordial, but that special bond between them had been dissolved. He had assumed the role of brother-in-law rather than best friend. Viktor was sad for that; he truly missed their companionship.

They had been given a private room in which to hold their celebration. The table was elegantly arrayed, with fine china, silver and candelabra. Heavy damask drapes covered the walls. Viktor stood and saluted the family assembled before him.

"I have been very proud Mr. Dzasokhov, Papa, to be taken in as part of this fine family. You treated me like a son, long before I was a son-in-law." They all laughed at that. "You have given me the loveliest jewel that your family possessed." As he said this, he took Tatyana's hand in his. "Now, I am proud to give her the honor she deserves by raising a salute in her honor, Tatyana Dzasokhova Gadayev—Madam Assistant Director!"

She looked stunning this evening, with her hair coiffured into three tiers. She wore a dark green dress and a single strand of pearls. Two pearls graced her ears. They all clapped for her and she blushed. In all her years she could not recall being made the center of such attention, not even on her wedding day.

Papa stood and looked at his youngest with pride. "Tatyana, you have always brought joy and pleasure to your Mama and me. You

honor us by the way you have managed a career and a fine family."
He made a gesture with his hand to include the three grandchildren
seated around their mother. Papa then turned to Viktor and continued
"And now, on behalf of our whole family, I wish to thank our gracious
host this evening." He raised his glass in the direction of his son-in-law.
"To Viktor Ivramovich, First Deputy!"

"To Viktor Ivramovich," the others echoed and they all clapped
again. Viktor noticed that Borz seemed less enthusiastic than the others.

It was a splendid meal. Tatyana was almost embarrassed by the
opulence; given the hardship she knew that the others must be experiencing. Food was even harder to find in the market these days. When
it came time for coffee the men excused themselves, adjourning to a
corner of the private room set aside for smoking and manly conversations.

"Borz, let your son come with us," Viktor said with a gesture to his
nephew, now nearing fourteen. "He is of an age that he, too, can be a
part of our discussions." The young man looked eagerly to his father
and sprang up as soon as he detected a nod of consent. Ivram pouted
at the table, wishing that he were older.

After some casual conversation, Borz turned to his brother-in-law
and said, "So, Viktor, it seems you have chosen to lead us all into the
great unknown. What hidden perils will we be called upon to face, I
wonder?"

Papa Dzasokhov looked dismayed. "Borz, you should not talk this
way to your host."

"Yes, my young friend is a gracious host. For that I must thank him.
Who would have thought that the young man I trained would rise to
such eminence? I hope, my friend, that you know what you are doing
this time."

Viktor put a hand on Borz's shoulder. Signs of gray were now visible in his friend's hair and his thick mustache was dappled now as
well. They were both a little heavier these days. "Yes, my good friend,
if you only knew how often I ask myself that very question."

Borz's son, unabashed by being in the presence of his elders, stated in a matter-of-fact manner, "My teacher says that the Russians will
surely send in their soldiers and that we will all be killed."

Viktor looked at the boy. What future would he have, he wondered? "We hope that it will not come to that," was all that he could
reply.

"But what if it does?" Borz added emphatically. "Viktor, how can
we withstand a move by the Russians. You have given us little room to
negotiate. The Ingush were wise not to sever the umbilical so quickly."

Grigor now spoke up. "I must agree with Borz. We depend on the Russians for almost everything. They certainly do not want to lose the oil fields. How many wars have been fought over oil in the past? They say that the oil runs red with the blood of our ancestors."

"I'm sure that President Dudayev has taken all of these things into consideration." It was Papa's way of trying to end a political debate.

Viktor surprised him by responding, "Consideration, yes. Resolution, I do not know."

"See, he does agree with me," Borz said with no cause to celebrate. "I'm afraid that we may all be called to arms and that the outcome is very much in doubt."

Grigor said, "I have no other family here, except for you. We are very afraid, Marika and I. We are thinking about leaving. There is no work in the oil field for me anyway."

"But where would you go?" Papa asked with some alarm.

"To Nazran. My mother is Ingush and I have cousins there. It is not that far away."

"You see what you have started, my friend." Borz looked directly into Viktor's eyes. "May the Almighty one be with us when this all ends."

"I also pray the same thing, Borz."

"Ah, but will our prayers be enough to withstand the Russian's tanks?"

"No, not if it comes to that. Then it will be up to people like you. Only if we all stand together can we hope to succeed."

23

For a while it did seem that The Almighty One was with them. Although Russia did not officially recognize their self-proclaimed independence, neither was any overt action taken against them. Perhaps Dudayev had been right.

Within a month from the day he had proclaimed independence for Chechnya the Union of Soviet Socialist Republics was dissolved. It was mind-boggling to say the least. One of the mightiest nations in the history of the world had simply disintegrated. Boris Yeltsin was left scrambling to preserve some semblance of the former world power. Even his rule was being challenged by Ruslan Khasbulatov. As Dudayev had observed, he was a native of Groznyy who had ascended to chairmanship of the Russian Supreme Soviet in 1991. Although deemed to be a conservative hard-liner, it was probably his influence that had kept Russian tanks at bay so far.

Each day brought yet another entreaty from Moscow for a peaceful re-alliance with the Russian Federation. In the Assembly, now that the Ingush dissenters were gone and many ethnic Russians were beginning to leave the country, a firmer resolve had been fostered. Surely it was the will of Allah that Chechnya be a free and independent nation. Had He not shown them a sign by bringing down the Soviet Union?

They were not to be the masters of their own destiny, however. In Moscow, Khasbulatov raised the ante in his battle with Yeltsin. He led a protest movement and with a group of about 100 deputies took control of the parliament building. Russian tanks were seen in the streets of Moscow itself, shelling their own government buildings. Khasbulatov was arrested, but a newly elected Duma saw fit to dismiss the charges. He was released and returned to his native Groznyy, intent on re-establishing his political power. In Moscow, Yeltsin solidified his own base of power and restored some semblance of order to the federation. He now directed his attention to this little annoyance in the south.

It was the morning of December 11, 1994. Sunday was Viktor's day to relax with the family. He had gone to bed late, looking forward to the chance to sleep in. When the phone rang at quarter to six he tried to ignore it. Tatyana answered it. "I'm sorry," he heard her say, "Deputy Gadayev is not available right now. Can he call you back later." After a pause, "Yes, yes I understand General, wait a moment please." He turned on the light and rolled over to take the phone, realizing that this interruption was unavoidable. Tatyana looked terrified as she handed him the receiver. "It is General Zumsovekyy—Russian troops are crossing the border!"

"This is First Deputy Gadayev speaking... Yes, General... Yes, I understand. How long ago?... Do we know how large a force?... Yes, I see... Casualties?... Yes, thank you for calling. No, it was no bother at all."

Tatyana was sitting up in the bed. She locked her arms around her husband as he talked to the general and took the phone from him to hang it up on the small table by the bed. "Viktor, have they really started a war?" She knew what the answer was but hoping against hope she was mistaken.

"Yes. I'm afraid our days of peaceful coexistence have come to a very abrupt end." He got up and began throwing on his clothes even as he spoke to her. "Two armored divisions are moving east from Mozdok and Nazran. We have mounted a resistance already. There are reports of heavy fighting and civilian casualties as well as to the militia. I must get to my office immediately."

She helped him straighten his jacket. "How long will you be gone?"

"I have no idea."

He kissed her quickly and hurried out the door. Later he would think about their parting and wish that he had taken longer to say good-bye. He never even stopped to look in on his children.

The sky was just beginning to lighten when he arrived at the Presidential Palace. This was no storybook castle or grand mansion. Rather it was an imposing ten-story building that housed the principal operations of the government. Its fluted white facade gave it the look of a Hilton hotel. Everything seemed in chaos. Sirens were wailing everywhere as police cars, military vehicles and emergency vehicles raced helter-skelter though the city streets. Government officials were hurrying in, all having received abrupt wake-up calls just as he had. Dudayev had secured himself in the command outpost with his senior military officials.

The Vice President was left to handle many of the more mundane administrative duties. "I have just received a report that more than

twenty thousand Russian troops may have crossed the border already,"
he was saying to a group of deputies and administrators as Viktor came
in. "We have attempted to establish road blocks at Kalinosvskaya and
Nadterechnaya. Also at these points just west of Groznyy." Two junior
officers were holding up a large map. Red arrows had been hastily
drawn in with magic markers to indicate the Russian advance. Double
green lines were slashed across several of the main east—west arteries.
"They have many tanks deployed against us, I am afraid, but no air
attacks have been reported as yet."

For the next three days he did not leave the building. He tried to
call home several times, but the service was erratic. He got through
once. Mama Dzasokhov answered the phone. "Hello, Mama, it's Viktor.
May I speak to Tatyana, please?"

"She has gone to the hospital."

"Yes, of course, I should have realized she'd be there."

"I was asked to stay here with the children. They are very frightened, Viktor."

Petruska grabbed the phone from her. "Father, is it true? Are we at
war with the Russians? Nadi just keeps crying and Ivram, he's so imma-
ture, he thinks he should join the army. I've tried to tell him he's just a
little boy."

Viktor closed his eyes and tried to imagine how this would all work
out. He had been so busy with the affairs of state he had forgotten the
real human consequences that were unfolding throughout the country.
"Petruska, you must all be brave. Do what Gramma tells you. I'll try to
get by and see you later."

In spite of their overwhelming superiority, the Russians were being
held in check. General Dudayev had assembled a sizable fighting force
of his own out of the Chechens who had previously served in the
Soviet Army and Air Force. Armed civilians, who saw this as their personal *jihad* or holy war, joined the regulars.

There was a lull in the action, so he took the opportunity to try to
see his family. He went to the Fourth Hospital, knowing that she would
most likely still be there. He found her right away. She was doing triage
at the main entrance, sorting out the casualties from bomb blasts and
rifle fire as they arrived by the truckload in a seemingly unending flow.

Her hair was pulled back and pinned up, but random strands had
found their way back down over her face. She wore a white smock to
cover her nurse's uniform, but everything had been liberally splattered
with blood by now. Her arms were bloody too. She threw them up
around him to give him a kiss, trying to hold them away from him so
as not to bloody him as well. "Oh Viktor, this is such a nightmare. All

of these women and children are being maimed." Her arm moved across the expanse of a reception area that was filled with badly wounded people. "They're saying that the Russians are deploying land mines on the mountain trails so the people can not flee the area. See," she pointed down at a young woman holding a toddler wrapped in a bloodstained blanket, "here is a small infant who has lost both of her feet. Is there anything you can do to stop this carnage?"

"No, this is the path we have chosen. I am afraid it is the one down which we must walk."

"I'm frightened Viktor. Not for me, but for our children. Can any of us get out of this alive?"

"I don't know," he admitted to her. "Can you get away?"

"No, not just now. There are just too many wounded coming in. My place is here."

"Yes, I knew you would say that. Try to get some rest. The children need you too." He pressed his lips to hers and held her in a long embrace. A tear formed in the corner of his eye. He hoped she didn't see it.

He drove by the house, but it was empty. Mama had taken them away from this place, hoping that her home would be out of the line of fire. He didn't have that much time. He had to head back to the palace. When he got there General Dudayev met him. He was dressed in combat fatigues. "Ah, Viktor, there you are. We have need of capable administrators in the field to coordinate supplies and funnel information back to our headquarters here. I understand that this is what you used to do for the oil company."

"Yes, general, but I thought that my duties required that..."

The general held up his hand to silence this protest. "No, Ivramovich, today your country requires you in the field."

24

There was snow on the ground. Viktor thought that it seemed appropriate. Hadn't all of the truly memorable, truly valorous battles of Russia's history been fought in the snow? He wore a great coat, a woolen cap and heavy gloves. His boots crunched on the snowy surface. He felt strangely alive, yet feared for the lives of those around him.

They were winning, or so it seemed. The Russian advance had been slowed. This was not only due to the resistance being mounted by the Chechens, but also to a lack of resolve on the part of the Russian Army. Memories of the bitter conflict in Afghanistan were still fresh in the minds of many seasoned veterans, officers and enlisted men alike. If popularity for that war had waned, then it never existed for this new onslaught. Once again the Russian citizenry watched images of old men and women, young boys and girls all in harms way. Only these people *were Russians too!* They were fighting their own now. Why? The action had stopped on several fronts because field commanders simply refused the order to attack. It was reminiscent of the events of 1917 when the Tsarist forces simply laid down their weapons and went home during the First World War.

General Babichev, commander of the elite Pskov airborne division spearheading the assault in the west, was reassigned. His replacement pressed the attack on to Groznyy. The Russians were able to establish several firebases above and around the city. The shelling was relentless.

The multi-storied apartment complexes spread across the city made easy targets for the Russian artillery. A dense cloud of black smoke hung over the city day and night, as fires burned unchecked. Building facades crumpled and spilled onto the broad avenues of Groznyy, now devoid of any traffic. The gunners were not seeking military targets. They were seeking to destroy the city itself and with it the will of the people. They were indiscriminate in the choice of objectives. Schools, mosques, apartments all fell to the shelling, as did the hospitals.

Tatyana was back at her post, sorting out the injured as they came in seeking healing and refuge. The air was filled with sounds of exploding artillery shells. It was similar to rolling thunderclaps, sometimes distant, sometimes very, very close. One particularly loud explosion rattled the room. A doctor working beside her said, "My, that was a big one! Tatyana, I don't know how you can keep at this hour after hour."

"I stopped thinking about it a long time ago. Sometimes, when they're close like that, I just close my eyes, take a firm grip on what ever solid substance I can lay my hands on, like this cot, and wait for the ground tremors to subside."

"Why don't you take a break, my dear. When was the last time you got some rest?"

"Who can rest in all of this chaos? No, with the constant sounds of the bombing I find it much better to stay active and keep my eyes open. Perhaps they will stop firing at us tonight." She resumed ministering to the current victim that lay mangled and torn on the stretcher in front of her. Gently she wiped the blood from his eyes and held his hand.

The doctor watched her with admiration. "Can I do anything for this one?"

"No, I'm afraid he no longer needs the services of a surgeon. He's dying. I was just trying to ease his passage into what must be a better place. Some pain killers might help."

"I'm sure they would. Unfortunately, our supply is nearly exhausted. We must save them for those with some hope of survival. It is barbaric, but also necessary."

"Yes, I understand.

"You are remarkable, my child," the old doctor said. "You still treat each of these poor wretches with tenderness, even now, after several weeks of seeing these same sights over and over."

"It's the children that really break my heart. Maimed and bloodied, some too stunned to even cry. They have no idea why this is happening to them."

"Yes, I..." This time, the sound of the explosion seemed closer than ever. In fact, the building shook before the ear-piercing noise, a bad sign she thought. Someone screamed close by and she turned to look. There was daylight where she knew a wall and ceiling belonged. The rest of the ceiling came down on top of her and she was killed instantly.

The Russians had launched a second offensive from the east, out of Khasav" Yurt, in Dagestan. Two Russian tanks had become separated from their column and were making their way along the road to Shali. They clamored slowly up a steep grade, the noise of the engines and metal treads on pavement reverberated off the surrounding hills. Clearing the top of the rise, they came into a small angular valley. In the center stood a solitary stone cottage. No one was about.

Captain Gargarin was new to the campaign and had not had a chance to engage the enemy yet. He was standing in the turret's main hatch and called down to the sergeant below, "What do you make of it?"

"Just an abandoned farmhouse, sir."

"Well at least we can get in a little target practice. That way the guns will not be untested when we are called upon for actual battle." He reached for his headset and said into it, "A bottle of vodka to the first crew to bring down this building." Both tanks stopped simultaneously. Their turrets turned ominously in the direction of their target, guns elevating. A sharp crack, crack echoed up the valley, as flame and smoke flashed out of first one barrel and then the other. Both found the intended target.

The old woman was asleep in her bed, which was now kept in the front room for convenience. Old age and poor hearing had kept her unaware of the approaching peril. The first blast sent a shock wave through the building, literally throwing her off the bed and slamming her frail body against the wall. If she wasn't dead immediately, she died soon after the second shell exploded. The first tank fired again. It brought most of the second floor down into the main room. Embers from the fireplace were tossed about and quickly began to kindle pieces of debris. A round from the second tank had been aimed at the second story window. With the structure collapsing before it, it passed through, exploding up the hillside, killing one of the goats that were frantically bounding away from the cataclysm below.

Myriana Gadayev had been out back feeding her little ones. She heard the muffled roar of the engines making their way up into her valley but thought there was little she could do about it. Best to stay out of sight and say a prayer for the people over in Shali. The sounds of the first two volleys startled her. So loud! So close! Then her home erupted behind her. She was knocked to her knees. The goats ran frantically up the hill. She scrambled to her feet and tried to run with them. Another roaring explosion behind her made her pause just long enough to turn and look over her shoulder. She saw her home, the family home for seven generations, crumbling in a cloud of smoke. She heard a screaming whistle and instinctively dropped to the ground. The shell passed almost directly over her head, exploding less than fifty meters beyond her. The noise was deafeningly loud. Dirt, rock and pieces of goat rained down on her.

"May the Almighty save me from this terror," she prayed softly and rose to run again.

In the second tank, the hatch flew open and a young sergeant popped up, chambered a round in the thirty-caliber machine gun and began firing. "Cease Fire!" came the command over the radio almost immediately. "We are not here to kill little old ladies!" Captain Gargarin felt suddenly sick to his stomach. Their little game had taken on real meaning now. My God, he thought, were there other people inside that house too?

It was too late. One thirty caliber round had ripped through Mama's hip. She fell to the ground one last time. She was not dead yet. Unfortunately, that would take some time. Alone in this little valley, there would be no one to find her and give her assistance. No one to pray for her departing soul. High above her on the mountainside, a lone grey wolf stopped, startled by the sudden tumult. He watched the human events unfolding below and then turned and continued on his way through the underbrush in search of his evening meal.

In the village of Chervlënnaya, Russian troops were going from house to house in search of rebel sympathizers. Mrs. Dzasokhov huddled in the kitchen with her two granddaughters. She heard someone pounding on her door, then the sound of crashing as it was kicked in. Her husband called out, "What do you want? We are just an old couple!"

"We are looking for the traitor Gadayev! Where is Viktor Gadayev?"

"I don't know who you're talking about," she heard Papa say.

"Then you must be a fool!" was shouted the reply. She could hear the sound of her husband being struck by the butt of a rifle. He fell to his knees, holding his head. Blood oozed through his fingers. "This fool does not know his own son-in-law!"

"You leave my grandfather alone!" Mrs. Dzasokhov's heart nearly stopped when she heard young Ivram's voice. She wanted to call out to him, but was afraid of calling attention to herself and the young girls she was clutching close to her. Ivram was just twelve. He had taken a large carving knife from the kitchen. In his brave young heart he saw himself as the defender of his family in the absence of his father. They hadn't told about his mother, but he had not heard from her in several days. He had seen the pictures of Groznyy on the television and he feared something terrible had taken place. He hated these men who were invading his grandparent's house. The young boy lashed out at the sergeant who had struck Papa, giving him a glancing cut above the wrist. Infuriated, the man turned his rifle at Ivram and fired several rounds directly into him.

"Ivram!" came the involuntary cry of anguish from the kitchen. Nadezcha began to scream, "Mama, I want my Mama!" Petruska wanted to silence her, but she too was shaking in terror and whimpering loudly.

"Kill them all, burn this fucking house down!" commanded the sergeant as he pushed passed his two colleagues. He held his wounded arm up to his chest. "A curse on all these damned people!"

Although he had no formal military training, Viktor quickly settled in as front line liaison officer. His primary duties involved marshaling supplies among the various units of regular and para-military forces that had been placed in opposition to the Russian advance. He also communicated directly with President Dudayev about the status of the war in this sector. Consequently, he was able to obtain immediate decisions on tactical matters that might otherwise have taken hours, possibly days, through the normal command chain. That saved several lives and the he won the admiration of the senior staff in the field. His comrades in arms regarded him as a seasoned veteran.

His current outpost was in the hills above Naderechnaya, about equidistant between Groznyy and the Russian base of operations in Mozdok. A large ridge of mountains provided a natural wall of defense for the capital city. He was with a unit charged with preserving control of the only major pass over them. The thrill of combat had quickly given way to the drudgery and misery of cold, mud and blood. He went for days at a time without sleep and ate only sparingly.

Their unit had again come under fire during the night. The Russians positioned several tanks along the mountain road below them and they were being shelled heavily. The air was thick with smoke from the explosions and from trees burning around them. This time they were hemmed in, unable to move out quickly and regroup in a new location as they had been doing.

The unit commander was an old army colonel named Mairbek Chermoyev. He had been called out of retirement to serve his native country and was a veteran of five years in Afghanistan. "Deputy Gadayev," he spoke gravely, " I am not sure that we can hold this position much longer. Is there any help on the way?"

"They attempted to get some more men through to us, but the Russians have us significantly out-numbered today. Dudayev asked, no, he implored us to hold out to the last man, if necessary."

"Well, my friend, it seems that that is exactly what we are about to do." The Colonel gave Viktor a hug. "Deputy Gadayev, it has truly been an honor to serve with you these past few weeks. If my son had not been killed in Afghanistan, perhaps he would be here to stand beside me today. I am grateful to have you in his place." Chermoyev kissed him on the cheek, as if to say 'good-bye, my friend' and headed back toward the line of revetments they had thrown up. He called back, "You had best pick up a rifle and join the fighting. You are more important to us now as a soldier, not as a liaison."

"Take care old man and may the Almighty guide your spirit," Viktor said too softly for the Colonel to hear above the din of battle. He had been given an AK-47 and had used it once before this. He threw it up over his shoulder, grabbed several bandoleers of cartridges and checked his nine-caliber pistol. He took a quick look around the tent that was both his office and billet. A picture of Tatyana and the children was tacked to the center post. He pulled it off and stared lovingly at her face. "I'm sorry, my love. Will you ever forgive me?" A sudden volley of rifle fire reminded him of the task at hand. He tucked the photo inside his great coat and ran down to join a small band of infantrymen in a trench line.

Russian infantry units were now inching their way up through the dense underbrush and fallen trees. The constant cracking of rifle fire assumed a strange rhythm, rising and falling in great swells as different units became engaged. This was underscored by detonating mortar rounds and even louder explosions from the tank shells. Interspersed with this were shouted commands, both in Russian and Nakh and the frequent screams from soldiers on both sides. The stench of battle filled his nostrils, nitre from the gunpowder, burning wood and those carnal smells emitted by human carcasses.

The battle raged on but the sounds seemed to fade from his consciousness. They were simply just too much for the mind to comprehend. For just a moment he thought that he saw her in the smoke and haze. Tatyana, just has she had come to him on their wedding day. Young and beautiful again. Her head draped in a fine lace shawl. She was laughing and calling to him. Her hand motioned for him to follow her. Then he felt the pain in his chest. He looked down and saw a growing circle of blood staining his coat. He saw the hole that the bullet had made as it ripped through the cloth. He looked up and she was gone. Viktor knew that he had to follow her and so he did.

Garyk II

25

The six-month leave of absence that was granted to Garyk to recuperate from his Afghan war wounds afforded him time to be with his young son. Georgi was a precocious four-year-old. He seemed as comfortable using a computer as either of his parents. While Katryn tended to the newest member of the family, the two *men* played in the park together nearly every day. Garyk told his son the stories he remembered from his own childhood. For the first time in many years he missed his own father.

Viktor's visit had been wonderful. Such a delightful family his brother had! Tatyana was charming and, he felt, just what Katryn needed at that time. Most of her friends were in the military. For the first time she had another woman to share domestic secrets with. During that brief visit he and Viktor also talked together more than they had for the preceding ten years. They took their sons to the park together.

"Viktor, I can't get over how content you look."

"I am, Garyk. The Almighty has truly blessed me with a wonderful wife and fine children." Viktor's attention was suddenly drawn to the two young boys running down a hill to a small stream. "Ivram, you take Georgi's hand and be careful by that water."

Both men screened the sun from their eyes to watch the boys frolicking. Garyk said to his brother, "I don't think I've ever heard you refer to the Almighty before. Is this something new?"

"New? No, I wouldn't say that. Reactivated perhaps. I always enjoyed going to the mosque with our father. Then, after he died, I simply stopped praying."

"We both did. I guess I just never felt the need to get back to it."

"Neither did I for some time. When we decided to get married, Tatyana insisted that the usman perform the ceremony. You remember him, don't you?"

"How could I forget. I thought Katryn was going to die of apoplexy or something. Strange how that affected her."

"Funny, I hadn't noticed that. Well, anyway, the usman insisted that I attend Morning Prayers. I agreed, reluctantly, for Tatyana's sake. Then, after the wedding, I just kept going. It gave me, I don't know, inner peace I guess. Now I say the prayers with Georgi every morning and we both go to the mosque each week."

While the boys raced around the trees and bushes in the park, the two men walked along a gravel path. People passing by were struck by the similarity of the two. In spite of Viktor's longer hair and close-cropped beard there was no denying that the two were identical twins. "I had almost forgotten that I was a Moslem until I went to Afghanistan. Of course Mama was quick to remind me when I told her about Kat." Both men laughed at the remembrance of that little scene. "Religion never seemed an issue up here while I was in school or even when I went to work full time for the Army. All of a sudden I found myself fighting in a war where the enemy's only crime seemed to be that he was a Moslem. Viktor, I tell you that I sometimes felt that I should be fighting with the Afghanis, not against them!"

Viktor stopped walking and wrapped his brother in a bear hug. "So my brother is not a Russian after all. We need to get you away from Moscow, Garyk. Can't you get a transfer back closer to home?"

"I don't think Katryn would ever agree to that."

That evening, after Viktor and his family had departed, he and Katryn made love for the first time since he had returned. It was not the wild, passionate lovemaking that had been a part of their earlier years. Instead, it was a gentle, compassionate affair, each needing the other's companionship and warmth. When they had finished, she lay close against him sobbing.

"Kat, what's wrong?"

"Garyk, I needed you so much, but you weren't there for me. I know that was senseless, selfish even. The baby was coming and I was all alone. At least, it felt that way. And then I thought that you were gone forever. It was just too much for me to handle. Please forgive me?"

"My dearest, there is nothing to forgive," he whispered softly to her. "You are all that I have ever wanted my whole life. I think I understand how you must have felt. I was afraid that I had lost you too. I don't know how much longer I could have gone on like that, but I knew I had to give you time to work things out. I hope things will get back to normal now."

"Just promise me that you will never, ever leave me again," she begged him.

He made no reply, other than to roll over on top of her. He pressed his lips against hers, their tongues working hard together. His fingers massaged her head. He was inside of her again, working slowly, rhythmically. They felt each other's deepest needs and came together, finally, in one explosion of ecstasy. After a long pause, he whispered "Kat, my dearest, I will always love you."

When they rose the next day it was as though he had never gone away. Their life seemed to be slowly coming back together.

He was reassigned to Satellite Uplink Interface for Nuclear Warhead Deactivation. As part of the ongoing accords with the United States, the Soviet Union had agreed to disarm, deactivate and decommission a specific number of nuclear warheads and their respective intercontinental missiles. In order to maintain control, a triangular network of command procedures was required to deactivate each warhead properly. The coded sequences were revised twice each day. It was not as challenging as his earlier assignments had been, but he welcomed the routine that permitted him to maintain a rather normal work schedule.

He missed working alongside of his wife. They made such an effective team in the past. And he deeply missed Alexandr. He found that he had no one he was close to, other than Katryn. Viktor was too far away. There was no close comrade to confide in and serve as a sounding board for his innermost feelings. No one to debate the events of the day with.

On the tenth anniversary of their commissioning, Katryn received the order promoting her to major. She came into Garyk's office sporting new gold shoulder boards. A small bronze star was mounted between the two narrow red stripes. Once again she was near the top of the promotion list. "Well, look at this!" Garyk was genuinely pleased that his wife had been promoted. "I suppose that this means I will have to salute you each night before I jump into bed."

"Nonsense, you've been promoted too, I'm sure." She naturally assumed that this would be the case, they had always advanced together in the past. In fact, she thought that his combat experience might push him ahead of her this time.

"Actually," he said rather matter-of-factly, "I was passed over this time around."

"Garyk, how can that be?" Her tone expressed a mixture of surprise and confusion.

"Well, I think that some of my superiors have taken umbrage to my views on the war in Afghanistan and about current affairs in general."

"Oh Garyk, no!" She was quite dismayed now. "You really need to be concerned about how this will effect your career. Mine too! They may decide that we should be split up. After all, we haven't actually worked together for some time."

He could see that she was becoming much too upset over his situation and losing the enthusiasm that her own promotion justly deserved. He pushed his door closed and pulled her into his arms, giving her a kiss. "Well," he said, as he broke away, "I've never actually kissed a major before. I think it might be something that I could get used to!"

"Garyk, you're impossible!" She pulled away and left his office. Her section was on another floor.

He was passed over again in 1987 and 1988. He took it in stride. After all, he was never really a military person at heart. He was quite content to work with his computer programs and take life one day at a time. With the release of each promotion list, however, Katryn's disappointment was more evident. She harped on Garyk to disengage himself from the political debates.

Her father also became more assertive in this respect. "Garyk," he would lecture him, "you must remember that it is not important *who* you are. What matters is *what* you are. And what you are is *Captain* Gadayev, an officer in the Soviet Army! Your first allegiance, no, make that your only allegiance, must be to it. You must also remember that political leaders come and go. When they go, those that were too closely associated with them have tended to go also. Do you understand this, Garyk? Make no mistake, my son, this Gorbachev will be gone soon, but the Communist Party shall remain!"

"Can you be so sure of that?"

"As sure as I am that the sun will rise in the morning. Some things in Russia will never change."

By now Garyk knew when it was unwise to continue to debate such points with Yuri Ivanovich Moldatin. He was a child of the revolution, born in '29, raised under Stalin and a member of the Communist Party ever since his fourteenth birthday. He was a member of the Congress of Peoples Deputies, the behind the scenes organization that appointed the Supreme Soviet and elected the national leadership. His jacket sported several lapel pins that represented the highest civic awards bestowed by the government. Moldatin could not see that a major tide of change was about to sweep his country. For that matter, who could have seen it in 1988?

Garyk continued to speak out for political and social reforms in spite of these entreaties from his wife and father-in-law. Aides to Ruslan Khasbulatov, a professor of economics turned political activist, took note of this fellow Chechen. They asked if he would like to be assigned as their military liaison officer in 1989. He agreed. As a result, he was immediately promoted to major. He joked to his wife, "You see, it does pay to be Chechen after all!"

She was not amused by this turn of events. "Garyk, I begged you to give up this political nonsense. Instead, you've given up your career for it."

"How can you say I've given up my career. Haven't I finally been promoted?"

"This isn't what they trained you for Garyk. My God, you've put your life in the hands of a history professor."

"Actually, he taught Economics," Garyk interjected.

Katryn was preparing a Stroganoff for dinner. At his last remark she shrieked in exasperation and banged down the pot for emphasis. Gravy splattered her blouse and most of the countertop. "Now see what you've made me do. History, Economics, what's the difference? Garyk, you are a computer specialist, a soldier, not a politician."

She became jealous of the time he had to spend away from her. Katryn felt that she was losing him again, that he had betrayed her, somehow. Once again their relationship cooled. Garyk was at a loss to understand her. Couldn't she see that changes were necessary? She refused to be drawn into any conversations about it. Soon, she refused to talk to him at all.

26

Things darkened considerably for them in the summer of 1989. Alexandra had been ill, on and off, for about three months. At first it was just a general listlessness, but this was in sharp contrast to the child's normal vibrancy. Katryn dismissed it as a childhood illness, a bad case of influenza that would not go away. When the fevers persisted she took her to the clinic. The doctor gave her some antibiotics to administer. When these showed no sign of improving her condition, Katryn became more concerned.

Alexandra's jowls became noticeably swollen. Bleeding started, from her nose first and then around her teeth. On her second visit to the clinic Katryn demanded that they perform more tests. Two days later she was called back to have further testing done. Her concern overcame her unwillingness to talk to Garyk. She called him at the office.

"Katryn!" he said with mock surprise upon hearing her voice. "Does this mean that I've extracted myself from the dog house?"

"I only called because I had to." Her voice was icy and, he thought, there was something else wrong. She continued, "I have just received a call from Doctor Kobichev's office. They want me to bring Alexandra back in for more testing tomorrow. They didn't say why, just that she would need to be in the hospital for three days. Garyk, I must insist that you to be there with me. You can make it, can't you?"

"Yes, of course I can. Do you want me to come home right away?"

"No, I'll see you tonight."

The next morning they both brought her to the hospital. Alexandra was not yet five. She knew that there was something terribly wrong and she sensed that her mother was very upset. It was rare that Mommy and Daddy would both take the day off. The hospital was a strange place. It was filled with people wearing strange clothes and there were all sorts of machines and computers. She thought that it was funny to be wheeled to her room in the special chair with large wheels.

"Why must I spend the night, Mommy?" she asked and "Why can't you and Daddy stay here with me?"

Her mother had the same questions for Dr. Kobichev when they met with him in the hallway outside of Alexandra's room. He was in his mid-thirties, with dark blond hair that was brushed back over the top of his head to well below his ears. Metal rimmed glasses were perched on top of an angular nose. With little emotion he explained, "The first series of tests were inconclusive. We have detected some abnormalities, but cannot make a final determination without doing more tests."

"What kind of abnormalities are we taking about, doctor?" Garyk asked first, but Katryn had been about to.

"Well, it is still too early to make a definitive diagnosis. It would be premature..."

"Tell us, doctor," Katryn said sharply, cutting him off in mid sentence. "We have a right to know what you think may be the matter with our daughter."

He looked at both of them, concerned only that they had broken his rhythm. "It is much to soon to say for sure, but there are certain indications. We think that your daughter may have leukemia, but let me assure you that it is not at all certain."

Katryn put both hands up to her mouth. "Leukemia! Oh God, no!" Garyk felt her weakening and wrapped his arm around her waist to keep her from falling. "When will you know for sure?" he asked.

"Not until tomorrow afternoon," the doctor told them. "Possibly not until the day after. There are several tests. If you like, I can arrange for the mother to stay overnight."

"Yes, please do that, doctor." Katryn said, pulling herself upright and pulling away from Garyk. Once again she mustered the strength she needed to go about her duty on her own.

When the test results came back they were painfully conclusive. It was acute leukemia and the worst kind. Dr. Kobichev called them into his office and explained that this was a disease that affected the blood forming tissues of the body. Something he called T-lymphocytes and white blood cells called leukocytes were overproduced. These cells would then invade other body tissue.

Garyk asked, "What could cause this to happen to Alexandra?"

"We still don't know the why of this disease. We are only beginning to understand the how. It is a viral infection and it can prove to be very deadly."

Katryn asked, "What course of treatment will you begin, Doctor?"

"If she were to undergo chemotherapy her life could be prolonged by perhaps a few months, maybe even a year. It would be very painful for her and, in the final analysis, it would be futile. Honestly, I believe it would do the child more harm than good."

"And without the treatments," Katryn asked, "what happens then?"

"She has six months to live, nine at the outside." Garyk felt as if the doctor had thrust a scalpel through his heart. For a moment he couldn't breathe. He stared at the large clock that hung on the wall. It's second hand jerked forward with each tick it made. It struck him that it was counting down the seconds in Alexandra's life. He loved his son, but he delighted in Alexandra. She was a cherub, with blonde-white hair just like her mother. She would run to him when he came home at night, leaping up into his arms, just as Kat had once done. She sang songs for him and "read" stories to him out of her picture book.

"Surely, doctor," he was finally able to speak, "the therapy can cause remission at least, even if not a cure."

"Major Gadayev, I really wish I could tell you that," the doctor responded. "Unfortunately, it is as I have already told you. We can delay the process by no more than six months. They will not be happy months, for you or the child. This is a particularly nasty strain of the disease. It spreads very quickly. All attempts to circumvent it by performing bone marrow transplants have been unsuccessful. Maybe that is just as well. I have seen other children who have been forced to endure this curse for several years. They suffer great hardships and then they die painfully. It will be better for her if she goes quickly."

"Thank you, doctor." Katryn spoke as she would to a clerk or junior officer who had just presented some routine report or evaluation to her. She rose from her chair in front of his desk, reached across and politely shook his had. "It is good of you to have taken the time to explain all this to us. I am sure that you have done the best you could under these circumstances. Now, I must go and attend to my daughter."

Her demeanor struck Garyk as unnatural. Was she really so detached from all this? Was this how she had responded to the news when he had been injured? He couldn't comprehend the totality of what just took place. Were they just to stand by and watch his darling little girl die? He wanted to lash out at something or someone. Katryn started to leave the office. Seeing that he was still seated, she turned back to him. "Come, dear, there is no reason to detain the doctor any longer. We must be going."

Garyk rushed to keep abreast of her as they hurried down the hall. "What is the matter with you?" He voice was strained with anguish.

"He's just told us that our little Alex is going to die and you act as if nothing is the matter."

"Of course something is the matter," she said rather brusquely. "Do you think that I don't feel it? It tears me apart, inside here," she said pounding her hand against her chest. "But that isn't going to help her, is it. All the pain that I could feel will not relieve one milligram of the agony that she is going to suffer. No, Garyk, this is not the time for us to grieve. We will have much too much time for that later on. Now it is time for us to comfort her and love her while we still have her here."

She was right, of course. She always was. Still he thought that it was remarkable that she could be so strong. He followed her down the hallway to the elevator that took them up to her floor. Down two more corridors to her room. In all that time, she said nothing more. When they got to her door, Katryn turned to him and said, "Don't let on that anything is the matter, do you hear me."

Alex was lying in the bed, cradling her favorite doll. She looked so small and defenseless in the big hospital bed with its steel rails pulled up to wall her in. When they came in she brightened up immediately. "Oh Mommy, Daddy I'm so glad you're finally here. I was afraid you weren't coming at all."

"I'm sorry, Sweetie," Katryn said, giving her a light peck on the forehead. "We were just downstairs talking to Dr. Kobichev. We didn't mean for it to take this long."

"They're not going to do any more tests are they, Mommy? I really don't like tests."

"No, my love, no more tests. In fact, you can get dressed now and we'll take you home."

"Oh, goody!" she shouted, hopping up and down on the bed. "Daddy, come here and help me, will you please." Garyk went to her on the bed and caught her in his arms. He hugged her tightly, fighting back tears he knew he couldn't let her see.

They enjoyed about a month of normalcy. He did not linger at the office and tried to cut out almost all of the evening engagements he would have routinely attended in order to spend as much time with her as possible. The relationship between Garyk and Katryn reverted back to the cordial yet distant association that had characterized the months following his return from Afghanistan. He needed her. He felt that she must be in need also, but his attempts to get close to her were rebuffed. When he reached for her at night, she turned away.

They were awakened one night by Alexandra's screams. Her pillow was crimson with blood flowing from her nose. It had begun in earnest and they rushed her back to the hospital. The doctors were able to control the pain and bleeding this time. Dr. Kobichev called in another doctor for consultation. Dr. Andropopokov was a pediatric oncologist. He suggested that they try a bone marrow transplant.

"We were told that there have been no positive results from such operations," Garyk reminded Dr. Kobichev.

Dr. Andropopokov was a few years older than Kobichev. He had a rounder, softer face with a receding hairline. He smiled politely and replied "Yes, that is true to a large extent. New advances are being made every day, not only in the Soviet Union, but in the west as well. The Americans have made much progress and we are attempting to keep up."

"Are you saying then, doctor, that you wish to experiment on my daughter?" It was Katryn's question, asked in a very clinical manner.

"Every operation in this area is an experiment, Major. That doesn't mean that your daughter will be a guinea pig, that she will not benefit from this procedure and find some relief from the pain she is experiencing right now. That pain will only intensify if we do nothing."

"What exactly is involved with this procedure, doctor?" It was Garyk's turn to ask.

"We must find a suitable donor first. That may take some time, but we would start with the immediate family. That is the most likely source."

They consented to be tested. Neither Katryn nor Garyk were found to be compatible. Georgi was. The boy was nine years old. Katryn explained, "Alex is very, very sick. You know that, don't you, Georgi?"

"Yes, Mama, is she going to die?"

"That is a very good possibility. But the doctors have told us that your body might hold medicine that could make her better. Do you understand? They will give you something to make you sleep and then they will take a very small piece out of your leg. There may be some pain when you wake, but it will go away."

The boy said "Yes, Mommy, if it will make Alexandra be able to play again, I will do it for her."

"That is a good boy!" his mother replied.

Alex was able to come home again about two weeks after the operation. She was confined to her bed and they needed the full time attendance of a nurse to look after her. Garyk read a story to her. Something in it reminded him of her plight and he was momentarily choked up. Alexandra caught the hint of a tear forming in his eye. "Am I going to die, Daddy?" It was such a simple little question; asked not unlike the hundreds of questions she had asked him before.

"Now why would you ask such a thing?" He tried to make it seem as if such a question was quite preposterous.

"Mommy says that I'm not, but I don't think I believe her. You will tell me the truth, won't you Daddy?"

He held her close to him. "We are all to die someday, Alexandra."

"Then, I would think it isn't such a bad thing if it's something everybody does."

"No, my little one, it isn't such a bad thing."

27

Alexandra's white cell count began to diminish and color returned to her cheeks. It appeared the transplant might have been successful. Georgi took pride in having played such an important role in the process. Their sibling bond strengthened and he spent hours reading to her and telling her stories from school.

"When can I go to school, Mommy?" she asked.

"Perhaps in the spring, dear. We will just have to wait and see."

The winters in Moscow are cold and dark. That year they seemed colder and darker than ever before as Garyk went about his duties as Khasbulatov's liaison officer. National events occupied his time, but not his consciousness. While Khasbulatov and his group of economic conservatives challenged Gorbachev's proposed free market reforms, Garyk remained preoccupied with the health of his little Alex. He lost interest in the public debate.

Khasbulatov himself called him to account one afternoon, summoning Garyk to come into his office. He was seated behind a desk piled high with reports. No offer was extended for Garyk to take a seat. "Major Gadayev, we are all concerned that you may have lost enthusiasm for our cause. It was your zeal which first caught the attention of my associates and led them to bring you into our inner circle."

"Forgive me, Comrade Khasbulatov. I admit my mind has been elsewhere. As you may know, my daughter is not well. She's dying, as a matter of fact."

Ruslan's expression changed to a look of genuine concern, rather than the stern, professorial image with which had begun the conversation. "Major, I am sorry. I was not aware just how serious the situation at home had become. Yes, you do have a right to be concerned for your child. However, I must tell you that we are at a critical time in the history of our country. 1990 may someday be looked upon as the turning point. We are in a position to determine the direction of that turn. It is important that I have people about me in whom I am able to give my absolute trust and confidence. We need to have your complete attention in the days ahead, is that clear?"

"Yes, Mr. Deputy." Garyk came to a rigid position of attention. "Please be assured that you shall have my absolute commitment."

"Very good, Major." Khasbulatov grinned that expansive smile of his. It revealed the full upper row of irregularly shaped teeth and three lines formed on either cheek. Another set accented his eyes. It was that smile that had first convinced Garyk to become part of the team. Ruslan stood up from his desk and reached across to take Garyk's hand. "May it go well for your daughter, Major. We are counting on you."

That evening Garyk told Katryn about the meeting. "I was called on the carpet today, by Imranych himself. He feels that I am not devoting enough of my time to the job. I'm going to have to start accompanying him on his trips around the country. That means I'll have to spend more evenings away from you and Alex."

"Yes, I understand. That is your duty," she simply responded.

When spring came, Alexandra was not able to attend school. The bleeding had started again. She was taken for yet another series of tests and it was found that once again her white cell count was increasing. In June Garyk returned home from a trip to Archangel to find that she had been readmitted to the hospital. He entered her room and was crushed by the appearance of this tiny thing, lying in such a big bed, tubes and electronic sensor wires all over her. Katryn stood by the bed, holding her daughter's hand. She was not in uniform, having hastily thrown on an old pair of jeans and a beige blouse, which she hadn't bothered to tuck in. Against the backdrop of medical equipment she, too, looked very small and fragile. "How is she?" He spoke in a hushed tone so as not to disturb Alexandra. Garyk came up beside her and put his arm around her. He leaned down to kiss her on the cheek, but she pulled away.

"She is sleeping now. It was a very long night for her. She kept calling for you. You should have been here."

"Kat, that isn't fair! You know that I just can't abandon my responsibilities. I came home as quickly as I could."

Without turning to look at him, Katryn said, "She is your responsibility too!"

There was no winning this. She was right once again. It was all so enormously unfair. Mercifully, the end did come quickly. He was able to be there for that, at least. He sat by her bed for twenty-four hours. She was not conscious for most of that time. Once, when she had woken, she looked over and asked weakly, "Daddy, is that you?"

"Yes, Alex, Daddy is here and Mommy is too."

"Oh good." That had been her final words to them. She stirred once or twice after that, opening her eyes and emitting faint, heart-wrenching little moans. Their silent vigil was finally broken by the intrusion of the electronic warning. It signaled that her little heart had finally stopped. Katryn allowed him to hold her as the nurses came in to check on her status.

The nurse bent over their daughter, felt for a pulse and then looked over to them. "I'm afraid that she has gone now," she said softly to them. "Can I get you anything, Ma'am?"

"No, thank you. That will be all." Katryn dismissed her.

Garyk could fight back the tears no longer. They streamed down his face as he stared at the lifeless form lying there before him. "Why," he cried out, "why did this terrible thing have to happen to her?" Katryn put her arm around his waist and rested her head on his upper arm. They stood together like that for several minutes, simply staring down at their child, at peace now after such a long ordeal.

After a pause, he felt Katryn straighten next to him. "Come, Garyk, there are now many things that we must attend to." Katryn spent the balance of the day immersed in the details of arranging for Alexandra's funeral. She approached the task in the same way as she would have performed any other special assignment. She prepared lists of people who needed to be called, schedules of things that needed to be done.

Garyk tried to keep up with the pace she set, but his heart wasn't in it. Finally he told her, "I think I'll take Georgi for a walk in the park. It will do us both good to get some fresh air."

28

After the funeral, Garyk found reasons not to come home. He rededicated himself to his job. That fall they were closely monitoring a series of elections being held throughout the various Republics. Khasbulatov needed to know how the public was reacting to the latest economic disasters.

"Major," one of his assistants called over to him one morning, "this Viktor Gadayev, might he be any relation to you?"

"I have a brother named Viktor. Why do you ask?"

"Well, it seems that your brother has just been elected to the Chechen-Ingush National Assembly!"

"You can't be serious," Garyk said with some surprise. He walked over to look at the computer printout the aide was holding. "My brother has never been involved with the Party as far as I am aware."

"Oh no, sir, he was not elected from the Communist slate. He won a seat representing the National Congess. It's one of the new opposition organizations."

Viktor had flown up for the funeral, of course. They had talked a little about what was happening to the country. It had not really been a time for political or philosophical discourse. So Garyk was only generally aware of Viktor's political involvement in the South. He had no idea that he had decided to run in opposition to the Party. As the day wore on, more and more of Garyk's associates learned of the news from the Caucasus Region. Not everyone was delighted with this new wave of political activism that was taking hold in the outer reaches of the country.

When he arrived home that evening, Mr. Moldatin was there. "I was not aware that your brother Viktor had taken an interest in government," was how Garyk was greeted as he walked in the door.

"And good evening to you too, Papa Moldatin," Garyk said rather sarcastically. He stopped to hang up his coat and hat, then turned back to his father-in-law and said, "Now, what was it you asked me about?" Mr. Moldatin was just about to speak, but Garyk continued, "Oh, yes,

Viktor, I remember. He said nothing to me about it when he was up here. Of course, I wasn't in the mood to do much talking then. I thought perhaps the two of you might have had a little chat along those lines." Garyk relished the thought of what kind of discussion that might have been.

"Do you think that it was wise for him to openly oppose the Party like this?"

"Mr. Moldatin, I don't think you realize what's been happening this year. I've been traveling all over the country. I can assure you that in many areas the Communist Party no longer holds the political power that it once did. This is particularly true in the South, where there are so many divergent ethnic groups."

"We've had these ethnic problems for years. It has only been because of a strong central party organization that we have managed to keep things in good order."

"Well," Garyk said, as he poured himself a glass of vodka, "I suppose that depends upon your definition of good order. Would you care for a drink?"

Katryn came into the room and sat beside her father. "Garyk, you mustn't be rude to my father."

"I wasn't being rude, Kat, it's just that he's less involved than he was five or ten years ago. Things have changed dramatically in just the past few months."

"That may be true," she continued, "But father says that we must be very careful. We cannot associate ourselves to closely with Viktor. It may have reprecussions for us here."

"How can I not associate myself with him? He's my brother!"

"Just be careful, young man," Mr. Moldatin said. "I may be getting old, but I have seen far too many purges and retributions in my 61 years. One can never be too cautious! Your actions, even the actions of your brother, could place my daughter and grandson in jeopardy, do I make myself clear."

"Yes, of course you do sir." Garyk did not want to argue with his father-in-law, or his wife, for that matter. He really wasn't sure where he stood in relation to these new developments back home. What Moldatin said was disconcerting, to be sure. He knew enough history to realize that Georgi's future could very much depend upon events taking place some distance to the south.

In the weeks that followed Garyk was forced to walk a political tightrope. The Khasbulatov camp was clearly opposed to Gorbachev. They espoused a return to the hard-line approach to Soviet economics. Gorbachev had aligned himself with the many liberal factions springing up all over the country. On more than one occasion Garyk found himself favoring the liberal ideas over those of his own associates. As to events in his native republic, Khasbulatov was clearly not enamoured with this upstart general who had taken over. Garyk found himself frequently forced to disavow any association with his own brother.

As if he didn't have enough problems, an entirely new family crisis reared up in the spring of 1991. He awoke one Sunday morning to find Katryn and Georgi all dressed and ready to go out. "And where might we be off to this morning?" Garyk intended it to be a casual inquiry, expecting that she was off to visit her mother. He was not prepared for Georgi's answer.

"We're going to church!"

"What do you mean you're going to church?" Gartyk couldn't imagine.

Katryn turned back from the door and said. "It's Easter Sunday! I thought I would take Georgi to church this year."

"You can't be serious about this, Katryn," Garyk said to her.

"Of course I'm serious, why wouldn't I be."

"Because in the fifteen years that I have known you, you have never once gone to church. It was never even an issue."

"That may be true, but it was never an issue because for most of those years it has never been permitted. Now it is!"

Garyk walked over to his son and put his hand on the boy's shoulder. "If you wish to go, that's fine. I can't permit you to take Georgi with you. Katryn, he's my son too, or have you forgotten?"

"No, I haven't forgotten. I just don't see how it would matter to you."

"Not matter! Katryn I am a Moslem. I will not have my son go into an Orthodox Church! Not on Easter Sunday or any other day."

Georgi looked up at his father. "Oh, Daddy, please let me go. Mommy says that there will be pretty flowers and candles. And there will be music and singing." Georgi was clearly excited about the prospect of going to the Easter service and very concerned that his father might not let him go.

"It seems you have done a good job of selling our son on this idea behind my back." There was more than a little sarcasm and bitterness in his remark.

She defended herself. "I don't think I did anything behind your back. Your back just wasn't here, was it? I don't see why you're making such an issue of this, Garyk. It's not as if you were out there doing your morning prayers every day. When was the last time you did? Don't tell me about your Moslem principles now."

Garyk couldn't believe that this was happening. They had spoken only in passing about religion over the years. It was not a topic one discussed in the Soviet Union. But she knew that he was Moslem, even if he had not practiced his faith for some time. The issue went beyond that.

"Why, Katryn? Why now? Are you doing this to hurt me for something? Please let me know what it is that you think I've done. It can't possibly justify your taking my own son away from me?"

"I'm not taking him away from you, I'm just taking him to the church with me."

"Kat, don't you understand. For me, it is the same thing. I cannot let him go!"

"Well, that's too bad, because we're going!" She grabbed Georgi by the hand and pulled him out the door. It slammed behind her. Garyk was left standing alone in the middle of the room. He stared at the door for some time after they were gone. His world was collapsing around him and he had no explanation for it.

29

Politically, things were coming to a head. That summer Boris Yeltsin emerged as a force in the Russian Republic in opposition to both Gorbachev's national reform program and Khasbulatov's conservative alliance. Ruslan Imranovich Khasbulatov called a meeting of his colleagues. Garyk was there as a confidential aide.

"Comrades," Khasbulatov began, "the time for rhetoric may have passed."

"Imranych, surely you aren't advocating a revolution?" one of his close associates responded.

"If it should come to that, yes." Ruslan's face broadened into his characteristic smile. "A peaceful exchange of power, I think. That is what is required."

Garyk stopped sorting papers. From his position in the back of the room, it was not possible to read the faces of those in attendance. He could feel the tension in the air though. He worked all night preparing summary reports for this meeting and knew its general intent. Still it was chilling, even for him, to hear such words being spoken. Granted, this was a closed-door meeting of a small group of people. But the people involved were all deputies in the Russian Supreme Soviet.

One of the deputies asked, "Are you sure that this is the right time, Ruslan?"

"Absolutely!" He shot back the reply. "Gorbachev has prepared this new Union Treaty to replace the one originally drafted to form the Union in 1922. The Republics will all be asked to sign it in two days. In the meantime, he has left the city and is on vacation. I merely suggest we make it an extended holiday. I propose that tomorrow we publicly declare that a state of national emergency exists and place him under house arrest. We will then move forward with our program to revamp the economy before it collapses completely."

The proposal was not met without debate, which continued for some time. Garyk listened to each deputy present his pros and cons as he moved about the room handing out one or another of the charts and schedules he had prepared. Without his knowing, Viktor had been briefed on a very similar proposal only hours before and fifteen hundred kilometers to the south.

On August 19, 1991, their plan was put into action. Unlike the reaction of the Chechens to their new political situation, not all of the Russian people were sure this insurgent group was in keeping with the rising tide of democracy. A reversion to more conservative programs was being proposed. Boris Yeltsin seized the opportunity to spearhead protest rallies in the streets of Moscow. The attempted coup failed, in as much as Gorbachev was permitted to return to Moscow. However, his base of power had been destroyed completely. Within a week he was forced to resign as General Secretary of the Communist Party. Days later, the Party itself ceased to exist.

Garyk had been spending long hours working on various reports for the conservative coalition. Many nights he had opted to catch a few hours sleep at the office, rather than head home. With the immediate crisis over, the forces of Khasbulatov and Yeltsin settled into a period of countervailing power. A normal routine was again possible. Garyk looked forward to arriving home early enough to be with Georgi before it was his bedtime. He had spent little time with his son the past month. When he entered their apartment, he stumbled over several suitcases. They were lined up at the door, along with several boxes.

"Katryn, what is all this?" he called out.

She came into the room from the bedroom carrying a few more boxes. "Well, to what do I owe the pleasure of your company?" she said derisively. She laid the cartons down and exhaled deeply. Her blonde bangs flipped upward from the force of her breath. "Actually, I am glad that you finally decided to come home. It gives me the chance to say good-bye. I think letters can be quite gauche, don't you?"

"What do you mean, say good-bye? Where is Georgi?"

"He's gone already, Garyk. My father took him this afternoon."

"Gone where? Kat, what are you talking about?"

"Did you think that you could play your little games of intrigue and not have it affect your family? We warned you about this months ago, but you were much too involved to listen to reason."

"You're not making any sense, Katryn. The fact of the matter is that the Party doesn't exist anymore. Khasbulatov is still in power. Please tell me what's going on here."

"We're leaving, Garyk. Can't you see that?"

"But why? I still don't understand what is happening here." Garyk was quite perplexed. He realized that he had not been attentive to the family for some time. Still, it was Katryn's coolness to him that had precipitated this. Whatever new crisis was lurking here, he did not understand.

"Garyk, wake up! Russia is in chaos and you have helped to stir the pot. Not only you, but also that damned brother of yours. Have you been too busy to notice? He's set himself up as a revolutionary leader down there?"

"Yes, I've seen the reports about him on the television. What has that got to do with us?"

"Oh, nothing, other than that I have been removed from my position, Garyk. They said that I could no longer be entrusted with classified materials or be left in a position that might jeopardize the security of the state. I've been labeled as a potential subversive!"

"Kat, that's ridiculous!" He was truly dumbfounded.

"Ridiculous or not, Garyk, you and your brother have destroyed my career!" Tears welled up in her eyes. "Everything that I have worked so hard for over the past fifteen years has been wiped out." She sat down on one of the suitcases and began to cry hysterically.

Garyk didn't know what to say or do. He started towards her, wanting to hold her in his arms, kiss the tears away and tell her everything was going to be okay. "Surely we've been through much tougher times than this. Here, let me..."

"DON'T TOUCH ME!" She jumped up from the suitcase and wiped the tears from her eyes. "This is all your doing this time. You caused this to happen and you placed your son in jeopardy. My father says that we must distance ourselves from you, Garyk. It may already be too late."

"Yes, I should have realized that your father had a strong hand in all this." Garyk dropped down into a chair and placed his head in his hands. He spoke softly and slower, hoping to calm her down. "Kathryn, he's still living in the past."

"It wasn't in the past that I lost my position, Garyk!" Her voice was still raised in anger. "And it wasn't in the past that they called me yesterday to take Georgi out of his school and have him reassigned. No, Garyk, I am afraid that you're the one who is not in touch with reality."

She gathered up the suitcases and boxes, arranging them on a carryall she pulled out of the closet. Katryn had completed her final diatribe and had nothing more to say to him. She was out the door. It slammed behind her with such force that several of the pictures on the wall slid off center and a stack of papers on the table blew onto the floor.

Garyk continued to sit in the chair long after she walked out.

Perhaps he should have gone after her; demanded that she stay with him. Would she have changed her mind? Not likely, after all, Georgi was already gone. It was more likely that an even bigger argument would have ensued, right there in the hall. He might even have hit her. No, he could never do that. But what if he had? What effect would that have had on both of their careers?

30

It was early in September, so it had still been light out when he arrived home. Now the room had darkened completely. He welcomed the darkness as it enveloped him. It helped him block out the world and left him free to drift in a limbo of thoughtlessness, devoid of any sensate stimuli. He had lost his daughter. Now his son and his wife were gone. Nothing else mattered.

The phone rang, startling him out of his trance-like state. It took several more rings for him to fully remember where he was. Stumbling in the dark, he knocked over a table lamp in his attempt to reach for the receiver. "Hello, Major Gadayev here."

"Garyk, is that you? Viktor here."

Viktor's voice jolted him back to reality. And reality was very painful. "Viktor, just what the hell are you doing down there?" He pounced on his unsuspecting brother because there was no one else on whom to vent his emotions.

"Well, I guess I could ask the same thing of you," Viktor came back, somewhat surprised at the vehemence of his brother's greeting. "It seems that we've both been involved in some pretty historic events the past few weeks."

"What I've been doing was working within the national government. Viktor, you've become a God-damned revolutionary!"

"Now just a minute, Garyk," Viktor was a bit annoyed with him now, "it seems to me that they weren't exactly rioting in the streets of Moscow in *support* of your Mr. Khasbulatov now, were they? From where I sit it would appear that Boris Yeltsin is the one working *within* the government up there."

"Yeltsin is a pig!"

Viktor chuckled at his remark. "Well, at least we can agree on that."

There was a brief pause then Garyk broke down. Desolate, he blurted out, "Viktor, she's left me!"

"Who's left you, not Katryn?"

"Yes, Katryn, and she's taken Georgi with her."

"My God, Garyk, why? Where did they go?"

"To her father, of course! He's a die-hard communist, I'm sure you realized that. He's convinced that the Party will take revenge on both of them because of you and that damned insurrection in Chechnya."

"Because of me, Garyk, that's absurd!"

"I'm not so sure. Katryn was removed from her position because they felt she represented a security risk. She's been black-listed, Viktor!"

"And what about you and your friends up there, Garyk? My God, they tried to put Gorbachev under arrest. Don't you think that got the Soviet Army brass just a little uptight?"

"Viktor, it's been so crazy here in Moscow. I really don't know where anybody's allegiance lies these days."

"Yes, I know the feeling. What I really don't understand is how you got involved in all of this. I mean, it's quite a leap from being head computer jockey to working for a conservative reactionary group like Khasbulatov and his crowd. Really, Garyk, his policies don't seem to mesh with you at all."

"Well, he is a Chechen, you know. I guess that's how this all got started. I was ranting on one evening about something or other to do with Chechens or Moslems, I can't even remember now. Anyway, some of his staff heard me and we were introduced. I had already lost interest in the military aspects of my job. This just seemed like a good way to make a difference."

"Do you still think so?"

Garyk didn't answer right away. He was giving it some careful consideration. "Yes," he finally said, trying to convince himself in the process, "yes, I think we can. Gorbachev completely ruined the economy. You agree with me on that, I'm sure. Yeltsin is an idiot. He's out for his own glory. Ruslan must balance out his influence or we will never survive this crisis."

"But you have forgotten one thing, my brother. You are not a Russian. Your interests lie in the Caucuses with your family, not up there in Moscow."

"Viktor, do you really think that Chechnya can ever be independent from Russia. Yes, I hear it all the time. All of the republics think that they should break free now. Economically, that will be suicide!"

"You may be right, Garyk, I wish I knew. I think that Dudayev is biding his time for now, but he will not wait too much longer. What do you think Khasbulatov will do if his own republic breaks away?"

"He's a hard-liner, Viktor, but at heart he is also a Chechen. I wouldn't want to find out."

"No, neither would I, But I think we both will in short order."

"Watch your back, Viktor!"

"I'll try. You do the same up there. I hope that things blow over and Katryn sees her way to come back."

"Yes, so do I. You know she's become a completely different person, Viktor. It started when I was wounded in Afghanistan. For a while, things got a little better. Then, when Alex got sick, I think it broke her. I've been living with a stranger for some time now. It's losing Georgi that really hurts."

"I'm sorry, Garyk, I had no idea things had gotten that bad. If there's anything I can do."

"No, I'm afraid what's done is done. At least for the time being."

By the end of that month, Khasbulatov was elected Chairman of the Russian Supreme Soviet. Shortly thereafter, Viktor was elected First Deputy in the Chechen Assembly. One of the first calls he made, after Dudayev announced the secession of the republic, was to Garyk. "Well, it seems that the die has now been cast," Viktor began.

"Viktor, this is insanity!"

"Don't tell me that you still think the Union will survive."

"The Union, no, but to break away from the Russian Republic. Viktor, does this Dudayev think he can succeed all alone?"

"That's what I've called you to ask, Garyk. Where do your people stand? Will Khasbulatov join us now? More important, will he fight us?"

"No, he will not join you, his base of power is in Moscow, not Groznyy. I don't think he's happy with your friend down there, but he can't side with Yeltsin either. I think there may be a standoff. For how long I can't say."

"And you, Garyk, will you come home and join us?"

"No, not now. I'll do what I can from here."

Over the months that followed, they talked from time to time. As he saw him develop as a leader of their people, Garyk grew prouder of his brother. In fact, he envied him. Not for his newfound political fame, but for his happiness. Viktor and Tatyana still had what he and Katryn had lost. Maybe he was right, Garyk thought, maybe I should have gone home when this thing happened. That wouldn't bring back Katryn or Georgi though. If he stayed in Moscow there was always a chance that he could see his son again.

When the Soviet Union ceased to exist, so did the Soviet Army. The newly formed Russian Army wouldn't accept him, since Chechnya had declared its independence, recognized or not. So he was now a civilian aide.

The year 1992 saw a series of political battles between Yeltsin and Khasbulatov to gain control of the new Russian Federation. Ironically, Garyk found an unlikely ally in his father-in-law. Moldatin was still a member of the Congress of Peoples Deputies. That body met twice a year to elect the Supreme Soviet, the Prime Minister and other officials of the national government. They would determine whether the forces of Yeltsin or Khasbulatov would hold sway. The latter's policies were more in keeping with Moldatin's conservative views than Yeltsin's liberal, free-market approach. Garyk called the old gentlemen to insure that they had his vote on a critical issue limiting powers granted to Yeltsin. Katryn answered the phone. "Kat, it's good to hear your voice. How are you and Georgi?"

"We are managing, no thanks to you," came her terse reply.

"Why must you fight me like this?"

"Garyk, they still won't clear me to do anything more than routine administrative duties. My rank has been permanently frozen. All because of your brother, the great Chechen revolutionary."

"You know that I have nothing to do about that, Kat. Your father is actually on my side right now."

"No, I think he is just against Yeltsin, he's still not for you."

Well, I've called to speak with him, nonetheless. After we're through, can I speak with Georgi?"

"No," she said curtly, "he's out with my mother."

Moldatin confirmed what his daughter had said. He didn't support Khasbulatov, he opposed Yeltsin. A majority of the Congress did also. For that reason Yeltsin began to put together a new constitution which would eliminate the Congress and give him control of the government.

Garyk still lived in the same apartment eighteen months after Katryn walked out. He hated being there alone, but just hadn't gotten around to doing anything about it. He found a few things in the freezer and was in the process of making himself a stew when someone knocked on the door. Opening the door, he was confronted by a man in his early seventies. Time had not been kind to him, especially these past thirteen years. Garyk barely recognized his guest. "Lemchenko, how long has it been?"

"Too long, my friend, much too long!" He offered Garyk his hand. It was large in relation to his height and the grip was as forceful as ever.

Garyk motioned for him to come in. "Don't tell me that you're still spying on me, old man."

"The spy business has ended, haven't you heard," Lemchenko said with a wry grin. The demise of the KGB had been a topic widely publicized on the national television. "I am, you might say, retired. Still, I try to keep track of my old acquaintances on occasion, just for old times sake."

"So, is that what brings you here, are you *keeping track* of me still?"

"When I can, yes. Now, will you offer an old man a seat and, perhaps, some vodka!"

"Of course, forgive me for being so impolite. You just surprised me, that's all, but you were always good at that." He led the man to the dining table and brought over a bottle and two glasses. Lemchenko's hair had turned fully gray over the past few years. It was a dullish gray, in keeping with the man's character.

"You know, I was always impressed with you, Garyk Ivramovich." Lemchenko took a good swig of the vodka that Garyk had provided. "You possessed so much promise. That is why I have come to warn you now."

"Warn me about what?" Garyk poured a drink for himself and noticed that his guest was already in need of a refill.

"Forgive this old man his little attempt at political assessment. It has been my responsibility to make certain evaluations, as you are aware. I have been doing that since the days of Nikita Khrushchev. I think I have been generally objective in this, do you understand, not biased by whatever the current political climate might have been." He took another long sip on his vodka. "Consequently, I have been quite successful at anticipating the major changes that have taken place over the years. That's why I believe that you are in a great deal of danger, my friend."

Garyk listened to his guest, trying to make some sense out of what was being said. This was only the third time in his life that he had been with this man. Garyk asked him, "Why, after what, thirteen years, are you suddenly showing up and professing such concern for me?"

"Yes, it has been that long since we last talked face to face. You were never that far from my attention, however. As I have told you before, it was my job to keep track of you. Believe me, my friend, I too grieved at the death of young Alexandra. Such a painful struggle that was. It wasn't appropriate for me to make an appearance at her funeral but, let me assure you, I was there." Lemchenko raised his glass to salute the young child and finished its contents. "I have also grieved with you these past few months at the break-up of your family. The two of you were so right for each other. What a pity."

Garyk interrupted, "I still don't understand why you're here now."

"Forgive me," the old man went on. "You have become a favorite subject of mine, I guess you might say. I am very concerned and, since the government no longer employs me, I feel that I need no longer stay in the shadows. No, I must warn you that the tide is definitely changing. Your allies in government will soon be disposed of, one way or the other. Do you understand this?"

"You mean Yeltsin is going to assassinate Khasbulatov?"

"No, I don't think it will come to that. However, he has strengthened his position and will continue to do so, of that I am certain. You are on the losing side, Garyk, and I am afraid that there may be repercussions."

"What sort of repercussions?"

"I can't be certain. Nothing is certain anymore."

"Well, I'm sure you have good reason to believe all this. I still think that we can succeed in controlling Yeltsin's crew. In any event, what else could I do now? Where would I go?"

"Out of the spotlight, my friend. It is never good to maintain a high profile in times like this. If I were you, I would return to my computers and in the private sector, not the government!"

"Yes, you may be right. I'll have to give that some thought."

31

Lemchenko's visit was disturbing to say the least. Garyk had some serious thinking to do. He needed someone to talk to. He realized again how alone he really was. He thought about calling Katryn, even now. No, that would mean having to admit that her father was right. He called down to his brother, but Viktor was out. The only other close friend he had ever had was Alex.

He sat at the kitchen table, playing with food that had long since become cold. "Just exactly what *am* I doing?" he asked himself. Lemchenko was right. Viktor had also questioned why he had gotten away from the computers that he loved. He realized that for some time he was merely *doing a job*. He had lost the enthusiasm that first led him to Khasbulatov. It was time to get out, go back down to Groznyy, maybe even teach at the State University. Yes, that would be the perfect solution. He resolved to start making plans the next morning.

He actually got to his desk early the next day. He was enthused again! This time it was over plans he was making to start his new life. In the back of his mind he hoped that when he had re-established himself, Katryn and Georgi could be persuaded to come down and join him. His phone rang and one of the other staffers was on the line.

"Gadayev, Niyazov here. We need you to bring Chairman Khasbulatov's briefcase over to the White House. He's going to demand to speak to the Assembly this afternoon and has to have certain documents that are in there right away."

See, I have become the errand boy around here, Garyk thought as he hung up the phone. I guess my planning can wait one more day.

Yeltsin had begun the process of eliminating his opposition by convening a special constituent assembly to draft a new constitution. Khasbulatov had publicly declared this action to be unconstitutional. However, he still needed to be present there to try to influence the delegates. For several days he had been seeking permission to address the assembly and had been routinely denied access by Yeltsin's forces. Today, he would demand to speak.

The White House, or *Byely Dom,* was what the parliament building was called. It had been built in 1980, a multi-storied white marble structure with a red granite base. It had become Yeltsin's base of operations in recent years. Garyk arrived just after ten. They had established a temporary office to coordinate the activities of their constituent group of delegates. He turned over his package to Khasbulatov personally. "Gadayev, I'm glad you're here. I think that this will be our day, yes I do. We can use your assistance to put together a press release. Copies of my speech text should also be made available to hand out once I have finished."

Khasbulatov was again denied permission to speak to the constituent assembly. They had prepared for this contingency, of course. All fifty members of the assembly who opposed Yeltsin walked out of the hall in a show of protest. The strike force staff went with them. They proceeded to the administrative wing of the building. Another fifty or more deputies and supporters had joined the group. There Ruslan Khasbulatov summoned the international press corps and announced, "Boris Yeltsin has acted in opposition to the duly elected Supreme Soviet of the Russian Federation. There are one hundred deputies here with me today. We are formally calling for Mr. Yeltsin to resign immediately. Until he does, we will continue to occupy the offices of the government.

Unbeknownst to Garyk, they had prepared for this moment by stockpiling a cache of small arms and ammunition in the building. Suddenly, he found himself in the middle of an armed takeover. "Hey Gadayev," someone called to him. "You were in the army. Here, take this and bring a group of six men down that hall and secure the stairways." The speaker threw something at him and Garyk realized that he was now holding an AK- 47 in his hands.

For the next several days, Russian television carried pictures of the White House under occupation. The two political factions seemed to be stalemated. Seeking to press the issue, forces loyal to Khasbulatov raided the mayor's office, located across the square from the White House. They also attempted to seize control of the television studios. Yeltsin branded his opponents as rebels of the state. He launched a full-scale attack to retake the parliament building and mayor's office complex. Garyk realized that this would be the ultimate showdown between the forces competing for control of the new Russian government. He was certain that Lemchenko's predictions were about to come true. He was trapped; working for a revolution that had failed to generate the popular support Khasbulatov had hoped would bring down Yeltsin. There was a sick feeling deep in his stomach. So much for starting a new life, he thought!

He'd lost track of the days. At times he felt that he'd lost track of reality. This whole situation was so illusory. There was shouting coming from the other end of the hallway. "What did you say, I couldn't hear you?" he shouted back.

"I said there are tanks coming up the Novy Arbat toward the building!"

"What do you mean, tanks?"

"Just what I said, Gadayev," the voice came back. "Look, it's on the television now. Shit, that son of a bitch is bringing in tanks against us!"

There was a television in the office next to Garyk's position. He went in and turned it on, then walked over to the windows. "This must be a nightmare," he muttered to himself. Yes, there were tanks rolling down the street, past the rows of new high rise buildings that had been erected in recent years. They were called "open-book" structures because of the way the two wings of each building angled out from the center. Images of the three tanks traversing the Novy Arbat were reflected in row after row of windows. The thoroughfare had actually been widened in the early sixties to accommodate the massive movement of troops and military equipment into Red Square for the May Day procession. This time, the tanks were not ceremonial. They were armed for combat and heading right toward him.

"Christ Almighty, will they really fire on their own parliament building?" He heard someone ask and wondered himself if they would. All of Russia, no, the whole world was watching this on television. At the command center, Khasbulatov was on the phone, refusing to yield their position. "General, let me remind you that I am the Chairmen of the Supreme Soviet. Are you prepared to open fire on your own government?"

Garyk stood to one side of the window, keeping an eye on the images being displayed on the TV screen and also watching the actual events unfolding in the square below. Suddenly, the barrels of three tanks flashed simultaneously. Yellow flames and black smoke spewed forth. From where he watched, there was no sound, at least not yet. "Shit!" he yelled out and dove for cover behind a desk. The sounds of the discharges came almost at the same time as the roar of the explosions as three shells found their marks against the side of the White House. It instantly brought back to his mind similar explosions many years before in Afghanistan. He couldn't believe it was all happening again!

One of the shells impacted directly below his position. The building shook violently. Books, pictures, glass, and paper all began flying around the room. It felt like he was in an elevator. The floor was dropping! The explosion had caused one floor to collapse down into the other. Sounds of rending metal, crashing furniture and breaking glass all mixed together.

He was engulfed in darkness. Here and there some streaks of daylight worked their way through the rubble. The air was thick with smoke and dust from the falling debris. He had survived again, somehow, but he was pinned under piles of building materials and furniture. His leg ached with sharp, piercing pain. Involuntarily, he screamed. "HELP, SOMEBODY PLEASE HELP ME," he called out, wondering if anyone could hear him. Faint sounds of gunfire filtered through to him. It all became muffled and at some point he passed out.

32

Garyk was awake, fully aware of his surroundings for the first time in several days. He knew that he was in a hospital bed and tried to remember why. The walls were tiled in white. About half way up the tiles gave way to gray paint. There were no windows. The only light came from garish overhead fluorescents. It was a ward of some kind, with six beds on each side of a center row. Eleven, including his own, appeared to be occupied. For a moment he thought he was back in Afghanistan. Then visions of the Novy Arbat and the White House filtered back into his mind. He remembered the explosion and had vague recollections about the events that followed.

Soldiers had finally come to extract him from the rubble. How many hours had he been trapped there? He had no idea. He remembered that they had not been gentle, pulling and tugging at his body to free him from the debris. He recalled the anguish and the pain, the excruciating pain. He looked down at his left leg. It was gone! The folds of the sheets ended just at his knee. He tried to move and pain shot through him, causing him to cry out. A male nurse appeared at his side. He was older than Garyk, possibly 50-55 and heavy set. He was a human slug, completely bald, his head as round as a volleyball with two large ears protruding on either side. "Ah, Mr. Gadayev. You have finally come back to us."

"How long have I been here?"

"Three days here," the nurse replied, "another day and a half up at the emergency center, I believe."

"Where am I exactly?"

"At the infirmary of the Moscow Correctional Facility. I'm sorry to say that in addition to all of your medical problems, Mr. Gadayev, you have also been placed under arrest as a revolutionary and charged with inciting mass disorder."

This must be some bizarre joke. He would have laughed if he weren't in so much pain. The pain served as an unpleasant reminder. He asked, "What happened to my leg?"

With little emotion and in a grating and irritating voice, the slug recounted what he knew of the patient's recent history. "I understand that a large section of the wall fell in on top of you. A steel girder crushed your left fibula. The bone was shattered into so many pieces it couldn't be repaired. The leg had been deprived of blood for a long, long time, I'm afraid. I've been told that you were pinned under the rubble for nearly a day. They had to wait for the fighting to end, you know, before any rescue efforts could begin."

"I understand," Garyk said in a barely audible voice. How ironic it was. All of the plans he was going to make for his *new life*. Well, he had a new life now. He was a paraplegic and a political prisoner!

Time passed slowly over the next few weeks. Garyk had sustained several other injuries, all less severe than the one to his leg, but all requiring time to heal. As a prisoner, he was not allowed any visitors. Even if he were, he wondered if Katryn would have come. His status also limited the amount of care and rehabilitary services that the state deemed that it was obliged to provide. In fact, he was being provided with no rehabilitation what so ever.

He was in a ward with eleven other prisoners. Six were also casualties of the October Incident. The others were convicted criminals. "Actually," he thought to himself wryly, "I'm a criminal now too!" The others were robbers and, he supposed, murderers. No one said anything about such things. They were all chained to their beds, as if he were going anywhere. The nurses were all male, better suited to guard duty than to being care providers. The overhead lights remained on constantly.

Word filtered in from the attendants about the fate of the other insurrectionists. One of the nurses let him see a newspaper. The photo of the White House, a gaping hole in its side and its white marble blackened by fire and smoke, had become a national symbol. Ruslan Khasbulatov, Chairman of the Supreme Soviet, and Vice President Alexander Rutskoy were both imprisoned. Many of their followers were dead. Yeltsin was now in complete control, although some dissension still existed. In a touch of irony, the area on the Novy Arbat where the White House and Mayor's office complex stood was referred to as "Free Russia Square."

Garyk spent nearly three months in the infirmary. Twice each day they came to change the dressings on his leg. In the beginning the pain had been excruciating. He was embarrassed by his own screams. They limited the amount of pain-killing drugs he could receive. Large squares of skin were removed from his right thigh to graft over the open wound left by the amputation. Consequently, he had to spend most of the time lying on his stomach.

At the start of 1994 he was deemed capable of moving into the prison population and assigned to a cell shared with two others. Yuri Furtseva was a big bear of a man. A pipefitter by trade, he had caught his wife *inflagrante delicto* with the local fishmonger. Unfortunately for them, he was in possession of a large monkey wrench at the time and had wielded it rather effectively. He was sullen most of the time but likable enough and willing to assist his one-legged cellmate when asked.

Igor Minsky was a black marketeer, convicted of hoarding food products during the national emergency. He reminded Garyk of a weasel, short and extremely thin, with a sharp angular nose that jutted out from a gaunt face. Despite his appearance, he was an amiable sort and went out of his way to help Garyk. When they went to the dining hall he held a tray while Garyk navigated on his crutches. If half of the stories Igor regaled them with were true, then he had led a truly amazing life.

On the outside, Yeltsin's newly restructured Duma met for the first time. Over his objections, a motion to grant amnesty to Khasbulatov and his associates was debated in February. By the end of the month Garyk was called down to the Prison Administrator's office. It was a testament to Russian bureaucracy. A modest steel desk with a leatherette swivel chair stood in front of two large windows that overlooked the prison yard. Photographs taken of the Administrator with various state functionaries filled one wall. He was invited to take a seat on one of the two metal folding chairs in front of the desk. Garyk realized that for the first time in months he was seated in an unlocked office with no prison guards in evidence.

"We have good news Mr. Gadayev!"

Garyk asked rather skeptically "And what might that be?"

"The State Duma has granted you unconditional amnesty. You are now a free man!"

"I guess I should be delighted, but right now I actually have no place to go. I wonder if I still have my apartment?"

"As far as I know, Mr. Gadayev, nothing was confiscated. Of course, the authorities have been known to make very thorough searches of private residences in cases such as yours. I cannot promise that you will find everything to be exactly the way you left it, if you know what I mean."

Garyk knew that the Administrator was trying to be helpful. The thought of what he might find upon returning to his apartment sent a chill down his spine. "Yes, I can imagine exactly what you mean. I suppose that I'll just pack what I can and head south. That's what I was about to do just before all hell broke loose."

"That may be a good idea." The Administrator was being very sincere and it struck Garyk as odd, considering how he had been treated hours before. He continued, "However, I would urge you to consider some further medical treatment before you leave Moscow."

"What kind of treatment are you talking about? I think that I've healed as much as I ever will by now."

"Healed yes, but they have done nothing towards rehabilitation. I must apologize for that, but such treatment is not permitted to prison inmates. I understand that you are a veteran, is that not correct. An officer, if I'm not mistaken.

"Yes, actually, I was a major in the Soviet Army," Garyk said this with a half-hearted chuckle. He had survived Afghanistan only to be blown up by the very same forces with which he had served.

"See, there you have it, my friend! As a former officer you can receive the best rehabilitation services that the state can provide. They will have you walking about on a new prosthetic leg in no time at all."

"You mean I'd have to give up these?" Garyk held up his two crutches in mock alarm. "Well, that certainly does give me something to think about. I'd sort of resigned myself to the fact that I would always be like this."

"Mr. Gadayev, Garyk, let me tell you that I am not proud to have had to keep you here these past months. That is my job, just as I know that your job put you into this place. Believe me when I say that many people supported you in that protest. The Duma has acted to make things right. I can only hope that things go well for you."

They shook hands and Garyk was led, not escorted, out to receive what few belongings had survived his ordeal. His wallet, identification papers and keys, along with a few coins that had been in his pockets when he arrived at the emergency room. He was also issued some casual clothing to wear in place of the prison garb he had on. After signing a dozen or more forms and releases, he walked outside. Garyk looked up and beheld the sky for the first time in nearly six months. He closed his eyes and took in three deep long breaths of cold fresh air.

33

Garyk had barely enough money to make it back to his apartment by means of public transportation. The trip took several hours and required that he transfer twice to different buses. With snow and ice everywhere he found it a more arduous trek than he'd anticipated. It was dark by the time he reached his apartment and he had a hard time fumbling with the key, while balancing himself on one leg. His hands were numb from having to remain exposed to the frigid air in order to grip the crutches. He hobbled inside and felt for the light switch. Nothing happened. Moving cautiously across the room, he found another switch for the kitchen. Again, no lights.

"Of course, they've cut off the power, stupid!" He said this out loud, as if he had to explain it to himself. There was just enough city light entering through the windows to allow him to make out the basic shapes within the room. He pulled all of the drapes open, letting in as much of the street light as he could. The room had been disrupted. He could tell that even in this light. He could also tell that someone had attempted to at least pick things up off the floor. Books and other papers were piled up on the table and a broken lamp, its shade all askew, was resting on the small table by the couch. Had Katryn been here, he wondered?

He found the phone and was glad to hear the dial tone. "Great, but who can I call?" He talked aloud to offset the loneliness he was feeling in this dark room. He thought a moment and then he dialed her number. Her mother answered on the fourth ring just as he was about to hang up. "Oh, hello Mrs. Moldatin, it's Garyk. I wonder if I might speak to Kat?"

"My God, Garyk!" Clearly Mrs. Moldatin was surprised to hear his voice. "Where are you? We heard such terrible things."

"Hello, Garyk, is it really you?" Katryn heard her mother say his name and pulled the phone out of her hands.

"Hello, Kat. Yes, it's me."

"Where are you?"

"I'm back in my apartment. They just let me go today. I've been in the correctional facility, did you know that?"

"Yes, we heard that. So did everyone in Russia. Garyk, my God, what were you thinking?"

"Actually, I was thinking it was time to pack it in. I was just in the wrong place at the wrong time, but that's another story."

"Are you all right? We heard that you were nearly killed."

"You know me, Kat, it seems that I'm quite a survivor. I was wondering though, if I might be able to spend the night there. They've shut off the power here and I've got no where else to go."

"I don't know, Garyk. Perhaps just for tonight. I don't want to have Georgi think that you're going to be coming back into his life."

"Kat. For God sake, I am his father!"

"See, you're starting already."

"Look, I'm not starting anything, okay. I just need a decent place to sleep for the first time in six months, that's all. There's no food, heat or light here, or else I wouldn't ask."

"You're right," she said, "I'm sorry. Can you come over now?"

"Well, that's another thing. I don't have any money. Maybe I can find some lying around here tomorrow. God knows what happened to my car."

"Actually, I have it here. We were allowed to pick it up from your office, once things settled down a bit. God, Garyk, you have no idea what it was like."

"I'm sure it was unbearable," he said rather sarcastically.

"I need to get dressed, so it will take me maybe an hour to get over there. Is that okay?"

"Hey, what else can I do?"

Garyk spent the time making his way through the apartment. He nearly vomited when he opened the refrigerator door. Nobody had cleaned it out, so without power, things had gotten out of hand in there. It was hard to be sure in the dark, but he was fairly certain that many of his personal papers had been taken away. His computer was gone. They probably wanted to see what political information he had stored inside. Meeting schedules and itineraries mostly. They must have been disappointed. It amused him to think that somebody had to spend two or three days trying to break his personal access codes, only to find out they had merely pulled up a calendar of family birthdays.

At long last there was a knock on his door. He opened it and found her silhouetted by the bright lights from the hallway. Bundled in a heavy winter jacket she looked like a child. Her hair was tucked under a woolen cap that she had pulled down nearly to her eyebrows. "Well, I'm here, are you ready to go?" She tried to remain distant and detached, yet his reaction to seeing her was the same as it had been so many years before in the Moscow train terminal. She smelled like jasmine and could still take his breath away.

"Yes, just let me get my wings." He reached for the second crutch that had been propped against the wall. Probably because he was standing in darkness, she hadn't really noticed him when he opened the door. As he placed both of the crutches under his arms and swung himself out into the hall light she saw his stump of a leg beneath the unbuttoned great coat. "Oh my God, Garyk, what happened to your leg? I had no idea!"

"What is it that the Americans say? Oh, yes, I gave at the office!"

"Really, Garyk, they never told us about this at all. I'm so sorry."

"Yeah, you and me both," he said, swinging his way quickly down the hall passage just to prove to her that he could.

It took a bit to get him into the front seat since he was so much taller than she was. Once he was in Katryn fumbled to get the crutches into the back seat. They drove for a while in silence. Then she turned to him and said, "You know, we did try to see you at the hospital. It took some time before they had a list of the casualties available. Nobody really knew who had been inside the building in the first place. By the time I was notified and was able to get to the hospital, they told me that you had already been transferred. At first, nobody could tell me where. Finally, we learned that you were being held at the prison. I went there twice. The first time they told me you were too critical to receive visitors. The next time I was told that you were being confined without visitation and I shouldn't bother coming back."

"I'm glad you told me that. I've felt so abandoned these past months, Kat, there's no way you can imagine what it was like. Knowing that you tried makes me feel better right now."

"Garyk, what will you do now?"

"I have no idea. You know what's really funny. I had just decided to quit that damned position and head back to Groznyy. Maybe teach down there at the university. Viktor's been after me for a long time to do that. I was hoping that if I did that, you and Georgi might come down there too." He looked over, hoping to see her reaction to this last remark. It had been almost a plea.

She said nothing for a really long time. Too long, he thought. "Oh Garyk, I wish I could tell you that something like that might happen. It's not going to. I don't know why. Something inside of me has changed. I'm not comfortable being with you anymore. I can't explain why or how that is. It just is. I'm sorry."

"Yeah, you and me both," he said with a sigh.

When they arrived at the Moldatin house, no one else was there. "Where's Georgi?" he asked.

"I thought it best that he not see you, Garyk. My parents have taken him to our cottage by the lake."

"Katryn, why are you doing this? Did I ever once do anything to deserve this?"

"Please, let's not start this again. I told you how I feel. I once blamed you for leaving me alone when I was pregnant with Alexandra. That was wrong but that's just how I felt. You almost died and I hated you for it. But damn it, don't you see, you did it again. This time it *was* your fault. You were in that building of your own volition and for the second time I had to live with the thought that you were dead. You put Georgi through that twice. Damn you anyway!"

She started to cry. Her whole body shook violently. He tried to hold her, but the stupid crutches got in the way so he just let them fall. He propped himself up as best he could, his back against the door for support and folded his arms around her. "Damn you, Garyk, damn you," she whimpered softly between heavy sobs. "I still love you, but I can't live like this any more." She looked up into his deep dark eyes. God, she loved those eyes. He bent down, closer to her then he had been in more than two years, and she was kissing his lips, probing deeply with her tongue. She pulled him towards her and he lost his balance. Hopping on his one leg to try to stay up right, he finally fell forward. They both landed on the floor and she rolled over on top of him. Her knee bumped against the stump of his leg. "Ouch!" he cried out.

"Did that hurt?"

"Just a little sensitive still."

"Good!" she said and proceeded to undress him, "I hope this really hurts!"

They made love right there on the floor. It was deeply animalistic lovemaking. They each had pent-up needs that had to be satisfied. She stayed on top the whole time, just as she had back in the boathouse in Novgorod. When they had both reached their climaxes, she collapsed down onto his chest and rolled over on the floor next to him. Still breathing heavily, she said, "This doesn't change anything."

"Yeah, I figured as much."

She stood up and grabbed up her clothes, then hurried out of the room to get dressed. He struggled a bit getting redressed where he sat and was finally able to pull himself up with the aid of a chair. When she came back it was as if nothing had happened between them. "Can I get you anything?"

"As a matter of fact," he said, "I'd love something to eat. I'm starved." They both laughed. It was the Katryn he remembered from so long ago. Why couldn't it just go on like this?

They had stewed beef and potatoes with brown gravy. It was the best thing he'd eaten in months, going back before the incident even. Over dinner, they talked about his plans to go to Groznyy. She asked, "Will you go right away?"

"I was told to check out the possibility of getting a new one of these." Garyk tapped on his good leg. I hear they're doing wonderful things with plastic these days!" He was laughing and that made her feel better. "Tell me," he then asked her. "When did you go to our apartment?"

"Tonight's the first time I've been there in over a year. Why do you think I was there?"

"You probably couldn't tell much in the dark, but the place had been trashed pretty good by the police or the KGB or whoever does that kind of thing these days. Anyhow, I think somebody came in after that and tried to pick things up. The police wouldn't have done that."

Katryn thought for a moment and then remembered. "Oh, I know, it must have been Viktor."

"Viktor?"

"Yes, he came up here about two months ago. Jesus, you'd think that he'd have enough pull to get in to see you. But then I guess he's not high up on Yeltsin's list of chums these days either. Anyway, he tried for several days and they refused to let him in to see you. Then he heard that they were going to evict you from that apartment because the rent payments had stopped. Viktor was sure that you would be released soon, so he paid them six months in advance. See, I guess you can stay there for a while."

"Those sons of bitches, I can't believe that they wouldn't let either of you in." Garyk banged his fist down on the table so hard that the glass of vodka she had poured for him nearly toppled over.

He spent the night sleeping in Georgi's bed. It felt strange knowing that this would be the closest he might ever get to his son again. The next morning she drove him back to the apartment. In the daylight it was quite a mess. He was glad he hadn't been able to see all this the day before. Viktor had picked up quite a bit, but many of the picture frames had broken glass and several of the cushions on the sofa and chairs had been slashed. "What did they think I was hiding here?" he asked her. No answer was expected.

A picture frame lay face down on the bookshelf. He turned it over and saw that it was a family photograph taken of the four of them before Alex got sick. The glass had broken and ripped through the picture. "God, Katryn, even my memories are being taken away."

He forgot to warn her about the refrigerator. "Oh my God, Garyk, open the windows!" she had yelled out to him, as soon as she opened the door. She did what she could to help clean up some of the worst of it, then said, "I'm sorry, but I've got to leave you now. Will you be all right here alone?"

"Yes, I guess I can get by, at least for now. Maybe you could drop by with some food later, after I kill the monster that's in there," he said pointing to the refrigerator.

"I'll see if my mother can do that. Oh, I forgot to tell you. I have a new job! I'm working for IKI-RAN, the Space Research Institute over at the Russian Academy of Science. We're setting up a whole network to allow all of the government agencies access to the Internet. Can you believe that? Russia is actually on-line!"

34

Garyk spent the next few days trying to get his life back in order. He sorted through piles of personal belongs with an eye towards eliminating as much as possible for a trip back to Groznyy. He did have some cash hidden away where even the search crew had missed it and his bank account had not been confiscated. It wasn't much, but he had become accustomed to modest living the past few months.

Mrs. Moldatin came by later that first afternoon with some basic supplies. She was cordial, but not entirely warm with him. "It is the best that I can do," she apologized. "There is not much available in the market right now and our resources have been drained considerably." Garyk suddenly realized that Mr. Moldatin's income had most likely been cut off with the collapse of the Communist Party. They would only have a modest state pension to live on, plus whatever Katryn was now making over at IKI-RAN.

He managed to get the lights turned on, but that had taken several days of bureaucratic hell. It was actually a blessing those first few days. At the prison the lights were always on and the guards walked the halls and woke the inmates for head counts every two or three hours. He slept for fourteen hours straight the first night. Getting heat back was an even greater accomplishment!

Garyk also made several calls concerning rehabilitation services. A doctor explained that the full process, to include a prosthetic device, would probably take at least six months from that point. He was scheduled for an initial evaluation in two weeks. Then he called down to Groznyy. "Hello, Viktor, is that you. It's Garyk!"

"Garyk, my God, I was beginning to think you were dead!"

"I guess I nearly was. In some respects, I think I am." Garyk went on to explain all that had happen to him, his recent release and his homecoming, of sorts, with Katryn.

"Well, my twin, will you be coming home to us at last?"

"Yes, Viktor, I think that's what I'm going to do."

"That's wonderful news, Garyk! Mama will be so pleased." Turning way from the phone, Viktor called out, "Tatyana, Garyk is finally coming home!"

"Viktor, there are some minor details that need to be taken care of first. It seems that I misplaced a leg somewhere along the line. I need to get that replaced before I can come down."

Viktor sounded quite disturbed. "Garyk, they did nothing for you while you were in prison?"

"Well, they cut it off and stopped the bleeding. Does that count?" Garyk's sarcasm did nothing to calm Viktor's growing rage.

"Damn them all, Garyk! Didn't I warn you not to get involved with these Russian bastards?"

"Yes, but what's done is done for now. I've been told that it may take six months before I'm really ready to travel. In the mean time, I've picked up a few odd jobs debugging some computer software. It's a whole new world and I need to get back in action or I'll be completely out of touch with the technology. Can you see if there may be a position available at the University this fall? Does the First Deputy have any pull down there?"

Viktor laughed, "Yes, I'm sure I can arrange for that. Do you want me to come up?"

"No, at least not right away. By the way, Katryn told me you were up here a while back. Thanks. I appreciate what you did."

"It was nothing, Garyk. I wish I could have done more. Let me know how things progress."

And so Garyk stayed in Moscow during the summer of '94. He met with the doctor, who expressed alarm that so little had been done to properly treat his wound. Still she was enthusiastic about the prognosis for getting him set up with a new prosthetic leg within the time frame originally established. The fittings began and he was soon learning to walk once again.

During this time he kept a watchful eye on events back home in Groznyy. Yeltsin continued to press Dudayev to sign the 1992 Russian Federation Treaty. Of all the former Russian republics and autonomous republics, only Tatarsan and Chechnya had still not come on board. Both constituted a significant portion of the country's oil reserves. Yeltsin, therefore, was under both economic and political pressure to bring closure to this situation. On the other side, Dudayev played to the Chechen's religious heritage. The evening news ran footage of the break-away republic's national hero, dressed in his camouflage field uniform and garrison cap, performing *zikr*, or ritual prayers.

A familiar face reappeared during that summer. Ruslan Imranovich

Khasbulatov was now in Chechnya, seeking to mediate a political settlement. He presented himself as the voice of reason. The friendly college professor turned statesman, in contrast to the militaristic Dudayev. Garyk wanted to trust his former associate but found he could not. This had become a *jihad* and no political resolution seemed likely.

He and Viktor kept in touch more frequently. He was Garyk's only close ally, even if they were fifteen hundred kilometers apart. They called each other at least once a week. Viktor did his best to get Garyk onto the Chechen State University faculty for the fall semester. The first opening, however, would not be until after Winter Recess. "That's okay," Garyk had told him. "I just started a new project that will probably run until the end of the year. I'm learning that capitalism can be very lucrative if you have the talent to develop computer software."

Moscow was getting cold and dark again. God, he really hated this place in the winter. He couldn't imagine why he lived here so long. Garyk wound down his free lance assignment and was looking forward to getting back down to Groznyy at last. He stayed up late Saturday night packing for the trip. Several boxes had already been shipped down to the farm, where he planned to stay for at least the first few months. Everything else essential was crammed into a Land Rover that he'd acquired for the trip. He let Katryn keep his old car.

He was going to drive down alone. With only the long three-day trip ahead of him, he slept in on Sunday. No need to get an early start, he'd be in the car long enough as it was. He finished some leftovers in the refrigerator and cleaned out the remaining contents. No sense making someone else go through that again, he thought. Ready to leave, he dialed Viktor's home number to let him know he was actually on the way. The line was busy. He tried again, with a similar response. He realized that this was not the normal line in use signal, but a general circuit busy tone, a faster louder pulse. "That's funny for a Sunday afternoon," he said to himself. He gave it one last try.

An electronic recording came on the line. A voice without expression advised:

"I'M SORRY, ALL SERVICE TO THE AREA YOU ARE CALLING HAS BEEN TEMPORARILY SUSPENDED DUE TO A STATE OF NATIONAL EMERGENCY."

This was immediately followed by the familiar busy signal. Garyk just stood there looking at the receiver. He felt strangely chilled and his stomach churned. Something was dreadfully wrong. The TV was already wedged into the back seat of the car. He looked around and found a small radio he planned to leave behind. He turned it on and fumbled to find the news information channel.

"...REPORT MINIMAL CASUALTIES AT THIS TIME. THE DEFENSE MINISTRY REPORTS THAT THREE ARMORED INFANTRY DIVISIONS ARE ADVANCING TOWARDS GROZNYY, THE CAPITAL OF CHECHNYA, AND ARE EXPECT-ED TO HAVE THE CITY IN THEIR CONTROL BY NIGHTFALL. PRESIDENT BORIS YELTSIN HAS ISSUED A STATEMENT REGRETTING THAT THE USE OF FORCE HAS BEEN MADE NECESSARY BY THE RECALCITRANCE OF DZHOKHAR DUDAYEV, THE SELF-PROCLAIMED LEADER OF THE INSUR-RECTIONISTS, TO AGREE TO THE TERMS OF THE RUSSIAN FEDERATION TREATY. WE REPEAT, AT 5 A.M. THIS MORN-ING, ACTING ON THE ORDERS OF PRESIDENT YELTSIN, FORCES OF THE RUSSIAN FEDERATION ARMY BEGAN AN ASSAULT ON THE BREAKAWAY REPUBLIC OF CHECHNYA. SOME LOCAL RESISTANCE HAS BEEN ENCOUNTERED."

"May the Almighty be with you, Viktor," Garyk whispered to the radio, as if it could carry back the prayer for him. Once again his well-intentioned plans had been postponed by national events.

He listened to the reports coming in over the radio for the rest of the afternoon. Radio Moscow was keeping the news as upbeat and pro-Russian forces as possible, but he realized that things were not going as easily for the Russian troops as the initial reports led one to believe. If they were encountering only sporadic small arms fire from local guerrilla bands, why weren't they advancing faster? By late after-noon, public sentiment was building against the military action. Even the Deputy Defense Minister had made a public statement denouncing the order to attack.

It grew dark again and he realized that he had not eaten anything substantial all day. There was nothing left in the apartment, so he went out to a little café down the street from his apartment building. There was a television mounted in the dining room and it was tuned in to the events in Chechnya. At first the pictures were reminiscent of those shown some ten years before, when Soviet troops were fighting in Afghanistan. Except this time he was looking at Groznyy. That was *his* city. He *knew* those buildings and they were *burning*! He thought, "God, this isn't some foreign news item, these are my people the Russians are killing on TV!"

As the scenes of battle flashed across the screen, the people seat-ed at the other tables were enjoying their evening meals. Occasionally, someone was overheard commenting on the events being shown up on the wall. A woman asked, "Why are we fighting our own people?" Her male companion said, rather derisively, "Those people aren't

Russians, they're damned Moslems and revolutionaries at that! It's about time something was done about this." Garyk almost said something, but decided against it. He gulped down the meal almost as soon as it came out to him. He couldn't watch anymore; couldn't listen to the remarks.

"What am I doing up here in this Goddamned country?" He was grumbling aloud as he strode back to his apartment. "I don't belong here anymore. My people are in Chechnya and the Russians are trying to kill them." He rushed into the apartment, grabbed up his things and headed for the Land Rover. He didn't know if he'd even be allowed across the border now. It didn't matter; he had to get down there somehow and as quickly as he could.

35

What should have been a three day excursion wound up being a seven day nightmare. The further south he went, the more congested the roads were. Military traffic heading south had the right of way. He was frequently required to pull over to let yet another truck convoy rumble past. The roads heading north were packed with people fleeing the battle zone.

He was detained several times at military police checkpoints. The authorities were not receptive to the idea of allowing another Chechen into the battle zone. "It is best that you wait until the military action has ended," he was told on more than one occasion. He traveled by night on country roads, making his way south by dead reckoning. In the end, he had to bear due west, around El'brus, the highest peak in the Caucasus and into T'bilisi in Georgia, then back north into Chechnya. He crisscrossed mountain ranges and rivers all along the way.

At the Georgian border the guards had no problem allowing Chechen nationals back into their homeland. He was glad that he had opted for the Land Rover rather than his old sedan. It was much more practical given the terrain he was attempting to pass over. In this part of the country a goat path was considered a major road. His route generally followed the Argun valley as it headed north.

Although he wasn't that far from home, Garyk felt he needed to get some sleep and clean himself up after a week of hard driving before dropping in on his mother and the Gran. He stopped for the night at a small inn near Sovetskoye. The innkeeper, an old woman with a worn and wrinkled face, gave him a cool reception. She had good reason to be wary of this stranger, arriving over a mountain pass so late at night. Although he spoke the Nakh language, Garyk had not used it for nearly eighteen years. He had simply forgotten many of the words and his accent was all wrong. His papers clearly showed he was from Moscow.

"There is only one small room available. We were keeping it available for cousins forced out of Groznyy. It really isn't up to Moscow standards, there's just a cot and a wash stand."

"That will be fine, really. I've spent the last three nights sleeping in the car."

"Perhaps you should find someplace closer to the city." A white babushka tightly ringed her face and disappeared under the collar of her frayed brown sweater. Garyk was about to give up and leave when her daughter came in. They spoke so rapidly in the local tongue that it was difficult for Garyk to follow. The younger woman, she appeared to be in her early forties, picked up his identification packet and looked at him curiously. Her hand worked at the knot of her own dark green scarf. Untied, it fell across her shoulder. "Mama, it's the First Deputy Viktor Gadayev!"

"No, actually he's my twin brother," Garyk hadn't bothered to shave since he left Moscow. His hair had also grown considerably longer the past several months. The brothers were now truly identical.

"Certainly, Mr. Gadayev, we would be honored to have you stay as our guest. My mama was afraid that you were a Russian spy! Please forgive us. There will be no charge for the brother of our distinguished First Deputy."

In the morning the two women treated him as if he were Dudayev himself. They made coffee and biscuits for him as well as some ham, apologizing that they had little else to offer. He felt guilty about not paying for the room, sure that they had little enough income to begin with. "This was a wonderful meal. I must insist that you allow me to pay you for it."

"Oh, no, Mr. Gadayev, it has been our pleasure to serve you. Your brother has done so much for our people. It is our way of saying 'thank you.'"

"Are the two of you all alone here?"

"For now. My husband and two sons left five days ago to join the resistance army. They're going to repel those loathsome Russians. Have you heard how the fighting is going? We have no television and the radio reception is poor at best up here in the mountains."

"When I crossed the border this morning I was told that the Russians had stopped their advance. I think that many of their soldiers are refusing to fight. That would be a blessing."

The woman sighed deeply. "Yes, I agree. My two boys, they are just seventeen and eighteen, too young to be fighting I told them. But they insisted. I can only pray that it is the will of the Almighty that they get safely through this. Are you going to join the resistance too?"

"Actually, I hadn't given it much thought. I'm just heading for my mother's farmhouse. It's out past Shali. I guess I'll hook up with Viktor after that and find out what needs to be done."

"May that Almighty One go with you."

He was on a real road. Although it was rutted and riddled with potholes, the travel was a little easier. This road led into Groznyy. There was a checkpoint at the intersection with the road to Shali. Chechen Militia manned this one. Beyond them he could see columns of smoke rising. He realized that the rumbling noise he had at first thought to be thunder in the distance was actually cannon fire.

"I'm sorry, sir, but we cannot let you go any further today. There are Russian tanks in the area and they've begun to shell the town." The man wore a corporal's uniform that looked new. His face was covered in a full black beard and long tresses fell from under his steel helmet.

"But my mother lives on the other side of Shali. I must get to her."

"Yes sir, I understand, but that would be very dangerous, impossible actually. The road to the east is impassable. We sent a squad out to try and take out the tanks. Until then, I'm afraid that they control the road and everything east of Shali."

The war was no longer on the television. It was in his back yard. For the first time he realized that his mother and the Gran might actually be in mortal danger. More rumbling in the distance underscored that thought. Certainly their farmhouse would not be a military target, but what could possibly be in Shali either?

"What is happening in Groznyy?" he asked the officer in charge. He, too, had a beard, but it had been kept neatly trimmed and his hair was a respectable length for a military officer. A regular in the Soviet Army before this, no doubt. In fact, most of their uniforms were old Soviet Army issue, with black and green arm patches hastily sewn on to distinguish them from the invaders.

"There's been very heavy shelling all day, sir. I wouldn't recommend a trip there either just now, but the tall buildings afford some cover. Be careful though, they like to home in on moving vehicles. There's also the danger of debris falling from the high rise buildings. It's no picnic, that's for damn sure!"

"Thank you, lieutenant," he said to the young officer. "I'll see if I can get through to my brother."

"Oh, one thing, sir," the lieutenant volunteered, "you may want to lose those Moscow license plates. No sense having one of our own people shooting at you, is there?"

"Yes, thank you!" Garyk got out and searched for a screwdriver that he'd seen rolling around on the back floor earlier. He quickly unfastened the bolts holding the license plate in place and threw them in the ditch beside the road.

A cloud hung over Groznyy as gray-black smoke rose all across the horizon. The rumbling of distant cannons and the closer thuds from exploding shells and crumpling masonry were almost constant. He had no idea where Viktor lived, not having been down this way for several years. Garyk suspected that he would most likely be at the command center anyway, so he made his way carefully towards the Presidential Palace.

The oil refinery had taken several hits and thick black smoke rolled slowly across the landscape just south of town. He drove through it and immediately his lungs filled with an acrid stench. He gagged and nearly retched right there in the car. The slimy residue blackened the windshield and it was impossible to wipe it away. Once through it he had to pull over and sacrifice one of his shirts in order to clear the greasy mess away. The wind changed slightly and he caught another whiff of that horrible odor. This time he did vomit.

In the city, the streets were generally deserted. Many were blocked with rubble from fallen buildings or with burning vehicles. There actually were bodies lying everywhere. Buildings that he had known as a child, places where he eaten and shopped as a student were all grotesquely misshapen, burning or gone completely. He found a place to leave the Land Rover a few blocks from the palace. He realized that if he left it on the street it would become an easy target, so he pulled into an open garage and hoped the building would still be standing when he came back.

To his surprised he was able to walk right past several of the sentry posts. When one of the guards saluted him, Garyk realized that they assumed he was Viktor. Someone actually called out to him, "Deputy Gadayev, be careful out here!" He was stopped at the entrance and asked for identification. The young soldier seemed confused. "I'm Deputy Gadayev's twin brother," he told him. "Actually, I'm trying to locate him, do you know where he might be?"

"No sir. I thought he'd gone up north the other day. I don't know if he's back yet. If he's here then he may be down in the command bunker. It's in the basement." The young man called in to the security desk. "Ye, Sergeant, this is Private Udogov at the front gate. I have a Mr. Garyk Gadayev outside. He's First Deputy Gadayev's brother. Yes, I'll hold." After a pause he told Garyk. The First Deputy is not here. However someone will be right out to escort you to in to see President Dudayev.

"Mr. Gadayev, or is it Major? I seem to recall Viktor telling me that once," the President began talking almost before he entered the office where Garyk had been waiting. He had seen the man on television many times over the past few months. It was quite different to be in his physical presence. He was actually much shorter than Garyk had expected but his bearing was much more commanding. A dynamo of energy packed into a combat uniform. Dudayev took his hand and shook it firmly. "Please excuse the mess here but we have been acting under some duress of late."

"Mister is quite correct, Mr. President. I have not been in the Army for some time. Thank you for seeing me. I didn't intend to interrupt such a busy person. I am merely trying to locate Viktor. I just got in from a very long trip down from Moscow."

"I'm amazed that you made it here at all," Dudayev said, truly impressed with his daring and perseverance. "Unfortunately, I have turned your brother into a military liaison officer. We needed him in the field more than in the assembly, as you can understand." Unconsciously, the general ran his forefinger quickly over his heavy mustache.

"Yes, I suppose that's true," Garyk answered.

"Viktor is up in the mountains right now, somewhere around Kalinovskaya. We have the Russians in check for the moment. The popular opinion is that Moscow will recall the troops but I am not counting on that."

"It is always wise to pray for the best, yet prepare for the worst."

"A good assessment, Mr. Gadayev. If I am not mistaken, didn't you work with Ruslan Khasbulatov?"

"As a matter of fact, sir, I did. I hope you don't hold that against me!"

"No, not if I can make that work to my advantage. It seems your friend is holed up in Tolstoy-Yurt right now. I think he's trying to mediate a truce and I'm not quite sure exactly whose side he's really on. Tell me, Mr. Gadayev, do you think that I could ask you to go up there and serve as a liaison between our two camps?"

"Certainly, Mr. President, but are you sure you know whose side I'm on?"

"It doesn't really matter, as long as you're fair. You're Viktor's brother, God, to look at you I'd swear you were Viktor. That is enough for me. Just keep a line of communication open so I know what that devil is doing up there."

36

The trip up to Tolstoy-Yurt was déjà vu in reverse. Garyk was once again part of a small convoy of military trucks carrying supplies. The main road was patrolled by Russian Army regulars who were keeping a watchful eye out for local insurgents in the hills above. Only this time, he was with the local insurgents and the army units below him were the enemy. With the home field advantage on their side, they made it through with little or no consequence.

The town had been converted into a fortress. Makeshift barricades of burned out cars and building supplies limited the access to two main checkpoints. Garyk had a personal letter of introduction from President Dudayev, which made a distinct impression on the young sergeant monitoring the gate. On the sleeve of the sergeant's mottled green and brown field uniform was the insignia of the special unit assigned to Khasbulatov. It was a black shield emblazoned with the wolf crest. The words "Never Forget!" were embroidered in white letters across the top. The sergeant was wearing common work shoes. Garyk realized that many of the militia did not have the luxury of standard issue boots. The young man shouted orders and three soldiers escorted Garyk to the house where Khasbulatov had set up residence.

"Garyk Ivramovich!" The former Chairman's face expanded into that well-known broad grin. Ruslan threw his arms around Garyk, kissing him on both cheeks in true Russian fashion. "So, we are together under fire once again it seems. I'm glad to see you looking so well. I had heard things did not go so well for you. Perhaps they were mistaken."

Well, I do carry this souvenir!" Garyk tapped his artificial leg hard enough to produce a rapping sound that could not be mistaken for anything human.

"I'm sorry for that. It seems there's a great many things I am sorry for these days." He made a dismissive gesture with his hand. "Well, we must save our regrets for another day. Now tell me, what brings you back to me today."

"President Dudayev sends his regards." Garyk handed a sealed envelope to Khasbulatov. It was addressed to him personally by the General. While Ruslan read through this, Garyk explained his mission, as he understood it.

"I went to the Presidential Palace to try to find my brother, Viktor. I discovered that he's serving with the militia in the west. President Dudayev called me into his office and suggested that I might serve as a liaison between the two of you. He wishes to keep a line of communication open."

"Yes, I'm sure he does!" Ruslan Khasbulatov finished reading the letter, and then he handed it over to his second in command, saying, "Now that he has brought the wrath of Yeltsin down on our country he seeks to make a new alliance. Well, it is always wise to protect one's flanks, is it not Zelmikhan?" The aide nodded in agreement.

Turning back to Garyk, he asked him, "So now you are to spy on your former associates, is that it?"

"No sir, that is not what I agreed to do. My brother may owe allegiance to Dudayev, but I don't. I will only tell the President what you wish for him to know, unless I feel it is not in the best interests of the Chechen people, of course."

"Ah, that is the point, Garyk." Another broad grin. Ruslan's eyes twinkled. "What exactly is in the best interests of the Chechens? Who can say for sure?"

They were distracted by a commotion outside in the street. The three of them walked over to a window to see what was going on. A group of about 20 Russian soldiers were being led through the town, towards Khasbulatov's headquarters. When they neared the entrance, they were ordered to their knees in three rows, their hands behind their heads. Garyk recognized by their insignia that they were members of one of Russia's elite armored units.

An aide came in to Khasbulatov's office to brief them. "It seems the militia successfully ambushed their unit. Many of their tanks took direct rocket hits and were burning. These crewmen attempted to surrender but the militiamen were intent on killing all of them, taking no prisoners. Fortunately for them, this band of local civilians intervened. They insisted that Chechens not be looked upon as butchers. They have brought them to you Imranych."

"Yes, it is better to leave the savagery to the invaders," Khasbulatov responded. "See if we can contact their headquarters in Mozdok. Tell them we have found some of their strays and suggest that they send a helicopter to retrieve them."

Garyk was a little surprised at the ease with which Ruslan apparently could communicate with Russian headquarters. But in this action, everyone had once been a colleague. It made for strange lines of communication, especially with Russian field commanders publicly speaking out against this invasion. When it became obvious that there would be no rescue mission from Mozdok, Khasbulatov went out to visit the crewmen. They had been kneeling in the street for several hours, although they had been allowed to lower their arms. It was dark, making it impossible to see their individual faces. As they walked through the ranks, one crewman began to sob violently.

The crewman to his right called to him, "Sergei, you must be strong! What has gotten into you?"

Khasbulatov stopped in front of the soldier. "Corporal, please understand that we do not intend to harm you. Hopefully, the war has just ended for you, that is all."

Still sobbing, the soldier looked up at the former Chairman and said, "You don't understand, sir. It was my tank that fired on you in the White House last year. I know that you're going to kill me for that."

The man's confession caused Garyk's entire body to shake. He could see the images of the tanks reflected in all of the windows on the Novy Arbat, their barrels flaming. Once again he heard the explosion ringing in his ears. His missing appendage throbbed with phantom pain.

"Gadayev," Khasbulatov called over to him. "It seems we have the young man who stole your leg! Come, tell me what we should do to him." He spoke as the professor presenting a classroom problem to one of his students. He was interested in hearing Garyk's solution.

Garyk walked between the rows of captured soldiers and stood by Ruslan's side. All eyes were riveted on him as he stood there and looked down on this pathetic, whimpering human being. Rage built within him. His first thought was to execute the man right there. The young tanker was clearly in anguish. "Oh God, sir, please forgive me!" The crewman fought to get the words out through his sobs. "We were only following our orders. We had to do it, sir."

Garyk could feel his own hands shaking. He raised one and let it rest on the corporal's shoulder. In a very hushed voice he said, "It seems that we may have both been in the wrong place at the wrong time, corporal. Tell me, have you had enough of this fighting with your own people?"

"Yes sir," was the whispered reply.

"Then I suggest you find a way to go home, corporal. Will you do that? Will you leave my country alone?"

"Yes sir, if I ever get out of here, I will do just that, sir."

Garyk turned and walked away. His leg throbbed with pain greater than at any time in the past month or so. He told himself he had done the right thing. Still, he knew that if he turned to look back at that soldier again he would probably grab a gun and shoot him where he knelt.

37

Every morning they watched the CNN *'World Report.'* "What a world we live in, gentlemen." Ruslan mused openly to all those assembled in the room. "Here we are in Tolstoy-Yurt, not 20 kilometers from Groznyy, and the best information about what's happening down there is coming via a satellite feed from Atlanta in the United States of America!"

They watched the scenes from Groznyy displayed on the screen. The Presidential Palace had been hit. Minimal damage to the top floors, but the sight of their capital building spewing smoke was a somber experience for most of those gathered in the room. "This brings me back to Moscow and the White House," Khasbulatov commented to those assembled. "Once again a government building has been set ablaze by our own guns!"

Other war scenes followed. The usual shots of old women with heads covered in shawls and children in agony and fear; streets littered with rubble and debris. One of the aides assembled in the room spotted a familiar structure. "Look, that is my cousin's apartment building!" Another called out, "Oh my God, that was our street!" More frequently the response was "Those bastards!" Garyk was pretty sure that he'd seen the apartment complex where he had lived as a student. It was hard to tell for certain, the façade had fallen away.

The picture settled back on the field reporter. He was standing in front of yet another crumpled and burning edifice. Garyk strained to catch the words that were being spoken in English. Each one pierced deeply into his heart.

I'M STANDING NOW IN FRONT OF THE FOURTH HOSPITAL, SCENE OF YET ANOTHER TRAGEDY IN THIS UNFOLDING DRAMA. YESTERDAY, ARTILLERY SHELLS FIRED FROM RUSSIAN POSITIONS ABOVE THE CITY STRUCK THIS PLACE OF REFUGE FOR SO MANY OF GROZNYY'S ALREADY WOUNDED AND DYING. THE IMPACT BROUGHT THE

ENTIRE CORNER OF THE BUILDING DOWN ON TOP OF THE HOSPITAL'S EMERGENCY TREATMENT FACILITY. AMONG THOSE KILLED, WE HAVE BEEN INFORMED, WAS ASSISTANT DIRECTOR TATYANA DZASOKHOVA GADAYEV, THE WIFE OF THE FIRST DEPUTY OF THE CHECHEN ASSEMBLY, VIKTOR IVRAMOVICH GADAYEV. HOSPITAL OFFICIALS TOLD US THAT MRS. GADAYEV HAD BEEN WORKING AROUND THE CLOCK TO TEND TO THE WOUNDED, ESPECIALLY THE YOUNG CHILDREN THAT HAVE BEEN STREAMING INTO THIS FACILITY. FOR CNN NEWS, THIS IS BERNARD WINSLOW."

Ruslan Khasbulatov walked over to where Garyk was seated and placed his hand on his shoulder. "Please accept my sincere sympathy, Mr. Gadayev, on the loss of your sister-in-law. Far too many of us are losing loved ones these days."

"Thank you, sir. Her family lives just up the road a bit, in Chervlënnaya. If you don't mind, I think I'll try to find them. See if there's anything I can do."

"Of course, Garyk. I'll arrange for two of my men to go with you. It isn't wise to travel alone."

Garyk had never been to the Dzasokhov home before. He had always met Viktor and Tatyana in their apartment, or at his mother's. He knew where she came from, of course. She often spoke about her home and family. These towns were small and most people knew their neighbors. He didn't think it would be hard to track them down.

What he had not taken into account was the affect the war was having on the people. Normally friendly and hospitable, the people of Chervlënnaya were now wary of all strangers, especially those toting guns. Since both sides had once been part of the Soviet Army, it was difficult to tell if these men were Russian or Chechen. Garyk himself had on an army six-pocket field jacket over his denim pants and green flannel shirt. Most of the people they approached to ask directions simply ran away. Those that would talk claimed no knowledge of the family. Finally, a shopkeeper was willing to give them directions, mainly because he had met Viktor and recognized his likeness in Garyk.

When they turned down the street on which the Dzosakhov's lived, they could see wisps of smoke rising from one of the houses. Garyk had seen so much of this in recent days that it had no real impact on him anymore. Then he realized that the house he was looking for and the smoldering ruins were one in the same. A few children ran about the wreckage in some macabre game. He searched their faces, hoping to find his nieces or nephew among them. When the children saw the three men approaching, they started to run off.

"Please, I'm looking for the Dzosakhovs. Does anyone know where they've gone?"

Without stopping, one of the little ones called back to him, "They're all dead!"

Garyk and his two companions walked around the wreckage of the house, looking for some evidence of the family. "Sir!" One of the men called out to him from the back. The back part of the house had not suffered quite as much fire damage. The man motioned for Garyk to look inside the window. It was difficult to make out at first, everything was charred and debris was everywhere. Then he made out the forms of three bodies huddled together in the corner of what had once been the kitchen. One was an adult woman, judging from the size. The forms of two younger children nestled close, with their arms wrapped around the adult.

Garyk dropped to his knees and began to throw up. Those bodies were part of his family. He had played with Petruska and held Nadezcha in his arms. The other soldier made an attempt to walk through the ruins. He came back to where Garyk knelt, the ground muddied by the snow that had been melted from the heat of the fire. "Best I can tell sir, there's five bodies in all. These three back here and two more up front. Those are burnt real bad. Couldn't even make out whether they were male or female. One looked smaller though, could have been a young girl or boy. No sense going in there, sir."

Garyk nodded that he understood. "Yes, thank you Mairbek." He thought about his brother. "My God, Viktor, I am so sorry for you. You've lost everything! May the God of our fathers be merciful to you." He spoke the words softly; letting them get carried away by the winds, to find his brother, wherever he might be.

They made their way back to his Land Rover in silence. His mind kept replaying images he had of Tatyana and her children. He wished he had taken more opportunities to come down here and visit with the family. They turned a corner and discovered that their vehicle had been stripped of its tires while they had walked through the town. "Well, it looks like we walk back down to Tolstoy-Yurt," Garyk remarked casually.

Mairbek walked the point. A light snow was falling and he had donned white rainwear over his other garments before they set out. This not only protected him from the elements; it provided better camouflage against the snowy terrain. He carried an old rifle in his right hand. With his left he motioned for them to get off the road. Up ahead they could hear a truck laboring up a grade toward them. Mairbek came back and whispered to Garyk "We can let it go by if you want. We'll just hide here in the bushes. However, if it's just one truck, we can take it out with these." He held up the front of his raingear revealing two grenades that were strapped onto his jacket.

The two militiamen looked to Garyk to make the decision. "Let's go for it!" Garyk unslung the AK-47 that he had been carrying over his shoulder and searched his jacket pockets for the magazine he vaguely remembered bringing with him. "How much ammo do we have?" Mairbek held up six magazines, as did his companion. Garyk took one from each man. "If the truck is carrying troops, we'll be severely out gunned. Can you throw the grenade into the rear first?"

"I should hope so!" Mairbek said, unhooking both and flipping one to his friend. "Ahmed, the two of you move back up the road a bit." He motioned towards a spot they had just passed. "When you hear the explosion, try to get this one under the cab."

"No problem." Ahmed grinned as he slipped the grenade under his white outerwear. He placed his hand on Mairbek's shoulder. "May the Almighty be with you!"

"May he be with all of us," Mairbek replied as he hurried back up the road. Ahmed motioned for Garyk to follow him. The truck was getting closer and they had little time. They split up, each taking up a position on either side of the road. Garyk wished that he had thought to bring along white outerwear too. His dark field jacket and blue denim jeans stood out too well, even against the forest backdrop. He could see the truck now, making its way around a bend and heading past where he supposed Mairbek was. Yes, there he was, running out into the road behind the truck and tossing his grenade. As he did, shots rang out from within the truck. Mairbek twisted around and began to fall. He hit the ground just as the grenade exploded.

The rear of the truck erupted in flames and smoke, pieces flying in all directions. No one got out. The truck continued on momentarily. The cab doors flew open and three occupants leaped out. Without hesitation, Garyk fired two rounds at the driver, dropping him immediately. He took aim at another and was about to fire just as Ahmed's grenade went off beneath the cab. He was too close. Pieces of the cab nearly hit him in the head and he was forced to take cover.

One of the fleeing Russians was hit with the shrapnel and writhed on the ground. Ahmed opened fire on the third, bringing him down as well. The truck was now a mere pile of twisted, burning wreckage. Garyk suspected that they had probably taken out a full squad, maybe two. The man rolling in pain was a lieutenant. Dark rivulets of blood streamed down his forehead and damp stains covered his jacket. As Garyk stood over him, all of the anger welled up from within, "Welcome to Chechnya, you son of a bitch," he shouted. He squeezed the trigger and emptied the remaining 28 rounds into the lieutenant's head and torso. He was about to reload another magazine and start again but Ahmed grabbed him by the arm. "Mr. Gadayev, I think that is enough! We may need those rounds later, all of this noise is sure to attract attention, don't you agree."

"Yes, you're right." Garyk lowered the rifle and stood over the bloody remains of the Russian soldier. At another time this could have been Alexandr, or even himself, for that matter.

"Sir, we must be moving. I'm afraid about Mairbek"

The mention of their own wounded comrade snapped him out of it. The two men trotted down the road to where Mairbek was still lying in the road, alive but bleeding badly. His white clothes had turned crimson. One round had found his shoulder, but the other had hit him in the gut. Garyk was sure he had major internal injuries. With considerable difficulty, Mairbek asked, "Well, my friends, how did we do?"

"We did well, Mairbek, very well indeed!" Ahmed cradled his friend in his arms.

Garyk knelt on his good knee beside them. A sound caught his attention and he stood and surveyed the area. "We must move him off the road. I can hear more trucks coming already!" They dragged their fallen comrade off into the brush. Ahmed ran back and did the best he could to cover the bloodstains, but the snow on the ground made it practically impossible to remove all of the traces.

"Go, my friends." Mairbek forced out the words. "There is nothing that you can do for me now. Perhaps I can take one or two more Russians with me though. Prop me up by that tree so I'll be able to see them when they come for me."

They did as he asked. Before leaving him there to die Ahmed knelt beside him, took out his cigarette lighter and made a flame. "I will say a prayer for you now."

Garyk and Ahmed made their way down into a ravine with a small stream of icy run off water coursing through it. They walked in the water to cover their tracks. Behind them they could hear the trucks stop. Soldiers were shouting orders. Three shots rang out, followed by a whole volley of rifle fire. "Yes, my friend, may the God of our fathers be with you," Ahmed prayed almost to himself.

They found a place that afforded them some adequate cover and hid out until it became dark. They then made their way cautiously back to Khasbulatov's headquarters in Tolstoy-Yurt. Ruslan was not there. He had gone off to try to persuade another Russian commander to cease his attack. Garyk was given some dry clothes to put on and he went to clean up a bit. His left leg was throbbing with pain, now that the adrenaline had stopped flowing through his veins. His right foot was not doing so well either after their trek through the frigid water. He found a cabinet with some first aid supplies and quickly gulped down four aspirin tablets to kill the pain.

He figured he had better touch base with Dudayev's staff, let them know the situation up here and all. They still had sporadic land line connections into Groznyy.

For the past few weeks Garyk had been making his reports to one of the President's aides. Therefore he was surprised when Dudayev himself got on the line this time. Garyk gave a brief account of events, leaving out his own trip to Chervlënnaya and recent encounter with the Russians. Dudayev's responses were terse. "Yes" or "Yes, I see."

When Garyk finished, the President thanked him, and then he said, "Mr. Gadayev, I'm afraid we've had some bad news from Nadterechnaya this afternoon. A company of our forces was overtaken up in the mountains there. They were badly outnumbered. As far as we can tell, no one survived. Mr. Gadayev, your brother Viktor was with them!"

Garyk closed his eyes and let this news sink in. He had nothing to say anymore. What could he say? After a pause Dudayev asked, "Mr. Gadayev, are you still there?"

"Yes, Mr. President, I am."

"Garyk," the President continued, "please let me assure you that I had nothing but the highest respect for your brother. Not just I, Mr. Gadayev, but the entire Chechen nation. It is a sad day for all of us and our most sincere condolences go to you and Viktor's family. Please tell them I said this."

"I would, Mr. President, but I'm sorry to report that they're all dead as well!"

38

Garyk lay on a cot facing the ceiling. His hands were clasped behind his neck for a pillow. Given the day he had just completed, he should have been fast asleep. Instead, he lay there staring into the darkness for several hours. No real thoughts ran through his mind. His whole being had been numbed. Earlier he tried to formulate a plan of action, but the thoughts "Why bother" and "What's the use" kept recurring and countermanded any thoughts about the future.

Daybreak passed and the room brightened. Ruslan's children had undoubtedly grown up here. Now the room accommodated Garyk and three other aides on old field cots. Their belongings were stored in various piles. The staff was rousing for another day. Soon they would hold the morning staff meeting; watch yet another report on CNN about the plight of their nation. Garyk could care less. Finally, someone jarred him back to reality with a firm, "Gadayev, are you joining us this morning?" He rose, threw some water on his face and grabbed a cup of the thick Turkish coffee they kept brewing there for the staff. It was sharp and bitter and packed enough caffeine to keep anyone or any thing awake.

Khasbulatov was explaining his plan for a cease-fire. "If we can convince enough of the Russian field commanders to refuse to press the battle, this will force Yeltsin to negotiate a compromise." Ruslan, of course, would broker the treaty. All of those in the room expressed general agreement with this plan.

Finally Garyk spoke up. "Ruslan Imranovich, please forgive me for disagreeing. I don't see how we can ever, in good conscience, negotiate a settlement with these bastards. Far too much blood has been shed for that."

Ruslan gave him a fatherly look. "Gadayev, I understand that you have reasons to be bitter right now. However..."

"Bitter? You're damn right I'm bitter! Losing my brother in combat, that was to be expected I suppose. Having his wife killed because those barbarians had to shell a hospital, that was tragic! But having my nieces and nephew butchered in the arms of their grandmother, tell me, Ruslan, what kind of savagery is that? These Russians have come to make war on our children and I won't let that go unavenged. The Nokhchii must not let this go, either!"

"Surely, Garyk, you must realize that not all of the Russians are in favor of this war. There is widespread dissension among the leaders down here and in Moscow as well. We cannot blame them all for the atrocities of a few."

"Yes," Garyk said, rising to leave the room, "we can and we must blame them! Tell your friends who disagree with Yeltsin to go back to Moscow and do their fighting there. If they choose to remain here, then I will do my best to kill them all myself!" He stormed out of the room and left the headquarters.

He had decided it was time to make his way back south to try to get to the farm. He wondered if his mother knew that his brother and family were all gone. He hated the thought of having to break the news to her. He walked over to the supply area and grabbed a rifle and some ammunition, as well as a small backpack to carry some essentials. He would be traveling on foot and by night to avoid being seen. Rather than head through Groznyy, he traveled southeast, toward Gudermoss, following the rail lines, rather than the road. From there he took the road south then moved cross-country to get to the farm. It was the area where he had grown up, so he knew it well and could avoid running into any Russian patrols.

It took him three days to travel the 50–60 kilometers. The distance, of course, was measured as the bird flies and did not include the up and down nature of the terrain.

At times he forgot that he had only one good leg. At other times, particularly when he tried to get some sleep, the throbbing would become intense. He wondered how long his stomach could take a constant diet of aspirin? He found places to sleep during the day and pilfered vegetables from the farms he traversed for food.

It was nearing dawn when he made his way into the lower end of their little valley. Several times he caught sight of a grey wolf lurking in the distance. "No, my friend, I am not going to be your dinner today," he called out to it. "Best to find yourself a little rabbit." Coming from this direction, he had to climb a fairly steep incline to get up to the road that crosses the valley. He used the butt of the rifle to support his artificial leg and made the climb with some effort. Panting deeply, he reached the road. The farmhouse was just on the other side.

Pulling himself erect, he looked over to the cottage, half expecting to see a light on in the kitchen already as Mama prepared for the day. The cottage was gone! Most of it anyway. One section of the south wall still stood. The rest of the building lay in ruins. "NO!" he screamed out in anguish. It was a long and agonizing cry. The sound echoed off the hills and mountains; rolled up and down the valley. After everything else, not this too!

He convinced himself that they must still be alive somewhere. In spite of his fatigue from the three-day trek, he half ran, half hobbled over the hill into the next valley. A group of cousins lived over there in a white two-story house rebuilt in the late fifties. He startled a woman in her late forties by bursting in upon her as she was kneading flour to make bread. Gasping for breath, he blurted out, "I'm looking... for Myrianna... Myrianna Gadayev." He was barely able to get out. "Is she here?"

The woman of the house wiped the dough from her hands and called anxiously to her father, "Poppa, come quickly. It is Viktor Gadayev!"

"No. I am Garyk... his twin... brother." The woman led him to the chair by the fireplace where he tried to regain his breath. An old man hurried in from a back room. His hair and beard were long and streaked with white. "Poppa, it is Garyk, returned from Moscow after all these years. He looks so much like his brother." While she spoke, the woman drew a glass of water from the tap and handed it to their surprise guest.

"Thank you. Please forgive me for barging in on you like this. I've been walking all night to get back home. But it's all gone! I was hoping that you might know where my mother and the Gran might have gone."

The old man seemed ashamed. He pulled a handkerchief out of his overall pocket and wiped his brow while he tried to think of what to tell him. "It's been several weeks now," he began. "We watched two Russian tanks coming right down the road out there." He pointed out the window to emphasize his story. "We thought we were all done for. I sat right here at this table and prayed to the Almighty One to watch over us. I guess he did, because those tanks just kept right on going. Next thing you know we hear them firing away with their cannons. Shook the pots right off the wall, didn't it, Lyomi?"

The woman nodded her agreement. "It was so loud, that shelling."

Her father resumed his story. "Three, maybe four big explosions and then we could hear gunfire. When it stopped we were all too afraid to go outside. When we did, we could see smoke rising up over that crestline, you know the one that separates our two valleys." The old man sat down and placed his hand on Garyk's thigh. "You must forgive us, Garyk, we were all too afraid to go over to assist our cousins right away. In fact, I am ashamed to admit, we did not go until the next day."

Garyk looked at the old man. His eyes reflected the grief that was in his heart. He could sense the guilt that both of these people felt. He grasped him firmly by the upper arm and looked him squarely in the eye. "I understand, old man. These are the times we live in."

His cousin again wiped his brow and dabbed away a tear that had formed. "I found the old woman, Nadezcha, right away. We suspect that she died instantly. She was inside the house when the shells hit. At first we thought that Myrianna must have escaped and hidden up in the mountains. Then my son found her lying up on the hillside. She was barely alive. How she lasted that long I couldn't say. We both picked her up and started to carry her over here." He paused, his head bent low and he closed his eyes. "I think the very act of moving her sapped whatever strength remained. She died in my arms." The old man sat there with both of his arms outstretched, as if his cousin was still clutched there and began to weep.

His daughter-in-law moved to his side and placed her hand on his shoulder. "It's all right, Poppa," she whispered softly to him. Then she turned to Garyk and told him, "My husband buried Marianna and Nadezcha. They are beside the stone tower, where the Gadayev ancestors have been laid for generations."

"Thank you." She offered him strong coffee, which he accepted. He refused their offer of food. He just sat there, staring into his cup. He began to shake and Lyomi covered his shoulders with a wool blanket. More than an hour passed before he roused from this trance. During that interval Lyomi's husband joined them. Garyk stood up. "I apologize once again for disturbing you this morning. Thank you for seeing to my mother and the Gran. I appreciate that." He firmly grasped the younger man's hand.

"You are welcome to stay here with us," the son volunteered.

"No, thank you, I've inconvenienced you enough already." Garyk pulled his hat back over his head and departed. Slowly, he walked back over the rise to what had once been his home.

Ivram

39

And so it was that Garyk Ivramovich Gadayev sat with his back propped against the remnants of a stone wall that had once been the home of his family for seven generations. This is how both the cottage and his life had come to ruin. He had turned his back on his heritage and his faith many years before by trying to mold himself into a Russian. Was he being punished for that? First his daughter. Then his wife and son had left him. Now Viktor and his whole family, as well as his Mama and the Gran were all dead. He was left to endure all of this alone. Surely there was a cruel curse cast against him.

The sun was going down and there was a definite chill in the air. A light dusting of snow seemed likely. He paid no attention to the cold; ignored the fact that he had not eaten since when, yesterday afternoon? What did it matter? He had gone immediately to the old stone tower upon his return from the cousins' house. The two recent gravesites were all too apparent. He stood between them, not knowing which was whose, and said, "Well, Mama, I've come home. Please forgive me for having taken so long." A chilling gust of wind blew down the valley and stirred the trees around him. He knew she was angry. He stood there waiting for another sign, but a strange calm settled over the valley and nothing moved. Finally he turned back to the ashes of the cottage and sat down. That had been before noon.

A car came over the hill and drove past the cottage ruins. It slowed and then, after a short distance, it stopped and backed up, turning into the front yard. It was an old car, a boxy, nondescript Russian model that had seen better days. It had once been white, but the luster was gone, as was the paint itself in several spots. The lone occupant got out and slowly walked around the rubble. He was a big man, not as tall as Garyk, but broader across the chest. Like most of the Chechen men these days he wore his hair nearly to his collar and sported a full beard. Touches of gray and white hairs clearly evidenced the fact that his forty-fifth birthday was soon approaching.

"My God, Viktor, is it really you? I was told that you were killed up north."

Garyk looked up at the sound of his voice. Without further motion he replied, matter-of-factly, "No, Borz, Viktor is dead."

"Yes, Garyk, I'm sorry, I should have realized it was you. But with that beard, by God, you look more like him than ever!"

He hadn't shaved for four or five days now. A dark growth of new hair was starting to cover his face. As it should be, he thought, it is time to mourn the dead. "Actually, I have decided that Garyk is dead also. At least everything that was ever Garyk has been taken away! He has ceased to exist."

Borz sensed the hopelessness in his voice. He feared that this despondency might threaten his very well being. "Well, my friend, what am I to call you then?"

Without hesitation the answer came, "I am Ivram. It is more in keeping, don't you agree?" Ivram looked directly at Borz for the first time. "Garyk and Viktor were Russian names. Our father chose them for us when we were born in the Ukraine. He felt we would have to learn to live as Russians in order to survive. Borz, I have been living as a Russian for too long. Look what it has brought me to."

Borz kicked over a stone and sat down on it. "Garyk, no, I apologize, Ivram, we have all made that mistake for too long. The time for change has definitely arrived."

"Tell me, Borz, what brings you out this way? You are far from home, I believe."

"Yes, what home I have left. I just took my wife and our children to stay with her Aunt. They live in Baku, down in Azerbaijan. She was terrified for our children after what happened to my parents and Viktor's family. Excuse me, you probably don't know about that."

"Yes, Borz, unfortunately I do. And it's you who must forgive me. I've been feeling so sorry for myself that I forgot that you also suffered the same loses. She was your sister; they were your nieces and nephew too. And of course, your parents." Ivram picked up a small stone and tossed it aimlessly out into the field where Mama would have planted her cabbages and beets. He stared at the spot where the stone landed and continued, "We went to see them, right after I'd heard about Tatyana. It must have been less than a day after they were killed. The bodies were still inside. I'm sorry, we did nothing for the dead."

"I understand." Borz picked up several small stones himself and jiggled them through his fingers, retaining the largest, which he also tossed into the field. "There are far too many dead these days for us to worry about such obligations. What is done is done. We can not dwell in the past, Ivram, we must begin to look to the future."

"And just what future do you see, Borz? Our country has been brought to ruin by these Russian bastards once again."

"All is not yet lost! For now we seem to be holding them in check. Beyond that, we shall have to see."

Ivram twisted himself around to fully face his visitor. For the first time some expression entered into his voice. "Borz, you seem to be unfazed by all that has happened. How do you manage that?"

"Faith in the All Mighty! We must abide by the will of Allah, Garyk, er... Ivram."

"I don't recall you having such a faith before, I'm sorry."

That evoked a chuckle from Borz, who threw his arm over Ivram's shoulder. "No, you're right. It has just been this past year that I met the usman. He has changed my way of looking at things."

"Really?" Ivram was really taking an interested in this conversation now. "Just who is this new usman?"

"He is called Mansur Shamil. He is of the Vis Haji brotherhood. I will have to introduce you to him, Ivram."

Without saying anything more, Borz stood up walked back to the car. Ivram, as he had now become, found himself riding with him. He had no where else to go, nothing else to do. He certainly had no commitments to either Khasbulatov or Dudayev. They rode in the dark. Borz kept only the parking lights on to avoid attracting too much attention. At night, either side would shoot first and ask questions later. The limited vision and rough roads slowed their progress considerably.

He half-expected Borz to take the road up to the village of Argun. Instead, they proceeded through Shali. He was more puzzled when they reached the main road up to Groznyy and Borz turned south, rather than north. It was the road he had taken coming up from Sovetskoye. "I take it we're not heading back to Chervlënnaya."

"No," Borz answered, "there is nothing there for me now. The oil fields have been shut down and we took most of our important belongings down to Baku. Hopefully, the apartment building will still be there when this is all done with. It's not safe there right now."

"Then may I ask where we are going?"

"Certainly, my friend. I have associates who are staying just beyond Urus-Martan. The Russians will not find us in the mountains."

"And just what kind of associates are these people?"

"Don't worry, Ivram, you will find them much to your liking. I'm certain of that."

They found a small café that was still open when they arrived in Urus-Martan. The proprietor gave them a wary eye. He was a rotund individual who clearly enjoyed sampling the fruits of his labor, not to mention the meats and vegetables. Samples of the menu were randomly displayed on the apron he wore. Four men sat in a back corner, their ages masked by the bushy beards that covered their faces. Ivram judged them to be younger than he was. They, in turn, appeared to be quietly assessing the newcomers.

"Good evening, gentlemen. What can I offer you at this late hour?"

"Some sausages and bread, if you have them," Borz requested in a loud, almost jocular tone. "Some hot coffee, too, to warm our freezing bodies!"

"Yes, but it may take a little while. We have not been getting many travelers this late since the invasion."

"That's no problem." Borz leaned towards the owner and in a mock aside confided, "My friend here has just lost his family. I found him over by Shali, just sitting by the ruins of his old house."

"Are you fleeing to Ingushetia then?"

"No, we'll head up into the mountains. I'm hoping to join up with Mansur Shamil."

There was some stirring at the table in the corner at the mention of Shamil. One of the group, the oldest perhaps, asked, "And just how is it that you know Shamil?"

Borz turned to his interrogator and explained, "I've been a student of his for about a year. He came up to Chervlënnaya and a colleague from the oil fields introduced me to him."

"I see," the inquisitor continued, "and is he expecting you tonight?"

"Not really. The last time I saw him was about four weeks ago. He told me that he was going to make camp up in the hills and to come and join him if I ever needed a place of refuge. Since that time, a lot has happened. I just came back from moving my family to Azerbaijan."

The man asked no other questions nor did he acknowledge Borz' responses. Through all this, Ivram hadn't said a word. He leaned over to Borz and whispered, "I'm surprised that you have spoken so freely. I would be more guarded around strangers."

Borz also replied in a hushed voice, so the others could not overhear. "I understand what you are saying. However, there are times when it is best for strangers not to have too many secrets, if you know what I mean. I have no way of finding my friends in these mountains. It is better to let them find us."

The proprietor reappeared with two plates heaped with sausages, potatoes and dark bread. Borz threw up his hands in delight. "Ah, a feast fit for the tsars!" They ate the meal in silence, save for a few casual remarks concerning the quality of the food. Ivram pulled out his

bottle of aspirin, nearly depleted by this time, and popped three more
tablets. "Forgive me," he said to Borz, "but I must take these for my little friend down here." As he said this he stuck out his left leg and gently rapped on the plastic.

"I was not aware of that, my friend," Borz said with mild surprise.

"It's no bother, so long has I can get more of these," he said, shaking the nearly empty bottle.

"Excuse me, sir!" Borz signaled for the proprietor, who had taken
a seat at a small table near the kitchen and was busy reading the
Groznyy paper. He came over to them and Borz asked, "Might you be
able to sell us a bottle of aspirin? It seems my friend has an old war
wound that requires some attention still."

"Not a war wound actually," Ivram interjected, "I was just unfortunate enough to have been in the White House with Khasbulatov last
year when the Russians decided to shell their own parliament."

The proprietor gave him a wry look, "So you were an enemy of
Yeltsin even before he decided to come down and visit us?"

"Yes, I guess you could say that," Ivram acknowledged.

The proprietor disappeared into another room. He came back holding a half-full bottle of white tablets. "These are stronger than aspirin.
I wouldn't sell them to you, but they're yours if you want them. Don't
take quite as many at one time, they'll knock you out if you do."

"Thank you" Ivram said saluting the man by raising up the bottle
before he slipped it into his jacket pocket. They finished their meals
and were settling up with the owner. All the while they had been eating the four other men had kept to themselves. If they had uttered anything, neither Borz nor Ivram had heard it. One of them rose and
moved to their table. He was not the man who had questioned Borz
before. A bit younger possibly, but not much. He was pulling on a
heavy brown rawhide jacket with a woolen liner. "If you are ready to
go, I will take you to Shamil."

Ivram was surprised by this sudden development. Borz, however,
must have been planning on just such a turn of events. "That would be
just great!"

Outside, their new guide told them to get what they needed from
the car. "You'll have no use for that up in the mountains. We will see
to it that it is stored out of sight. The keys will be back inside when
you need them." Borz had a small bag that he took out of the back seat.
Ivram had a brown backpack. They crossed the street and crowded
into the cab of an old farm truck. Borz was barely able to pull the door
shut. After ten or fifteen minutes on back roads the driver pulled off
onto a narrow path. Underbrush and tree branches scraped along the

sides of the truck as it bounced along into the woods. They entered into a small clearing and the truck came to jerking halt.

The driver opened his door and said, "Come, this way." They were the first words spoken since they left the café. He started off down a footpath and the three men were soon into heavy foliage. The going was slippery and a bit treacherous at times, what with the snow and all. Ivram did his best to keep up. The guide stopped and turned back to him. "I'm sorry about your leg, but we need to move as quickly as possible to get up to the camp before daylight. It isn't good to be seen."

"Yes, don't worry about me. I'll be able to keep up."

40

They needed to stop several times to permit Ivram a chance to catch up and then get a brief rest. "Borz, I'm sorry about this. This damned contraption is giving me a lot more trouble than I anticipated. You should have left me with the rest of the rubble back in Shali."

"Nonsense." Borz found a small tree limb and quickly broke off the smaller branches with the aid of a pocketknife. "Here," he said tossing the limb to Ivram, "use this as a walking stick. It will give your good leg more support."

They walked, climbed actually, for nearly four hours. The guide stopped and Ivram was about to tell him it was okay if they went on, when two other men suddenly emerged from the surrounding forest. It was difficult to make them out in the dark. Both were wearing camouflage jackets and pants. At least one had a beard. A hushed but fairly animated discussion was held between the three, during which the two newcomers turned frequently to eye Ivram and/or Borz. Finally, their guide came back to them. "These men will take you the rest of the way. Don't worry, it is not far." He laughed at that and patted Ivram on the shoulder. "You have done well, my friend, much better than I had expected. Now I must be getting back."

Ivram was amazed to think that he had come all this way just to lead them. "Surely you're not going all the way back to Urus-Martan now!"

"Not to worry, my friend, I can move much faster when I travel alone. Besides, it is nearly all downhill!" With that he was gone.

Fortunately, they were within a kilometer of a small base camp. It consisted of an old stone cottage with several wooden sheds about it. These had recently been augmented with four tents, each about four meters square. Center poles supported the pyramid roofs that sloped back from the four walls. Three were dark, but a Coleman lantern hung at the center of one. Inside, Ivram could see tables and chairs. Obviously, this was the mess hall and someone was already preparing for breakfast. One of the escorts asked them if they would like some coffee. Suddenly, Ivram realized that he was famished after the long trek up into the Caucasus Mountains. "Yes, that would be marvelous," he answered.

They were led into the mess tent and directed to have a seat. There was a small kerosene fired stove, which provided much appreciated warmth against the cold night mountain air. The two other men left them and disappeared into the darkness. Someone approached them with two mugs of steaming coffee. Ivram looked up to say "Thank you" and was surprised to find that their server was a young woman. She had on well-worn jeans and a heavy brown sweater. Her long dark brown hair was pulled back into a ponytail, which she had secured with an elastic band. "Here, this will warm you after the long trip up our mountain," she said. Her voice was soft and mellow, pleasing to the ear. As she handed them their mugs her eyes met Ivram's. She had delightful brown eyes, he thought, and a very pleasing smile.

Ivram reached into his pocket and pulled out the bottle of pills the café owner had given to him. "Let's hope that these work as well as he claimed," he said to Borz, and popped two into his mouth. He took a big swallow of coffee to wash them down and let out a little cry, "Youch, this stuff is really hot!"

The young woman, they learned that her name was Tapa, apologized profusely and hurried back with a towel to wipe up the coffee that had been spilled onto the table. After they had finished the coffee, she led them out to another tent. Inside were two rows of four cots each. Four were occupied, as evidenced by the piles of bearskin blankets that covered the recumbent bodies beneath. "Sleep well, gentlemen, and may the Almighty bring you peace," she said as she left them.

They slept for three, maybe four hours. The camp was alive with activity when they made their way back to the mess tent. At this time of day little light filtered down through the trees above them. It was soon apparent that there were other encampments close by, as the number of people passing through the mess tent could not all have come from this compound. All the tables were full. People sat on stones and tree stumps. Some even sat cross-legged on the cold ground. Breakfast was nothing more than coffee and biscuits with gravy. Everyone seemed to be enjoying the day. The air was filled with the happy sounds of men and women talking and children laughing.

As they passed among these people, Borz recognized several and introduced them to Ivram. "I would like you to meet Gar– no, I keep forgetting, *Ivram* Gadayev. He is the brother of my brother-in-law, you know, Viktor Gadayev." They all greeted him warmly. Most expressed their deepest sympathy over the loss of his brother. Several even spoke of Tatyana. Ivram suspected that many had stories similar to his own, although no mention of their recent hardships was made.

A stir of excitement passed through the camp when two men emerged from the cottage. They both seemed tall, perhaps because one wore a high fur cap, which extended some six or eight inches above his eyebrows. The other was clearly a leader, for he passed through the groups of people greeting each one personally; hugging some, firmly clasping the hand or forearm of others. He wore a heavy gray-blue jacket, opened at the front to reveal a green flannel shirt and blue sweater. For pants he wore the same camouflage pair that was now common for most men. A black turban was wrapped about his head, which draped down over his shoulders. The sounds of laughter followed him as he moved through the camp.

He came up to them and threw his arms around Borz. A broad smile clearly visible through his bushy black beard and mustache. "Borz, my good friend, I see that you have found your way to our little mountain retreat. Now who is this new friend you have brought with you?"

This is the brother of our slain First Deputy, *Ivram* Gadayev. Ivram, please let me introduce you to Shaykh Mansur Shamil."

"Ivram Gadayev, welcome to our assemblage. I hope that you will choose to make yourself a part of our little family." Shamil took his right hand firmly in both of his. They were strong, powerful hands, sending what seemed to be a charge of electricity throughout Ivram's body as he grasped him.

When he completed his rounds through the crowd, he called out to everyone, "Come my children, it is time for our morning zikr." With that he entered the cottage and all the others began to follow him in as well. As Kathryn had been blunt enough to point out several years before, Garyk had not been one to practice his faith. A Moslem in name only, he could not remember the last time that he performed zikr, or "remembrance." He was reluctant to do so now, but Borz grabbed his arm and they were in the midst of a group of twenty-five or thirty people crowding into the cottage.

The inside was roomier than he'd expected, given the throng. There was one large room, devoid of furnishings. The walls were light gray, with ornamental prayer rugs hung as tapestries. A woven burlap carpet occupying the center of the wooden floor, leaving little more than a meter between the carpet and each wall. As they entered, the people removed their shoes and outer garments, piling their coats in a small anteroom. The men and boys all pulled skullcaps out of their pockets, or had already been wearing them under the winter hats. The women draped their heads with brightly colored shawls. Ivram had been wearing a woolen ski cap. Realizing he had nothing else to wear, he pulled it back on to cover his head.

Inside the room someone began to play a violin. This was soon augmented by the rhythmic beating of a drum. The first people into the room had begun to circle in a counter-clockwise direction. They stayed close to the walls, not stepping on the prayer carpet. When the music started, they began to clap. Everyone was now circling the room in procession. Shamil commenced a chant, which was soon picked up by all the others. The chanting increased in tempo as it increased in volume. They weren't just walking anymore. What they were doing, Ivram had no idea. It wasn't exactly what he would call a dance, sort of a rhythmic trot, interspersed with leaning to one side and then the other, all the time the clapping and chanting continued.

Shamil clapped his hands loudly, three times. Suddenly everything stopped! Ivram's head was awhirl. Three more claps and everyone hustled to find space on the prayer rug. Ivram, too, was on his knees, prostrating himself and offering prayers to the Almighty.

After going through the Morning Prayer ritual they were dismissed. Back outside, their boots crunching the snow beneath them as they made their way back to the tent, Borz turned to Ivram and asked, "Well, my friend, what did you think?"

Ivram hadn't spoken at all since the zikr had ended. He was left in a state of unexplainable euphoria. He had a sense of well being and happiness that he hadn't experienced for many years. Borz' question pulled him back into the world. "I'm sorry," he said to Borz, "what did you say?"

"I asked you what you thought of our little zikr."

"I don't honestly know what I think. It was unlike anything I've ever experienced before. The zikr that my father introduced me to as child was certainly not like this!"

"Yes, I can imagine," Borz said with a little laugh. "Many things have changed over the past thirty years. You have been away far too long!"

41

Borz and Ivram returned to the tent where they had stashed the few belongings that they had been able to carry up into the mountains. No one else was there. The others had all busied themselves with whatever tasks and duties had been assigned to them. Ivram lay back on the cot, his hands folded behind his head, deep in thought over this morning's experience. He had woken up completely fatigued. The brief sleep was not sufficient to erase all of the effects of his recent physical activities. Now he was at rest, save for the constant throbbing in his left leg. Even that was more tolerable than it had been before.

He heard the sound of someone entering and glanced over to see Tapa coming toward him. She was again holding two mugs of coffee for them. He sprang up, as best as he could, nearly losing his balance as his artificial leg gave way to the sudden pressure placed upon it. "Excuse me," he said to her, somewhat flustered, "you must think us lazy brutes to be lying about like this while everyone else seems to be making themselves useful."

"Not at all," she assured them both. Her head was still draped in a ceremonial shawl, purple and white, which extended in folds down the full length of her sweater in front of her. "We know that you came in late last night, actually early this morning. There will be time enough for you to be assigned some regular duties. The usman must first learn what it is that you have been sent to do that is best for our community."

"I'm afraid you pre-suppose that we're going to being staying. I don't know if I've made that decision as yet."

Borz turned to his friend, a little surprised by this last remark. "Garyk, no Ivram, sorry I keep forgetting, where else would you go?"

"Let's just say I'm keeping my options open for now."

Tapa smiled at them both, handing each the coffee she'd been holding. "I have learned that those who come to this camp have usually been sent by the Almighty. Who are we to question his judgment in such matters?"

"So you think that I may be on some divine mission," Ivram asked half-joking.

She looked into his deep dark eyes and simply answered, "Aren't we all?"

Ivram had no response for that. Borz, however, laughed heartily, slapped his comrade on the back and said, "I think she has you on that, my friend!"

Tapa lowered her eyes, blushing and afraid that she had offended their guest. Without looking back up at him, she pulled a brightly colored skullcap out from under her sweater where she had tucked it into the waist of her jeans. "Please forgive me if I am being too bold again. I noticed that you did not have a cap to wear this morning. This belonged to my brother and I thought you might like to have it."

Ivram reached out to accept it. In doing so his fingers touched her hand. It sent a tingle up his arm that took him by surprise. "Thank you very much. It is a gracious offer and a beautiful one besides. Are you sure that your brother won't mind?"

"I'm afraid not," she said very softly. "He was killed three weeks ago." She turned away quickly and hurried out of the tent.

The two men stood and watched her hurry away. She carried herself well, which gave her the appearance of being taller than the five foot seven she actually was. Her arms were folded around her to ward off the chill. "How strange," Ivram finally remarked to Borz.

"Perhaps, but I think that you may have a new admirer in that one. And such an pretty one at that!" Borz poked Ivram in the arm and had a good laugh at his expense.

Ivram made no response. Absently, he lifted the mug up to his lips and took a swallow. "Aiyee, how does she make this stuff so hot! You'd think this cold air would have cooled it down by now." He set the mug down to let it cool a bit longer. Fumbling through his pockets, he found his bottle of painkillers. He shook it to better gauge the extent of its contents. There were about a dozen tablets inside. "I guess I'd better save these for a rainy day," he said to Borz, rattling the pills inside for emphasis. "That's just more pain that I'm going to have to learn to live with."

At midday a group began to reassemble outside of the cottage. Ivram noticed that this time there were only men and older boys included. He wondered where all of the women and children had gone. Shamil's assistant, still wearing that high fur hat, opened the door and ushered them in. Again coats and shoes were piled in the anteroom, but now they moved directly onto the prayer rug and assumed a position on their knees. Shamil was already in his place at the center of the front row. Following his cue, they proceed through the prayer ritual.

Prayers done, Shamil turned and sat cross-legged before them. The men formed a series of semi-circles around him. With a hushed voice he began to speak to them in their native language. "We come today, as we must do every day, to bring ourselves into a mystical union with the Almighty, the One True God," he began. For the next hour he spoke extemporaneously, often quoting in Arabic from the Qur'an, than explaining the intricacies of the passages to them in Nakh. "And how does one achieve such a union with the creator," he counseled them. "It is by seeking spiritual peace and rectitude, apart from the world about us."

As his talk progressed he gradually became more animated and agitated. His voice became more powerful as his focus turned away from the divine mysteries of life and became a diatribe directed against the invading horde of Russians. He recited the litany of past abuses that their people had suffered at the hands of the Russian and Soviet rulers over three centuries. Ivram was stirred as he recounted the massacre of 4,000 Qadiri Moslems at Shali in 1864. They were among his direct ancestors.

"And let us not forget the genocide and deportation of 250,000 under the reign of terror imposed by that depraved butcher Stalin. He tried to purge the land of all Chechens and Ingush, all believers in the One True God, repopulating it with immigrants he shipped down from the north. We still serve the One True God! We must be prepared to sacrifice for the cause of truth!" Shamil was standing in their midst now, entreating them to remain politically active and not to yield to this current oppression. "Remember what has been written on the stone memorial to our fallen brethren," he raised his voice to its limits as he reached the conclusion: "We shall never forget! We shall never forgive!"

Led by Shamil's assistant, all of those assembled inside the cottage rose and began to chant these final words, "WE SHALL NEVER FORGET! WE SHALL NEVER FORGIVE." Louder and louder their incantation was raised up to their God. Finally, Shamil clapped his hands together loudly. "Enough, my brothers! We have nourished our souls, I think it is time to find nourishment for our bodies." The group began to disperse, each man reclaiming his boots or shoes and putting on his coat or jacket. They filed out into the bright, crisp afternoon and made their way to the mess tent. Many of the women were there already and the aroma of a hearty stew drifted through the camp.

Mansur Shamil came and sat down next to Borz as they were eating their meal. It was a long wooden table that could accommodate ten on either side. Ivram sat across from them. "So you are the brother of Viktor Ivramovich. He was a good man. It was a tragic loss for our people."

"Yes, I believe he was," Ivram said. "I regret not having spent more time with him."

"That is a sad realization that too often comes to us after a loved one has passed on. Still, we must never regret what has or has not been done in the past. One can only live for the present. You can make amends to your brother by dedicating your life to what he believed in."

"And I suppose you know what Viktor believed in."

Ivram's sarcasm alarmed Borz, who saw it as a great disrespect for the teacher seated beside him. "You must not talk this way to our esteemed usman," he scolded.

"That's quite all right," Shamil assured him. "Your friend speaks from the heart. A heart that has borne much grief of late I think. At such times we must give counsel and compassion, not admonitions. Actually, I did have the opportunity to meet with Viktor on several occasions." Ivram seemed surprised at this. Shamil, noting his upraised eyebrows, laughed softly and continued, "No, Viktor was not a murid, a follower of the way. But we shared a passion for our country and our people. I can tell you quite truthfully, Mr. Gadayev, that what your brother believed in was the Nokhchii!"

Ivram smiled at that. "Yes, you're absolutely right." They had the table to themselves at this point. Those who had been eating finished their meal in a hurry, realizing that their leader wished to have a private audience with the two new arrivals. Shamil surveyed his guest, studied his face and, it seemed to Ivram, looked into his very soul. "So tell me, what brings you to us, Mr. Gadayev?"

Ivram began to give him some sketchy details of his recent travels. Shamil pressed with questions, turning each answer into yet another more probing inquiry. By the time they had finished, Ivram had bared his whole life to this man. "Yes," Shamil concluded, "I can see where you would seek to become a new person after all of this. I, too, assumed the names of our two greatest shaykhs when I felt compelled by the Almighty to lead his people. But you must be careful. You say you have chosen to be called Ivram to give honor to your ancestors and that is a good thing. But if you have stopped being Garyk to turn your back on the past, then you turn your back on yourself. That is not a wise thing to do, do you understand? Everything that happens to us molds us into what we become. It is the Almighty himself that does the molding and his work is never completed."

He turned to Borz who had been sitting through all of this in silence. "Borz, you have had the opportunity to see into a man's heart today. That is a rare privilege my friend and carries with it a grave responsibility. You have now become this man's true brother." Shamil rose from the table and the two of them rose with him. "Examine your heart, Mr. Gadayev. I will talk with you again tomorrow. If you choose to remain with us, I am sure that there is much that we can do together."

Ivram spent the balance of that day reflecting on all that he had seen and heard since coming into the camp. He had many questions for Borz, who apologized for not being a skillful teacher. Still, he was able to explain that Shamil was an adherent of the *Vis Haji*, an outgrowth of the Qadiri order of mysticism. This had developed in the camps of exiled Chechens in Kazakhstan. Since the Gadayev family had been shipped to the Ukraine, they had continued in the more traditional Moslem fashion, which among other things excluded women and eschewed vocal or musical accompaniment to zikr. Even here the women were required to attend separate noon prayers and afternoon instruction. Because the senior Ivram had assumed that his sons would be assimilated into the new Soviet Union, he had limited his own faith practice and after his death in 1966 the two boys received no religious instruction.

The next morning they attended the group zikr again. Ivram found it just as exhilarating as he had the day before. Some inner need was clearly being satisfied. As they were leaving the cottage, Shamil caught his arm. "Come, my friend, let us continue our talk in private." He led him into a small room off the main meeting area. This apparently served both as his office and sleeping quarters.

Shamil's assistant joined them. He was introduced as Buvais Murat. Even indoors he wore his fur cap and leather jacket. Unlike his usman, Murat's face was without a beard, just the hint of reddish brown whiskers to highlight his cheeks. Shamil and Murat sat on an oversized couch and indicated to Ivram to take a seat on a smaller sedan chair at right angles to theirs. "So, my friend, have you decided to join us? Are you prepared to begin training as a murid?"

"Yes, I believe that I am."

"Good, that is as I expected. The Almighty has led you to us for some great purpose, I am sure of that. We must now try to find out what He has in mind."

Murat picked up the conversation here. "As you may have already detected, the most immediate need is to provide sufficient supplies for our community. There is an ever-growing group of people fleeing the

Russian onslaught. Like you, most come into the Caucasus for refuge, bringing little but the clothes on their backs."

"Yes, I'm sorry for not..."

Shamil held up his hand to stop him. "You entered your new life just as an infant enters the world. He has no need to apologize and neither do you."

Murat continued, "Our second mission is to press the attack against the invaders. We do this through clandestine operations, you understand. We are not capable of making direct confrontations. The militia can do that."

Ivram sat forward in his seat. "Perhaps I can help you there. The best way to attack the enemy is to know where they are going to be ahead of time and in what strength. Most of the Russian troop and supply deployment is coordinated via satellite transmissions and retained in a central database. We need only access that and we will be able to execute surgical strikes that gain maximum effect at little risk."

Shamil shook his head and said, "I know very little about computer technology, Mr. Gadayev. However, I do know that you are talking about breaking into the most secure data system in all of Russia. Even if we were to gain access, I'm sure that everything is encrypted. We could never crack those codes."

"You couldn't," Ivram said with a broad grin. He teeth gleamed through the full week's growth of beard that now graced his face. "But who do you think designed their whole system of satellite communications? Who do you think it was that laid the foundation for whatever codes they may now be using?"

Shamil gave him a curious look. "I suppose you're going to tell me that it was you, Ivram."

"Yes!"

"But surely they have made changes to the system now." Murat sounded skeptical. "You said you left the army how many years ago?"

"Actually, I've been away from computer operations since 1989. What's that, six years? Certainly they change the codes every day, but the basic system is still the one that I put together for them during the Afghanistan operation. When you design a computer system as complex as that, you always create little doors and windows that allow you to get back inside to perform system upgrades. I can assure you that they are still in place. What's more, I'm the only one that can gain access through them!"

Murat probed further, "There must be a considerable amount of computer equipment required to achieve this access. As you can see, our resources here are very limited."

"That's the beauty of it all. Get me a good lap top, you know one of those little computers that looks like a small attaché case, and a cell phone and I'll be into their system in less than half an hour!"

Shamil looked at his associate with a broad smile. "What did I tell you, Buvais." He gestured with his arms held out from his sides. "The Almighty has sent us a very special gift indeed!"

42

Ivram made a list of the specific equipment that he thought he might need. He included some small extras just to make sure he had back up materials to modify the system. With Groznyy under constant attack, they were not certain where they could go to get what was needed. However, two men were dispatched on a procurement mission that afternoon. Borz and Ivram remained at the camp. They spent most of their time helping to clear ground for an expansion of the present encampment. A large building was being erected to house many of the families with smaller children. A larger tent had also been located which would serve as a new mess hall.

Late in the afternoon of the following day the two men came back from their expedition into Groznyy. They had liberated a number of items from classrooms at the State University. The main buildings had been closed temporarily as they had all sustained significant bomb damage. "We brought back three computers and four cell phones, just in case some don't work."

Ivram was given one of the tables in the mess hall to work on. True to his word, he established a satellite up-link almost immediately. Within ten minutes he had accessed the Central Army Database. It actually took him another half-hour to bypass the security systems and decode the data.

With Ivram's guidance over the next three weeks, small bands of three or four men and women were dispatched as raiding parties. They targeted lightly guarded supply convoys, sometimes actually commandeering the vehicles themselves. These were then driven back up into the hills beyond Urus-Martan and hidden from view. Once, Ivram located a deployment of two tanks with no supporting infantry. These had been positioned to intercept a Chechen supply convoy. Instead, three of their own were able to take the tanks out with two hand-held rocket launchers obtained just the day before.

Spirits in the camp were very high. They were now better armed and had obtained several Russian field radios. These allowed them even greater access to troop movements and also permitted them to communicate with the Chechen National Army units operating in the area. However, they still lacked some basic food and medical supplies, especially things for the younger children. It was Tapa who brought this to Ivram's attention one afternoon. Ivram was seated at the table with Buvais and three of the commando team captains. They were reviewing plans for that evening's forays and she brought coffee over to them. "A word of warning, gentlemen, this young woman makes the hottest coffee in all of Chechnya!" Ivram joked to his colleagues.

By now Tapa was accustomed to his little joke and could laugh along with him. She overheard them discussing an attack on an ammunition convoy. "Are guns and ammunition all you men can think of? Bullets will not feed those small children over there. They need milk! We could all use some flour to make bread and fresh vegetables. Oh, and there's another thing. Everyone is getting sick living out in the cold like this. We need some antibiotics."

Buvais started to wave her away. "We can only gather what the convoys carry, woman. This is not the Gum Department Store!"

"Wait," Ivram said, "she has a good point. You are correct also, Buvais. But nothing says that we can't arrange for these convoys to be carrying exactly what we need. Tapa, go and make a list of those items that we need the most."

One of the captains asked, "Ivram, what are you going to do now?"

"It's so simple, I should have thought of it before. I can access their supply requisition system. That will generate a packing order to place everything we need onto those trucks. Then we just have to route them along a section of roadway that we can control. This is much too easy!"

They all shook their heads in amazement and laughed. Tapa hurried off to talk to the other women in charge of feeding the community and tending to the ill. Her heart fluttered from the thrill of having been taken seriously by the inner circle of men charged with running the camp. In spite of their inclusion in the morning rituals, it wasn't often that the women were taken into account. More than that, however, was the fact that he had taken notice of her. He remembered her name!

It took her about forty-five minutes to gather the information and compile a precise list. When she returned to the mess tent, he was there alone, seated in front of his computer. She was amused by the way he rapidly tapped out commands. With each stroke it seemed that new images flashed on the small screen before him. Ivram looked up and saw her standing there, peering over his shoulder. "And just what do you thing is so funny?"

"I've never seen anyone work so quickly on the computer. They tried to teach us how to use the word processor at technical school. I was never very good at it. My girl friend Maya was. But even she was never this fast! There's another thing. I don't think I've seen you so happy since you came here."

"You're probably right. I've been working with computers for more than twenty years now. God, were you even born then? I think I've always been happiest when left alone to play with my friends."

She was hurt by his remark about her age. Did he only think of her as a child? "I'll have you know that I'm twenty-three years old. I'll be twenty-four at the end of next month!"

"My, an old woman," he said with a pleasant laugh. "Where is your babushka and shoulder shawl, gramma?"

They both laughed. She presented him with her 'shopping list.' "My, we have been busy," he said. "Tell you what, bring me another cup of that tongue-scalding coffee of yours and I'll see what I can do about this." When she brought the coffee over to him he motioned for her to sit down next to him. "See, I'm into their systems here. That's a schedule of all of their food rations. All we have to do is click on the items we want. Would you like to try?"

She was elated. Not only was he taking the time to show her what he was doing, he was going to let her use the computer too! He pointed out the items that they were looking for, explained what she needed to do. Her hand was on the mouse, tentatively moving it. "Like this," he said and took her hand in his and guided it across the pad. For a brief moment she closed her eyes and held her breath. This really wasn't happening. She could feel her heart pounding and wondered if he could hear it too. Tapa, get hold of yourself!

It was the first time Ivram had been this close to a woman in years. Yes, he and Katryn had made love, well, they had had sex, he wouldn't call that love, less than a year ago. Before that he'd forgotten when the last time was. There had been no others before or since. He wasn't looking for a relationship even now. He just felt comfortable being around her. Other than Borz he had no close associates in the camp, no family anywhere. He hadn't really thought about it when she sat down. He just enjoyed sharing his love for computers and no one else seemed to take any interest in that. It was natural for him to take her hand. He'd done that many times before when he was training some assistant. He'd done it with Georgi and Alexandra. Funny she should remind him of them. This is crazy, he told himself. I'm almost old enough to be her father! Sitting next to her he could feel her warmth. He sensed her smell. I thought only Katryn could make me feel this way, he mused.

"I'm afraid the Russian Army isn't stocking infant formula just now," he said as they finished checking off another item. He removed his hand and slid away from her on the bench. "We don't want to put all of our eggs in one basket, or truck. That might raise some suspicions up there. Make a note, though, we should look for some cases of eggs the next time."

"Oh, will there be a next time."

"I don't see why not. If this one works we should do it again every week."

The next day the Russian supply garrison located at Nazran in Ingushetia received a communiqué from the main command head-quarters up in Mazdok and began loading three trucks with supplies destined to the border patrol outpost. "This is crazy," the sergeant major in charge muttered. "How much food do they think ten men can eat? Such fools we have running things these days!" But orders were orders and who was he to argue. He complained again when the three trucks were ready to leave. No provision had been made for any military escort. He stormed into the supply garrison office. The officer in charge was a wet behind the ears lieutenant, fresh from the training academy. "Lt. Kasakov, this is insane!"

The young officer looked up from the supply manual he was try-ing to master. The sergeant had a broad face with large ears and very little hair. All of that exposed skin was turning crimson, reminding him of a big red balloon ready to pop. "Settle down sergeant. Just what seems to be the crisis now?" The lieutenant had only been there a few weeks, but already he was use to his supply sergeant's frequent bouts with exasperation.

"Sir, it's bad enough that they want us to send five times more food and medical supplies than normal, but they're not even giving us an armed escort to deliver it!" With that he threw the orders and requisi-tion forms down on the desk in front of Lt. Kasakov.

Kasakov readjusted his eyeglasses and studied the documents. He hoped that he might detect some glaring error, obvious typo or the like that the sergeant had overlooked. "Well, sergeant, everything does seem to be in order as far as these documents are concerned. I'm sur-prised that they chose not to send any support troops. However, the trip is almost entirely within Ingushetia. I don't think the Chechen mili-tia has ever knowingly crossed the border. I suppose the infantry is needed some place else today."

The lieutenant handed the paperwork back to the sergeant, who snatched them back in disgust. "Yes sir, thank you very much sir," he grumbled as he strode back out to the waiting convoy of three trucks. "What has this army come to," he said to the corporal driving the lead truck as he climbed up into the cab.

"Excuse me, sergeant?" The driver clearly had no idea what was eating the sergeant this morning. He did not cherish the thought of having to share the truck cab with this disgruntled old veteran all afternoon and envied his two buddies in the rear trucks who would have the luxury of listening to the radio or perhaps a cassette player rather than the sergeant's complaints.

The trucks lumbered along making comparatively good time. There was little reason for civilian traffic to be heading into Chechnya these days. It was late in February and the sun remained low in the sky. It would soon disappear behind a ridge of mountains. The day was dark and dreary enough as it was, with a lingering cloud cover obscuring much of the light that was available. They had been on the road for about an hour and the sergeant had kept up a running monologue about the good old days in the Soviet Army and how everything had gone to hell the last two years. The corporal was obliged to interject "Yes, Sergeant" or "You're right, Sergeant" at appropriate intervals.

They approached the Assa River crossing, about ten kilometers from the border, when something exploded on the road twenty meters in front of them. The corporal slammed down hard on the brakes, stalling the engine in the process. "Son of a bitch, what was that?"

"A grenade, I think," the Sergeant Major said. The truck was struck in the rear by the second vehicle and lurched forward. The combined effects of the sudden stop and rear end collision thrust him forward into the windshield. Blood appeared above his right eye. "Damn, I think I just broke my fucking arm! Didn't I tell them that we needed an escort detail for this trip!" He tried to push open the door; cursing and screaming at the pain it caused to his arm. Someone on the outside pulled the door open and he nearly fell out.

"Good afternoon, sergeant. I'm sorry for this little inconvenience but there has been a slight alteration to your plans. Get out please. You too, corporal. If everyone follows orders then no one need be hurt."

"Tell that to my fucking arm, you son of a bitch!"

"I'm sorry, sergeant, we didn't mean for that to happen. Borz, come see if you can help the sergeant here."

The three drivers were led to the rear of the convoy and told to stand with their hands clasped behind their heads, facing the back of the last truck. Their captors, they noticed, were all wearing the same

Russian army uniforms that they had on. The leader shouted up to Borz, who was tending to the sergeant's bleeding forehead, "Borz, try not to let too much blood get on that jacket. You'll need to be wearing it at the border."

"There, that should stop the bleeding nicely," Borz told the sergeant when he had finished applying a makeshift bandage to his head. "Now let's get this jacket off so I can see to that arm of yours." Although he was trying to be gentle, the movement sent a shock wave of pain through the wounded arm, evoking a shout from the sergeant. That was followed by "Damn you, you fucking idiot!" Borz was not a trained medic, but he had worked in the oil fields long enough to have become well acquainted with resetting broken limbs. "This may hurt just a bit," he said, pulling quickly on his arm. The sergeant cried out again, closely followed by yet another string of expletives directed at Borz.

Fortunately for the Sergeant Major, the medical supplies had been stored near the back of the second truck. They found a splint to put on his arm and placed it into a sling. Borz found a carton containing some pain capsules and pulled out a bottle. He tossed it to the sergeant and said, "You might find these useful."

This whole encounter lasted about ten minutes and the leader was getting a little edgy. "Hurry Borz, they will have cleared our little diversions by now and traffic will be coming soon!"

"I'm done," Borz called back. "Now Sergeant, if you don't mind I just need to have your documents and we'll be on our way!"

They had brought a driver for each truck and Borz was to replace the sergeant. The plan was to get across the border using the Russian documents. Then they would simply drive past the outpost and make straight for Urus-Martan. Two men would remain behind to guard the Russians just long enough to detain them from making any premature report. That way, the border guards would not receive word about the highjacking until the convoy had already passed by. If all went well no shots had to be fired on Ingush soil. The most amazing thing about the plan was that it actually worked! By the time the Russians realized that the trucks were not heading for their proper destination, the convoy was well into friendly territory. Any attempt to pursue them would likely result in further ambushes and real lose of life. When informed about what was happening, the border outpost commander merely shook his head and had a good laugh.

As they neared Urus-Martan the three trucks each took different side roads that led up into the mountains. It was not wise to concentrate all of the vehicles in one place as the Russians had satellite surveillance cameras that could pinpoint their location. Borz and his driver made their way slowly along a network of little country roads and tractor trails to a point where they could travel no further. Several trucks had been stashed there previously and as they pulled in a team was already beginning to unroll a camouflage tarp to drape over this one. The arduous task now began of carrying the crates and boxes of food and medical supplies on foot to the main encampment. Poles were strapped onto some of the crates, allowing two bearers to heft the load. Borz grabbed the back end of one such set. He was delighted to finally make it into the clearing and set his burden down outside of the mess tent.

Ivram was working on his computer when they arrived. He looked up in time to see his friend lumber into camp. "How did it go?" he called to Borz.

"Like a charm, my friend, just the way you planned it! Here, I needed to break into some of the supplies down there and found something you might find useful." He tossed a full bottle of extra-strength pain relievers to Ivram.

A group of the women began taking stock of their newfound inventory. Tapa was among them, gleefully dancing from box to box as she counted off the items from her "list." She asked about some of the items that had not yet been hauled up the mountain and was ecstatic about the success of the mission. She dashed about thanking each of the men who had gone on this expedition and found herself standing in front of Ivram. "I can't believe that you made all of this possible. How can we ever thank you," she said to him. Then, without thinking, she threw her arms up around his neck and kissed him.

Ivram received her kiss, but then put his hands around her waist and gently eased her back from him. She blushed and put her hand up to cover her mouth. "Oh, I'm sorry, I shouldn't have done that," she said with considerable embarrassment. Her eyes looked into his for some sign that he had not been offended by her rashness.

"Perhaps not," he said to her "or perhaps you should have, who is to say. I'm the one who must be sorry though, not you. I'm just not ready for this right now, Tapa. I'm not sure if I ever will be."

43

Shamil sought Ivram out after morning zikr the next day. "I wanted to tell you what a splendid job you've been doing for us, Ivram. I was certainly right when I said that the Almighty had blessed us by your coming!"

"I wouldn't call that a blessing, but I am glad to be useful." Ivram felt uncomfortable having such praise bestowed upon him by the usman. "I just hope that I can continue to do so."

Shamil's expression changed to one of concern. "Why, is something wrong?"

"I'm beginning to see indications that my visits to the Russian data banks have not gone completely unnoticed. Someone is starting to close down my doors and windows."

"Does this mean that you've lost access?"

"No, not entirely. Still, it may be best to lay low for a little while and not pique their interest. To wait until we have a special project."

"Yes, that seems logical. In fact, we may all need to lay low for a while. It seems that Groznyy has fallen to the Russian onslaught. What's left of it anyway. Dudayev has escaped, of course. He and his staff will keep on fighting from the mountains, just as we do."

"This was inevitable, I'm afraid." Ivram's expression was grim, but not one of despair. "We must press on, one day at a time, and see what each new day brings."

Shamil threw his head back and laughed heartily. He slapped Ivram on the back and said, "Excellent! You are learning well, my friend, and have become a good murid!"

Borz caught up to Ivram after Shamil had gone on to another group. "It seems that my brother remains in good favor with our usman. Hopefully, that should bring blessings on both of us!" His eyes twinkled and his face was graced by a broad grin. Both men had allowed their beards to grow in fully, although Borz seemed to be doing a better job at keeping his trimmed.

"I didn't think you had to rely upon me to bring you blessing, Borz. From what I hear around the camp you've become quite the accomplished commando!"

"I just do what I can," Borz replied, not so meekly. They both laughed at that. "Now, Ivram, tell me what have you done to that delightful young woman of yours. I hear that you may not be in Tapa's good favor this morning."

Ivram stopped in his tracks. He looked directly at his friend and asked, "Borz, what are you talking about?"

"Perhaps I should not repeat these things." Borz looked at the ground for a moment, trying to decide if it was right for him to interfere in this matter. "It's just that some of the women were talking this morning. You know how they can be. From what I could gather Tapa spent most of the night crying. She refused to come down with them this morning. I just assumed that you two must have had a fight. I'm sorry for jumping to conclusions."

"I wasn't aware that we had become a topic of conversation. Borz, do people really think that we are, what would you say, involved? Is that what you think?"

Borz reached his arm up around Ivram's shoulder and they began to walk again. "You are truly the little brother I never had, my friend. Even with Viktor there was never such a bond. If you could only see yourself when she is around you, Ivram, you glow! As for her, I think she finds ways to be near you. They call her your little coffee girl!"

"Yes, I guess that I knew or at least suspected as much. I honestly don't know what I should be doing about this, Borz. I am still a married man! Granted Katryn seems to have dissolved it. However, that was not my doing and there's been no official divorce, none that I'm aware of anyway."

Borz took a hard look at his friend. "Ivram, do you still love that woman?"

"Someplace inside of me I always will, yes. It's as if I were to ask you if you still loved Tatyana or your mother, only Katryn is not dead. Neither is Georgi!"

"Ah yes. It is quite a dilemma. Still we all have needs, my friend. Sometimes it is best to take sustenance where the food can be found!"

"Is that what you are doing while your wife is in Baku?"

Borz shook his head. "No, you know me too well. For now we will just go on being celibate together. At least I can anticipate the time when my separation will come to an end!"

"Yes, you are lucky for that," Ivram said. "I've resigned myself to the fact that my time will never come again."

Borz stopped in front of their tent. "So tell me, Ivram, did you tell all this to Tapa? Is that why she was crying last night?"

"No, not really. We kissed yesterday. Actually, she kissed me, but I didn't try to stop her. Then I told her I wasn't ready. I think I may have said that I might never be ready."

"Well, my little brother, I think she deserves to know the reason why."

Ivram looked for her, resolved to do just that. However, several days passed before he actually saw her. When he did, it was not possible to exchange more than a simple greeting. She was making a point not to be near him, just as she had earlier found ways to be close. She either absented herself from the morning prayers or surrounded herself with other women. She stayed close to the camp where the old women and orphans were housed and ate infrequently. Her absence grew on him. He no longer wanted to talk to her, he needed to. He found that she consumed his thoughts as much as Katryn ever had.

After almost a week he came upon her alone in the mess tent one morning. She had been sent to fetch some supplies and hoped to get in and out while he was engaged in the daily staff meeting inside the cottage. Those who had sent her actually hoped that this would not be the case. "Good morning Tapa," he said, coming up on her from behind.

"Oh, Mr. Gadayev! My, you startled me. I didn't know anyone was nearby."

"If I'm not mistaken, it seems that you have been avoiding me lately."

"Now why would I want to do that?" She was doing her best to act indifferent, but it wasn't working. She could feel her whole body trembling and hated herself for it.

"That's just what I've been asking myself. I've been hoping to have a chance to talk with you, Do you have a minute?"

"No, actually, I need to run these back up the hill. There are children waiting for their milk right now."

"I'm sure they can wait a few moments longer. Please, sit down for just a minute." Reluctantly, she agreed to do that. "Tell you what, why don't *I* get *you* some coffee for a change!" His offer made her blush. She had also heard the comments being made about her. He sat down across from her and slid a cup of coffee over to her. "It seems that I have done something to offend you. For that I am very sorry."

"No, you did nothing wrong. It's just that I behaved like a young schoolgirl. It's all too embarrassing to even think about. Please forgive me." She picked up her cup and made a pretense of drinking from it.

"You must not think that way, Tapa. I realize that I must have been encouraging you. No, I know that I was. I have become deeply attached to you."

She put her cup down. "Attached, now that is an interesting word you've chosen."

"I'm sorry," he said with an apologetic little laugh. He reached his hand across the table and tried to take hers, but she pulled her hand away. "What I meant to say, Tapa, is that I have fallen in love with you. But I'm not in a position where I can act on that love, not honorably or fairly to you." She looked at him intently, trying to understand what he was telling her, why he was telling her. He sensed that and reached for her hand again. This time she allowed him to take it. "Believe me, I truly wish that I could, but that would be much more harmful to you my dear."

He told her about Katryn: about how they had first met and fallen in love; about losing Alex and having had Georgi taken from him; about how she had somehow fallen out of love because of the ethnic and political walls that had mysteriously sprung up in their lives. When he finished tears rolled from her eyes. She bit down hard on her lip, trying to make them stop.

During his narrative he had removed his hand from hers as he gestured to emphasize one or more of his points. She reached across the table now and took both of his hands in hers. Looking directly into his dark brown eyes she said softly, "You still love her deeply, I can see that."

"Yes, I'm afraid that I always will. I'm sorry."

"Please don't be, because I shall love you more for that than for any other reason." She got up from the table, wiping the tears away with the end of her apron. "Thank you for telling me all this." She bent down and kissed him on the cheek, then slowly walked back up to the other camp.

44

Days and weeks passed by without significant event. The Russians installed a puppet government and generally occupied the more populous areas of the country. It was estimated that somewhere around 40,000 Chechens had been killed. At least another 300,000 had fled the country. Dudayev ran his government in exile, mounting periodic raids against the occupying forces, while Khasbulatov continued to speak in opposition to him, urging reconciliation with the Russians and a return to the Federation.

On three occasions Shamil and his followers were forced to relocate. Fortunately, word usually got to them before the Russian's sweep patrols to locate and destroy the roving bands that continued to harass them. The cottage was torched and they lost a number of tents during this process, being unable to carry everything on such short notice. The move further into the mountains fragmented the followers into several separate camps. They might go for days or weeks without seeing members from the other groups. Shamil and his main confidant Murat were the only ones who routinely visited each location, staying one or to days at a time. Borz and Ivram stayed together, of course, but neither of them saw Tapa for several months.

Summer was in full swing and the mountains were alive with a multitude of colors from the flowers in bloom. Borz joined up with Ivram at the evening meal. He seemed downcast. "Is something wrong, Borz? I don't recall you ever being quite so grim."

"Undecided might be a better word, Ivram. I have been talking to some of the other men. They say that the war has ended and a state of normalcy is beginning to return to the country, while we remain up here in the mountains. Look what someone brought up with them the other day." Borz reached into his shirt pocket and pulled out a folded piece of paper. He opened it up and flattened it out on the table and then slid it over to Ivram. It was a flyer proclaiming the reopening of the oil fields. The Russians seemed intent on restoring the production capabilities of the Chechen oil reserves as quickly as possible. Crews were desperately being sought to go to work. No questions were being asked of anyone with experience. Borz watched intently as Ivram read through it. When he finished Borz asked, "What do you think I should do?"

"We can't stay mountain goats forever. This phase of the battle is clearly over. The war may continue, as it has for hundreds of years. Who knows, we may be called upon to fight again, but in the meantime, we have our own lives to live. Actually, I have overstayed my usefulness to these people."

"That's just what I've been thinking. The sooner things can get back to normal, the sooner I can get my family to come home again. What are you going to do?"

I hear that the university will reopen in the fall. That's where I was supposed to be heading when this all started. I think I'll see if I can get in there now."

Shamil was in their camp that afternoon and they discussed these plans with him. "Yes, I agree with you. Many others have already made similar choices. What better way to prove to the Russians that they cannot defeat us! I would go back myself, but I'm a wanted man. Keep the faith, my friends and know that I will be here if you have need of me."

They made their way down from the mountains on foot. These journeys were still hard on Ivram, but he had become more expert at maneuvering on the artificial leg and had also developed a greater tolerance to the discomfort. What he really needed to do was to get back to a hospital and have the damn thing cleaned and serviced. At Urus-Martan Borz inquired about the fate of his car.

"Ah yes," the café proprietor replied, "we have been keeping it safe for you. Not here, of course. I will make a call and have it ready for you by the time you arrive in Groznyy."

They joined up with a group of other refugees also seeking to get back to their homes. A truck was available to taxi them into the city, where other transportation could be found to bring them to the outlying regions. With some effort, Ivram climbed up onto the bed of the truck and sat down next to Borz. "You haven't said a word all day, my friend. What's wrong?"

"It's as if my whole life is about to start from scratch. I have no home, no job, no family now except for you."

"You know you can stay with me as long as you like. That's assuming that I still have a home!"

"Yes, I am grateful for that. But I will need to find an apartment close to the University if I can teach there. It will be easier for me with this," he said, rapping on his leg.

"There's something else, isn't there Ivram?"

"Yes, you know me well enough by now. It's Tapa. I haven't seen her for over two months. She must have gone home already. I don't even know where that might be. I wonder if I'll ever see her again?"

"That, my friend, is a matter best left to the Almighty to determine. If it is his will, then it will be. If not, it is all for the best."

There were twenty men, women and children aboard the flatbed truck. A general hubbub of happy chatter persisted throughout the ride into Groznyy as they anticipated their return to home and family. The truck entered the city and immediately a pall was cast over all of the people. They had seen pictures from time to time and heard stories, but the overall magnitude of the devastation was totally mind numbing. Tears welled in the eyes of many, men and women alike. It was like seeing a once beautiful young woman suddenly transformed by illness into a withered old hag. And there was a stench, the smell of death and decay.

The truck drove past block upon block of destroyed buildings. Whole apartment complexes without front walls like massive dollhouses open to expose the furnishings inside. In other cases it was only the front wall that remained, just like theatrical props Ivram had seen in stories about movie making. A few children scampered over piles of debris and here and there old men and women picked through the rubble seeking lost treasures of a bygone era. Mostly, however, those they passed simply stood and stared back at them with vacant eyes.

The driver stopped not far from the old railroad station. Other trucks and buses congregated here to exchange riders. "I am going to Gudermos," the drive called back. Several of the riders stayed in place. The others clamored down and Borz went to find his car. Ivram stood in the midst of confusion and watched the unfolding vignettes of tearful family reunions. People carrying all sorts of possessions milled about seeking rides or family members.

Shortly Borz returned waving a set of keys. "We are in luck. The car is just down that alleyway, running better than ever!" As they headed back towards the alley Borz ran into some old acquaintances. They greeted each other with the customary hugs and Ivram was introduced all around.

"My God, Borz, you look so thin," one of the newcomers said.

"And what about you, my friend," Borz came back. "Are we not a strange collection of ghosts?"

They drove through Tolstoy-Yurt. Things looked about the same there as when Ivram had walked away seven months ago. Khasbulatov's presence had undoubtedly saved the town. Chervlënnaya had not been as fortunate. Many of the buildings bore the scars of artillery or tank shelling. Some burned out shells stood eerily next to perfectly undamaged homes and stores. There was no logical pattern to the destruction.

Thankfully, Borz' apartment building was still standing and relatively unscathed. The apartment itself had been broken into and generally ransacked. Anything of value had gone with his wife and family, so Borz was not too upset. The beds were still intact, which was all they really hoped for. "I think our days of sleeping on those terrible field cots many finally be over," Borz said with great satisfaction.

Things actually got better after they had spent about an hour trying to straighten up the place. There was a knock on the door. Since the lock had been forced open many months before, the door swung open on its own. A woman's voiced called into the room, "Hello, Borz is that you?" She was a frail old woman, probably in her late seventies, but who could be sure of such things these days. She carried herself well, considering all she must have gone through this past year.

Borz came to meet his visitor. "Mrs. Zakayev, do come in. Please pardon the mess. It seems I've had visitors while we were away!"

"Yes, I'm sorry about that. We did our best to keep the vandals out of the building, but the soldiers came through and demanded access into every apartment." The woman was holding a pile of bed linens and some towels. She had two pillows tucked under her arms. "Forgive me Mr. Dzasokhov, but after they broke into your door we thought it best to salvage as much of your belongings as possible. Here are some of your bed linens. When you're ready, please come downstairs and take back what you need. There's no hurry though. Make sure you get that door fixed first!"

"Mrs. Zakayev, you are an angel!" Borz gave the woman a big hug and relieved her of her burden. "Ivram, can you believe this, soft mattresses and fresh bed linens! Oh, excuse me, Mrs. Zakayev; allow me to introduce my good friend Ivram Gadayev. He will be staying with me for the time being. Ivram, Mrs. Z and her husband oversee this building, what's left of it anyway."

She eyed Ivram carefully. He was quite a vagabond these days, with unkempt hair and whiskers, not to mention the tattered and smelly clothes he was wearing. "You'll have to excuse us, ma'am. Borz and I have been camping in the mountains for several months. I guess we both could use a good bath."

"There's no hot water, I'm afraid, but the showers still work." Mrs.

Zakayev turned and made her way out of the apartment. Halfway down the hall she called back, "You must let the police know that you've come back, unless you're not planning on staying."

"Thank you, we will do that right away. We don't need any midnight visitors, do we?" Ivram continued the clean up, thinking back to how his own apartment looked after his release from prison. Borz sought out the local police patrol to report that he and Ivram would now be living in the apartment again. He returned waving a padlock and door hasp he had been able to buy at the local market. "This will have to do until I can get a new door installed."

Ivram retired that night and tried to recall the last time he had actually slept in a real bed. Before he could remember, he was sound asleep.

45

Borz was immediately hired on to begin the arduous task of rebuilding the oil fields. Chechen saboteurs seeking to deprive the Russians of this valuable natural resource had destroyed many of the pumps. Others had been the early targets of the Russian tanks. Now, both sides had an interest in putting things back in order as quickly as possible. This required sixteen-hour shifts, so Borz was rarely back in the apartment.

Ivram quickly tired of sitting around the apartment alone. He made his way back to Groznyy. He had held on to just enough money to rent a small room and retrieved what was left of the boxes he had stored at the Presidential Palace months before. The TV was gone of course, as well as most of his books, but his clothes were still there and a few pictures.

The Chechen State University occupied a stately three-story red brick building. Six large white columns graced the front portico. The upper façade was marred by the damage incurred from the artillery shelling and the columns were riddled with bullet holes. Many of the windows were still broken and black smoke stains clearly marked those rooms where fires had broken out. Still, the building remained serviceable and classes were scheduled to begin almost immediately. The Rektor was delighted to have Ivram join them in the computer sciences department. "I'm afraid, Mr. Gadayev, that you will be discouraged by the condition of our equipment. Much of what wasn't damaged seems to have been stolen."

"Really," Ivram replied. He thought it wise not to let on that he may have been responsible for at least a part of that. Classes began and the primary area of study the first few weeks entailed a crash course in computer repairs. With a handful of systems finally deemed operational, he began the more exciting part, at least for him, to teach DOS programming.

Ivram's classes were over for the day, but he was still in conference with one of his more promising students. He glanced up and noticed someone standing in the doorway of his office. It was Buvais Murot, wearing that same fur cap with an old army great coat unbuttoned and draped over his shoulders. The combination presented a massive figure. Ivram hurriedly dismissed his young charge and waved Murot in. "Buvais, it's good to see you again. The usman is well, I hope. I'm sorry that I'm not able to get back out there to see him. I still have no transportation."

Murot accepted his hand in greeting and then pulled Ivram into a tight bear hug. "Yes, the usman is well and sends you his blessing. You are missed, but we hear good things about you still."

"And just what brings you to the University? I don't suppose that you're planning to enroll."

Buvais laughed. "No, I was never a good student, I must confess. Shamil thought that you might be willing to serve as an intermediary. You've performed such services in the past I understand."

"What type of intermediary do you have in mind," Ivram asked rather cautiously.

"You are well acquainted with Ruslan Khasbulatov, is that not so?"

"Ruslan again! Buvais, my poor leg throbs every time I hear that name."

"I am sorry for that. As you must know, new elections are scheduled for the end of this year. Khasbulatov has announced his intention to seek the Presidency in opposition to Dudayev."

"Yes, I am aware of that much, although I really haven't spent much time following the news."

"We have no real love for Dzhokhar Dudayev either, I'm sure you know that too. He likes to wear his religion the way he wears his uniforms. It makes a nice impression for the people, but he can take it off when he retires to the privacy of his home. He is, however, the favorite of the people. A symbol of our national pride."

"Yes, I always deemed him to be a little too fanatical."

"Well, we are very concerned about many of the positions Ruslan has been taking. You must realize that he has stated his intention to renounce the secession as soon as he is elected. With Dudayev forced into the mountains and many of his followers still afraid to return to their homes, there is a very strong chance that he will be elected. You know what that would mean."

"Yes, we will once again be part of the Russian Federation. There was a time when I would have agreed with Ruslan, but that time is long past."

"There's more to it than that, I'm afraid. There are many Nokhchii who would rather die than see their homeland returned to the Russians. There are many who would kill any one who tried to make that happen. Do you understand?"

"You're telling me that he is going to be assassinated."

"Hopefully not! That would certainly not be in the interests of our country. It would only bring harsher reprisals from the Russians. That is what you must warn him about. He has a big ego, but he also has the best interests of the people at heart."

"I'm not sure that I would be welcomed back by him now, so I doubt if I could be an effective emissary."

"We think that you might. If anything, they will respect your neutrality in this matter. We need you to extend a warning to Mr. Khasbulatov. Tell him this is not a threat; please make that very clear, but it is a very important warning."

"Yes, of course. I'll have to find some way to get up there. If I can, I'll go tomorrow."

"Good. We have already arranged for someone to be outside your apartment tomorrow morning. Is nine o'clock too early?"

Ivram laughed at their efficiency. "That will be just fine!"

He tossed and turned all night. It was difficult to sleep with this new intrigue weighing on his mind. He rose early and reheated some coffee that had been left in the pot. It was terrible, but it did the job of rousing him. At nine he went downstairs and found a well-worn sedan waiting for him right in front of the door. He recognized the driver from the camps, a clean-shaven young man with sandy brown hair that he neatly parted across his forehead from right to left. Ivram climbed into the passenger seat of the car and nodded an acknowledgment to the driver. Little was said on the way up to Tolstoy-Yurt.

As expected, he received a cool reception. Several aides questioned him concerning the nature of his requested audience with Khasbulatov. They too were concerned about the possibility of an assassin finding his way in to their chief. Exasperated, Ivram said firmly, "Just tell Ruslan that I have come representing parties interested in the well-being of our country, parties not directly involved in the current political campaign."

At last he was ushered into Khasbulatov's office. Ruslan remained seated behind a large desk, piled high with papers. He wore a white collared shirt, open at the neck. A brown suede jacket was draped across the back of his chair. Without offering any formal greeting he began, "So Mr. Gadayev, or is it Professor Gadayev these days, am I to understand that Dzhokhar Dudayev has not sent you back to us as his lackey?"

"First, it is instructor, not professor, but thank you for the promotion. Second, I was never Mr. Dudayev's lackey and I think you know that. I have not seen the man since before I left here. Lastly, I am here representing independent parties, persons with a concern for both the national and the religious interests of the people."

"Of course, the religious zealots! I was not aware that you were now among the murids."

"Whether I am or not isn't a concern. Actually, our concern is your own personal well-being."

That full-faced grin emerged, displaying a row of white, but crooked teeth. "My well-being?"

"Yes Imranych. Now please hear me out. I have not been sent to issue any threat against you, I want to make that perfectly clear. But I have been asked to convey a very strong warning. Very strong, is that clear?" Ruslan nodded in the affirmative. The smile disappeared from his face. "Good! Whether you win or lose the upcoming election does not immediately concern certain people. They are convinced, and so am I for that matter, that if you should win you would not live to be sworn in as president."

Ruslan started to get up in anger. "How dare you come in..."

Ivram held up his hand and continued, "Remember, I have not come to make threats! Your assassination would benefit no one except, maybe, Yeltsin. Such an event would only trigger further military action by the Russians. That is something we all hope to avoid."

Khasbulatov sat back in his large leather desk chair and studied the man standing before him. "Garyk Ivramovich Gadayev, I have always admired your willingness to speak frankly. I thank you for that. You have said little but it gives me much to think about. Tell your friends, whomever they may be," he added with a smile, "that Ruslan Imranovich understands their warning and will take it under advisement." He rose and took Ivram's hand firmly and walked him out to the waiting sedan.

On the way back down to Groznyy the driver turned to him and said, "Things must have gone well for you to be smiling like that."

Ivram laughed and said, "I have no idea about that. It's just that he called me Garyk. It's been almost a year since I heard that name!"

46

Any doubts Ivram may have had concerning the viability of his visit to Tolstoy-Yurt were quickly put to rest three days later. Reading from a prepared statement, Ruslan Imranovich Khasbulatov appeared on the national television channel. In marked contrast to his customary boyish charm, he looked older, weary and downcast. He told his countrymen, "After long and careful consideration, I have decided to withdraw from the presidential contest. I can assure you that this decision was made with the best interests of our country in mind. I have decided to return to Moscow to write and possibly resume my former duties as a professor of economics." He endorsed no other candidates.

Ivram's life settled into a routine best described as mundane. He taught classes five days a week. Since he only had the lap top as his own equipment, he remained at the university long hours after his classes were completed to utilize the facilities there. He began to surf the net; amazed at the unlimited access this gave him to the entire world.

When he wasn't at the university, he was generally holed up in his apartment. This was a dreary one-room efficiency unit that was entirely sufficient for his personal needs. Two well-worn armchairs, a pedestal table and lamp graced the corner to the left as you entered. They suited his need for a comfortable place to read and provided Borz a place to sit on his infrequent visits. A single bed, rarely made, was pushed into the rear corner and next to that a modest chest of drawers. His one extravagance was a TV, which sat atop the dresser. A folding table with a single wooden chair occupied the center of the room. This served as desk, dining table and repository for anything and everything.

There was a small kitchen unit along the right side. The counter extended almost to the door. He rarely utilized the small stove and oven, choosing instead to frequent the few local restaurants that remained in business near the school. The refrigerator was stocked with only the bare essentials. The only window was on the left wall. It looked out onto a row of devastated buildings, so he tended to keep the shade pulled down as much as possible.

On the floor under the window he kept his prayer rug rolled up when not in use. He made a point of using it each morning as he began the new day and whenever he happened to be home during prayer times. At the university he participated in group prayer sessions with the other faculty and students who cared to join in. His new found faith was providing him with a sense of oneness with the Almighty and with the world about him and made it possible for him to go on day by day.

From time to time the Russians became targets for another round of guerrilla attacks. One could never be sure if this was Dudayev's doing or the work of one of the many splinter groups that had been spawned during the hostilities. Ivram sometimes thought he could detect the hand of Shamil at work and wondered how they were fairing up in the hills. At those times he would think about Tapa and about what she might be doing right then. He hoped that she had found someone new who would give her the love she deserved.

In April a new series of attacks on the Russians garrisoned in Groznyy began. Supply depots and motor pools were bombed during night raids. Ivram was detained at length for questioning. His relationship to Viktor, past association with Khasbulatov and suspected affiliation with Shamil made him a primary suspect. They held him at the police headquarters for close to 48 hours with little food and no sleep. His story remained consistent and they could produce no evidence against him, so the local authorities pressed for his release.

He returned home and immediately went to bed. When he finally woke up he wasn't sure how long he had been asleep. He wasn't even sure what day it was and hoped he hadn't jeopardized his position by missing too many classes. He flipped on the TV to orient himself. The screen filled with a picture of the president, dressed in his formal military uniform. It was his official state photograph. Somber music was playing and the off-screen announcer was reciting the official obituary of the national hero. Ivram learned that he had been killed the night before in a Russian rocket assault.

He had only met this man once and was never sure whether he liked him or not. He was too brash and arrogant at times. Ivram felt that the path he had chosen for his people was much too perilous. One need only look at the devastation in Groznyy to realize that. Still, Dudayev was the embodiment of Chechnya. The people referred to him as 'The Grey Wolf' because he was the symbol of their thirst for freedom and national identity. Now he was gone. Those bastards had killed him, just as they had killed Mama and the Gran, Viktor and all of his family. All of that pain rushed back into his soul. Ivram dropped to his knees and cried.

In honor of the fallen hero, a day of national mourning was declared. The university would be closed for two days. Ivram decided that he needed to get away; needed to reach out for the spiritual comfort he had found in the camp. He needed, he finally admitted, to find her.

Vlad was a young medical student who lived down the hall. After some cajoling, he agreed to give Ivram a ride down to Urus-Martan. All the way there Vlad harped on the sad state of current affairs. "I hate these sons-o'-bitches for what they're doing to us! How am I supposed to become a doctor when the university keeps shutting down like this? I've lost three whole semesters of work already. Even when we are in session there's barely enough equipment and supplies."

Ivram kept his thoughts to himself. Had he been like this young man once, he wondered. Hadn't he reacted to Colonel Pushkin in much the same manner? "You're interfering with my life!" Their country lay in ruins all about them as they drove; yet this youngster could only see that it was interfering with his life. How terribly disconcerting it was. He debated whether he should say something, not wishing to get into an argument with the boy. Finally, he asked, "What about your family, how have they faired through all of this?"

"All right, I suppose. My mother lives up north, near Kamyshev. We have a small farm. My sisters live in Volgograd. They're both doctors up there and I was planning on joining them. I should just transfer to the university there, but I'd probably lose all of the credits I have now and have to start all over again."

Ivram realized that this young man's family was most likely ethnic Russian. That would account for his indifference. Still, it was hard to imagine not being emotionally involved in the human drama that was being played out daily. As soon as they reached the outskirts of Urus-Martan, Ivram had the young man drop him off. "Thank you for the ride. Good luck with your classes!"

"Yes. If they ever start up again!" The young man executed a sharp U-turn and sped off back towards Groznyy.

"How very sad," Ivram said the words out loud. He shook his head and turned back toward the town. Actually, he didn't have a clue about where he should be going. He had heard little from anyone who belonged to Shamil's group since the meeting with Ruslan. He knew only that they continued to move about to avoid detection by the Russian authorities. He began to walk the streets of Urus-Martan, hoping that he might run into a familiar face. At first, he walked right past the small café, not recognizing it in the daylight. Something caused him to turn back and check it out. "Yes, this is the place!" He said with an air of triumphant discovery.

It was near mid-day and the place was crowded but subdued. A small television was on and the day-long eulogy for the fallen Dzhokar Dudayev continued. A young woman, a girl really, came to take his order. He suddenly realized how hungry he was. He ordered the chicken and potatoes and a large cup of coffee. The owner was not in sight. Ivram assumed that he was busy in the kitchen cooking for all of his guests. He asked the woman for a newspaper to read while he waited for his meal. Dudayev's picture, bordered in black, occupied the entire front page.

He sat reading the paper and sipping the strong black coffee she brought. It coursed through him and revived his senses. He kept a watchful eye on the room, searching each face to find someone he might know, someone who might let him know where Shamil's camp was. The meal was excellent, much better than what he had become accustomed to back in the city. He ordered more coffee and wondered how long he could stay here before they asked him to leave. The room emptied as the diners finished their meals and got back to their daily chores. About an hour passed. He had long since finished the paper; it was not very big to begin with. The waitress was no longer in the main room either, having retired to the kitchen soon after delivering his third coffee.

The kitchen door swung open and the owner peered into the room. His gravy stained apron protruded in front in keeping with his sizable girth. Slowly he approached Ivram, wiping his hands on a dish-towel. "Is there anything else I can get for you, sir? The young one's gone off for her break before we start up again for dinner."

"No, thank you. I realize that I've probably overstayed my welcome."

"Not at all, sir, you can sit there as long as you like. The coffee pot's back there, if you don't mind serving yourself."

"That's very kind of you," Ivram acknowledged by raising his cup. "I had hoped to run into some friends of mine. I'm sure you don't remember me, but I stopped in here one night over a year ago. I was with another man then and you let me have some painkillers. Someone from here was able to take us to where our friends were staying. I was hoping to do that again."

"Yes, I see," the owner said. He gave Ivram a good looking over. "So many strangers pass through here. Perhaps your friends may be in tonight, although what with all this funeral talk... You're welcome to stay on if you'd like." He threw the dishtowel over his shoulder and sauntered slowly back into the kitchen.

More time passed. Ivram tried not to look at the clock hanging on the wall by the kitchen door. He could swear that it sometimes moved backwards. Reluctantly, he availed himself of a fourth cup of coffee and found the place where he was able to relieve himself of the first three. He just got back to his seat when the door opened and three men entered. Ivram was delighted to recognize one of them as Aslan, his driver to Tolstoy-Yurt.

The three men stood by the door for a moment; each eyeing Ivram and exchanging whispered comments. They walked over to a corner table and sat so that they could all see him. Ivram realized that this was part of the security process. He assumed that the owner must have contacted someone, alerting them to the stranger looking to find his friends. These three had then been dispatched to check him out. He wasn't quite sure what the next step should be, but he decided it was time to take the initiative. He couldn't stand to drink another cup of coffee right now.

Without standing, Ivram looked over at the young man he knew and said, "Aslan, isn't it? I think I had the pleasure of your company not too long ago. Didn't you give me a ride up to Tolstoy-Yurt one morning?"

"Of course, Mr. Gadayev! Forgive me for not remembering where I had met you before."

"That's understandable," Ivram said, relieved that the wait was concluded. "I was wondering if you might still be available for a little chauffeur assignment?"

The driver rose from the table and walked over to Ivram. "I think that can be arranged, sir. Let's go outside where we can talk."

Ivram explained the purpose of his visit and the young man agreed that he could bring him up into the mountains. They drove for about an hour on dirt roads that twisted back and forth through the forest. After crossing a small stream the car entered a clearing. Several trucks and four-wheel drive jeeps were parked just into the tree line. "I'm afraid the road ends here," the young man said. "I've got to get back to town before it gets too dark. Just follow that foot trail. It'll take you a good forty-five minutes to an hour, but I'm sure someone will meet up with you along the way."

"Probably more like an hour I would imagine, thanks to this

damned leg of mine. But that's not your problem is it. Thank you very much."

Ivram began the ascent, keeping a lookout for a nice walking stick to help him on the way. The day had clouded over and the sun was now below the line of mountain ridges. What light filtered down through the trees created a patchwork of golden haze and darkness. He began to worry that he would soon be completely enveloped in the dark and unable to follow the trail. "Ivram, is that you, my friend!" His heart leaped, startled by the unexpected sound in this vast forest, as well as by the sheer joy of hearing a familiar voice. He looked up and saw the massive figure of Buvais. Two other men stood behind him.

47

As they walked up to the camp Buvais and Ivram discussed the major topic of the day—Dzhokhar Dudayev's death and its likely impact on the country. "It will be very difficult to find someone with his zeal to step forward and take his place," Murat said. "The Russians will certainly keep a tight rein on the political system for some time to come. We've become too fragmented for anyone to gain the same broad base of support. He was necessary and he will be missed."

They reached the present campsite as the evening meal was winding down. "I'm not sure if there will be any food left, but I'm sure there will be coffee if you'd like," Buvais offered.

Ivram held up both hands. "No coffee, thank you. I believe I had enough to last me a week down in the village this afternoon. Perhaps they might have some soup left."

There were many familiar faces in the mess tent. Ivram was greeted warmly, exchanging hugs with old acquaintances and getting introduced to new ones. He couldn't remember another time in his life when so many people had showed so much sincere friendship. "It is good to be home," he thought. Two old women scoured the kitchen and found what food was left for him to eat. All these faces, yet the one he hoped for wasn't among them.

Even sleeping on the cot again felt good. He slept soundly and woke to feel the brisk mountain air. Instead of the four walls of his apartment cramping him in, he was surrounded by the grandeur of the Caucasus. The aroma of fresh brewed coffee wafting down from the mess area woke him. There were more people gathering this morning then he had seen last night. He again received warm greetings from old friends. Again he looked for her but she was nowhere to be found. He started to drink his coffee, but in this old familiar environment it made him think about her that much more. He grabbed up a biscuit and left the tent.

Shamil was making his customary rounds. He saw Ivram and threw up his arms in delight. "Greetings, my brother. The Almighty one has again blessed us with your presence. It is good to see you." His arms enfolded Ivram and he held him in close. He whispered into his ear, "Your coming back today is confirmation that He has blessed the plans we have been making. We will talk later."

It was time for the morning zikr. There was no building at this site large enough, so the ceremony was held out in the open. A field had been cleared for the purpose. The music had begun already and there were over forty men, women and children coming into the field from various mountain paths. Ivram reached inside his jacket and pulled out the cap she had given him. He had acquired others during the past year, but always saved this one for special occasions. He clapped his hands and began repeating the mantra. He swayed and danced around the circle with the others. He was supposed to be moving ever closer to the mystic unity, instead, he found himself searching the faces looking for Tapa. He lingered on the prayer rug after the others began to disperse. Ivram knelt with his eyes closed, seeking the Almighty's forgiveness for not being able to empty his mind completely of the things of this world. "Make me one with you," he prayed.

He rose to find Buvais and Shamil standing on the main path waiting for him. As usual, Shamil's head was wrapped in a black linen headdress that fell over the shoulders of an old gray jacket. Buvais' head was crowned as usual by his fur hat. "I'm sorry. I didn't realize that you were here."

"Never apologize for being in communion with the true God, my son. That is our primary purpose in life." Shamil put his arm around Ivram and they walked back towards a small building. It looked to be of recent construction, thrown together quite hastily Ivram imagined. The exterior was unpainted plywood, with a minimal amount of finishing just sufficient enough to keep out the elements. Tar paper covered the roof. The interior was not much better. The wooden studs were still exposed, although a few tapestries had been hung to block the drafts. The door opened into a small central room with several chairs and two long folding tables. One was in the middle of the room and Ivram guessed it served as the conference table for staff meetings. The other was pushed back against a side wall and piled high with papers, books and boxes. Four doors, one on each side and two in the back opened into small living quarters.

The usman took a seat at the head of the table, facing the door. Buvais pulled up a chair and sat to his right. Shamil motioned for Ivram to take a seat on his left. Two men dressed in camouflage field uniforms and army boots came out of one of the side rooms and also sat down on either side of the table. Ivram recognized them as the ones who had accompanied him back up the hill last night.

"Gentlemen," Shamil began, "we have been discussing ways to bring the plight of the Nokhchii home to the Russian people. They watch on the television as our buildings burn and our women and children bleed before their eyes. They say that they are greatly shocked about all this and they march in protest. What good has that done?" Shamil slammed his hand down hard against the table for impact. "None! Their soldiers still patrol our country and now they have killed Dzhokhar. That pig Yeltsin will soon be pressing harder than ever for us to sign his fucking treaty and subjugate us to them once again. It is time for us to press the attack in earnest. Are we not agreed?"

Ivram looked around the table, realizing that the others had all heard this speech before. Buvais was staring at him, looking to see what his reaction to this proclamation would be. Other eyes were also focusing in on him. "I assume that you would like to hear my opinion on this. I don't know why. I am just a visitor today. Surely there are others in a better position to give you counsel."

The usman tapped on the back of Ivram's hand. "You humble yourself unnecessarily, Ivram. Remember that I said it was the will of the Almighty that brought you back to us, just as it was his will a year ago. You were of great service to us then and I think that you will be of even greater service now."

"If that's the case, then he certainly knows much more than I do." Ivram forced a laugh but realized how seriously the others had taken the usman's remarks. "To be honest with you, I just don't see how we can be anything more than a minor inconvenience to our oppressors. What little remains of our country will be completely destroyed in retaliation. I'm afraid that in the end more Chechen blood will be shed than Russian."

"Well said, Ivram, that is exactly our thoughts on this matter," Shamil's eyes gleamed. He reminded Ivram of an old professor he once had. He was laying some foundation for Ivram to build upon, but Ivram had no idea where this was going to lead. Shamil went on, "You are right, too much Chechen blood and too many Chechen homes. It is time to burn Russian homes and spill Russian blood on Russian soil. We must strike outside of our own country and let those bastards know first hand what pain and grieving are all about."

"Our military force may be able to fight a holding battle, popping in and out of mountain hideaways to surprise the Russians from time to time, but surely you can't think that it could launch a major offensive."

"Not an offensive, not even a series of guerrilla attacks. No, Ivram, I am talking about one sudden and devastating blow, struck deep in the very heart of their country. I'm talking about detonating a nuclear device in one of their major cities. Let them die by the tens of thousands for a change!"

Ivram was sure that his mouth must be hanging open as he looked hard into Shamil's eyes. He realized that the man was very serious, as were the others around him. He shivered involuntarily from a sudden chill. "That would mean instant reprisals. No one would be left alive!"

Shamil again tapped lightly on Ivram's hand. "Don't be so sure. That is a distinct possibility, of course, but are we not engaged in a jihad already? If it is the will of the one true God, then so be it. However, I think that such a blow will so horrify the Russians that they will realize the foolhardy ways of Mr. Boris Yeltsin in dealing with all of the Moslem republics. He will be dragged out of office, possibly even executed in public. Remember, there are still many Chechens with great influence in control of Moscow's underground economy."

Ivram knew about the so-called Russian Mafia. They had developed a parallel government in many ways. He also knew that a number of Chechen nationals were rumored to be in charge. In fact, he had worked with some of them on Khasbulatov's staff. Still, he was not convinced that they could dissuade a massive retaliation if Shamil's plan were to be carried out. No one spoke for some moments. Ivram looked around the table, studying each of these men. They, in turn, fixed their gaze on him, anxious to learn his response to the proposal. Ivram returned his focus to Shamil. "Do you actually have such a weapon at your disposal?"

With a broad grin, Shamil fired back his response. "Actually, Ivram Gadayev, we were thinking that this is exactly where you might be of assistance. We were about to send for you to come here, but the Almighty led you back to us himself."

"You're kidding, aren't you! You can't honestly think that I can lay my hands on an atomic bomb just like that." Ivram knew that they weren't kidding. He could see the look in their eyes. These four men were serious, deadly serious! Eight eyes bored into him, waiting.

"Oh my God." Ivram brought his hands up to his forehead and placed both elbows down on the table for support. He stared down at table without actually seeing it, mustering all of his conscious thought to the issue before him. Right or wrong was not the issue; it was strictly a matter of feasibility. The others sensed that and allowed him the time he needed to think. Without looking up, he finally began to speak again. "This isn't the same as ordering supplies to be loaded onto a delivery truck. The requisition forms don't have a line marked ATOM-IC BOMB that you can just check off. You realize that of course?"

Shamil spoke as if to console a petulant child. "Yes, my friend, we understand that this will be a very difficult task indeed. It is a job that requires your special abilities. It is perhaps the one for which you have been training most of your life.

Ivram thought about that for a moment. Could the Almighty have had this plan in mind for such a long time? Was this the reason he had been selected to receive all of the special military and computer training? Was it the will of the one true God that he had been assigned to the deactivation task force? He alone knew more about the security codes and sequences needed to deactivate and remove nuclear warheads from missile silos scattered across the old Soviet Union than any two or three others did.

He looked up, brushing one hand over his beard. When he spoke, it was as the instructor. "The security for these things is incredibly tight. Even now with so much chaos rampant through out the system. We need to find the weakest link. Actually, we must first identify where these devices are still deployed. It's been a long time since I had anything to do with that. However, I doubt that they've revised the procedures. If significant changes have been made to the programs, I may not have any access at all."

Shamil and the others concentrated on him intently. They had become the students and he was the master, dispensing his vast store of knowledge. Shamil smiled, knowing that Ivram had already identified the problems and was already focusing on finding the proper solution.

"For any plan to have the slightest chance to succeed there's the secrecy issue. The fewer people that know about this and are actually involved with this project the better. At the same time, we are going to need assistance along the way. We can't just jump in a truck and drive across the border, especially these days. We'll need reliable allies who can supply us with a truck and shielding to avoid radiation detection devices."

Buvais spoke for the first time. "Yes we have given that some thought already. It was mentioned that we have certain friends in Moscow these days. Those friends have a great interest in certain procurement matters. If I am not mistaken, the item we are discussing here usually comes packaged in clusters of three or four. Is that correct?" Ivram nodded that it was. "Yes, I thought so. We have need of only one device or bomb, if you chose. There are those who would welcome the opportunity to acquire the others for their inventory value. Such a commodity would command a very hefty price in the world market I am told."

"This is incredible. It isn't enough that you want me to find an atomic bomb, you want me to get my hands on four!" After a momentary pause, Ivram snorted a chuckle and shook his head. "Actually, the logistics may not be altogether different. If we can find one, we most likely will find the others!"

"Good, so we are all agreed!" The usman stood up, an obvious sign to those present that the meeting had been dismissed.

"Please understand," Ivram added as an after thought, "I have only agreed to undertake a feasibility study at this point. I have no idea if this is even possible."

"I understand," Shamil told him as they walked toward the door. "Just let us know what you will require."

"Time, mostly. The equipment I need is all at the university. It will be better for me to work from there. I think I'm being watched. They arrested me last week to investigate any possible involvement I may have had in recent raids. They know or at least they suspect my ties to you. For that reason alone it's wise that I don't just disappear right now. Don't worry, they won't be able to detect what I'll be working on."

48

Ivram's mind was racing. As he developed each new series of mental checklists, he became more excited about the challenges that lay before him. This was a computer problem that needed to be solved, nothing more. Once he had a solution, he would leave it to the others to carry out its implementation.

As anxious as he was to get back and get started, he still had others reasons for remaining. He had come for religious solace and wanted to attend the afternoon instruction. He had also come hoping to find her. It was apparent that Tapa wasn't here, so he sought out anyone who might know where she had gone. He ran across several of the women with whom she used to be friendly. "No, we have not seen her for many months," he was told. It was the consensus that she had gone to live with some aunt or cousin. Some said it was in Ossetia, others south, in Georgia or Dagestan. He met a man who had a brother. "I seem to recall him telling me that she was with them, but I can't remember for certain. He's fighting with a band of guerrillas off in the east, near the border out past Kirovauya. That area has come under heavy attack in recent weeks. I haven't heard from my brother for some time."

He stayed in the camp until late afternoon. There was a contingent heading back down the mountain. Most lived around Groznyy, so he was invited to join them. On the walk down the mountain and in the truck that evening he said little. He responded to their direct questions and laughed at the little jokes, but his mind was occupied elsewhere. He had come seeking companionship and spiritual renewal and had been granted that. He had come seeking some purpose for his life and that also had been given to him. He had come hoping to find her and realized that he had missed the opportunity months ago and would never see her again.

Ivram determined that caution was the best criteria for the job at hand. He suspected that his past forays into the army's database had been detected, since his access had been immediately shut down. This time he needed to be more circumspect, so as not to arouse their interest until it was too late to deter the mission.

He began to build an elaborate network of interlocking web sites through which he could channel his activity. This would mask both the number and duration of hits that the Russians might detect and diffuse the points of origin. To accomplish this, he decided to work through the government's own web server at IKI RAN. To the casual observer this would create the impression that his inquiries were merely the result of one government agency seeking data from another.

He spent several hours each day laying the initial groundwork. With this completed, he logged onto the main web site at the Russian Academy of Science. Katryn had told him that she was working there, but he suspected that she might actually be in charge of setting up and overseeing the internet system. If so, she would have almost unlimited access. Since they had worked together as a team for so many years, he knew how she thought. Consequently, he would be able to figure out and by-pass whatever security systems and access requirements she had built in.

He began by searching for her name. Katryn Gadayev wasn't listed anywhere. Odd, he thought. Then he tried under Moldatin. The information burst onto his screen. He sat there for a while staring at the name—KATRYN YURIANA MOLDATIN. All of the old emotions rushed back upon seeing her name emblazoned on the screen. It was one final slap in the face, the fact that she was denying even his name now. What about Georgi, he wondered.

Over the course of several days he logged on and off, never staying on-line for more than five minutes at a time. Occasionally he down loaded parts of her programming onto one of the school's computers. This allowed him time to study its composition in greater detail. Her personality conveyed itself through them and gave him a sense that he was once again working alongside of her. In fact, he caught himself one afternoon in the middle of dialing her number to ask her why she had chosen a certain programming format.

He created his own web site and installed it within her system. It was officially designated as the home page for the Federation Center for Ethnic Studies and Autonomous Governance. He was able to back date its existence for more than a year and downloaded a series of erudite papers and studies covering a wide range of ethnic issues, all readily available on other government databases. It included page upon page of statistical spreadsheets and census data.

Buried in all of this was an article on the mass deportation of the

Chechen and Ingush peoples under Stalin. The commentary was fourteen pages long. Double-clicking on the page number found at the top of page six opened a link to the Russian Federation's Supreme Ballistic Missile Command. It gave immediate access to the total deployment of strategic nuclear weaponry. Through this any active site could be reprogrammed using the access codes he had originally installed years before. He ran a test of the program to insure it was operational, then waited three days to see if his access had been detected and closed down. It was still live. They were ready to proceed!

Buvais had given him a telephone number to call whenever he needed transportation to the camp. Ivram cleared time on his schedule and made arrangements to head up into the mountains. The next day he rose early to prepare for the trip. Just as he was rinsing out his coffee cup there was a knock on the door. It was Aslan, the same young man who had served as his driver in the past. "Well, hello there. I'm sorry to make a habit of requiring your services!"

"It's no problem, Mr. Gadayev. I guess you could say it's my job. I'm one of the few people with a car these days and they help me get enough gasoline to keep it running. Can I help you with anything?"

"Yes, actually," Ivram said, turning to several bags that he had arranged by the door. "This one contains some computer equipment and printouts. I'm afraid it's a bit on the heavy side. I hope someone can assist me on the final leg up the mountain."

"You're in luck today sir. I'm going up to the camp myself."

They were at the camp in time for the mid-day prayers and instruction meeting. When it was over Ivram made his way to the mess tent to get something to eat. Before he had a chance to find a table, one of the captains who had taken part in the earlier discussion called him aside. "Come, you can eat while we talk." He motioned for Ivram to follow and they headed for the small building that served as the conference room.

Buvais was there already, as well as the second captain. Ivram had never been formally introduced to either of those two. They were seated in the same positions they had occupied four weeks earlier. Ivram joined them at the table. There was a light rapping on the door and Buvais called out, "You may enter." It was a young woman carrying a tray of food. At first Ivram thought it might be Tapa, silhouetted as she was by the bright light in the doorway. His heart fluttered for a moment then suffered a striking blow as he realized that it was not her. The girl brought in a large crock filled with the hearty stew that was being served outside, along with a basket of biscuits and a pot of fresh coffee. There were bowls and utensils for five.

"I see that you have gotten yours already, Buvais said, but you are welcome to take more if you like." He served himself from the crock set before him and passed it along to the others. "I hope you don't mind mixing business with the midday meal."

"No, not at all," Ivram responded.

As they began to eat the door opened again, admitting the usman. The streaks of white were becoming more prominent in his beard and mustache. He still wore a black headdress, but had opted for a long white linen robe in deference to the warming season. Shamil walked across the room and Ivram noticed that beneath the robe he wore a pair of military camouflage boots. "Good, I see you have started without me. It's always difficult to get away from the afternoon meetings without having to stop and talk to at least ten different people." Shamil took his place at the head of the table and reached for the stew pot. "Ah yes, I see we have another gourmet treat today." He piled the stew high atop a biscuit. "So, Ivram Gadayev, I see you have finally rejoined us. Tell me what our procurement specialist has been up this past month."

"I have not been idle, rest assured of that, Mansur. For this plan of yours to be successful we must be very circumspect. Any detection by the Russians will close all of the access I have gained into their system."

"Yes, of course, Ivram, we understood that this would take time." The usman patted him on the shoulder to assure him that he had only been kidding him.

"But it was time well spent, I think you'll all agree. I was able to locate a number of sites that are suitable for our purpose. I was looking for small installations with a minimum of security. I would recommend one that's just north of Qyzylorda."

Shamil shrugged his shoulders and looked about the room at the others. "I don't know this place, what did you call it, Kwazilora?"

"Qy-zy-lor-da," Ivram repeated slowly, not sure himself of the correct pronunciation. "Here, let me show you." He pushed away his bowl and cup to make room for his laptop computer. Flipping it open he quickly tapped out some keystroke commands and a silver-green map flashed onto the screen. "Here it is, on the Syr Darya."

Shamil studied the map for a moment, then pushed the computer around so that Buvais could get a better look. His adjutant located the objective and looked over to Ivram with some surprise. "Ivram, that's in Southern Kazakhstan! It's got to be more than fifteen hundred kilometers away. Couldn't you find something a bit closer?

"Closer yes, safer no." Ivram had anticipated this objection and was quite ready to defend his decision. "Certainly anything close to

Chechnya will be heavily guarded these days. They are concerned that someone will try to do exactly what we are attempting. Even further north the Russians have maintained a well disciplined security system. Things are a lot slacker in the independent republics. The Kazahkis are responsible for the overall security, with only a small contingent of Russian troops permitted to perform the on-site surveillance. They just entered into a twenty-year lease agreement to keep the Baikonur Cosmodrome under Russian control. The site I've selected actually falls within that agreement. It's been less than two months, so the lines of communication are still being redrawn. In the interim, most of the Russian resources will be concentrated on the space center and the Kazahkis won't be allowed near the missile sites."

Shamil nodded his head in agreement. "Yes, you may be correct in that assessment, my friend. I think that you used your time well!" Now, tell us what resources you will need to bring with you on this little expedition."

Ivram suddenly went pale. "Surely you weren't thinking that I was going on this mission? With this damned leg of mine, I'd only serve to slow things down. I've set up the computer so that almost anyone with a little training can handle it."

"Nonsense, Ivram. We all know that in operations such as this you must always be prepared for the unexpected. You, my friend, are the best person, no make that the ONLY person who can immediately adapt to such unforeseen developments of a technical nature. You have both the technical and the military training to accomplish the mission. You will be in charge!"

49

Once they agreed upon the broad concept of the mission, Shamil excused himself. "Gentlemen, I can see that there are many details that will need to be worked out. The four of you are much better equipped for this than I am. Please continue working while I go about my other responsibilities here. Buvais will keep me informed of your progress." He rose and shook Ivram's hand. "Once again I thank the Almighty one for bringing you to us." They spent the rest of the day discussing the tactical plans and logistical requirements of the mission.

The man seated to his left had gone into the back room and could be heard rummaging around looking for something. He came back carrying several tubes containing geological survey maps. "I'm sure we'll find something in here better than that computer screen of yours. I was going cross-eyed trying to make anything out on that."

As he started to spread one of the maps out on the table Ivram said, "I'm sorry, but you know I don't think I ever learned your name. It's not a secret is it?"

"Certainly not. I am Ilyas and this is my cousin Hadzhi." He turned and shook Ivram's hand. Hadzhi rose and reached across the table to grasp his hand. It was a strong firm grip from a large hand. Hadzhi added, "We come from the region around Naderechnaya. Both my cousin and I served as officers in the Soviet Army special commando forces."

"Then you saw action in Afghanistan also?

Hadzhi' expression became grim. "Yes, we had a hand in the slaughter of fellow Moslems, I'm afraid. That's when I decided to get out. I joined the Chechen militia and was commanding a company at the outbreak of the hostilities here. I spent several days with your brother Viktor. He was a good man."

"So how did you wind up here?"

"I guess you can blame that on me," Ilyas said. "I stayed in the army until three years ago. I drifted back down to Chechnya after that. When the Russians invaded, I linked up with group of independent guerrillas and joined in the resistance outside of Urus-Martan. Our usman was killed so we joined forces with Shamil's followers. A few months back I ran into Hadzhi and convinced him to come along with us."

"That didn't take much convincing." Hadzhi picked up the narrative. "The militia were content to just hold the Russians at bay by that time. I still wanted to press the attack. The independent groups are the only ones doing that."

"Well, we are delighted that you joined us." Buvais' tone indicated that it was time to end the small talk and get on with the business at hand. Turning to Ivram he continued, "Hadzhi will accompany you on the procurement mission to Qyzylorda. That part of the trip entails the greatest likelihood for conflict. I anticipate that no more than two additional members will be required for the team."

"Yes, that sounds good." Ivram nodded toward Hadzhi and added, "I'm delighted to know you'll be alongside of me. Might I suggest that one of the other team members be fluent in the local Kipchak dialect."

Hadzhi looked over to Murat, who shrugged his shoulders and responded, "An interesting request. I can see where that might come in handy. Still, it may be a difficult order to fill."

"As long as we're speaking about filling orders..." Ivram shuffled through the stack of papers he had brought with him. "Here's a laundry list of items I thought the team would need. Of course, I wasn't planning on going along when I made this up. The plan I envisioned calls for us to travel as a Russian Army inspection team. This will require proper uniforms and documentation. The most important thing is a means of transportation, particularly for the return leg. Since we will be carrying four nuclear devices by then, we will need shielding from radioactivity, not only for our protection, but to prevent possible detection along the way.

Buvais took careful notes. He would have to coordinate the acquisition of these items and their delivery to some central meeting point. The list was embellished by Hadzhi, who added the small arsenal that they might need to meet any and all contingencies. Ivram had been correct several weeks earlier when he said that they couldn't just ride out of Chechnya armed to the teeth and ready for bear. No, they would need to slip away individually, then meet up someplace near the Russian-Kazakhstan border. This is where their allies in Moscow would be needed.

They worked into the early evening. Buvais made a final run down of what had been agreed upon. He looked at Ivram and Hadzhi sitting across from him and shook his head. Laughing, he told them, "One thing is certain. If the two of you plan on passing yourselves off as Russian Army officers you're going to have to lose those beards!"

Ivram ran his hand over the full growth of hair covering his cheeks and jaw. He smiled and nodded in agreement. "Yes, I guess the time for mourning has finally come to an end. It is now time for action."

Ilyas began to gather up all of the papers they had spread before them. He ripped them up and tossed the pieces into the small stove that provided heat to the room. As they were leaving, Buvais caught hold of Ivram's arm and said, "I hope that no one ever gains access to that little black box you're carrying." He tapped lightly on Ivram's laptop.

"Don't worry yourself. I've set it up to immediately erase all my files if the proper access sequences haven't been entered within sixty seconds. You just have to hope I never forget what those are!"

Ilyas and Hadzhi invited Ivram to stay with them in the small cottage they shared up the mountain. The offer was graciously accepted. There was a wood stove in one corner of the main room. It not only provided heat, but also permitted them to keep a pot of coffee brewing at all times. Even though it was nearing the end of May, they were about 3,500 feet above sea level here and a night chill had settled in. Ivram welcomed the warmth of the cottage. It was similar in composition to the one they had just left. Ilyas occupied the small room to the left of the main room and Hadzhi the one to the right. Aslan, his frequent chauffeur and another young recruit named Mairbeck, shared one of the larger rooms in the rear. The other room was set up with four bunk beds, so it could accommodate as many as eight. Tonight Ivram would be the only occupant.

"I guess you'd call this the bachelor quarters," Ilyas said. "People tend to come and go a lot around here. It's been quiet lately. The men have either relocated their families to new homes or gone back down to the city to resume their lives."

Ivram slept soundly, thanks to the refreshing mountain air, and arose the next morning to find that three of the others had already left. Aslan sat at the long wooden table in the front room, sipping on his coffee and reading. "I didn't realize it was so late," Ivram said as he entered the room.

"No, it's only a quarter to seven. The others had to go on a reconnaissance mission this morning. They left here hours ago."

In spite of his own reason for being here, Ivram had almost forgotten the duel function of this community. Not only was this a religious retreat, it also served as a para-military outpost. It was a strange mixture of the insane and the sublime. He removed his artificial leg to take advantage of the small shower unit and nearly fell when the initial blast of icy water hit his body. He hopped out and began toweling off. From the other room Aslan called in, "Sorry, I forgot to warn you that we have no hot water. We keep a tank up on the roof. The sun does a good job of warming it during the day, but first thing in the morning, it's really quite cold."

"Yes," Ivram called back, "I certainly I found that out!"

Ivram made his way down to the main area of the camp and found it to be in quite a stir this morning. He joined a group of men he knew informally and learned the news. The interim president had agreed to accept Yeltsin's offer of a cease-fire. Peace negotiations were scheduled to begin in two weeks. From the tone of the announcement, it was likely that Chechnya's proclamation of independence would be withdrawn.

After morning prayers Shamil and Buvais came over to Ivram. "I assume you heard the news," Murat inquired.

"Yes, but I'm not sure what it all means."

Shamil placed his arm across Ivram's shoulders. "It means, my friend, that we have far less time than we counted on. It means you must be ready to implement our plans before the end of June!"

In the afternoon they met again to go over the plans. Ilyas was no longer part of the group, since he would not be going with them. Shamil was apprised of what had been discussed and agreed that they had developed a sound strategy. "All that remains is to decide where we intend to deliver this little surprise of ours."

Hadzhi spoke up first. "Isn't it Moscow? Certainly it's the obvious choice. The Russian's have destroyed our capital city. Shouldn't we do the same to theirs?"

"Yes, the thought of Moscow reduced to ashes has a certain appeal," Ivram agreed, "but I do still have a wife and son there."

The usman shook his head to discourage the idea. "Unfortunately, we are going to have to rely upon alliances with certain individuals whose base of operation is in Moscow. I don't think they would respond kindly to our returning the favor by destroying their homes and families. Besides, we will need to have a government in place with which to negotiate our terms."

Buvais was in favor of Volgograd as the objective. "Remember that this city was once named Stalingrad. What could be more fitting than to invoke the memory of that bastard butcher of our people? We would finally gain retribution for the Great Repression."

The historic connection did seem to favor this choice. It was Ivram who finally turned their attention away from that city. As usual, he had his laptop open on the table in front of him and was keying in commands as the others talked. He was looking at terrain and atmospheric maps. "According to these projections, it would be possible for the radioactive fallout from an explosion in Volgograd to carry southwest. The probability is small, but Chechnya could be placed at risk. It's more likely that Dagestan would be affected. It's certain that Kazakhstan would suffer. Can we alienate all of the independent Moslem states?"

"No, we can't," Shamil affirmed. "That is a very good point. We are seeking to gain world sympathy for the unjust oppression of our people. We cannot alienate any other country, especially a Moslem one."

They threw out names of other cities, discussing them as they would an article of clothing or a menu selection in some restaurant. There was no thought at all given to the fact that their decision would impact the lives of hundreds of thousands, perhaps millions of people. Genocide had been inflicted upon them for centuries, it was simply time for some payback.

Ivram couldn't recall who mentioned it first, probably because they had called it by its old name, Leningrad, initially forgetting that this had been changed in 1991 to St. Petersburg. The more they talked about it, the more they liked the idea. "It is the second largest city and a primary seaport," Hadzhi stated. "It is a major component of the Russian economy."

Ivram concurred, "It is far enough north not to pose a threat to anything other than Russian soil. More important, it's the embodiment of Russia's heritage. It was the home of the tsars, the very root of the oppression of our people. The fact that the city has once again assumed the name St. Petersburg symbolizes the end of the Soviet era and the reemergence of Russian ethnic supremacy.

Shamil stood and looked at the other three men seated at the table. "So, we are all agreed, it is to be St. Petersburg?"

"It's the perfect target," Buvais agreed. He stood and the others followed. "St. Petersburg!" He thrust out his right hand into the center of the group. Shamil, Ivram and Hadzhi clasped their hands over his. "ST. PETERSBURG!" they all repeated in unison.

"I'm just glad I'll be going there in June," Ivram said. "It's the coldest fucking place I've ever been to in my life!"

50

With the military and logistical details in the hands of Hadzhi and Buvais, Ivram headed back to Groznyy to await the go ahead. The term had nearly ended and he advised the Prorector of the Science Department that he would be away for the summer. He didn't mention that it was unlikely that he would be back at all. By mid-June the cease-fire had all but failed. In spite of, or more likely because of the on-going peace negotiations, the various radical groups increased commando raids on the Russian forces. This led inevitably to Russian reprisals, not always targeting the parties involved in the hostilities. On two separate occasions Ivram was again brought into police headquarters and interrogated. After several hours of grueling questioning, he was released each time.

Ivram was alone, as usual, one evening reading in the corner of his room. The knock on the door puzzled him, coming as late as it did. He was delighted to find Borz standing outside when he opened the door. Borz had rid himself of his beard, but he still sported a full mustache that curled around his lips and dipped down below his mouth. "Borz, what a wonderful surprise! What brings you here so late at night?"

"Ah, my little brother, it is good to see you again!" Borz clasped his friend in a great bear hug. "I'm sorry, it's been too long since my last visit. I've been working extra shifts and when I'm not in the fields I'm usually asleep." Ivram ushered him inside and offered him the other chair. "No, thank you, I can't stay long. I plan on driving all night, if I can. I'm heading down to see my family. Can you believe that a year and a half have gone by? I've taken a month's leave that I've accumulated and plan on reacquainting myself with them. If all goes well with the peace talks, I may actually bring them home again!"

"I'm happy for you, Borz. You're lucky to have a family to return to and I wish you good luck." Ivram gave him another hug, holding him close for a long time. "I don't know if I've ever thanked you for all you did for me."

"What I did was nothing special. Certainly I owed that much to the memory of my sister and my friend Viktor. You have thanked me already by your friendship. I look forward to introducing you to my wife and the children. I've written them often about their 'Uncle Ivram.'"

"Yes, I would love to meet them. Unfortunately Borz, I don't know if I'll be here when you get back. In fact, I don't know if we will ever meet again."

Borz was stunned by this news. "Ivram, what are you talking about? This sounds much too final for my liking." Now he did take the seat that had been offered to him. "Come, my friend, tell your big brother what has been happening since we last met. I suspect that there have been some very strange developments."

Ivram brought some coffee over for both of them and sat down next to his friend. Without divulging too many of the specifics, he related some of the recent events concerning his return to the camp and the fact they were about to set out on a journey that would strike a blow for the Nokhchii in the very heart of the Russians.

"I can imagine that such a plan entails great risk, Ivram, but you make it sound inevitable that you will not be coming back when it's over."

"Yes, Borz, I have the feeling that it is His will that I shall not be returning. I can see no purpose for my life beyond this mission. It's odd, but I am truly at peace with that."

"But surely your position at the university has given meaning to your life."

"At one time computers *were* my life. Lately, I've just been going through the motions. At least as far as my classes are concerned."

"And whatever became of your young friend, what was her name?"

"Tapa. I told you once that there would never be room in my heart for anyone other than Katryn. I told her that too. I was wrong, Borz, but by the time I realized that she was gone. This, too, seems to be the will of the Almighty. If she were still here . . ." He paused for a moment then sighed with regret, "but she isn't."

"Who am I to argue with the will of the Almighty one. Still, I think I shall pray that He shows you some other path Ivram. A path, I hope, that leads you back home again."

"Ah, there's the point, Borz! Where is my home?"

June was drawing to a close and Ivram hadn't heard from anyone. He was beginning to wonder if the camp had come under attack and the usman either captured or killed. Perhaps they had simply abandoned this plan as foolhardy and just not bothered to let him know.

His classes ended and the idle time was beginning to grow on him. He debated whether to make contact and go back up into the mountains. He decided against this, suspecting that he was still under surveillance.

He spent the morning at the university logged onto the computer. At least he could enjoy himself while they made him bide his time. He briefly ran some spot checks on his programs. If they didn't hurry, security at the missile site would be beefed up.

No one he knew was in this morning, so he attended to his midday prayers alone in his office. Then he decided to go for a walk and get something to eat along the way.

He tried to walk at least five kilometers each day. He was also doing sit-ups at night trying to get his body in some semblance of good physical condition. The plan didn't call for any strenuous activity, but he wanted to be ready just in case. If he could, he preferred walking without a cane. However, on these long walks he found he needed the support after the first two or three kilometers.

Ivram made his way down to the Sunzha River and decided to forego the paved walkways. Better be ready to walk cross-country, he told himself. He followed the river as best he could, forcing himself to ascend and descend the steepest embankments. He fell twice, cursing his leg and the Russians who'd caused him this aggravation in the first place. His hands were muddy, not to mention his pants. "Well, that's enough of this for today," he said aloud. He struggled up to the street and looked around, trying to get his bearings. That task was made difficult because so many of the old landmarks had been destroyed. He could see the Presidential Palace rising high above the other derelict buildings and made off in that general direction. He soon passed a small café and decided that he really was quite hungry so he went inside.

A heavyset woman of indistinguishable age greeted him at the door and showed him to a small table. He imagined that in better times this would provide a magnificent view of the river. Unfortunately, the front windowpane had been the casualty of one or another bomb blast and was now replaced with plywood. "I wonder if I might wash up a bit before I sit down? I was walking by the river and I'm afraid I was a little clumsy," he said holding up his muddied hands.

"My goodness, you should be more careful, with a cane and all that and still walking down there!" The woman showed him where to wash up and left his menu on the table. When Ivram returned he could see the back of someone seated at his table. "Excuse, me, but I believe... Ilyas! How did you ever find me here?"

"Don't get mad or think me rude, but I've been following you for more than an hour. I must say that you impressed me down there."

"Yes, I do fall well, don't I?" They both laughed.

"I think I would have too. That last slope was quite steep and slick. I'd say that you are ready, my friend."

"I've been ready for some time. I thought you'd called the whole thing off."

The woman came back to take their order, so they stopped talking for the moment. When she was out of hearing range, Ilyas continued, "Yes, from what I understand, there were some delays in getting the support you will need. Our friends in Moscow are taking a wait-and-see attitude, what with the negotiations still going on. I also think they were somewhat skeptical about your ability to actually deliver, Ivram. I'm sure that they thought we were either fools or government agents trying to trap them."

"So I've been put on hold, is that it?"

"No, actually I've been sent to tell you it's time for you to leave. I've left a small van back at your apartment; here's the keys." Ilyas slid his hand across the table and left a set of car keys next to Ivram's plate. "All the paperwork is in the compartment. Tomorrow head out on the road to Malgobek. When you get to the border, just tell them you're going up to Moscow to stay with your family. You still have family up there I understand."

"Not that they'd admit to, but yes, I do."

"Good, they can check that out if there should be any questions and it won't present any problems. I doubt it will come to that, but you never know these days. Before you get to Malgobek head north. You shouldn't have trouble at any of the border crossings. If you do, stick to that story. Make your way up toward Volgograd. Check into the White Swan, it's a small inn not far from the city on Volga-Don Canal. Use your own name. Someone will contact you within a week."

"A week! What am I supposed to do in the meantime?"

"Relax and enjoy yourself. Take in the sights. You're an instructor from the university on holiday so no one should be suspicious of your activities. The rest of the team will join up there when everything is ready."

The meals came out and several other patrons came in and were seated at the table across from them. They spent the rest of the time in casual conversation. When they finished eating Ilyas looked at his watch. "I suggest you may want to get to the bank before it closes. Do you have everything you'll need?"

"Yes, I think so."

"Then may the Almighty go with you." They both got up from the table and Ilyas clasped his hand in both of his. "Until we meet again," he told him and left the restaurant.

The walk home was an emotional journey for Ivram. He recalled many of the sights and sounds of his student days. He remembered the city as it once had been. He recalled the joyous times with friends and, most of all, with Viktor. Those memories were juxtaposed against the actual sights of the war scarred and ravaged city that lay before him. Ivram tried to fight back tears, but was unable to do so. He had blocked these images out for too long. He knew he was looking at his city for the last time and it grieved him.

Jihad

51

Ivram rose early, packed what few essentials he owned and ripped up and discarded most of the not so essential things he'd accumulated. He started to do the same to a picture he kept of Katryn, Georgi and Alexandra. It had been taken right after they'd learned of her illness. The smiling faces belied all of the unpleasant memories that were to follow. Ivram sat down on the edge of his bed and gazed at the photo for a long time. He could almost hear Alex laughing and calling out to him. No, he thought, some memories can never be destroyed. He tossed the photograph into his open suitcase and snapped it shut.

Looking around this tiny apartment, he had to laugh. It had never been so neat. He wrote a brief note to the building superintendent explaining that he had been called away to Moscow on a family matter and was not sure how long he'd be away. He folded the key inside the note and slid it under the superintendent's door.

The van was parked behind the building. It was old and nondescript; its dull gray finish had suffered numerous dings, dents and chips, the casualty of having to exist in a war ravaged city. Ivram checked the glove compartment and saw the documentation just as Ilyas had promised. He was amazed by their efficiency. Everything was in his name, back dated several months.

He drove out of Groznyy and headed west towards Malgobek in Ingushetia. It was warm already this early in the day. The road lay in the valley between the two northernmost ridgelines of the Caucasus Mountains. The sun lit the mountains in glorious splendor and momentarily cheered his spirits. Then he passed by the ruins of a building and was immediately reminded of the purpose for this trip. Large patches of charred earth replaced the foliage in many places along the road, ever-present reminders that this was where the militia had stood their ground against the initial wave of Russian armor. At one point it was apparent that an entire village had been leveled by Russian artillery and burned to the ground.

His heart beat faster as he approached the Ingush border. Russian soldiers manned the gate, with armored troop transports and tanks parked along the side of the road poised for action. A blonde-haired Sr. Sergeant ordered him out of the vehicle and took his papers. In a very brusque tone he demanded, "What is your name?"

"Ivram, Ivram Gadayev."

"It says here that your name is Garyk. Why is that?"

"Yes, I'm sorry. My name is actually Garyk Ivramovich Gadayev. I haven't used the name Garyk for some time. I almost forgot."

"Yes, I see. And what is your destination this morning, Mr. Gadayev?"

"I'm on my way to Moscow. I have family there. I haven't seen them for a long time either. Actually, I thought I might stop in Volgograd along the way."

"So, you are on holiday then, Mr. Gadayev?"

"Yes, from the State University. I'm an instructor there."

"Very good. Welcome to Ingushetia, Mr. Gadayev. Welcome back to the Russian Federation." The sergeant gave him a curt nod and handed back his document folder. All this time two other soldiers had been carefully searching the contents of his van. With the sergeant's interrogation now completed, one of the young men called over to Ivram, "Excuse me, sir, I wonder if you wouldn't mind opening this suitcase for us." They made a cursory search of the contents, satisfied that there was nothing more than clothing and personal belongings. The Sr. Sergeant observed from behind. "You travel very lightly, Mr. Gadayev. For such a long trip one would expect you to have much more clothing."

"Actually, sergeant, you're looking at everything I own!"

The sergeant raised his eyebrows a bit at Ivram's disclosure. "That is enough. Let him pass," he commanded the two privates. Ivram climbed back into his van and pulled back onto the road. On each side of him rose six flagpoles on which were alternated the white, blue and red striped standards of the Russian Federation with the flags of Ingushetia. Those were white, with top and bottom bars of green. In the center was the national emblem, a violet circle with triune tines. They all flapped gently in the morning breeze. How strange, Ivram thought, not to see the red flags with their gold hammer and sickle emblems anymore.

Once across the border the scenes also changed. The land no longer bore the scars of war. There was no charred earth, no bombed out buildings. Occasionally a military convoy passed by, heading west with supplies and replacement soldiers, but essentially he had entered a land at peace, only kilometers away from so much destruction.

He turned north and passed from Ingushetia into North Ossetia without incident. At Mozdok he stopped for lunch. Here was a city less than half the size of Groznyy, yet it was alive and vibrant. Its shops were busy with mid-day traffic. The streets were actually congested. The Russian command was based outside of the town, so there were many men in uniform walking about. He chose an out of the way restaurant and sat sipping his coffee. He was ill at ease surrounded by so many cheerful people going about the normal daily tasks.

After lunch he crossed into the Stravropol' Territory. As an administrative territory or *kray,* the area was less autonomous than the republics he had just traveled through. Ivram was now officially back in Russia. Consequently, he was again made subject to an extensive search of his vehicle and an interrogation as to the purpose of his travels. This time he was escorted inside the administrative building and made to wait in a small cubical that contained only a metal desk and two chairs. He was seated in the chair facing the desk, his back to the door. Some ten minutes slowly passed by before an administrative sort in a brown suit and blue bow tie entered the room and took a seat behind the desk. Without acknowledging Ivram, he spread out the documents Ivram had turned over to the officer outside, pulled out a pair of heavy plastic rimmed glasses from his jacket pocket and spent a few moments examining the papers. When he was satisfied, he looked up. His face had no expression whatsoever. "Yes, everything seems to be in order, Mr. Gadayev. Just a few questions and you can be on your way again."

After several border crossings, the questions had a familiar ring to them. Ivram could almost recite the next before his inquisitor could ask. When he reached the point at which Ivram expected to be excused, the man pulled a computer printout from his folder and started a new line of questions Ivram had not heard before. "Tell me Mr. Gadayev, your brother was Viktor Ivramovich, a former First Deputy of the Chechen Republic, is that not correct?"

"Yes," Ivram responded cautiously.

"He was killed fighting against our Russian forces, I understand, is that not so?"

Ivram grew uneasy, not sure where this line of questioning was going. "Yes, he was an administrative liaison officer at the time. The unit he was with came under attack and he was killed."

"How very unfortunate," the functionary said with little or no emotion. "And your trip to Moscow, you will be staying with your wife, Katryn Yuriana Moldatin Gadayev?"

"Probably not. We haven't exactly been close the past few years. I suspect I will stay at a hotel."

"You have reservations for that then?"

"Actually, no. I more or less decided to make this trip at the last minute. My duties at the University were finished and I found myself with some time."

"It's not always easy to find rooms available in Moscow I'm told. Perhaps you'll be able to stay with an old associate. You will be seeing Ruslan Khasbulatov on your visit?"

"No, I certainly don't plan on that."

"Really, I would have thought that the two of you would have much to talk about."

Ivram fought the uneasiness that was growing inside of him. "Not any more. I think that our views have diverged as time has progressed."

"Yes, that does happen. How unfortunate for you that it came after the loss of your leg. Your time could have been better spent not having to be detained in the Moscow Correctional Facility for six months."

"What is done is done. One can not dwell on the events of the past."

After each response the interviewer wrote copious notes on the printout, not bothering to look up as he posed his next question. Still writing, he asked, "You are a follower of Mansur Shamil, are you not? I see that you were detained for questioning several times by the authorities in Groznyy." This time the man glanced up to watch Ivram's reaction to his query.

Ivram told himself to remain calm and not show any reactions to these questions. "Yes, I have been called in for questioning by the Russian military police, not the Chechen authorities. They found no reason to detain me. The usman is my spiritual leader, nothing more. He took me in when I had lost everything and helped to put my life back in order."

The man seated across from him jotted down a few more lines without saying anything then began to reassemble the documents that lay before him. With a bit of a flourish he picked up his official stamp and loudly affixed the seals to his papers. He handed Ivram's packet back to him. "Thank you, Mr. Gadayev, I trust that your current trip will not result in anything that might require further inconvenience to you. I'm sure you have seen enough of our correctional facilities." The inquisitor smiled for the first time. "You are free to go."

52

The remainder of the trip to Volgograd was uneventful. The Volga—Don Canal, which links the two principal rivers, lies just to the south of the city. It was getting on towards evening, but at this time of year there was still several hours of daylight remaining. He drove by dead reckoning and came upon a sign that announced the White Swan Inn. It possessed all the charm of a by-gone era. Inside, he approached a small counter and rang a bell for service. No one seemed to be about. He was about to ring again when a tall young woman with long blonde hair falling in curls over her shoulders hurried in from what may have been the kitchen. "Excuse me sir, I didn't hear you arrive. We're just preparing for dinner. Will you be joining us?"

"Yes, my name is Gadayev, Ivram Gadayev."

"Oh yes, Mr. Gadayev, we were expecting you." He received a very pleasant smile from the girl. She reached under the counter and pulled out a form that she placed down so that it faced her guest. "Please fill this information card out, if you would. Can I get someone to assist with your bags?"

"No, that's not necessary, everything I have is in this small one here."

The young woman showed him up to his room. After the long trip, his good leg had stiffened up quite a bit, making the ascent a little painful. It was a lovely room, larger actually than the one he'd lived in the past number of months. Two windows opened out onto a view of a spacious lawn, which sloped down to the canal. A wide variety of flowers were in bloom including a stand of giant sunflowers. They reminded him of his mother.

He washed up and put on a clean shirt and badly wrinkled tweed jacket, wishing now that he had acquired a better wardrobe. He made his way slowly down the stairs for dinner. He could hear bustling sounds coming from the dining room and was surprised to see that there were quite a few guests already seated. "Would you like to be seated now, sir?" It was the same young woman as before, only now she had pulled back her hair into a bun on the back of her head and had donned a light blue blazer with a white swan crest. It was more in keeping with her duties as hostess.

"Give me a moment. I think I had better retrieve my cane. I left it out in the van."

"If you'd like, I could have one of the boys fetch it for you, sir." She had a delightful smile and obviously worked hard at trying to please her guests.

"Yes, if you don't mind, that would be very kind." Ivram sat by himself, but was soon drawn into conversation with several of the guests seated at other tables. They were all on holiday. Most were down from Moscow. Teachers and middle level managers mostly, in their late forties and fifties he'd have to guess. When they learned he was from Chechnya they all expressed their concerns that such a terrible fate had overtaken one of their own republics. "I hope that these recent events haven't affected you much," one of the women dining with her husband asked politely.

Ivram smiled at the irony of her question and just replied "I suppose we've all been affected in one way or another."

An older woman then said, "I hope that your family hasn't been harmed in any way."

"Actually," he responded, "they're all dead." This sent a noticeable chill throughout the room and the conversation stopped quite abruptly. When it began again, the talk was of other matters and not directed his way at all.

After dinner he walked through the garden and down to the canal. It was a busy seaway, alive with both ships of trade and pleasure boats. The sun was setting, but the air retained the heat. The next day he ventured into Volgograd. The city had been destroyed almost completely during the war, so it embodied the architectural style of the fifties and sixties, functional socialism. He heard the whistle of a passing train and recalled his first glimpse of this vast metropolis. It was hard to believe that had been twenty-three years ago. Where did the time go? How much had he changed since then? Feeling melancholy, he spent the afternoon seated at a small table in an outdoor bistro overlooking the Volga River.

When he returned to the White Swan the young woman met him as he was heading up to his room. This evening she wore a red blazer and again allowed her hair to flow in ripples over her shoulders. "Oh, Mr. Gadayev, your friend arrived this afternoon. If you don't mind, I've arranged for him to sit with you at dinner this evening."

"No, I don't mind at all," he told her.

By the time he had freshened up a bit and come back downstairs Hadzhi was already seated. It was the first time Ivram had ever seen him not wearing combat fatigues. He looked quite striking in a blue blazer with khaki pants. His blue and gold striped shirt was open at the collar. Like Ivram, he had shaved off his beard several weeks ago to allow the skin underneath to attain a natural color. He rose when he saw him coming. "Ivram, my friend, it is good to see you again!" The two clasped forearms and Hadzhi slapped him on the back. Several of the other diners made casual nods of greeting, but none seemed inclined to reestablish communications this evening.

"Hadzhi, you can't imagine how glad I am to see you. How soon will we begin our journey?"

Hadzhi held up his hand. "Be patient a little while longer. There will be time enough to discuss that later." He lowered his voice and added, "This is neither the time nor the place for that." Louder, he said, "Right now it is time to eat. I'm starving!"

During dinner, Ivram did learn that Hadzhi had left the same day he had, only he had taken an easterly route at first, traveling up through Dagestan. It was better not to risk having too many Chechen travelers pass through the same border points. After eating, they both walked down by the canal and found two lawn chairs well away from any others where they could talk. "So tell me what's happening," Ivram began, anxious to learn about the mission.

"All is finally ready. I think Ilyas told you that we had encountered some resistance, but that has all been resolved. I believe that some discreet inquiries may have been made concerning your abilities with the Russian computer system. Don't worry, it was nothing that might compromise you or the mission. Just to assure people that we could deliver. Speaking of that, they believe that we will be delivering all of the nuclear devices to them, that this is merely a financial matter for us. They certainly would not have agreed to participate if they knew our true intentions."

"Yes, that makes sense. What will happen when we only have three to turn over?"

"By then, it will be too late. You will already be on your way to St. Petersburg. I'll tell them we had a problem with one of the devices and abandoned it. Believe me, they will be delighted to get their hands on just one. Do you have any idea how much money certain parties will be offering to get one of these things?"

"Yes, I do. That's what so scary about the whole thing. So when do we leave?"

"We'll be contacted shortly by one of their representatives. He will have some of the things we've asked for and information concerning how we obtain the rest of our supplies. We'll be going north first, up to Saratov. That's where the other team members will join up with us. Right now a large group might attract attention."

"How large a group are you talking about?"

"Just two more. You know Aslan. He has worked with me in the past. He's good in very tough situations. The other one I haven't met; it's the linguist you requested."

They returned to their rooms and Ivram sat up late expecting the contact person to come at any time. At midnight he decided to get some sleep. The next morning, Hadzhi came to his door and knocked. "Are you awake, my friend?"

Ivram opened the door to let him in, again expecting to see that their guest had arrived. Hadzhi was alone. "I've come to see if you'd like to join me for morning prayers. Down by the canal, perhaps?"

"Yes, that would be fine," Ivram said. "I believe I have a prayer rug in the van." Although Russia prided itself on its ethnic diversity, the sight of these two men kneeling in prayer was still cause for some attention and discussion among the other guests. By mid-morning, the long-awaited knock came as Ivram and Hadzhi were chatting in Ivram's room. Ivram opened the door and stared at a weaselly little man in a flashy tweed suit standing in the hallway. "Igor, is it really you? Please come in!"

Hadzhi was puzzled by the fact that Ivram knew the messenger sent from the Moscow cartel. Igor was also trying to figure out who this man was that claimed to know him. Granted, he had called him by name. "Excuse me, but you have me at a disadvantage. Have we met before?"

"Igor Minsky, we lived together for how many months? I'm surprised that they ever let you out of that prison!"

"My God, Garyk!" Igor embraced his former cellmate. "Please forgive me. I was told I would be meeting someone named Ivram. I just didn't make the connection. And without the crutches too, I'm happy to see!"

Hadzhi was still bewildered by all of this. Ivram led the new arrival over to him. "Hadzhi, allow me to introduce my good friend, Igor Minsky. I don't know if I ever told you about my experiences up in Moscow. Let's just say that I spent some time in the correctional facility after I lost my leg to the Russian tanks. Igor was there over some misunderstanding about chickens, I believe."

"Yes, a very big misunderstanding. Fortunately, I survived and so did you, Garyk. You are looking much better these days, my friend."

"And so are you." In addition to a suit and Italian shoes that probably represented more than six months' wages for the average worker, Igor sported a shiny Rolex and several large rings. His hair was heavily coated with styling gel and combed straight back over his head. "You should know that I have chosen to be called by my father's name, Ivram. It seemed more in keeping with the times."

"What's in a name, a friend is still a friend," Igor proclaimed.

"And I can see by the fact that you are here that you have resumed your old business, that you are a *commodities* trader."

"Yes, you might say that business is better than ever!"

53

Igor brought four new sets of military documents and identification. "Here's the name and address of an associate of mine in Saratov," he told them, handing the package and separate slip of paper over to Ivram. "You'll find that he's very *artistic*. When your group has been assembled he will insure that the proper photographs are affixed to all of those documents. You are soon to become officers in the Russian Army. Congratulations on your promotion, Colonel." Igor gave Ivram a mock salute.

Unannounced inspection visits were almost a routine and would account for why no one would recognized these newcomers to the area. The orders, which Ivram would be able to down load from his computer, would give them almost unlimited access to the missile site. Ivram busied himself reviewing all of the documentation. "I'm a bit confused, Igor. This set is made out for a Corporal Elaina Dolstekaiya."

"Yes, is something wrong? I was told only to be prepared for three men and a woman. They gave me some approximate sizes. If there's been a change in those plans, no one relayed that information to us."

"Hadzhi, do you know anything about this?"

"All I know is what I told you last night. Aslan certainly is not a woman. As to the translator, I have no idea. I know only that he *or she* is a proven commando fighter fluent in Kipchak. I suppose we'll just have to wait and see when we get to Saratov."

"Yes," Ivram said, I guess you're right."

Igor said, "Come, I will take you to where we have a full supply of all of the military uniforms you will need." He road in the van with Ivram while Hadzhi followed them. They drove to a small store on the outskirts of the city. Igor told them to park in the rear and they loaded several boxes into the back of the vehicle. "Here's a packing slip and shipping invoice," Igor said. "Just in case anyone should ask, you're delivering these goods to a shop up in Saratov. These days no one really asks."

Hadzhi gave him the keys to the car he had driven up from Groznyy. Igor looked at the battered vehicle and said, "Well, it certainly needs some work. Hopefully I can find a desperate buyer."

Ivram snickered. "Knowing you, Igor, I'm sure you already have one in mind who will give you a nice profit."

Igor shrugged and just said "Perhaps." His sly grin affirmed Ivram's suspicions. He rapped on the side of Ivram's van. "As for this, my friend in Saratov will know what to do. We have a nice military Hummer that's been fully equipped for your journey. I must say there were some peculiar specifications for that one. I had quite a time putting that together, let me tell you."

"You are truly amazing, Igor," Ivram avowed.

Igor reached into his jacket and pulled out a map. He handed this to Hadzhi. "You're to head over to Orenburg, then south into Kazkhstan from there. It's better that you enter the republic from the north, rather than taking a more direct route." Igor traced a path with his finger. "Follow the mountains south until you come to Aral. That's where the heavy equipment has been stored for you. You'll have directions in the vehicle. After that just follow the Syr Darya upriver. Once you've acquired the merchandise, keep following the river down to Toshkent in Uzbekistan. Here's a contact number to call to arrange for the transfer." Igor handed over a slip of paper with the number scrawled across it.

After an exchange of hugs they headed north with Hadzhi behind the wheel. Ivram was grateful for that. It allowed him to stretch out his good leg. He found that he had developed a tendency to transfer most of his weight off the prosthesis and unto his natural appendage. This was affecting the joint in his right knee and also causing some back pains lately. The route generally followed the Volga valley and afforded them spectacular views of the river's broad expanse. They stopped along the way for midday prayers and found a restaurant for lunch. It was nearing four in the afternoon when they arrived in Saratov and found the shop Igor had directed them to. They greeted the old man tending the counter and explained that they had a delivery from Volgograd.

"Wait here please," he instructed and quickly vanished into a back room. A few minutes passed and a younger man entered from the back. He had crooked yellow teeth and reeked of garlic. "Yes, gentlemen, how can I help you?" He studied the papers that Igor had given to them and then motioned for the two men to follow. "We have been expecting you. Your associates arrived about an hour ago. As soon as we get you all properly dressed I'll take the photographs

I need. The papers will be ready for you tomorrow morning."

He led them down a flight of stairs to a photo studio set up in the basement. Two young people were sitting there, engaged in casual chatter. Ivram recognized Aslan and assumed that the other, who was sitting with her back turned to him, was their woman linguist. They rose upon hearing them entering the room and she turned to greet them. Ivram stopped dead in his tracks. It was Tapa! Her hair was cut shorter and she was wearing the uniform of a Russian Army corporal. His mouth dropped open and he sucked in a vast quantity of air, forgetting to exhale.

Her face beamed with a broad smile. She tilted her head coyly to one side, taking in the man standing before her. "Why Mr. Gadayev, I didn't realize you'd been hiding such a handsome face behind those whiskers. I must say it seems quite an improvement."

The sound of her voice caused a titillation throughout his entire body. He realized that he was holding his breath and released it noticeably. "Tapa, I can't believe that you're here. How is this?"

"I received word last month that Shamil had need of a trained fighter who knew how to speak Kipchak. I wasn't really sure I should volunteer for this. Then I learned that you were to be in charge."

Hadzhi looked at Ivram with mild astonishment. "Well, it seems there's no end to your acquaintances that keep popping up. What other surprises do you have in store for us?"

"Truly, Hadzhi, I have no idea!"

Ivram pulled out the officer's uniform that they provided for him. The uniform would have to be pressed, of course. Such creases might not show in the ID photograph, but an officer in the Russian Army certainly would not tolerate them. It had been a while since he had last put on a uniform and it took him a few moments to remember how to assemble the various accessories. His shoulder boards had two blue stripes on a gold background. On each stripe was a small bronze star denoting the rank of a lieutenant colonel. If things had gone differently, he would have become a colonel by now. The collar tabs bore the crossed rocket insignia of the strategic weapons command. He pinned on the rack that contained several rows of ribbons, including awards for valor and meritorious service in Afghanistan. In an ironic touch, the campaign ribbon for service in Chechnya was also included.

He put the jacket on and stood in front of a full-length mirror. It was as if he had been reintroduced to an old friend, Garyk Gadayev. Even without the beard, the image reflected back to him was older than he remembered. Lines were evident around his eyes and the line of his jaw wasn't quite as sharp. His hair was shorter than it had been for several years. Here and there a silver strand was evident among the black. "Time hasn't been kind to you," he told the man in the mirror sadly. He turned back to the others and addressed Aslan without even thinking, "Sergeant, please see to it that all of these uniforms have been properly tailored and pressed before we leave tomorrow."

Aslan stared back at him, not quite sure whether this command had actually been intended for him or not. Then Hadzhi started to laugh. "Well, Ivram, no, excuse me, Colonel, it seems you have adapted quickly to your new role." The others laughed too and Ivram was embarrassed by the fact that he had so naturally assumed the position. He started to laugh along with them and admitted, "Yes, I guess putting on this uniform had its effect on me. Funny, I don't recall that I was ever such a stickler for formalities when I was an officer. Perhaps I just never realized it."

Hadzhi became serious again. "Actually, my friends, if we are to succeed in this mission we must all begin to think and act like the soldiers we are supposed to be." He nodded in Ivram's direction, "The Colonel is correct. These uniforms need to be fitted properly and that is the sergeant's responsibility. Corporal," he said, turning to Tapa, "you will see to it that everyone's boots have been properly shined and that all of the equipment is in good order. From this moment on we are Russian soldiers. Is that clear?"

Tapa and Aslan both nodded that it was. Hadzhi looked sternly at both of them and repeated in a harsher tone, "Is that clear?"

"YES SIR!" they both responded this time.

"Good, remember that. All of our lives may depend upon it."

54

The rest of the day was spent separately in final preparations for the trip. Hadzhi arranged for three rooms at a small hotel that was close by. The documents that Igor had provided to them included an authorization card and vouchers that permitted their expenses to be charged directly to a special military account. Hadzhi took great pleasure in signing off on those. They regrouped at about seven that evening and ate together in the hotel dining room. The fare was modest and the talk was subdued, appropriate for a mixed company of officers and enlisted personnel. After the meal Tapa excused herself and retired to her room. Ivram was disappointed that he did not have a chance to speak with her in private. It would certainly not be proper to visit her room.

They rose early the next morning and retrieved the *artwork* from the shop. None of the ID cards looked new, but rather had the appearance of being well used and worn with age. Then they were on their way, heading east into the morning sun. As befit their newly assumed identities, Tapa did most of the driving, spelled occasionally by Aslan. Ivram and Hadzhi made themselves comfortable in the rear of the oversized vehicle. The roads were not heavily traveled and Tapa was able to make the 600-kilometer trip in eight hours, stopping along the way for something to eat. The plan was to stop there in Orenburg for the night and cross over into Kazakhstan in the morning.

They ate an early supper together and prepared to go their separate ways for the evening. Ivram caught up to her as she was leaving the restaurant. "I thought I'd try to explore the area while there's still some daylight, he said. "Would you care to walk with me? I think the Ural River is somewhere nearby."

"Yes, I'd like that," Tapa answered.

As they walked he told her, "I'm still at a loss to explain how you got here."

"I told you, they asked for volunteers."

"Yes, I know that much. But we were told that you are a seasoned guerrilla fighter. That's not the Tapa I remember from the camp."

"My cousins belong to a group that follow the usman Muhammad Haji. He's based near the Dagestan border. They had been after me for some time to join them, but I was happy with Shamil. And then you came along."

"I'm sorry, I..."

"No, it was my fault. I decided it was best if I joined my cousins. They're a much more militant group than Shamil's, if you can believe that. I've become quite an effective commando this past year." Her hair was cut evenly just above the nape of her neck and a few strands had blown across her face and ear as they walked. She brushed them back and smiled, proud of her accomplishments.

"I would never have suspected." Ivram shook his head in disbelief. He admired the cockiness that the experience had obviously instilled in her. "But where did you learn to speak Kipchak?"

"Oh, my grandmother was originally from Kazakhstan. She met my grandfather at one of the camps in central Asia and came back to live with him in Groznyy after the war. As a child she would tell me stories in her native language. When my parents died, I lived with her until it was time to go to technical school.

They found a bridge that spanned the many rail lines that converged along the river and worked their way along its bank until they found a small park. The river flowed west here, having come down from the mountains, which were visible to the east. It would roll on for several hundred more kilometers before turning south again and making for the Caspian Sea. Ivram stood looking across to the opposite shore. "Did you know that Europe ends here? Everything to the east is now officially in Asia."

"It looks the same from here," Tapa replied. "It's extraordinary, isn't it?"

"Yes, people are always putting some kind of label on everything and we just expect that nature will conform."

They started to walk again and Ivram slipped his hand naturally over hers. She pulled it away and turned to him. "Do you think that would be considered proper conduct for an officer and an enlisted woman, Colonel?"

"No, I'm sure it wouldn't. But do you consider it proper?"

"There was a time when I hoped it might be," she said to him. "I should never have let that happen. I understand that now. Still, I was very relieved to get another message from my family that I should come and join them. It made for a very convenient escape."

"I came back several times looking for you. Did you know that?"

"No, I didn't know that. And just why did you do that?" It was a pertly put question, part of the new self-confidence.

"Now you're being a tease," he said. "You know why. It was because I couldn't stop thinking about you."

"And what about your wife?"

"I don't know, Tapa. Katryn will always be my wife and a part of me will always be in love with her. But she's removed herself from my life and taken my son with her. I should hate her for that, but I don't. That isn't fair to you, I know, but I need to have someone standing beside me. There's a tremendous emptiness that needs to be filled."

"Yes, I know that, Ivram. I want very much to be that person. I also need to be a wife and a mother someday. Can you promise me that?"

Ivram looked down into her brown eyes. They were warm and compassionate eyes, yet they probed deep into his very soul. He searched himself for the honest answer to her question. Finally he said to her, "No, I'm sorry, but I can't."

She stopped walking and turned to face him. Then she put her hands on his shoulders, stretched up on her toes and kissed him softly. "Yes, I knew that and I love you for being honest." Tears formed in both of their eyes. "Damn! It certainly will not do for a corporal to be seen crying in public." She wiped hers away with a finger, then turned and hurried back towards the hotel where they were to spend the night.

Ivram stood there, alone and motionless. He watched her disappear into the darkness. A strange tightness gripped his chest and he realized that he had not taken a breath since she turned away. He sucked air in and then released it in one loud, forceful exhale. "Timing is everything," he spoke softly to himself. "Yours, my friend, is really lousy!"

55

The Kazakhstan border was manned by a unit of Russian soldiers on one side and Kazakhis on the other. Sky blue flags bearing yellow sunbursts above a soaring eagle flapped gently in the breeze to greet them. The Kazahk sergeant who met them was curt, not particularly happy about having to allow Russian Army officers into his country. The fact that the Russian driver was not only able but also willing to converse with him in Kipchak and not force him to conduct the interview in Russian seemed to ease the process. It didn't hurt that she was rather attractive as well.

He reviewed the document package that the sergeant presented to him and peered into the vehicle to compare the photographs to the occupants seated within. Satisfied, he walked around in front of the vehicle to return the package to the driver. They chatted briefly and he waived them through with a cursory salute.

They proceeded south along the edge of the Ural Mountains until they came to the Aral Sea. Near the town of Aral they found the abandoned factory building where Igor had told them they were to find the balance of the equipment. The packet of directions that was left for them contained a key. Hadzhi used it to unlock the padlock that secured the overhead door. Tapa drove the Hummer into the building and Hadzhi pulled the door down behind them. There were few windows to let in light and Ivram's eyes took a while to adjust to the dark surroundings. He groped along the near wall until he found the switch to turn on the overhead lights. Even these did little to brighten the place.

They found themselves in a large storage bay. Except for a few old cartons and broken crates, it appeared empty. "Over there." Aslan said to Tapa, pointing to a pile of tarp against the rear wall. She drove the vehicle further back into the building and Aslan got out. He pulled back the tarps and uncovered several wooden boxes. He opened one and it was filled with those annoying plastic capsules for shipping. He dug his way through the peanut shaped pellets until his hand touched metal, then he pulled out an automatic machine pistol and held it up for the others to see.

There were three more machine pistols and enough rounds of ammunition to supply a full squad in the first crate. The second contained four brand new AK-47 rifles, two with telescopic sites, and the third contained six hand-held disposable rocket launchers. Tapa looked at Hadzhi and asked, "Are we really planning to use all of these?"

"Hopefully, no. But we need to be prepared for any contingencies."

"Well prepared, I would think," she said. While Hadzhi and Aslan loaded the crate containing the rockets into the back of the Hummer, Ivram inspected the three larger boxes that contained the communications and computer equipment he had requisitioned. "Yes," he said looking over to Hadzhi, "I think everything I asked for is here. It's really quite amazing that they could get their hands on all of this stuff."

Ivram unloaded some of the equipment and began to set it up inside the vehicle. The rest was loaded in back by Hadzhi and Aslan. Tapa opened the case that contained food supplies and began to prepare a meal. The three ate while Ivram busied himself with his computer. After some time he let out a little shout of exultation. "Yes, there it is, we're up and on line now! I've reestablished access to the missile control program."

Tapa called in to him, "Colonel, would you care to join us now for something to eat?"

"Just give me a few more minutes," he called back. He was like a young child with a new toy. The three looked at each other and shook their heads in amusement. They were long finished when he finally came out of the truck to join them.

"I'm sorry, sir, but I think you'll find everything has gone cold," Tapa said. "Would you like me to reheat it for you?"

"No, I suppose I deserve to eat it cold. Actually, I don't think I've ever had the opportunity to drink any of your coffee without having to worry about being scalded." Tapa blushed at the reference to her coffee making and Ivram turned to the other two and explained, "This young woman makes the hottest coffee I've ever encountered."

Aslan nodded in agreement, saying, "Yes, we found that out a while ago!"

Ivram turned back to her and said, "I'm sorry for taking so much time, but everything depends upon that equipment. In fact, it also depends upon either you or Aslan being able to enter certain commands when the time comes." He turned to the young man. "Aslan, you do know how to use a computer, don't you?"

"Me, oh no, sir. I was never much good at anything technical. If that Hummer over there breaks down, I can fix it in a second. But I wouldn't even know how to turn on one of those computer gizmos of yours."

"Well, Tapa, I guess that makes it your job. It's no more difficult than ordering up medical supplies."

"Are you sure?" She looked at him with concern, afraid that the mission might fail if she couldn't do what he required of her. "I didn't think I did that very well and it was some time ago."

Ivram smiled at her and said, "You were very good, don't worry. As soon as I finish this, what is this stuff I'm eating anyway?" He held the slab of cold meat up to look at it. The others all laughed and Hadzhi tossed over the empty can for him to see. He read it aloud, "Processed Beef Supplement, Daily Field Ration. Okay, so now I know what it says it is, I still can't imagine what it is!"

"I should have reheated it for you," Tapa said, still laughing. It doesn't taste quite so bad when it's hot."

"It's hard to imagine it ever tasting good," Ivram said. "Anyway, I was starting to explain that we'll have time to run through the procedures tonight. The whole security system is based upon a series of commands being entered from three separate locations to gain access to the missile nose cones. One inside the command bunker, one in Moscow and the other at Strategic Command Headquarters. The trick is to reprogram the satellite communications system into thinking that the computer in the truck is Moscow and the one I haven't unpacked yet is Command Headquarters."

"Ah, but can you do that? There must be access codes required." It was Hadzhi who had voiced what the others were thinking.

"Of course I can. I was the one who installed those systems in the first place. When the time comes, I'll first reprogram their main computer to accept our own set of clearance codes."

Hadzhi knew enough about computer systems to ask, "Won't that deny access to everyone else? Surely they'll know something is going on."

"You're right, once someone else tries to gain normal access to the system they'll find they've been locked out. They'll try again several times before the call is made to report a problem. Then someone else will have to punch in all of the access commands to see that the system really isn't functioning. The next step will be to call in the Officer-In-Charge. He'll also try to access the system at least once before authorizing a total lock down and instituting the backup codes. We'll be doing this around 0200 hours, when activity is minimal. I'll be able to detect when they run a routine system scan. Those checks are done randomly, but never more than once every half-hour. Once it's completed, we will begin. We'll have a short window of opportunity."

"Very short," Hadzhi emphasized.

Tapa looked at Ivram and said, "You make it all sound so simple."

"It is, if you have access to the main program, which I hope I still do."

They spent the night in the building. Ivram and Tapa rehearsed on the computer inside the track, while Hadzhi and Aslan secured all of the supplies and cleaned up the area where they had been stored. Anyone coming upon this room in the future would find only a stack of empty boxes under a pile of tarp. Tapa was given the luxury of sleeping in the truck on one of its fold-down cots. The men availed themselves of the sleeping bags that had been provided and slept on the floor. They rose early the next day and joined together for morning prayers. They asked the Almighty to guide them and grant them a successful mission. After a hasty breakfast of coffee and crackers they started on the final leg of the journey.

The road from Aral to Qyzylorda transverses the delta region of the Syr Darya. This semi-arid area relies heavily upon an irrigation system that pulls water from the river to cultivate rice. They drove for several hours with nothing more than rice paddies extending from either side of the road. As the day progressed it grew hotter and the air conditioning unit inside the vehicle was having difficulty keeping up. They came upon a small inn about ten kilometers before the expected turnoff to the missile site and Ivram told Tapa to pull in. "I think it would be wise for us to all freshen up a bit before we make our surprise visit. We'll make a better impression if we're not all hot and sweaty from the trip." They all agreed that it was an excellent idea.

It was not a prosperous looking establishment, inside or out. Ivram couldn't imagine why anyone would want to frequent the place except out of dire necessity. A toothless old woman finally came to greet them after they had been seated at the largest of four wooden tables for some time. She walked in a shuffle, partially bent at the waist and neck. In spite of the heat, she was dressed all in black, to include the shawl that covered her head. She spoke in a shrill voice words that were completely incomprehensible to Ivram, Hadzhi or Aslan. Tapa said something back and the woman repeated the string of syllables, this time apparently more slowly, although Ivram could not detect any difference.

Tapa leaned into the table and explained, "She apologizes, but the kitchen is not open until this evening. She can offer us some goat cheese and bread, some cold meat if you'd like. There is coffee or tea."

Hadzhi asked, "Does she have anything cold to drink?"

After another exchange with the old woman, Tapa said, "I'm not sure it will be cold. Apparently the refrigerator isn't working very well. There is some bottled soda available if you want to try that."

"Yes, why not. It's a wonder that anything will be safe to eat in this place."

"You obviously didn't grow up on a farm, Hadzhi," Ivram said with some amusement.

The old woman returned holding a tray in front of her. It trembled with the shaking of her hands and they were glad to see it arrive safely on the table without being dropped. It was piled high with pungent cheese and heavily spiced meats, a large round loaf of black bread and several rice cakes. She reached into her apron pockets and pulled out four of the ever-present green *Coca-Cola* bottles, only these had the name written in Aramaic. It was a simple meal, but clearly the best that she had to offer to them.

The toilet was a located in a shed out back that overhung the river. It provided a flushless system of instant drainage, which was fine unless, of course, you were immediately down river from it. The woman did offer them a room where they could wash up. Ivram wondered whether she drew the water out of the river above or below the little shed. Still it felt good to wash the sweat off his face and arms.

They returned to the Hummer and found it hotter than ever inside. It had been sitting under the mid-day sun while they ate. As they neared Qyzylorda the frequency of structures along the road increased. Shortly after passing a sign that advised them they were 14 kilometers away from the city, they passed an unmarked side road that headed off into the rice fields on the left. "Stop, that was it!" Aslan had a military terrain map spread open on his lap.

"Are you certain? It doesn't look like anything bigger than a tractor could travel on it," Tapa said to him."

"Yes, that's the whole point," Hadzhi agreed. "Once the construction of the site was completed they cut back the roadway. All that's required now is the few small jeeps and trucks that bring supplies and change the guard."

Tapa executed a U-turn on the tight roadway, careful not to drop down into the muddy paddy that hugged the side of the road. Looking around at the rice fields that surrounded them, Aslan asked, "How could they have dug a missile silo down into all this muck?"

"Once we move away from the river the land will rise up just a bit," Ivram assured him. "The land becomes extremely dry if it isn't close to an irrigation canal." Aslan wasn't quite sure that was going to happen.

They headed north, away from the river, for more than fifteen minutes. The paddies were still close on both sides of the road. At times Tapa wasn't sure whether the truck's wide wheelbase would remain on the narrow path. Then the road began to gradually rise above the fields. The water level was soon about ten feet below them and they were riding along a narrow dike. After another ten minutes the paddies stopped and the land about them went quickly from lush greens to yellow brown.

56

"So that's what a missile launch pad looks like." Tapa had stopped the Hummer and was staring at a chain link fence that marked the end of the road. It rose about four meters high and marked off an area about fifty meters square. Inside, the ground was covered with crushed stone. Six structures, concrete blocks actually, rose about three meters high. There were three of these on either side of the complex, well in from the fence line. Each was about five meters square.

"Yes," Ivram answered, "Each of those blocks holds a missile launching tube with an intercontinental rocket poised to carry four nuclear warheads. Each warhead has enough capacity to destroy a good-sized American or European city. Collectively, this complex is capable of eliminating a good portion of Europe or the Eastern Seaboard of the United States." That thought was overwhelming. A sense of dread filled the vehicle and Tapa shivered involuntarily.

At the far end of the complex was a one story wooden building with a tar papered roof. There was a single door in the center with two double windows on either side. The building was painted a dull gray, with red trim. A soldier had come out and was casually walking across the complex to the front gate. Ivram and Hadzhi disembarked as he was approaching and they came around to the front of the truck. As the young man neared, he was able to make out their insignia of rank. Realizing that he had deal with a lieutenant colonel, he straightened himself and finished the walk in proper military style. "Can I help you sir?" he barked out and snapped a formal salute.

Ivram and Hadzhi returned his salute and Ivram responded, "Yes Corporal, thank you. I am Colonel Romanov and this is my aide, Captain Plushenko. We are with the Russian Federation Supreme Ballistic Missile Command and are on a routine inspection tour of the facilities in this sector. Captain Plushenko has a copy of our inspection authorization order for your commanding officer. Would you please advise him of our presence."

"Sir, yes sir!" The corporal again offered them a salute and reached out to take the envelope, which the captain was passing through the gate to him. "That would be Senior Sergeant Kalamanov, sir. There is no officer assigned to this unit right now."

"Thank you, Corporal, I understand." Ivram again returned his salute informally and the corporal did an about-face and double-timed back to the office. The sergeant was already coming out the door, buttoning up the blouse of his uniform, as the corporal approached. He had observed the process on a television monitor that carried pictures from eight surveillance cameras scattered around the complex. "Oh shit, it's another God damned inspection team," he had muttered to himself as he watched the exchange.

"Sergeant, it's a Colonel Romanov from the SBMC. He says it's a routine inspection tour." The corporal handed the official envelope over to the senior sergeant and then followed behind him back to the gate. The sergeant tore open the envelope and scanned the document as they walked. "Christ Almighty, you'd think these people would find better things to do. They were just here three weeks ago!"

He came to attention at the gate and saluted his guests. He addressed the colonel in a nasal voice. "Senior Sergeant Sergei Kalamanov at your service, sir. I am the acting officer-in-charge. Would you please have all of your team exit the vehicle sir. We need to check your identification and inspect the vehicle before I can allow you access."

"Certainly Sergeant, that is the proper procedure and protocol."

The corporal opened the gate and allowed Kalamanov to pass through. Then he secured it behind him. He reached down and unsnapped the holster on his belt and drew out the nine-caliber machine pistol strapped to his leg. This would be held at the ready position until the sergeant verified the authenticity of the team.

Tapa and Aslan climbed out of the truck and formed ranks with the two officers. They stood in ascending order by rank. Starting with Tapa, they each handed over their ID cards to Sergeant Kalamanov. He stood in front of the woman and compared her to the picture. "And who might you be?"

"Dolstekaiya, Elaina Nikolaiva, Corporal 678 9887 0405, Sergeant!"

Kalamanov smiled as he checked the information on the card. "Yes, and a pretty one at that. Colonel, I compliment you on your staff," he said as he handed back her identification. He proceeded down the line with Aslan and Hadzhi, then came to Ivram. "And Colonel Romanov, again I apologize for the delay. Please, sir, your name, rank and serial number."

"Romanov, Anatoli Petrovich, Lieutenant Colonel, Army of the Russian Federation O97 9356 6978."

"And tell me, Colonel, just where did you receive your military training?"

"Why at Novgorod, Sergeant, in 1976."

"Ah yes, you were one of the 'Wunderkind,' were you not?"

"Yes, Sergeant, I guess they called us that back then, it seems so long ago."

"I see that you spent some time in Afghanistan. Tell me, Colonel, with what unit did you serve?"

"I was with the 14th Communications Detachment, Sergeant.

"Is that so? Odd, a ballistic missile officer being assigned to a communications unit, wasn't it?"

Ivram realized he had made a technical blunder and Kalamanov had immediately picked up on it. He smiled at the sergeant. "It was a special technical command. That was very quick thinking Sergeant. You are very good. Actually, my expertise lies in the field of computers and satellite communications. I seem to find myself in whatever branch of service that my particular talents are needed the most. Right now that happens to be SBMC."

"Yes, I'm sure it is." The sergeant turned and walked back towards the truck. "Corporal, you will please open the rear of the truck for me."

Tapa remained several paces behind him until they reached the rear of the truck. She stepped around him and pulled up the hatch. The sergeant peered inside, noting all of the computer instrumentation that was set up. "What is in these boxes corporal?"

"Supplies, mostly. We've been on the road for several weeks. There isn't always a good place to sleep or eat."

"Yes, that's for sure. This is a God forsaken place. Please open this crate for me." Tapa opened the crate and the sergeant looked at the four sleeping bags and cooking utensils that were neatly stored inside. "And all of those boxes. This is more computer equipment, is it not?"

"Yes, Senior Sergeant."

Colonel, it seems that you have quite a lot of electronic gear with you. Why is that?"

"On our last trip the computer went down half way through. We lost an entire week. This time I decided to bring along a back-up system as a precaution."

"Yes, I can see where that would be a problem. Very good! Corporal," he called up to his associate inside the gate, "you may allow our guests to enter. All is in order."

Tapa drove the Hummer through the gate and up to the control building while the others all walked back. She took advantage of what little shade the building provided to park the vehicle out of the sun. Ivram found walking on the crushed stones a little difficult and concentrated on keeping his balance. An artificial leg was not exactly standard military equipment. It would be hard to explain why this hadn't earned him a full disability discharge. He made a point of stopping by each of the three bunkers to ask some questions of the sergeant.

They reached the building and the two officers followed Senior Sergeant Kalamanov and the corporal inside. Aslan went to retrieve some equipment. Tapa remained in the truck and was already booting up the system.

Inside was a small office that contained the sergeant's desk and the panel of video screens. One camera was mounted over the front gate and could be panned up or down to view either the road approach or the area directly in front where they had been screened. Four were mounted at each corner of the compound, facing inward, and panned the complex continuously, while two others were mounted on a pole atop the building and made 200° sweeps of the terrain surrounding the compound. At twilight, these converted to infrared night vision automatically. The final screen display showed another sergeant seated at a computer console. The seat beside him was vacant. It was not immediately apparent where that room might be.

In addition to the office, the building contained a metal table with some magazines and the remnants of someone's lunch. Four molded plastic chairs were grouped around it. The rear was partitioned off to form two rooms, one a utility kitchen and supply room and the other a bunkroom that could sleep up to six. Between the entrances to these two rooms was a door. At first glance it might lead to the toilet or a closet, except for the double set of locks that secured it.

"You'll have to forgive us sir," the sergeant was explaining to his guests as he led them in, "we're operating at about half strength these days. We man this post on a 24-hour shift that changes at 1800 every evening. There's supposed to be four technicians to man the control boards, two on, two off, every four hours. And we should have an OIC and two security guards. Instead we just have four, myself and the corporal here; Sergeant Kepka, who you see down there now and Sergeant Gorki, who is back there sleeping. She's due up in another forty minutes."

"But don't you need two men to man the control boards at all times?"

"To activate the rockets, yes sir. All four of us are board qualified, sir. During an alert we can get a second man down there right away. I was down there until the corporal called me up to cover while he went to the gate."

"They've left you critically short-handed. Is this normal or is someone missing today?"

"I'm afraid its been like this for several months now sir. The

Kazakhis have limited the number of Russians they'll allow into the country and we certainly don't want to let any of them in here."

"I understand, Senior Sergeant," Ivram said. "How long does it take to get a replacement out here if you need assistance?"

"A good hour, sir! We're garrisoned out of the Space Center back at Leninsk. Now, if you'll excuse me a moment sir, I just need to verify your visit." Kalamanov picked up the phone and punched out the numbers to the main base back at the Baikonur Cosmodrome. "Yes, Senior Sergeant Kalamanov here, post CV4995, the clearance code is 'Daybreak.' Yes, I'll hold... Yes, I authenticate with 'Red Fox'... Yes Captain, this is Senior Sergeant Kalamanov. We have an inspection team here from SBMC and I need to confirm... Yes, Colonel Anatoli Romanov, that's confirmed then? Yes, thank you sir."

The sergeant hung up the phone and smiled at the colonel. "Well, the computer back at the base confirms your visit sir. I guess we can get started." He walked over to the door in the center of the room and inserted a key from a chain that hung around his neck. The corporal also took out a key and unlocked the second lock on the door. Kalamanov pushed a button next to the door and the man on the TV screen could be seen looking over his shoulder. He reached over and pressed a button on his console. "Kepka has another set of TV monitors down there," The sergeant explained. "Except he has one that displays this room instead of the board room."

A buzzer sounded when Kepka pushed his button and the sergeant opened the door to reveal a small room. Actually, it was an elevator. "Come, I think we can all fit in," he said motioning to both Ivram and Hadzhi to enter with him. Once the door closed the room began to descend slowly. "We're only down about five meters here," the sergeant began to explain when the door opened into a concrete walled room. Three of the walls were lined with computer screens and control boards. The forth contained the elevator and two couches. Sergeant Kepka remained seated at his board position, just glancing over his shoulder to check out the visitors. "These walls are 50 centimeters thick, reinforced concrete with steel plates and lead shielding above and around the sides. It may not withstand a direct hit to the center of the compound, but anything more than 1,000 meters off won't harm us down here. We don't have any supplies, of course, so we'd die in a matter of days, but the mission would have been carried out by then."

They were introduced to Sergeant Kepka and Ivram began his inspection. "I'd like to run a few diagnostics, if you don't mind," he informed them. They agreed and Ivram laid his laptop down on the control board and ran some connection wires between them. As he

entered keystroke commands his screen came to life. He had pre-pro-
grammed his computer to run a diagnostic while his computer screen
displayed a series of images unrelated to the actual tasks it was performing. In actuality, it was down loading all of their security codes and
installing a special set of access commands that they would rely on
later. Ivram kept the two NCOs occupied with questions concerning
their daily routines. Hadzhi opened a notebook and checked off their
responses to the Colonel's questions.

Midway through the interview a bell rang. It startled both Ivram
and Hadzhi. "Don't worry, sirs, that's just Sgt. Gorki ready to relieve
Kepka." He pointed to the bank of monitors and they could see that
Gorki was a woman, slightly overweight, it appeared, with short
blonde hair. She was standing by the elevator, waiting to come down.
Kepka reached over and pressed a button. Hadzhi noted its position in
his book. They could hear the elevator ascending. When it was in position at the top, they heard the buzzer go off. Kepka flipped another
switch and the elevator returned down to them.

"The door upstairs won't open until someone down here throws
that switch and the elevator is in position," Kalamanov explained.

"What if the person on duty down here becomes ill or is disabled
somehow?"

"If there's no one down here to throw the switch, we need to call
in the security team from Leninsk."

"Yes, I see," the colonel said in a rather official tone. "That makes
it all the more important that there always be two of you down here,
doesn't it, Sergeant?"

"We try to do that, sir. Believe me, if Sgt. Gorki hadn't been up all
night, I'd have had her down here as soon as we saw you at the gate."

Again Ivram said, "Yes, I see." And nodded to the Captain, who
made further notes in his book.

The elevator door opened, revealing a rather heavyset woman in
her late thirties. She had been introduced to the sergeant upstairs and
was still trying to straighten her uniform in preparation for meeting the
two visiting officers. She snapped to a position of attention. "Sergeant
Gorki reporting for duty, sir."

"Ah yes, sergeant." The colonel extended his hand to greet her.
"There is no need for such formalities. Please go about your duties as
if the Captain and I weren't here."

Easy for him to say, each of the three noncoms thought. Kepka
briefed his replacement on the current status, which was inactive. He
excused himself and entered the elevator. Gorki now pushed the button
that sent it back up to the top. Hadzhi made a note that you could not

exit this room unless there was someone else here to activate that switch.

Ivram completed his diagnostic. "I wonder if the two of you could run this test for me now?" The colonel motioned for Kalamanov to take the other seat as he handed a printed sheet of instructions to Sergeant Gorki for her to follow. She took the paper from him with a toothy grin. Kalamanov nodded his approval to Gorki and she began entering the data. Her short, fleshy fingers moved quickly over the keyboard. "I need to speak to my sergeant. Is this a line up top?" Ivram had his hand on a red telephone and Kalamanov nodded an affirmative.

As soon as he picked up the receiver he could hear that the connection was made upstairs. The corporal answered almost immediately. He had been watching them on the screen while chatting casually with Aslan. "Yes, corporal, this is Colonel Romanov. I need to speak with my sergeant if you don't mind. Thank you. Yes, Sergeant, we are ready to run the test on one of the missile silos. Number four, I think should be okay.' Ivram looked over to Kalamanov, who again gave him a nod to indicate that silo four was fine for this test. "Yes, silo four, sergeant. Could you and the corporal up there please go out and insure we have the proper opening and closing sequences? Thank you."

The procedure to activate a silo hatch door normally required joint data entry from both the launch site and the Strategic Ballistic Missile Command Center. Ivram's diagnostic routine had temporarily shunted the satellite link away from SBMC to the computer set up in the Hummer. Tapa was now on line with them, going through the routines she had learned the night before. Everything went smoothly. The silo hatch swung open and Aslan was able to verify that he could gain access to the missile nose cone. Using a radio, he advised his colonel that all was satisfactory and the hatch swung closed with a loud clang of steel on concrete.

Down in the board room Ivram made a few more entries into his computer. These returned the site to its normal control without anyone at SBMC ever detecting that they had been off line for fifteen minutes or that the silo hatch had been activated. The Colonel turned to Kalamanov and shook his hand. "Thank you Senior Sergeant. Everything has gone very well this afternoon, I believe. If you don't mind, I would like to leave Captain Plushenko with you this evening. He will be merely an observer of your routine and of your replacement team. Let them know I will be by in the morning to retrieve him."

"Yes Colonel, that will be no problem," the sergeant replied. Son of a bitch, he thought, I'd like to see one of these desk jockeys try to man a missile station with half a crew for six months. He was glad their shift would be ending in less than two hours. This frigging inspector would be someone else's problem tonight.

57

Katryn Moldatin liked to think of herself as a survivor. She had survived the loss of her daughter, the unraveling of a military career, the dissolution of her marriage and the outright collapse of her government. Still the troubles continued to break upon her, in wave upon wave, like the relentless pounding of a tempest sea. Georgi was sixteen now and much taller than she was. As if that weren't trouble enough for a single mother, he and his friends were constantly being bombarded by the flood of western fads, fashions and faults that swept over the country after the fall of the Communist regime. On several occasions she had caught him drinking, too drunk to even stand up or talk to her.

Over the past year her father's health had failed dramatically. The doctors told them it was Alzheimer's Disease, but she knew that he had simply lost the will to live. All of his life Yuri Ivanovich Moldatin had been an active participant in the Communist Party. A member of the Youth League at fourteen, he was vice president of the local chapter by the time he was sixteen and a national officer by his seventeenth birthday. He had served as a delegate to The Congress of People's Deputies for forty years and every national leader since the death of Stalin had known him by name. If ever he or his family had need of something, he had only to ask and it was taken care of.

All of that changed abruptly. He woke one day to find that the Union of Soviet Socialist Republics was gone. Red flags no longer flew over his city. He was simply an old man without political connections, unable even to provide food for his wife, daughter and young grandson. His vulnerability crushed his spirit and he just simply stopped thinking.

At times Katryn felt like screaming. Such an emotional outburst would be unseemly and she fought to remain in control. She took pride in the fact that she had always been able to present herself in a professional manner, no matter what the adversity. Her office became her refuge. Of course there were always problems, crises even, but these were solvable and reconcilable. She was always in control there, not like the situations at home.

She had been invited to come to the Space Research Institute to assist in the implementation of an integrated computer network that could link all of the activities of the Russian Academy of Science. She was soon managing the project and expanding it beyond the original scope to include access to all governmental agencies. Within a year she was named Director of Computer Operations. This required that she spend more time on bureaucratic paperwork and less actually working on the computer. That was a hard change at first, but she was getting used to the new role.

She had to rely on others to do the work for her and only periodically spot-checked their reports to keep a finger on the pulse of the operation. That's why she had not been completely concerned several weeks back, when she found what appeared to be a glitch in the monthly activity report she was looking over. It listed the number of new agencies (5) that had come on line the previous month and stated that the total now stood at 47. "That can't be right," she muttered to herself. "I'm sure we only had 41 last month."

She turned to the computer console at her desk and made a few entries. Everything seemed to be in order. Still, she was certain that the number had only been 41. In fact, she'd given briefings to that effect. She pulled up the list of agencies and ran down the names. One caught her attention, the Federation Center for Ethnic Studies and Autonomous Governance. "Odd," she thought, "I don't remember seeing that one before." She checked to be sure it was not one of the five new agencies and then pulled up its file.

According to the records, this particular file had been active for over a year. "It's not possible." She liked to talk out loud to herself; the dialogue helped her think more clearly. "I would have had to set this up myself. I simply don't recall ever seeing this account before." She clicked unto the web-site and surveyed the documents that were included. Technical papers and statistical reports, many very dated, were all she could find. "This is really strange." She made a note to herself to investigate this account further; using one of those new sticky pads that had made their way into her office. She attached the note to the printout and flipped it into her "To Do" box, where it was gradually buried under other, more pressing matters.

This morning she was reviewing her notes for a presentation on the needs of the space exploration staffers. Her buzzer sounded and the voice of the young woman seated outside her office came over the speaker. "Madam Director, there's a gentleman here to see you. He's from the Military Security Service."

Katryn told the young woman to show him in and decided that she would remain seated behind her desk as a sign of her authority. The man who entered had a familiarity about him, but she couldn't immediately place the face. "Good morning, Katryn," he said in a friendly and informal manner. "It's been a long time. Fifteen years, I think. I'm delighted to see you looking so well."

Her mind raced back fifteen years and then she remembered. "Sergi, my God it *has* been a long time. I thought that you'd dropped off the face of the Earth for sure!" She rose and came around to give him a hug. "Look at you. A little heavier perhaps, and a lot less hair I might add."

"Thank you, Katryn, you always were one to be perfectly frank. But look at you. My God, Katryn, you're as lovely as ever." Katryn was not used to such compliments and blushed noticeably. Sergi was being serious. Her hips had filled out and her facial features were more striking with maturity. She was wearing a neat little steel gray suit. The skirt cut nicely above her knees to reveal quite shapely legs. They spent a few moments reliving old memories about life at Novgorod.

"I was assigned almost immediately out of the training center to work for Army Intelligence Operations. Back then it was a counterpart to the KGB. Believe me when I tell you that I *can't* tell about most of what I did back then. Lately I've been involved primarily in developing security systems for our computer networks and in detecting attempts by hackers to log onto the system. That's why I'm here today," he told her.

"Surely you don't suspect me of any tampering now, do you?"

"No, but I was hoping you might be able to give me some help. You're still one of the best damn computer people in the country."

"Sergi, I'm not one of the best, I AM the best," she said dryly, then broke into a hearty laugh. He joined in.

"Ah, Katryn, always the same. I was shocked to hear about you and Garyk.

She stopped laughing and became businesslike again. "Well, those things happen. Now, how can I be of assistance?" She directed him to a chair and moved back to sit at her desk.

"For some time now we have suspected that someone or some group was attempting to gain access to military records. In the beginning it was crude, but still sophisticated enough to break into some of the more classified operations going on down south. We were able to secure each breach has soon as it was detected but we always seemed to be one or two steps behind. Then the activity stopped completely. We assumed we had succeeded in closing all the doors and windows.

"Lately, we have detected new activity. This time it's subtler, a lot more sophisticated too. In the past we know that certain information must have been used to coordinate guerrilla activities, based upon subsequent raids that were carried out against our supply convoys and tactical units in Chechnya. For now, they just seem to be probing. However, we're sure that this is being done in anticipation of some major break into one of the security nets. Whoever it is has access at the highest levels. In fact, we think it must be someone on the inside."

"Yes, I share your concern." Katryn unconsciously blew her bangs out of her eyes, causing the platinum blonde strands to flip up a bit. "What do you think I can do?"

"To begin with, there are certain signatures, characteristic traits if you will, that every hacker has. Even though there have been several different types of probes detected, we feel that it may be the work of only one person. Perhaps you can help us determine who that might be. Of greater importance, however, is to try to determine what the next move is likely to be. We can't stay one step behind this guy."

"Sergi, you've been trained especially for this kind of detective work. I've been out of the intelligence field completely for some time. This is what I do now," she said, sweeping her arm around the office.

"Yes, Katryn, and that's just the point. Recently, many of the hits on our system have been run through here. Someone is using IKI RAN access to enter the nuclear weapons database!"

"You're kidding! We have no direct links into that type of information here."

"Perhaps not officially, Katryn, but I can assure you that inquiries have been processed through your network on several occasions." Sergi had brought a number of diagnostic printouts with him. He walked around and stood next her, laying the spreadsheets out across her desk. "See, here are the dates and times that IKI-RAN's computer has logged into the SBMC data base."

It annoyed Katryn to think that someone had used her project to hack into the highly classified military network. Actually, she had to admit it was the fact that by beating her security systems someone had actually beaten her. That's what really got her mad. After Sergi left she buzzed her secretary and summoned her two chief programmers to her office immediately.

"We may have had a serious breach in our security system," she told them. "Here is a list of programs I want run immediately." She handed the list to a nervous middle-aged technocrat who stood fidgeting in front of her desk. She handed another to the more casual, heavyset woman standing next to him. "Anastashia, I want you to get me all of those files. This is a number one priority. Do you understand?"

They both nodded that they did and hurried out of her office. Katryn planned to spend a few hours each day on the project. The more she got into it, the more intricate she realized that this system actually was. This prodded her into spending more time to unravel the puzzle. Someone had spent an enormous amount of time creating a series of switchbacks and blind alleys to discourage detection. She was impressed that Sergi had actually been able to detect this pattern in the first place.

Because of her involvement with the IKI RAN side of this problem, she paid little attention to the earlier break-in material. Sergi was right, it had been a clumsy job. Nothing had actually been done to mask those attempts. Someone had simply stumbled unto unprotected entry ports and doorways. She was much more interested in finding out how her systems had been breached so she could close those gaps. Her job might depend upon it!

58

The colonel ascended the elevator and took leave of Sergeant Kepka. The corporal walked slowly out to open the gate while the inspection party, less the captain, climbed back into their vehicle and made their way out of the compound. The corporal snapped to attention and saluted as they passed through the gate. It was returned by a gesture that was more like a wave than a salute. They heard the gate clang shut behind them.

Neither Aslan nor Tapa said anything as they drove back along the gravel road. Both decided that it would be better to allow Ivram the first comment. He was seated in the front passenger seat and turned back to address them both. "Well, I think that went very well, don't you?"

"Does that mean I can finally breathe again? My God, Ivram, no excuse me, Colonel, my hands were shaking so much back there. I was afraid I wouldn't be able to enter the proper computer commands."

Ivram and Aslan both chuckled at her remark. Ivram patted her hand lightly as she steered down the path. "Tapa, you did very well. You both did very well indeed. I'm proud of you. However, the biggest task still lies before us."

They continued on to the point where the dry ground began to give way to rice paddies and Tapa stopped the truck. "All right, Aslan, you can get out here and check the supplies we left behind. Stay out of sight, but keep an eye out for that truck bringing in the change of watch. They should come by in about an hour. If you count more than four people, give me a holler on the radio. It's best for us to be seen leaving this place now, but we'll be back before midnight. Any questions?"

Aslan shook his head to indicate that he had none and stepped out of the Hummer. He walked over to a clump of underbrush and signaled back that the weapons stash they had unloaded earlier was still undisturbed. Tapa eased back onto the path and proceeded to retrace the route back to the main road. "Are you sure we can pull this off, Ivram, excuse me again, sir?"

"Well, *corporal,* if the next group is as lax as this one, there's no doubt about it."

When they returned that night, Tapa was a nervous wreck. It wasn't the mission that concerned her, but rather it was trying to keep this oversized vehicle on the narrow dirt road without the benefit of head-lights. It had been hard enough earlier in the day and she was certain that they would soon end up on their side or possibly even upside down in the rice fields. Fortunately it was a clear night but there was a less than half a moon to provide any illumination. She kept her eyes riveted to the road ahead. Suddenly, there were two sharp raps on the door next to her. "Oh my God!" she cried out as she slammed on the brakes. "Did I hit something?" Turning her head to look back over her shoulder, she was immediately confronted by a face peering back at her through the window. Startled, she screamed involuntarily. She shrieked again when she felt the hand come down on her arm.

"It's all right, Tapa." Ivram said calmly. He was patting her hand to calm her down. "It's just Aslan. I believe you drove right by him in the dark."

"Thanks be to the Almighty, I'm glad that's over," she said, once she had finally composed herself.

Back at the compound activity had shifted into night mode. The new crew consisted of a Master Sergeant, two sergeants and a corpo-ral, none of whom had been delighted by the news that they would have a visiting officer monitoring their watch. The captain kept pretty much to himself, only occasionally joining in on their casual conversa-tions and for that they were thankful. What unsettled them most were the constant notations he was making on his workpapers. At midnight the crew completed the routine security check with missile command. One of the sergeants, a Mongolian by ancestry, advised their guest, "Well, we're good now until 0600 tomorrow morning, unless of course we go to war before that!" He chuckled drolly at his little attempt at humor. Pushing his chair back from the control board, he said, "I'm heading up top to get some sleep. Care to join me sir?"

"No, thank you, Sergeant. I'll probably catch a few winks on one of those couches. Hopefully I'll catch up on some sleep tomorrow afternoon. That's a hazard of this inspection detail, I'm afraid."

Hadzhi marveled at how these men could do this night after night. The room remained the same, hour after hour, except for the panning action displayed on two of the security screens. Those pictures were now an eerie green, the cameras long since switched over to infrared mode. The other cameras remained stationary, focused in on the compound where nothing had moved since the last watch had departed over five hours ago. The final screen now displayed a picture of the elevator door being opened and the sergeant walking out of view, all in absolute silence. Random red, white and green lights were illuminated on the control boards. Their small, steady beams, combined with the faint hum emitted by the computers, had a mesmerizing effect. The digital date-time display provided a monotonous pulse to the whole setting.

The two sergeants were both asleep in the bunkroom and the corporal was somewhere up stairs, probably asleep at the table. At the control board the Master Sergeant donned a headset and was listening to classical music, whistling loudly in accompaniment. He was older than Senior Sergeant Kalamanov by about ten years and seemed qualified to retire. Single, and given the state of the Russian economy, he had opted to remain on active duty for as long as they would have him. "Hello, what do we have here?" He sat upright in his chair and pulled the headset off with his left hand, reaching for the red phone with the other. "Come on, Mensenko, wake up, you idiot," he muttered to the TV monitor.

Hadzhi was about to nod off on the couch. He noticed this activity and walked over behind the sergeant to see what the cause of this stir might be. The monitor carrying the picture from the front gate showed a moving image approaching the compound. The sergeant manipulated some controls and the camera panned up and zoomed in. It was difficult to make out in the dark, but there appeared to be a woman walking a bicycle up to the gate. The infrared cameras both stopped their pans at the detection of this motion and were displaying similar images.

"Damn it, Mensenko," the Master Sergeant yelled into the phone, "it's about time you woke your sorry ass up. Get outside and find out what the fuck is going on. It seems we have a night visitor at the gate. Wake up Sergeant Ivanof before you go."

The sergeant turned around and spoke to the captain. "Sir, is this part of your inspection drill?"

"No, Sergeant, I have no idea what's going on."

Corporal Mensenko was still trying to shake the effects of his cat-nap as he walked quickly across the compound to the front gate. The night air was hot and dry. The stones made a loud crunching sound as his boots dug in. He'd been assigned to this post for almost five months and this was the first time that he could recall ever having someone approach the gate after dark. Behind him Sergeant Ivanof was stretching and yawning in the doorway. "Excuse me, ma'am, this is a restricted area, I must ask you to leave immediately," he advised the stranger as he neared the gate. His hand worked to find the snap that unloosened the pistol at his side.

The woman began to speak. He had no clue what she was saying; it was that Kazakhi mumbo jumbo. "This is a Russian military compound. Do you speak Russian?" He repeated the last question slowly, using the little Kipchak that he had picked up. "Do...you... speak...Russian?

"Yes," she answered haltingly, "I speak it a little. Please to forgive me, I was looking for road to the house of my cousin. I have turned, I think, down wrong path. These small roads they all the same in dark."

"Well there's no one living along this road, that's for damned sure. You're just going to have to go back the way you came."

"Please, sir, it is so dark. I am terrified coming down here. I am so happy when I see lights. Can I not stay here until morning? I not want to go back alone."

"That's impossible. I told you, this is a restricted Russian military base. You must leave at once!" The young woman began to cry. The corporal realized that under the shawl she had wrapped around her head was actually a rather attractive young thing. Her sweater swelled over the fullness of her breasts. What the hell she was doing out this late he couldn't imagine. Too bad he couldn't meet someone like this at the local bistro when he had a night off duty.

She was talking in Kipchak again and he motioned with his hand that he couldn't understand. "I cannot go back," she sobbed in Russian. "Not across fields at night. I not be able to find my cousin house until it is light. I cannot, how do I say, understand the land. I am not from this place. I am visitor."

The corporal turned back and motioned for Ivanof to come out and join him. The sergeant flipped the butt of a cigarette off in the direction of Block One. He had thrown on his shirt, not bothering to button it. It hung down over his trousers and exposed his chest and modest potbelly as he sauntered towards the gate. "What's the problem, Mensenko?" he asked as he came across the compound.

"It seems we have a stray sheep that's lost her way. Not only that, but she's afraid to be out alone in the dark."

"Well, that is a problem, now isn't it," Ivanof said. He cast a leering eye at the young woman standing on the other side of the gate. "What do you suppose we should do with her, Mensenko?"

"Maybe we could get her some blankets and let her stay here by the fence until it gets light enough for her to go back."

"Such a kind heart you have, corporal. How do we know she's not a terrorist or a spy?" His tone was condescending, mocking both the corporal and the peasant girl. "Come, let's have a look." The sergeant opened the gate and went out to the visitor. He drew his pistol and pointed it at her head. The woman's eyes reflected sheer terror, not knowing what this man might have in mind. Again she said something to him in Kipchak. "Don't talk that babble to me, bitch," he said crudely. "Let's take a look and see what weapons you've got concealed here." Holding the gun to her head he ran his other hand up and down her sides, pausing to fondle her breasts. "These seem fully loaded, what do you think, Mensenko?"

The corporal laughed nervously. He looked back in the direction of the building, realizing that they were most likely on camera. "Sergeant, remember we have an inspector downstairs."

"Fuck him. He can have a turn with this one if he wants, after I've finished with her." He moved his hand down massaging her thighs and buttocks as he did so. "And what might you be concealing under here?" His hand was under her skirt, moving up the inside of her leg.

Sobbing deeply, she bit down on her lip and closed her eyes to shut out the embarrassment. Anxiously, she said, "Please, sir, it was mistake. Please, I go now."

"Sure, babe, we'll let you go. Just as soon as I've finished my little search." His hand was up between her legs and he was happy to find that she wore nothing else beneath the skirt. His fingers began to probe inside of her. He pushed three of them in has far as they could go moving them about slowly. "Yes, I really think I've found something here. What do you think, my dear, does that feel good?"

Mensenko watched this with growing anxiety, embarrassed that his own penis had grown fully erect as the scene unfolded before him. Everything in his head told him that this was wrong, yet something more carnal down deep inside longed to become involved with the seduction. She was crying hysterically and called out "PLEASE, NO!" or words to that effect in her own language. He stood transfixed, watching as the sergeant pinned the woman against the fence. Ivanof raised her skirt higher and pushed the barrel of the revolver between her legs and up inside her while he groped for the fly of his pants. Mensenko heard a strange pop—pop and watched as blood suddenly exploded from the sergeant's chest, splattering over the woman's sweater. Before he realized what was happening, he felt his own chest collapsing under the weight of a mighty blow. He dropped to his knees. Vaguely he could make out two men running up the road towards the gate. Then he fell face forward into the crushed stones.

The master sergeant had been watching all this on the TV monitor. "Jesus, what the fuck does he think he's doing out there?" He was more concerned that the captain was watching this episode unfold than he was with the event itself.

"Getting a little pussy, it looks like," the captain had replied with a crude laugh.

Without the benefit of sound, the sergeant watched, as both of his men fell to the ground. Before he could react to this unexpected development, the captain had the blade of a knife at his throat and quickly split his windpipe open. On the monitor, Hadzhi watched as Aslan pulled the keys out of Ivanof's pocket and made his way into the compound. Ivram was holding Tapa with his arm under hers to steady her. She was noticeably shaken and appeared to be still crying as he walked her slowly toward the building.

59

Sergi swung by Katryn's office late in the afternoon to see how she had progressed. "So how is my newest detective getting along?"

"Very slowly, I'm afraid. I still don't understand how you picked up on these so quickly."

"Every hit on one of our special access programs is re-analyzed every day and compared to all others over several time intervals. Actually, it's the short time hits that concern us the most. One random access hit might be attributed to accident. Someone just keying in the wrong information and getting through by sheer chance. It's unlikely, but it does happen. These hits have a pattern only when studied as a group. Someone is popping in for a quick look and getting out before an alarm can be triggered. Why?"

"Have you figured that out yet?"

"Originally, to gain access to troop and supply deployments. I think I told you we identified several guerrilla attacks on our Army units by Chechen para-military forces that seem to coincide with the break-ins. It looks as though they may have actually gone so far as to order up the supplies that they intended to hijack. Now we think that something big is being planned for. The fact that they got into the nuclear weapons program is a major concern."

Katryn looked very concerned. "You don't think they can launch a missile, do you?"

"Highly unlikely. Do they think they can steal a warhead—possibly, but that would require multi-point verifications, with one or more people on the inside. To be safe, though, we have beefed up our security at certain critical launch sites, as well as at SBMC."

"Yes, but won't they know that?" Katryn was annoyed before. Now she was scared. The fact that the nuclear missile command system had been so readily breached raised the specter of all kinds of craziness.

"Possibly. It depends on what systems are being monitored and on who it is they've got on the inside."

"Do you have any ideas along those lines?"

"Some, but we really can't be sure we're catching every attempt. It's a well designed program."

"I know. I think I'm really quite jealous actually. Whoever did this is very good. Are you really sure that those earlier break-ins were by the same person?"

"100% certain, no I'm not, but my gut reaction is that it was the same guy. That was a field operation. Christ, he accessed the system using a God damned cell phone! The computer was limited in its capacity too, based upon what he did and didn't do. You've got to be good to do that!"

Katryn looked at Sergi and asked, "But certainly they needed a powerful computer just to run the algorithms to break the access codes."

"No, that's why I think it's the same person. See this guy isn't trying to break the codes. He's never on line long enough to be doing that. No, I told you the other day, this guy seems to already know how to get into the system by bypassing the codes. It's as if he's got his own access key."

Her eyebrows raised when Sergi said this. How could she have missed it the other day? She turned to her computer and started to bang out a whole series of commands. The fingers of her left hand moved quickly over the keys and she whipped the mouse back and forth with her right. She paused and ran her finger down the first set of printouts he'd given to her, sorry now for not having looked at these more closely before. She clicked one more time and displayed a screen that listed the various access points that Sergi had discovered. Sergi stood behind her, trying to figure out what it was that she obviously saw in that pattern.

"My God, Sergi, I should have realized this right away. It's Garyk!"

"Are you certain?"

"Absolutely! He designed that system, Sergi. I helped a little, but that was his project. God, look at this. These are all his favorite catchwords. That's my fucking birthday! He built all of those windows into the system so he could get in to perform maintenance updates without having to log on and off all the time. He hated that part of it. Sergi, Garyk was responsible for the security programs for both the satellite communications system *and* the nuclear warhead deactivation program. He won't need a three-way hook up to access those missiles. He'll know how to do it all by himself!"

Katryn called home and told her mother not to expect her for dinner. "When will you be here?" her mother asked.

"I really can't say for sure. Something very important has come up and I'm not going to leave here until I get to the bottom of it. Late, very late, I'd guess. Tell Georgi I love him."

Sergei also made some phone calls. He alerted his staff about this breakthrough and spoke directly to the commanding general of SBMC.

"I'm sorry Sergi, I should have realized this was Garyk's handiwork from the very beginning, especially with the Chechen tie in. I've tried to put him out of my mind this past year and I guess I succeeded. My god, do you think he's really going after a nuclear warhead?"

"It seems all the more likely now, given that it's him we're dealing with." What we need to know is where will he attempt to do this."

"Of course, there's another very important question, Sergi," she said with some apprehension. He looked across at her from the other side of the desk and slowly nodded in agreement, without having to ask what that was. "Yes, I know. Assuming he can get his hands on one of those things, just what the hell is he planning to do with it?"

They worked together for several hours analyzing all of the known times he had accessed any of the military data sites. They hadn't all emanated from IKI RAN and she took some comfort in that. By working backward through the maze of interconnections he had put in place they finally determined that he was using the State University as a base of operations. "Well, we can shut that down first thing tomorrow," Sergi told her. "I'll have our people down there bring Garyk in for questioning as well. Unfortunately, the Chechen government still considers itself a sovereign entity, otherwise I'd just have him arrested."

Sergi packed up his briefcase. "I think it's time to call it an evening. It's nearly nine o'clock. Why don't you go home too? Of course, if you'd like, I'd be delighted to buy you a late supper."

Katryn smiled at the offer. When was the last time she had gone out on a date? That was the offer, wasn't it? "No, thanks anyway. I think I'll keep at this a while longer. I still want to know how he's using my computer."

She worked at the computer for two more hours. Just before eleven she was about to give up. "Damn, he's good!" she told her computer screen. He had disguised his actions in so many different ways that even now, when she knew what she was looking for, it was still difficult to find the trails. There had to be some common link, but where was it? "Screw you, Garyk!" she said aloud and took a big stretch. She ran her fingers through her hair, rubbing her scalp vigorously to stimulate the flow of blood to her brain. Her eyes moved randomly around her office, just trying to get a break from the computer screen's glow. She wound up staring vacantly at her 'to do' box. Then it hit her. "What was that I was looking at?" She stood up and ruffled through the stack of documents, reports and briefs that had accumulated and found what she was looking for almost at the bottom of the pile. "I'll be a son of a bitch!" she muttered, followed by. "Katryn, you were supposed to follow up on this last month. Shit!"

The Federation Center for Ethnic Studies and Autonomous Governance was a bogus agency. She could see that now. When she started to analyze the recent hits to that web site they almost all led back to Groznyy. She ran several diagnostics and finally found that one article seemed to be attracting the greatest attention. It was entitled "*The Mass Deportation of Chechen, Ingush and Alan Nationals During the Stalin Era of Repression*" and represented a scholarly research paper written almost fifteen years earlier. She scrolled through this several times looking for some icon that might open onto whatever program she knew Garyk must have planted. After the fourth time through, she began randomly clicking on words and phrases.

Nothing was happening and she was finding it hard to keep her eyes open. She scrolled onto page six and, without thinking, clicked the page number displayed at the top. She was already moving the cursor to something else when her screen suddenly turned completely green. "What the hell is this?" She was watching a dog caricature trot across the screen. No, it was a wolf! It moved from left to right, reappearing slightly lower each time it completed a trip and disappeared off the right side. On the fourth trot across the screen the figure was close to the bottom and it stopped midway across, sat down and looked out at her, panting. Curious, she clicked on the wolf. Immediately, the screen changed and she was now staring at the official seal of the Russian Federation's Supreme Ballistic Missile Command. It was a sky blue screen, with the crest emblazoned in white. A prompt asked for the user to enter the access code and password. Below it flashed a warning in large bold red letters.

THIS IS A RESTRICTED ACCESS PROGRAM
SECURITY CLEARANCE REQUIRED

TOP SECRET
VIOLATORS WILL BE SUBJECT TO ARREST!

"Son of a bitch!" She quickly clicked off of the screen. No sense in getting the Army down on her back. She looked at her watch. It was just after midnight. She thought about calling Sergi, but decided that it really was too late. She was about to log off and call it a night when she realized that the Ethnic Studies program was currently in use. "Garyk, you bastard, are you on-line now?"

60

Aslan slipped quietly into the building. Tonight he was wearing a black tee shirt, his face and arms liberally covered with lampblack. No one was in the main room. He held a machine pistol in front of him with both hands. On the TV monitor he could see Hadzhi down below, propping up a body at the control board. He made his way cautiously to the back room. It was completely dark inside and he waited for his eyes to fully adjust. The sound of someone turning over in the far top bunk caught his attention. He moved silently to the side of the bed and fired once, directly into the head of a sleeping sergeant. "That is for the soul of my brother," he told the corpse.

Ivram ushered Tapa inside and helped her to a seat at the table. Still shaking and sobbing slightly, she looked up at him and apologized. "Look at me. Some commando I turned out to be."

"Hush, you have nothing to be ashamed off, my dear." Ivram had also changed into night combat attire. A black woolen cap fit tightly over his head, causing perspiration to bead on his forehead, streaking the black compound on his face. " I just wish Aslan hadn't waited so long to shoot that bastard. I was about to do it myself. I'm sorry for putting you in such a dreadful position. Are you sure you can continue?"

"I'll be fine. Just give me a minute."

Aslan came up to her and laid his hand on her shoulder. She shuddered at his touch. "I'm sorry," he said, removing his hand. "You did just fine. I waited until I could see him release his hand from that pistol. I didn't want that going off when I shot him."

"Thank you for that." She almost sounded herself again.

Ivram told Aslan to bring up the truck and then picked up the phone to talk to Hadzhi. "What is the situation down there, Captain?"

"Everything is in order sir. I hope all this blood doesn't short out the control board."

"I wouldn't think so. I'll be down in a little while. Tapa still needs some consoling I'm afraid."

"God yes, what the hell was that all about? At first I didn't really think it was her. Where did that bicycle come from?"

"Just something we commandeered in town this evening. I thought that might catch them off guard. I just didn't figure on that sergeant being such a pig."

Tapa had gone into the small kitchen to get some coffee. She came back cradling the cup in her hands. "I hope you two aren't talking about me," she said, forcing a smile to reassure him that she was okay.

They had left the Hummer several hundred meters down the road from the compound to avoid being detected. It took Aslan some time to jog down and drive it back. He stopped and secured the gate behind him, just in case another unexpected visitor should come along. Tapa came out when the truck stopped by the building and climbed inside. "Are you okay?" he asked her.

"Yes, why is everyone so concerned?"

"Well, it could have something to do with the blood splattered all over you."

"Oh, I hadn't realized," she said, looking down at her sweater. "God, what a mess you made." She took a seat in front of the computer terminal Ivram had set up and started switching on the equipment. The second system had been set up earlier that evening and she booted it up as well. She ran over all of the procedures he had taught her, hoping that she wouldn't forget anything when the time came.

Ivram took his laptop and a radio with him and descended to the board room. He utilized the key taken from Ivanof and another, conveniently left around the neck of the dead man in the bunkroom. Hadzhi greeted him with considerable relief. "I hope you don't need me down here. I've explained everything in my notes. Sorry, but I'm about to go claustrophobic. I need to get outside for some fresh air."

"I'll be find. You've done a good job."

After working through the elevator procedure, Ivram hooked up his computer. It was set to monitor the system to detect the random electronic sweep that emanated from SBMC and assured headquarters that the system was fully functional. Once they got the signal, he knew he would have at least thirty minutes to take the site off line, remove the warheads and go back on line again.

His computer beeped twice and the display read:

SECURITY SWEEP IN PROGRESS

He called out on the radio. "Okay, Tapa, it's time to get started."

"Roger, I hope I don't screw this up."

"Nonsense, you'll do just fine. Take a deep breath and do everything just as we rehearsed it this afternoon."

He began keying in some commands when his radio squawked again and he heard her voice calling. "Ivram, I think you better get up here. Something is terribly wrong!" Her voice had urgency about it and it caused a knot in his stomach. What could possibly have gone wrong at this point? He grabbed the phone and told Aslan to come down so he could go out and see what it was.

He entered the truck and found her just staring at the computer screens. She turned to him and said, "I did everything just the way you showed me, Ivram. I swear I did nothing wrong!" Ivram could tell that she was frantic. Tears welled in hers eyes once more.

"I should never have put you through all this, I'm..."

"No, that's not it. I got into the Ethnic Studies web site okay and clicked onto page six, just like we did the other night. Only this time I'm getting a completely different screen. It happened both times."

He looked over at the two monitors and gasped in disbelief. In bold letters across both screens were inscribed:

GARYK
WHAT ARE YOU
DOING?

He tried several entries but he was locked out. Each time he tried to re-enter the web site he got the same message. And then the screen simply read:

ACCESS DENIED

Concerned, Tapa asked, "What is it, Ivram, did I do something wrong?"

"Not at all. I think it must be Katryn. She's on to my little game somehow."

"Does that mean we can't access the system anymore?"

"Well, not through IKI RAN at least. Hopefully they still haven't found all of my other back doors yet. It will just take me a little more time. Unfortunately, we don't have much of that left. Better tell Hadzhi there's been a slight alteration to our time schedule."

Sergi's people had been successful in closing down most of his secret windows, but not all of them. It took him over an hour, but he was finally able to hack into the SBMC net and they were back in business. He wished that Hadzhi had been briefed about running the system at the control board so he could stay up top and monitor any new problems that might pop up. Fortunately, everything else started to fall into place.

At 0410 the SBMC computer system made another random sweep and they put the plan into action. Tapa was able to direct the satellite communications system to switch over to her commands. Between the two of them they directed the computer to open the hatch on block number 6, the one closest to the truck. Hadzhi and Aslan ascended the steel steps embedded into the concrete and watched, as the missile tube was revealed to them. Performing just as he had programmed it to several years earlier, Ivram and Tapa executed the three-way commands that released the locking mechanism on the warhead and allowed Hadzhi and Aslan to slowly unscrew the devices.

Ivram had warned them that these would be heavy, but they still were not prepared for the massive weight associated with plutonium. Aslan tried to reposition himself to better handle the weight on his arms, but lost his grip. The warhead they were pulling up started to slip away. Hadzhi slammed it against the side wall and pinned it there long enough for Aslan to grab hold again.

"Christ, be careful Aslan. That damn thing nearly crashed down inside the missile silo.

"These things can't detonate by being dropped, can they?"

Hadzhi shook his head and cast a stern glance at his companion. "I don't think so, but let's not try to find out, okay."

It took them nearly twenty minutes and their uniforms were saturated with perspiration. Ivram anxiously called to them on the radio. "How are you guys getting on up there? Time is running out on us. We're going to have to shut this hatch again in five minutes or risk being detected."

There was an uncomfortable pause before Hadzhi responded. "We're just a little busy right now. On the last one." His voice sounded strained.

The warhead contained four separate nuclear devices, each a small rocket in its own right. If deployed, the nose cone would open at high altitude and allow each to be ejected and self-propel to different targets. They were removing each rocket, unscrewing the nuclear device in its cap, and replacing the rocket unit back inside the main missile. It was a lot of effort, but the security program wasn't designed to detect missing components. If they could mask the actual theft for as long as possible it would give them sufficient time to get out of the country with the goods before an alarm was sounded.

Inside the van, Tapa held her breath as she watched them struggle with the last one. The sweat on their hands made it that much more difficult to manage. Ivram's voice came over the radio impatiently, "Time, gentlemen!"

Aslan answered this time. "Yes, Hadzhi is screwing the nose cone back in place right this minute."

Another twenty seconds ticked agonizing by on the control board. Finally Ivram heard the words, "Okay, we're clear!" Tapa exclaimed, "Praise to the Almighty!" She and Ivram quickly entered another series of commands. The hatch cover slowly moved down and clanged into position. Aslan was sure it could be heard all the way back to the Cosmodrome. Tapa reprogrammed the satellite. "We're back on line!" she told Ivram over the radio. Thirty-seven minutes had ticked by on his stopwatch. No sooner had they completed the final entries than Ivram's laptop signaled that the sweep program had again kicked in. "That was just a bit too close," Ivram said to himself.

Earlier, Hadzhi had carried the two bodies in from the gate area while Ivram was trying to regain access. He told Aslan, "Load our friends here onto the elevator. We'll store them down below so when the next watch gets here at 1800 there won't anyone in sight."

Aslan dragged Ivanof's body in first and was about to haul in the corporal's when Tapa said, "Wait!" She entered the elevator and stood over the body. Lifting her skirt, she urinated on Ivanof's head. "May you smell that for all of eternity, you bastard," she said and walked back out to the truck.

Ivram received the three bodies and propped them up on the two couches along the back wall. They had to wait an agonizingly long hour until 0600 for the morning sign-on and security check. Hadzhi came down to work the codebook with Ivram, using the notes he had taken when this was done at midnight. Once this was finished, they hoped that no one would be checking back with the site until the watch change. Then it would take at least another hour for the security team to come out from Leninsk and gain access to the lower chamber.

Hadzhi tied a rope around the master sergeant's arm and looped this over a pencil, which he jammed into the control board. They both stepped into the elevator and Hadzhi gave the rope a quick tug. The pencil pulled away, dropping the sergeant's arm down onto the elevator release button. The door closed and they were on their way up top.

61

It was 6:30 in the morning back in Moscow. Mrs. Moldatin was trying to rouse her daughter. "Katryn, wake up! There's a telephone call for you. The man said it was urgent."

Katryn moaned and opened one eye to look at the clock. "God it's only 6:30," she mumbled. She had not gotten home until after one and it had taken her a while to fall asleep. Her mind kept replaying the incidents of the passed few hours. She shuffled into the kitchen where they kept the telephone; her eyes still half closed. "Yes, this is Katryn Moldatin, who is this please?"

"Katryn, it's Sergi. Sorry to have to wake you. It seems Garyk was very active last night. This morning actually. We've detected several unsuccessful attempts to enter the system, all between midnight and about 2 AM."

"I'm not surprised, I caught him on line at IKI RAN right about midnight and terminated his access."

"You're kidding, you were actually on line with him!"

"I have to assume it was Garyk. I found out how he was using our system. He'd set up his own web page and it linked directly to SBMC. Who else would be into an obscure site like that at that hour?"

"And you shut him down?"

"Oh yes, I made sure of that!"

Then that explains why he was making all of those other attempts to get in. It's a bit strange. We've never seen him try to access the system this late before. He's always come on line during the day. He's never made that many attempts to get in before, either. You must have really spooked him."

"I hope so. Are you completely certain he didn't get in this morning?"

"No, not really. We only know about those entry codes we had detected and shut down beforehand. We're still running searches. That's why I called. Do you think you could meet me at my office in about a half-hour?"

She looked at her watch and thought for a second. "Give me forty-five minutes. Where the hell are you, anyway?"

It took her nearly an hour because she changed her mind twice while dressing, opting finally for a sheerer blouse and dark blue skirt that accentuated the curve of her hips. She giggled when she paused in front of the mirror and asked the image, "What are you thinking about? Then she undid the second button and headed off to her office to pick up some of the information she'd printed out the night before. Sergi worked at a highly classified bureau and she needed to be screened before they let her in. Katryn found him sitting at a desk stacked high with various papers and printouts. He looked disheveled, his shirt opened at the neck and his tie loosened and askew. A forgotten cigarette with a long train of ash was balanced between his fingers. He didn't rise to greet her but remained staring at one particular spreadsheet that was spread out over all of the others.

"I brought some of my things over to show you what he's been up to," she started to explain as she sat down in the chair in front of his desk.

"Oh Katryn, hi." As he moved to acknowledge her, the ash fell off the cigarette in a pile on the printout. Absently, he brushed them away.

"Sergi, my God, you look like you've just seen a ghost. What's the matter?"

"We're too late Kathryn! Whatever it was he was planning, I think maybe he pulled it off last night."

"You're kidding, aren't you? Please tell me you are," she said rather alarmed.

"I wish I were. I told you we detected a series of unsuccessful hits on our security system early this morning. We kept checking and found several unexplained hits. The first was about 0210, Moscow time. I guess you spooked him enough so that he didn't cover his tracks quite as well this time. The entries were made via satellite links. He's not in Groznyy anymore, Katryn. He was somewhere in central fucking Kazakhstan!"

"Kazakhstan? What could possibly be there?"

"Oh, not too much. Just six of seven holdover ICBM launch sites with less security than the Moscow train station."

Katryn didn't say anything. In fact her complexion paled noticeably. Sergi glanced up at her and realized that she looked ready to pass out. "God, Katryn, can I get you something, water, coffee?"

"Yes, some coffee would help right now. Sergi, I can't believe I had him on line. I should have held on and sounded an alarm right then. I was just so mad. All I wanted was to get him out of MY system. I never gave a thought to national security."

"No, don't blame yourself. I was the one who packed it in early last night. This was my project."

"Have you figured out what he's up to?"

Sergi exhaled loudly and answered, "Not really. We do know that the satellite link between all of the SBMC outposts in that entire sector was taken off line from 0211 to 0247 hours this morning. That's our time. Out there it would have been two hours later. The system is programmed to make random status sweeps. That son of a bitch timed it exactly in between two of them. He couldn't have had the system back on line for more than ten or fifteen seconds. If they had detected that the system was down then, all hell would have broken loose. All of the missile sites came up this morning for their 0600 security sign-ins too. Either nothing untoward happened out there or he stayed around long enough to enter the daily security codes. I'd put my money on the latter. SBMC is trying to reconfirm that all of the bases are operational first, then they'll have to do a site by site inspection. Of course everything has to be cleared through the Kazakhi chain of command. If there's been any breach at all they'll probably go running to the Americans to make sure they don't take the fall for this."

The phone rang and Sergi picked it up. "Yes... How long will that take?... Yes, I see. Thank you and please keep me informed."

He hung up the receiver and looked at his watch. "Son of a bitch. That was SBMC. They can't get any answer at one of the launch compounds. It will take them over an hour to get a security detail to check it out. It's what, about ten in the morning out there now, which brings them to eleven, another frigging hour or so to figure out what the hell happened. Christ, he'll have a six hour jump before they tell the Kazakhis to shut down the borders!"

62

The four devices were loaded into the four special containers Igor had provided for this purpose. They were lined with lead to shield most of the radiation being emitted by the plutonium cores and they fit neatly under the rear seats. Anyone making a cursory inspection of the vehicle wouldn't realize that they existed. When they were all in place Tapa began to climb into the driver's seat. Aslan grabbed her arm and asked, "Are you sure you want to drive?"

She looked at him indifferently and responded dryly "Yes, why shouldn't I?" When she reached the gate, she kept her gaze fixed down the road ahead, not once glancing over to the spot, marked by a crescent of dried blood, where Ivanof had accosted her.

Aslan secured the gate behind them and called in to Ivram, "What should we do about this bicycle?"

"Leave it. It will give them something else to try to figure out!" Aslan propped the bike up against the fence, walked in front of the Hummer and climbed into the front passenger seat. It was about 0630, local time, the sun was all ready well up in the sky and it was a beautiful day. They drove into Qyzylorda and stopped to pick up some coffee and fresh bread for breakfast. While Hadzhi made the purchase, Ivram and Aslan used the opportunity to rid themselves of the greasy black cream that covered their face and arms. They used their black tee shirts to towel off and disposed all the dirty field uniforms in a barrel behind the shop. They all ate in the truck, not wanting to chance leaving their precious cargo. Hadzhi said, "With any luck at all, we shall be in Uzbekistan before they even realize something is amiss."

"Yes," Ivram said, "I wish you all a safe trip. May the Almighty One ride with you."

"Ivram, it sounds as though you're not coming with us," Tapa said.

"Yes, that's true. My journey lies to the north. You've all done your jobs very well, my friends. It has been a distinct honor to have served with you."

"But how will you travel?" Tapa sounded apprehensive. "Certainly you aren't planning on walking back to Russia?"

He laughed. "No, I don't think my leg would stand up to that. Igor gave me the name of an associate of his who specializes in dealing merchandise. I think he will happily trade all of this computer equipment for an old car or truck."

"You're not seriously thinking of driving an old truck across the Urals now are you?" Hadzhi voiced the concern and the others all concurred.

"It doesn't need to take me all the way. I plan to drive across the border and head for Sverdlovsk. Actually, I think they just changed the name of the city back to Yekaterinburg. Everything is so confusing these days. No matter what it's called, you can still board a train there that takes you west."

With Tapa's help in asking directions from the locals, they were able to locate the man Igor had recommended. The sign in the window said the shop didn't open until 8:30 and he was about fifteen minutes late after that. After an exchange of introductions, he examined the computers Ivram was offering to trade. "Yes, these are wonderful machines," he told them. "Unfortunately, there are not too many people sophisticated enough to have need of such things in Qyzylorda or in most of Kazahkstan for that matter. It will be a difficult exchange."

Hadzhi didn't have the time or patience for horse trading this morning. They should have been more than half way to the border by now. "Perhaps these may trade better!" He pulled out a crate, opening it to reveal the machine pistols. I would like to keep one of these. As a souvenir, of course," he added with a broad grin. "I'm sure you understand."

The trader's eyes brightened considerably when he saw the weapons. Ever the shrewd businessman, he said, "To carry such merchandise is illegal, I'm sure you realize that."

"Illegal and highly profitable too, no doubt," Hadzhi countered.

"Well, that might be. Who is to say," he said, shrugging his shoulders and offering a condescending grin. They haggled some more and finally agreed upon a fair exchange price for all of the merchandise. "I may know someone willing to sell his van. It will take some time to have the paperwork prepared for the vehicle though."

"That is to be expected," Ivram acknowledged. "I'll return this afternoon to pick it up, say about two o'clock?"

"You give me little time. I will see what I can do."

Ivram smiled, certain that the dealer already had a vehicle he was dying to unload. "I'm sure you'll do your best." Back in the Hummer,

Ivram told Hadzhi, "There's no need for you to remain here while I wait for the car. Let's find a place where we can store one of our little friends back there and you can be on your way. It's better for you to be out of the country by nightfall."

"Nightfall! I had hoped to be across the border already." Tapa located a small grove of fruit trees along the banks of the Syr Darya and pulled off the road. They secluded one of the special containers in the underbrush. Hadzhi and Aslan each gave Ivram parting hugs. "May the God of our fathers walk with you, my friend. It has been a privilege to serve with you," Hadzhi said softly. Aslan snapped to attention and smartly saluted him. "Yes, Colonel, it has been an honor."

Tapa stood to one side during this exchange, staring off at the river flowing past them. She had her arms tightly folded in front of her. What little breeze there was played gently with wisps of her hair. "Come Tapa, we must be on our way," Aslan called back to her as he climbed into the truck.

"No, I'm not going with you. I have decided to go on with Ivram."

Ivram turned to her in surprise. "Tapa, that is neither wise or necessary. The journey I'm planning doesn't have a happy ending. I won't be going home."

She did not move to look at him. Keeping her gaze fixed on the flowing river she said, "I suspected as much. But I have no home to return to myself, Ivram, only a few cousins who will not miss me all that much." Now she turned her face to him. "When I first met you, I knew that my destiny was to be with you. For a while I chose to walk a different path. Now the Almighty has brought us back together and I will not be deterred again."

Ivram placed his hands on her arms and gently turned her toward him. "Are you really sure, Tapa?"

"I am absolutely certain."

Hadzhi looked at his watch impatiently. "I will miss you both. My prayers go with you, but if you're not coming, I need to be on my way." He took the keys from her and the Hummer pulled away.

Ivram moved his arm around her waist and the two of them were left standing alone beside the river as the truck roared out of sight. He could feel her body quivering as she stood next to him. Looking at the young woman whose destiny was now interwoven with his, he asked, "Tapa, are you all right?"

"I will be." She spoke in almost a whisper. "I can still feel that awful man's hand inside of me. Come, let me feel you inside of me instead." She took his hand and led him to a grassy recess, hidden from the road by a copse of bushes. There, with the sounds of the river to soothe them, they lay down and she began to unbutton his shirt.

At first, she was above him, kissing his lips, his neck and his chest. Her tongue worked its way through the thick hairs on his chest and explored his navel. She undid his trousers and caressed his penis. He moaned with deep satisfaction and then rolled over on top of her. Now it was his turn to undress her. She had discarded the bloody sweater in exchange for the camouflage blouse of a uniform. He undid each button, kissing the skin as it became exposed.

She still wore the skirt and his hand worked its way up the inside of her legs. At the first touch her body trembled and gasped. He stopped and looked into her eyes. "I'm sorry, if that's too painful for you, I'll stop."

"No, it's over now. I feel wonderful."

Still, he thought it best not to use his hand there. Instead, he mounted her and gently inserted his penis inside of her. With soft thrusting motions he worked it in and pulled her close into him as he released. She wrapped her hands tightly around his neck and held him locked in an embrace for a long, long time. When she finally released him there were tears in her eyes.

Ivram pulled himself up to look at her and started to speak, but she put a finger to his lips to silence him. "Nothing needs to be said except thank you," she told him.

They sat side by side without speaking and watched the river flow by them. The sunlight danced among the ripplets and the water lapped gently against the embankment below them. Nearby a cluster of butterflies flitted about a bush. Ivram felt more at peace than he could ever remember. Finally he made a move to get up and had to steady himself by placing his hand on her shoulder. She started to get up as well. "No, you better wait here and keep watch on our 'little acquisition.' I'll walk back into Qyzylorda to pick up the van and a few other incidentals I asked for.

"Are you trying to get rid of me already?"

"Of course not." He bent down and gave her a kiss.

"That's better. Remember, I'm the one that knows how to speak the language." She sprang to her feet and began walking towards the city. "Besides, it's nearly noon and I'm famished!"

They walked together without saying much for some time. His leg was bothering him more lately and that annoyed him. She offered to let him lean on her, but he refused and hobbled along, trying to push himself to walk faster. "Ivram, what's the big rush? The van won't be ready until late this afternoon."

It wasn't that far to walk to get back into the city. The city itself was not all that big, having a population of about 150 thousand or so. They found a café that seemed a little more antiseptic than the one they'd frequented the morning before. The building looked ancient and had probably served as a caravansary in its prime. Tapa ordered a light lunch. The temperature was soaring and not conducive to a hearty meal. He had discarded his officer's jacket in favor of a summer poplin shirt before Hadzhi and Aslan had taken off, so at least he was better dressed for the climate. Still his shirt showed massive splotches from the sweat on his back and chest.

Ivram consumed a large quantity of iced tea made with coarse sugar crystals. Tapa just swirled hers with her index finger. "What happens next, Ivram?"

"I believe that the waiter brings us our food, we eat it, pay the man and leave."

She kicked him under the table. "No, seriously."

"Seriously, we pick up the van and head north. We've got a pretty long drive ahead of us. If we both drive we can possibly make it in one night without stopping. I have no idea what the roads are like."

"And just how do you plan on getting across the border with our 'little acquisition' in the back of the van?"

"Oh, hadn't you heard? My sister just died. I'm bringing her body back for burial." She looked at him inquisitively. "I don't have the slightest idea what you're talking about."

"Don't worry, you'll find out soon enough." He gulped down several pain pills before eating, so by the time they finished his leg was feeling much better. "Shall we tour the town a bit while we wait?' he asked her. It was not much of a city. Agriculture seemed to be the principal reason for its existence. At one time, during the twenties, the city had served as the capital of Soviet Kazakhstan, but those glory years were a faded memory now. They walked for about an hour and he could feel his stump throbbing again. He asked her, "Do you have any idea where our friend's shop might be?"

"Actually, I do," she said with a gay little laugh. "It's right around the corner!"

The dealer was not in when they got to the shop so they were obliged to wait. A clerk, possibly the man's son, offered them two chairs to sit in, for which Ivram was very grateful. Nearly a half-hour elapsed before he finally entered the store. He had a dark olive complexion, which served to accentuate the whites of his eyes and teeth, especially when he smiled. "Ah you are here already. If I had known I would have hurried back sooner. There's a bit of excitement apparently. I don't know exactly what it is, but the Russian army people have been running through the city all afternoon. Ah, but then you probably know more than I do."

Tapa cast an alarmed look in Ivram's direction. He remained impassive, however, and asked casually, "Really, I would have thought that the Kazakhi Army would be running things these days."

"We like to think so, but the fact is you Russians still have a number of bases here. I think some of them have to do with nuclear missiles, but no one wants to admit to that officially." He gave Ivram a knowing wink, believing him to be the Russian officer he was dressed to be. The man was obviously fond of betel nuts, because the smell of them filled the air when he spoke. "When it comes to such things, your people remain in complete control."

"Well, that is interesting to know," Ivram said. "Anyway, how did you make out on our little project?"

"Very well, I must say. Here are the keys to your van. It's parked out back. Here are the ownership papers, made out to Anatoli Romanov. I believe that's correct."

"Yes it is," Ivram said accepting both the keys and papers he was handed.

"The other item you requested is already in the van. And this is the death certificate. That took a little extra effort, I'll have you know."

"Well, it is certainly appreciated," Ivram said, taking the man's outstretched hand and giving it a thankful shake. The trader obviously was hoping for more than a handshake. To dissuade him from reopening the negotiations, Ivram quickly added, "I'll be sure that my friends in Moscow learn how efficient and trustworthy you have been."

"Yes, that would be appreciated." He led them through the rear of his shop and out the back door to a small alley. Ivram climbed into the driver's seat of a van in slightly worse condition than the one he had surrendered to Igor's associates in Saratov. It may have once been shiny dark green, but was now a faded blackish-gray. Tapa joined him in the passenger seat. Something caught her eye as she got in and she looked into the rear of the van and realized that there was a metal casket in the truck. She gave Ivram a puzzled look and he simply nodded back at her.

They drove back to the spot by the river where they had concealed the 'little acquisition.' It was heavy, even for the two of them, but they managed to hoist it up and into the casket. Ivram closed the cover and fastened all of the bolts. "It really is a shame about my poor sister. She died at such a young age."

63

Katryn left the information she'd brought with Sergi and headed back to her office at the Russian Academy of Science. There would be no new information for at least an hour. Besides, what more could she do now anyway. It seemed that the horse was already out of the barn and well on its way through the meadow. She tried to work on the routine matters that came under her responsibility but found herself disinterested this morning. She took several calls, from section heads mostly, all clamoring for trivial information or pressing her to resolve petty jurisdictional conflicts. Her answers were hollow.

Printouts from last evening were still strewn about, a constant reminder of the more immediate problem out east somewhere in Kazakhstan. She put her head between her hands, propped her elbows up on the top of her desk and closed her eyes. When she opened them again she was staring at the information she'd left for herself concerning the Center for Ethnic Studies. In frustration she grabbed up the papers and flung them across the room. In mid-flight the paper clip came off and the individual pages fluttered to the floor. "GODDAMN YOU, GARYK!" she yelled out.

Her assistant rushed in to see what was the matter. "Are you all right, Miss Moldatin?" She was a young woman, a teenager really, just out of the technical school but normally quite efficient. She, too, was out of sorts today, picking up from her boss that something was not right.

"Yes, I'll be fine, Mishka," Katryn assured her. "If you don't mind, could you just get me some coffee, please."

"Yes, ma'am," the young woman responded and hurried off down the hallway.

Time dragged on. She thought about calling Sergi to find out what new information he might have, but decided against it. After all, he would be spearheading the effort to uncover whatever plot Garyk had hatched out there. She was no longer an essential element to the crisis at hand. At 11:30 her phone rang and Mishka advised her that there was a Colonel Minkov holding for her. It took a second to make the connection. "Oh yes, Sergi! Please put the call through."

"Hey, Kat, sorry I couldn't get back to you sooner. It's become a madhouse over here."

"I can imagine it is."

"I thought you'd want to know. We got word from the security detail that was sent out to post CV4995. When they got there no one was in sight. They did find traces of blood on the ground, both inside and out of the compound. Apparently the missile control room is located below ground, with some sort of security elevator linking it to the building up above. Anyway, unless someone down there activates a switch the elevator is virtually inoperable. They had to fly a goddamned specialist out by helicopter to gain access. That took another forty-five minutes. When they finally got in they found the bodies of all four of the crew. All dead of course."

Katryn closed her eyes again, trying to visualize the carnage caused by her husband, "Yes, I understand. Please go on."

"Initially, all of the missiles seemed to be in tact. They had to open each tube and make a physical check. They did the search one at a time. Can you believe this, it was the last fucking silo! All four of the nuclear warheads are gone."

Katryn said nothing and there was an extended pause in Sergi's recounting of the events. Finally he asked, "Katryn, are you still there?"

"Yes, I'm here. I'm just at a loss for words right now. Do you have any leads on where they've taken them?"

"Not really. It seems they disguised themselves as an inspection team. The previous watch is being interrogated right now. They were off duty until this afternoon and hard to track down. Christ, there was computer authorization for the visit! We're getting word out now to all of the border patrols to be on the lookout but that takes time and the Kazakhis really run that part of the show. We know they were still at the compound at six, their time. Shit, that was over seven hours ago. They could be anywhere by now!"

"What's the most likely escape route?"

"The prevailing wisdom is that the thieves will make for the closest way out of the country. That would be south, into Uzbekistan or possibly even Kyrgyzstan. Those countries are hotbeds for political intrigues, ideal for black marketeers. They're closer to the tumultuous Middle East, where there's likely to be an eager market for nuclear weaponry and plenty of oil money to subsidize such an acquisition."

"So you think they're just looking to sell them then?"

"Jesus, Katryn, I hope so. As an alternative, if the raiding party really was Chechen, then they might head for the Caspian Sea. A boat could be found to bring them back to Dagestan where they could attempt to get back home."

"What about Russia? You don't think they'd come here?"

"It's considered highly unlikely. But we're alerting all of the border stations, just to be safe."

"Sergi, is there anything I can do to help?"

"I'm afraid not, unless you want to pray. It's allowed these days, I understand, and we could certainly use that kind of help right now."

"Yes, maybe I will. Thank you for letting me know all this. I know how busy you must be." Katryn hung up and suddenly felt a bout of nausea coming on. She rushed out of her office to the women's room, arriving barely in time to throw up several times into the toilet. Someone's arms were about her waist, supporting her from collapsing to the floor. It was Mishka.

"Miss Moldatin, my God, you scared me so. Are you going to be okay?" The girl was terrified. She always admired her supervisor for being the calm "I'm in control here" type.

Okay? God, was she ever going to be okay after this?" Katryn whispered. "Yes dear, thank you very much. Let me just rest here a minute. Then I think I'm going home."

Mrs. Moldatin was concerned to see her daughter coming in the door so early in the day. She asked, "Katryn, is everything all right?" but got no response. Instead, her daughter walked straight into the kitchen, opened the cabinet, stretched to her fullest and took down a bottle of vodka. She poured a good four fingers into a glass and chugged it down, then started to refill the glass again. "Katryn, my God, what is wrong with you?" Mrs. Moldatin was extremely alarmed now; this certainly was not usual behavior for her daughter.

"There's no sense in trying to explain. Christ, Mama, I can't explain it to myself!" A torrent of mixed emotions surged through her. Foremost was the dread of what Garyk was actually planning to do with these weapons. The best case scenario was that they were just looking to raise funds for his Chechen revolutionaries, or maybe just for himself. The worst case—she didn't want to think about that. And what about her? God, his brother's political activity had destroyed her military career. What future did she have now as the wife of a nuclear terrorist? What made it even worse was that he had used her to make this happen. "You son of a bitch!"

"What was that, dear?" Her mother paced anxiously in the other room, wringing her hands. She wished that her husband were better. Yuri always knew what to do.

Katryn was well into the fourth glass of vodka and feeling the full effects of it. Funny, she used to be able to down several bottles of this stuff, but that was a long time ago. Actually, she rarely drank at all these days. She was vaguely aware of some activity at the door and droopily responded to the presence of her mother standing before her.

"Katryn, dear, there's a gentleman outside to see you. Actually he was looking for Mrs. *Gadayev*. I think he said his name was Dzasokhov, Borz Dzasokhov."

Her mind swirled, or was that her whole head, she couldn't be certain. Somewhere in the past she knew she'd heard that name before, but for the life of her she couldn't place it. Even as the man came into the room she had no clear recollection of where or why she might know this person. He appeared rather good looking, in a rugged sort of way. Broad shouldered, a bit too heavy perhaps, with thick dark eyebrows and a mustache to match. "Yes, Mr. Dathocop is it?" She remaining seated at the kitchen table and raised her arm in a half-hearted attempt at shaking his hand. "You'll haf to excuth me, I've had a really shitty day. Oh. Excuth me, I thudden talk like that to a stranger."

"Actually, Mrs. Gadayev, I'm really not a stranger. We met several years ago at my sister's wedding. She married Viktor, Viktor Gadayev."

"Oh yes, Tashyana. Such a delightful young woman. How ith she theeth days." Katryn's head was really spinning now. She could barely make out his response. "I'm sorry, wha did you shay?"

"I'm afraid she's dead, ma'am. The whole family was killed in the war."

"Oh, I'm thorry. I hadn't heard or if I did I don't remember. And what brinth you to Moshcow? I hope you're not looking for that thon of a bitch brother-in-law of yourth."

Borz ran both of his hands back over his head, flattening down the long strands of dark brown hair. He responded timidly, "Actually, I am. I believe that he plans to do something really quite terrible. I'm hoping I may be able to stop him before it's too late. I was also hoping that maybe you could help me do this."

Borz' request for help hit her like a bucket of cold water. She had been sitting there feeling sorry for herself, largely because she felt so helpless not being able to do anything about the situation. Could the two of them actually work together to stop this madness? It was worth a shot. She fought to pull herself back together and concentrated on getting each word out correctly. "Yes, I would like... to help, if... you really think... we can do it. God, look at me. I'm a dithgrace."

In actuality, Borz thought that she looked pretty good. Even in her present state. His faith discouraged drinking, especially for women. He sensed that this was not her usual practice, possibly because of the way the old woman was reacting in the other room. He had not remembered her as being this attractive when they met eighteen years before. But she had been in uniform then. He recalled her being rather cool and detached. Now she seemed vulnerable and quite stunning in that tasteful but revealing blouse. He could see why Garyk had remained so much in love with her all these years.

Katryn staggered just a bit as she rose from the chair. She braced herself by holding on to its back. Borz reached out to give her a hand, but she waved him off. "S'okay," she slurred, shaking off the dizziness. "Give me some time to clean up."

Mama was standing near the doorway in the other room nervously listening to what was going on. Katryn still had not told her what the cause of her sudden melancholia was, but it was clear, with Borz' arrival, that something was terribly amiss and that it had everything to do with Garyk. Maybe it was better that Mr. Moldatin was sleeping through most of this in the bedroom. Katryn called in to her, "Mama, I'm going to take a quick schower. Please offer our dinner some guest. No, please offer our guest some dinner."

Borz declined anything to eat, but accepted a cold soft drink. He felt quite awkward, sitting in the front room with Mrs. Moldatin. He was not comfortable wearing the black suit and tie normally reserved for special occasions and he was really not good at making small talk. Mrs. Moldatin was not volunteering any either. The sound of the shower running was underscored by the tick, tick ticking of a grandfather clock. It was about the only noise to be heard. Katryn stayed under the cold water a good fifteen minutes before she felt she had fully cleared her head. Then she hurried to towel off and threw on some clean clothes, a pair of denim jeans and a soft pink summer sweater. She came out still shaking water from her not-quite-shoulder length hair. Borz stood as she entered the room.

"Please forgive my behavior when you arrived. I'm so embarrassed." She reached for his hand and held it with both of hers. "Borz, you were right. Garyk isn't just planning something terrible; he has already put his plan in action. I was indirectly involved in that process and was feeling bitter about it I guess. That's why you found me the way you did. Your coming here was just what I needed to snap out of my self pity."

"I'm glad to hear that, Mrs. Gadayev."

"No, please call me Katryn. There's no need for you to be so formal. After all, we are related somehow, aren't we?"

"Perhaps that's true, I'm not really sure what you'd be, my sister-in-law twice removed maybe? You said he has already put his plan in motion. That can't be true, can it?"

Katryn realized that her mother was still sitting in the room, trying to take all of this in. At just that moment the door opened and Georgi came in, all sweaty and ruffled from a late afternoon football match. Borz was amazed at the likeness of Georgi to his father and uncle. He towered over his mother and grandmother and looked exactly the way Borz remembered Viktor the first day at the oil fields. Katryn didn't want to bring the whole family into this, at least not at this moment. "Oh Georgi, this is a friend of your father's, Mr. Dzasokhov. He's up from Groznyy and needs to discuss a few things with me at my office. Mama, we'll be gone for a while. Please eat without me."

Borz barely got out a greeting to the young man when Katryn pulled him out of the apartment. She led him briskly down the corridor. "I'm sorry Borz, but I don't have time for pleasantries. To get back to your question, the answer is yes; Garyk apparently led a raid of some sort on a nuclear missile site early this morning. That was someplace in Kazakhstan. He has been in possession of four nuclear warheads since four o'clock this morning. As far as I know, nobody has any idea where he is or where he may be going. Do you?"

"I think I do. A friend told me that he was going to blow up St. Petersburg!"

Katryn stopped walking and ran her hand across her forehead and back over her head. "Oh dear God! Well, he can't have gotten there yet." She grabbed him by the arm and began walking again. "Come, I need to introduce you to someone."

64

They drove all night. Tapa dozed off almost as soon as they had gotten underway. Ivram was grateful for that. He preferred not to talk when he drove. When the ache in his back and the throbbing in his leg got too bad he pulled over and let her take a turn at the wheel. After fourteen hours of nearly nonstop driving they reached the town of Qostanay. It was morning, so they stopped to get some coffee and breakfast. They parked in front of the restaurant and took a seat by a window where they could keep the van in sight.

Ivram went to the restroom and splashed water on his face, cursing when he realized there were no towels to dry off with. "It's only about a hundred kilometers to the border from here," he told her when he returned.

They traveled along the Tobol River up to the crossing. No one at this particular border post had any reason to be searching for nuclear materials. Word of the theft had not been disseminated to the far outreaches as yet.

"My sister died suddenly while visiting friends from school," Ivram explained to a disinterested border guard. "Unfortunately, the family could not afford to fly the body home to St. Petersburg, so I was enlisted to drive her back." The inspector made a cursory search of the van and asked if he could open up the casket. "I suppose, if you think you must. She's been dead for almost five days. In fact we've driven all night to try to get the body back home before it starts to smell too bad." The border guard quickly stamped their documents and sent them on with heartfelt condolences.

The first major Russian city they came to was Chelyabinsk. Tapa asked him why they couldn't board a train there.

"We could, actually," he replied. It's pretty close to the border though. We got across without any problems but there's no sense risking heightened security checks at a terminal this close. Sverdlovsk is not that much further north, but I'm counting on a lot less security there."

He was right. They purchased two tickets for a train bound for St. Petersburg and consigned the casket to the baggage handler. The old porter assured him that they would treat the remains of his departed sister with due respect. Tapa managed a few sobs as she patted the coffin on her way out of the freight section.

They had several hours before the train was schedule to depart. Ivram saw this as another opportunity to go exploring. Tapa was more concerned about leaving their cargo unattended. "Are you sure no one will go snooping around back there? My God, Ivram, we just left a bomb, no, we just left an *atomic* bomb sitting in the station's baggage office!"

"If there's one thing I've learned, Tapa, it's that people have a great respect for the dead. More so than for the living it seems. They also harbor fears concerning the dead and death. That porter will take great pains to insure that no one gets too close to that casket and happily push it onto the train as quickly as he can get rid of it."

Sverdlovsk, or Yekaterinburg as it was once again being called, combined the charm of an Eighteenth Century imperial frontier town with the inelegance of an aging industrial complex. Many of the factories and other buildings dated to the Second World War Era, having been hastily built to relocate industrial complexes away from the western front with Germany. Little had been done to update them since. The city's one major claim to history was the fact that Nicholas II and his entire family had been executed here. Reflecting the current political trend of the country, the city had purged itself of the name that gave honor to a Bolshevik hero and reclaimed its tsarist heritage.

They walked for about an hour, arriving at the station with half an hour to spare before the train arrived. Ivram found a compartment in one of the passenger cars that was unoccupied and claimed it for their own. Tapa curled up on the seat facing Ivram and was asleep almost immediately. He tried to get some sleep as well, but found he was so over-tired by the activity of the past 48 hours that sleep became difficult. He had taken some of the pain pills when they had first settled in. That was less than two hours ago, but he reached into his pocket and pulled out the tiny bottle. There were six pills left inside. More than enough for the job at hand, he thought and swallowed down two more. They finally had an effect and he was asleep within fifteen minutes.

When Tapa awoke several hours later she found him sleeping soundly. The sun still blazed high in the sky and she was surprised at how late it actually was. She nestled herself into the corner where the seat met the side of the car, pulled her legs back under her and leaned her head against the window. She sat that way for a long time, just looking at him. His broad chest and chiseled jaw were still quite striking. He was, in fact, handsome, in spite of the two-day growth of stubble that was again encroaching on his face. "What is it about you, Ivram Gadayev, that makes me love you so much?"

Tapa thought she had said these words to herself, but he startled her by muttering a muffled "What?" and tossed about a bit, before dropping back off to sleep. What did she really know about this man to whom she had tied her destiny. That he was married with a child living somewhere in or near Moscow; that the Russians had killed his brother and presumably most of his family and that he was a former Army officer and a computer whiz at that. But what did those facts tell her about the man sleeping so soundly across from her. Softly she said, "Ivram, what is in your soul?"

He blinked his eyes and said, "I'm sorry, did you say something?"

"No, I'm sorry. I was just musing out loud. I didn't mean to wake you."

He straightened himself in the seat and looked at his watch. "God, it's after nine o'clock. I don't suppose the parlor car will still be serving at this hour."

"Would you like me to go and get something for you?"

"No, that's okay. I need to make a trip down the corridor anyway. How about you? Do you want anything if it's still open."

"Some coffee maybe, nothing else."

He was gone about ten or fifteen minutes and she was beginning to worry. He came back balancing a small carton with two cups of coffee and some sweet breads. "I saw these and thought you might like one." He handed the little box over to her and smiled broadly.

"What's so funny?"

"Nothing funny, it's just that you look so charming sitting all curled up like that."

"Oh God, Ivram, I look terrible! I'm sure I must smell terrible too. Promise me a bath when we get to St. Petersburg. By the way, just exactly what is our plan when we get there?"

"Honestly, I really haven't got a clue. To tell you the truth, I never expected to get this far!"

65

Katryn drove Borz to Sergi's office. She found it impossible to get past the security people, since her name was no longer on the list of expected visitors. "Look, will you please call in to him, this is extremely important," she implored the senior security guard, a sergeant, stationed in the main lobby. The man let her know that he felt this was highly irregular, but he finally picked up a phone and dialed into the special surveillance section.

"Yes excuse me but there's someone at the front gate who wishes to see Col. Minkov... Yes, I understand." The guard held the phone against his chest and said to Katryn, "I'm sorry, ma'am, but the Colonel is tied up in a very important meeting right now. I understand it's been going on all afternoon. Perhaps you could come back tomorrow."

"No, I can't come back tomorrow, tomorrow will be too late! Tell them to let the Colonel know that it's Katryn Moldatin and I need to see him right now."

The man relayed that information and received a similar response, to which he gave Katryn a shrug of the shoulders and said, "I'm sorry, they say he simply cannot be disturbed right now."

Katryn's frustration turned to anger at the stupidity of the situation. She reached over and grabbed the phone from the startled sergeant. "I don't know who this is, but I am Katryn Moldatin, Director of Computer Operations for the Space Research Institute. I've been working with Col. Minkov on his current project for the past few days. Go tell him that Katryn Moldatin is here and that I've got Garyk Gadayev's fucking brother-in-law with me. He knows what Garyk is going to do with that goddamned bomb! ... Yes, thank you, I'll hold."

Katryn stood at the security desk cradling the phone between her neck and shoulder. Her right foot tapped impatiently on the tile floor while she waited for the speaker to return. The sergeant remained behind the counter, looking quite perplexed. "I'm sorry sergeant, but this is a matter that goes beyond national security. There are four million lives at stake." The poor man did not know what to make of this and looked over to the gentleman standing behind Katryn as if to gain some additional insight.

Borz' face bespoke his grave anxiety. He gave the sergeant a single affirmative nod and said, "Yes, my friend, I'm afraid she is absolutely correct."

Katryn held the phone for about two minutes. Her frustration rose with every passing second. It was Sergi's voice that finally came on the line. "Katryn, my God, I had no idea they were detaining you down there. What is this about a brother-in-law?"

Borz Dzasokhov is with me right now. He's Garyk's brother-in-law. He flew up from Groznyy to try to stop Garyk. Sergi, he thinks he plans to detonate at least one of those bombs in St. Petersburg!"

"Christ almighty, Katryn. Are you sure?"

"He is!"

"Let me speak to the security guard." Katryn handed the telephone back to the bewildered sergeant. "This is Colonel Sergi Minkov. Katryn Moldatin has just been temporarily assigned as a special agent of this office. So has the gentleman with her. Do you understand?" The sergeant indicated that he did. "Good, please pass them through immediately!"

He not only passed them through, he told his assistant to take over and personally escorted Katryn and Borz up to Sergi's office. After a brief introduction, Sergi invited Borz and Katryn to have a seat and allowed Borz to tell him what he knew of the present situation.

"Please forgive me, " he began, "but I am not used to such high intrigue. Ivram, that is what Garyk chooses to be called, is now like a brother to me. I do not want to bring him any harm. Still, I am very concerned that he has selected a path that will not only bring harm to him, but to many, many people as well. It may very well prove extremely damaging to our entire country."

Sergi cast a quick glance over at Katryn and then refocused his attention on the man seated before him. "Yes, I understand Mr. Dzasokhov. Please continue."

"Some time ago I introduced Ivram to a new spiritual leader. A shayk or usman we call them. You have to understand, Ivram was a completely devastated man when I found him down near Shali. He was sitting in the rubble of his ancestral home, which had been destroyed by senseless shelling from a Russian tank unit. Both his mother and grandmother had been killed."

Katryn had not heard of this before and raised her left hand over her mouth in response to an involuntary gasp. Borz looked across to her. "You did not know this, I'm sorry. His whole family is dead now, did you know that?" Katryn shook her head. Borz turned back to Sergi and continued, "Viktor, his twin brother and the First Deputy of the Chechen National Assembly, was killed in action against the Russian invaders. Then the pigs, I'm sorry, you'll have to excuse me for that, the Russia soldiers came to my house, the home of my mother and father, and assassinated my parents and Viktor's three children. The bastards burned the house down." Borz had to stop. Tears welled up in his eyes and the words caught in throat.

"I'm sorry," he said after a brief pause, "but they were so young, my nieces and nephew. There was no need. My sister Tatyana, Viktor's wife, had already died in the shelling of the hospital where she worked. So you see, Ivram, or Garyk if you will, had no family left except for you." He turned to Katryn, adding, "Do you realize how much it hurt him to have lost your love?" She was crying and bowed her head a bit at the question.

"Forgive me, this is not what I came here for. Let me get to it. Ivram became involved with the usman Mansur Shamil and it restored him to life. He became a devote Moslem and, I must admit, we both became involved in certain activities for the liberation of our country. You must understand, Colonel, our people did not seek this war, only our freedom."

Sergi shook his head in agreement. "I will not judge you for that, Mr. Dzasokhov."

"Eventually I went back to work in the oil fields and Ivram began to teach at the Chechen State University. Apparently, he also remained active with Shamil's group. Last month I went to visit him on my way to Baku to retrieve my family. Ivram was planning to go away and I got the distinct impression that he did not plan on returning. That he expected he might be killed. When I returned he was gone. Three days ago I met one of our former associates from Shamil's camp. He confided in me that Shamil had devised a plan to strike a blow for the Chechen people directly at the heart of the Russian invaders. Somehow, he was going to launch an attack against the city of St. Petersburg. I asked him 'How is such a thing possible?' and he told me that Ivram Gadayev was leading a team that would procure a nuclear weapon and detonate it in the city. Surely, he can't do such a thing, can he?"

"He not only can, he apparently has. The procurement part anyhow." There was a long period of silence. Borz and Katryn remained focused on Sergi, waiting for some assurance that the situation was under control. Sergi knew that it wasn't. "Well, we knew how Garyk got hold of these devices. Now we know why. From what I just heard, Garyk Ivramovich Gadayev is a man on a mission." Looking at Borz he asked, "What do you call it?"

"A jihad?"

"Yes, a jihad. He's out to avenge his family, his country and his god. Clearly he has proven he is capable of obtaining such a weapon, so clearly he intends to use it!"

Sergi made arrangements for the three of them to fly up to St. Petersburg that evening. He also ordered his staff to put the police in St. Petersburg on notice that a suspected terrorist plot had been detected and to place all of the points of entry under strict surveillance. He wanted to go to a full military alert, but his superiors felt it unwise to do so. The presence of military personnel patrolling all of the terminals would raise too many questions. The answers could lead to mass panic and that would make their efforts to track down Garyk even more difficult.

They arrived in the very early morning and went to an office that had previously housed the local KGB operation. "We've more or less taken over all of their operations," he told them. Katryn raised an eyebrow in response to that remark and he quickly amended it. "Well, maybe not ALL of their operations. We're a lot less intrusive in private affairs."

A young brunette in a junior sergeant's uniform entered carrying a stack of papers. "Good morning Colonel. These are the reports that came in while you were enroute."

Katryn and Borz sat facing Sergi while he flipped through the reports. "I'll be damned!" Sergi held up one of the sheets of paper. "This is incredible. An army inspection team consisting of two men crossed the boarder from Kazakhstan into Uzbekistan near Toshkent. Their vehicle was searched, but nothing seemed amiss. The names of the two individuals are listed as Captain Josef Plushenko and Sergeant Mikhail Federof. Those were two of the names used by the alleged inspection team at post CV4995. That information was not made available to the border units until some hours after they had been passed through!"

Katryn asked, "Do you think they had the weapons with them?"

"Some most likely. Garyk certainly doesn't need more than one. We're missing four. The fact that the team split up might confirm that they have a double agenda."

There was little else they could do at this point except to hope for some lead on Garyk's whereabouts. All three of them took the opportunity to catch a few hours of uneasy sleep. Katryn stretched out on one of the leather sofas in the office, while Borz and Sergi shared the other, propping their feet up on a small wooden coffee table. By 0830 they were finishing their second round of coffee when a clerk walked in and handed Sergi a report off of the fax machine. He read through it quickly and then advised the others. "There's a report out of Yekaterinburg that an Anatoli Romanov purchased two tickets on the afternoon train to St. Petersburg. Romanov was the name used by the inspection team leader. I think we may have found our man!" Katryn jumped up from her chair and came around behind Sergi to read the paper over his shoulder.

Borz walked over to a large wall map that still depicted the old Soviet Union. He ran his finger along the Kazakhstan border. "I can't seem to find any place with that name. How do you spell it?"

Sergi looked over and said, "Oh that's an old map. Try looking for Sverdlovsk, I think that was the old name.'

"Yes, here it is. It's a long way from Qyzylorda but it is almost due north. I guess that makes sense."

Sergi picked up his phone and asked for someone to look up the arrival time for that train. When the phone rang back and he grabbed up the receiver before the first ring had finished. He got the information and looked at his watch. "Son of a bitch, the train is going to be here in seventeen minutes! Let's get over to the station right away."

66

The train arrived at St. Petersburg around nine in the morning. Ivram felt exhilarated, having had the luxury of a full night of sleep and an early breakfast in the dining car. Tapa was more concerned about her personal appearance then anything else. "Look at me, Ivram, I'm such a mess. My God, the little provincial girl comes to the big city and this is all she has to wear!" Tapa was still wearing a field uniform top tied at the waist over the skirt she had on back at the compound. Caked blood was embedded in the fabric. She had only been able to splash some water on her face and upper torso in the small lavatory provided on the train and had completely neglected to bring a comb with her.

Ivram tried to reassure her. "Don't worry, you look just fine."

"What do men know of such things?" she shot back. "Remember, you promised that I could get a bath as soon as we arrived. I think that a change of clothing is also in order. I'd like to burn these."

He laughed. "I'll see what can be arranged."

Ivram noticed right away that there were far more policemen on patrol this morning then on any of his previous visits. He wrapped his arm around her and whispered, "Act like we are lovers. I think they're looking for us."

She looked up at him and said, "I thought we were," but he did not respond.

He had planned on looking into renting a van or truck right there at the station but decided against that. A security guard was stationed right next to the counter, which proclaimed **AVIS** in bold red letters. He knew that the casket would be taken directly to the baggage handling area and held there until someone came for it. They ducked outside, utilizing one of the smaller side exits, and were greeted with a blast of hot air and brilliant sunshine. "This certainly is different than my first visit to Leningrad," he told her. "I froze my butt off then."

The morning traffic moved slowly and the train had already arrived by the time Sergi got to the station with Katryn and Borz. A large number of people were milling about. "Look for someone carrying something heavy," Sergi suggested as they pushed their way through the throng of people. Borz went to check out the baggage claim area, on the off chance that Garyk would have allowed the package out of his sight. While he was there he noticed two porters manipulating a hand truck into the back holding area. The truck contained a coffin. Borz had seen so much death the past year that the sight of another body had little impact on him.

Borz returned to the center of the waiting area and found Katryn. She was exasperated. "Damn, where the hell could he have gone to so quickly?" Sergi soon joined them, shaking his head to indicate that he too had no luck finding their man. He held a radio up to his ear and was shouting directives into the mouthpiece. People passing by turned to see what the commotion might be about.

They stood looking in all directions hoping to catch a glimpse of him somewhere in the crowd, but to no avail. Borz remembered something Sergi had said earlier. "Didn't I hear you say the this Romanov person bought two tickets? Who was he traveling with?"

Sergi reached into his back pocket and pulled out the sheet of paper. Looking at it he said, "Apparently he was traveling with an Elaina Dolstekaiya. At least that's the name on the manifest."

"So that means we're supposed to be looking for a couple," Borz concluded. Somehow the though that Garyk might be traveling with another woman was unsettling to Katryn. They followed Sergi as he walked over to the baggage area. He still had the radio up to his ear and was in communication with the security patrol out on the street. "Yes, alert everyone. We may be looking for two people, a man and a woman. No, I have no description of her. Just look for a couple!"

There were several pieces of unclaimed baggage still waiting to be picked up, as well as a number of crates and boxes that had been forwarded on to St. Petersburg. Sergi walked over to one of his security people and told him, "I want every one of those packages searched and accounted for. Get someone in here with a radiation detector and screen the damned things first. Don't open anything suspicious until its been cleared for booby traps, is that clear?" The man responded with a crisp, "Yes Colonel!" and headed off to follow through with the detail. He, too, held a radio in his hand and called for the radiation team.

Outside, Ivram sensed that the authorities had intensified security throughout the city. "How could they know this?" he asked himself. Trying to avoid the main thoroughfares and transportation centers, he led her to a less frequented area he had visited on several of his business trips for Khasbulatov. "We can get a room over there," he told her, pointing to a small guest house across the street from where they were walking. "While you wash up I'll see about getting you some new clothes."

"Oh no you don't. I may be a country girl, but I have some dignity too. You can't think I'm going to let you pick out what I'm going to wear. Come, I see a little shop right down here."

She literally dragged him down the street and into a small store that specialized in women's apparel. A matronly woman in her mid to late fifties came down an aisle to greet them. Her broad smile quickly turned into a dour scowl as she surveyed this ragamuffin couple. Looking down her nose at Tapa, she said, "Yes, how can I help you?"

"As you can see, I desperately need to get out of these rags. I just lost everything I owned in a fire. My cousin lent me these things. Aren't they dreadful?"

Immediately the shopkeeper's attitude changed again. "My poor child, that's terrible. Come, I'm sure we can find something better for you in back." Ivram was amazed at the selection of western apparel that was available in Russia these days. He was even more amazed at the price tags for items that boasted that they were Calvin Klein or Aeropostale. Capitalism had surely won the battle for the economic well being of the people. She bought jeans, a blouse, sweater, some undergarments and a pair of white tennis sneakers. It nearly wiped out all of the cash he had held in reserve. "Remember, we need to rent a truck and you still want your shower," he whispered into her ear, trying to restrain her enthusiasm over yet another acquisition.

"What about you," she asked, "surely you'd like to get into some fresh things too."

"These will be fine," he answered.

"My God, Ivram, you men have absolutely no class at all! I hope you'll at least let me wash those out for you."

They completed the transaction and headed back to the guest house. The man behind the counter smiled sheepishly at them, suspecting that they were yet another couple on an illicit rendezvous. In his business it was not discreet to make too many inquiries. They entered the room, which was rather small, containing only a double bed with a white metal headboard, a bed table, chair and small desk. It did feature a private bath, however, and that was delightful. Ivram suggested that he would go out and find a vehicle while she showered. "Oh no," she scolded, "you're not going anywhere until I wash those clothes."

She made him strip and took the clothes with her into the bathroom. Ivram was embarrassed by his nakedness. He felt awkward standing there like that and was particularly conscious of his prosthetic left leg. He pulled the sheet off the bed and draped himself with it. He could hear her singing to herself over the sound of the shower and heard her call out, "Damn, I should have remembered to get some shampoo." It had been quite some time since he had been a part of such domestic activity.

After the water stopped running he could hear the splashing sounds as she was presumably washing his clothes. Funny that things like that should matter so much to her he thought. If things went according to his plans they might both be dead before nightfall. He would be anyway. He resolved to send her back to Chechnya before that happened.

She came out with a towel wrapped over her head and nothing else on. It surprised him to see her like that. Her body was lithe and her breasts stood out firm and full in front of her. She blushed at his look and he felt himself quickly becoming erect beneath the sheet. "I've hung your things in front of the window in there. Hopefully, they will be dry in about two hours. You weren't in a hurry, were you?"

Before he could answer she wrapped her arms around his neck and began to kiss him. He grasped her around the waist and pulled her close to him, feeling her breasts press against his chest. She smelled of fresh soap, fresh and clean. Tapa shook her head and the towel fell of. Damp hair ringed her head and he ran his fingers through it. She pushed against him and they fell back unto the bed, causing her to land against his artificial leg. She let out a little cry of pain as her knee struck the hard plastic. "I'm sorry, that damned thing is always getting in the way," he said, annoyed about his deformity.

"No, that's all right," she whispered into his ear and then twirled her tongue inside of it, biting gently on the lobe. They made love slowly and passionately and she held him tightly long after they had finished.

He rolled over on his back, staring up at the ceiling and tried to comprehend why the Almighty had placed her in this situation. "Tapa, I want you to leave now."

She sat up, pulling the sheet that he had worn up over her breasts. "What do you mean?"

"I mean that there's no reason for you to be here."

"Oh, excuse me! I thought what we just did was reason enough. I guess I was wrong. Are you finished with me then?"

"Tapa please don't do this. You know what I've come here to do. There's no reason for you to die with me. I don't *want* you to die."

"Ivram, I told you back in Qyzylorda that my place was by your side. If you are to die, then I must also. I won't let you send me away like this. But why can't we both go? Surely the device can be set off by some timing mechanism. You don't need to be here, do you?"

"To insure that nothing goes wrong I do. Besides, they know who I am. Katryn or someone identified me on the computer the other day. Whether I live or die, I will have no life after this. They will track me down for sure. But they don't know about you Tapa. You are so young and have a lifetime ahead of you. Please, you must do this for me. If you truly love me, you'll go."

"I do truly love you and that is why I will stay. I won't hear any more of this" She got up from the bed and walked back into the bathroom. A few minutes later she emerged wearing her new ensemble. She looked marvelous, so chic and cosmopolitan "Your clothes are still drying. Let me go and secure a van for us while you take a shower. I hate to say this, Ivram, but you do smell rather bad!" Again she didn't let him respond but grabbed his wallet and headed out of the room.

67

Sergi reviewed a list of all of the recent automobile rentals. "Lieutenant, please have your men follow up on each one of these, he instructed the police liaison officer. Turning back to Katryn and Borz he said, "It's no use. He's either slipped through here somehow or else he never came in on that train. They're talking with the train crew now to find out if they noticed anything out of the ordinary."

They had been at the terminal for over an hour. Out of desperation, Sergi began to cruise the city in the car provided to him. He tried to drive in ever increasing circles, but kept running afoul of the Neva River, which coursed its way through the center of the city. Borz sat in the rear seat, anxiously looking from one side to the other in hopes of sighting a familiar face. Imperial palaces and Eighteenth Century architecture made an impressive backdrop, but the present situation did not call for sightseeing.

"Wait, can you slow down a bit? He had caught a quick glimpse of a young woman walking briskly down the sidewalk. She reminded him of that young woman back in the camp, what was her name. They drove past her and he tried to study her face. That did seem familiar, but her hair had been much longer. The clothes were all wrong too. The woman he remembered had never been smartly attired. This woman seemed so self assured. She must be a local, he thought. "Sorry, I was mistaken. She's not the woman I thought she was."

Tapa was gone for nearly two hours. Ivram's clothes finally dried. Well, his shorts were a little damp in spots, but he put them on anyway. The man at the desk seemed surprised when he called down and asked for an iron. After all, this was a lieutenant colonel's uniform and it did need to be pressed. Tapa was right, he should have gotten some civilian clothing to wear. There was a knock on the door and he let her back in. She was bubbling with excitement. "Ivram, I never imagined what a marvelous city this is! I'm sorry to have been gone so long, but after I rented the van I just started to drive around to look at all of the buildings. My God, Ivram, there's so many people!"

She was right. The population of St. Petersburg was five times greater than all of Chechnya's had been before the start of the war. Of course over 300,000 people had fled their country by this time, not to mention another forty or fifty thousand dead. So that meant that the city was nearly ten times larger now.

"Ivram, I drove past the Mariinsky Theater and both the Summer and Winter Palaces. They're beautiful! I'll have to show them to you later." Ivram remembered that many years ago, sitting in a bus very late at night, another young woman had enthusiastically described all of the wonders of this city to him. She, too, had promised to show him the sights one day, but that had never happened. The thought of Katryn sent a chill throughout his body. Why did he have to think of her now while Tapa stood right beside him?

"Ivram, is something wrong? You look so distant all of a sudden."

"It will pass. It is better not to be so taken by this city. Remember why we are here."

She sighed deeply. "Yes, you're right. How foolish of me."

Ivram followed her downstairs to where she had parked the van. It was a sleek looking black one, in much better condition then any of the others utilized on this journey. Tapa was eager to drive and Ivram was more than happy to oblige her. It would give him more time to concentrate on the problem at hand, which was exactly what to do next. It amused him that he had spent so much time planning the logistics of the operation in Kazakhstan, but had utterly failed to devise a plan for the actual detonation of this device. Were they really such crass amateurs he wondered?

As they drove back toward the train station he also realized that just blowing up the city was not enough. No one would have any idea why it had happened. The government would devise some fabrication to cover up the true cause. On the other hand, there were many ethnic freedom groups these days and all of them might look to claim this action for their own cause. He needed to issue a public statement before the device was detonated and he had to insure that it was given the widest possible dissemination, not just in Russia, but across the world.

They were driving by a large department store. "Stop!" She slammed on the brakes and irate drivers honked behind them. "Sorry, just pull over and park the car." By the time she turned off the ignition he was already out of the van and she had to run after him. "Ivram I thought you said there was no money left for shopping sprees."

"Only for necessities and what we need right now is a video

camera." The prices for even the simplest cameras were insane. Ivram wondered where people got the kind of money that was required to buy all of the electronic and photographic equipment that was on display in this store. The clerk was a youngster in his mid twenties who knew all about these wonders from Japan and the cruder Russian knock-offs. He was very helpful in explaining the different features available on each model. Ivram realized that he was eager to close a sale in order to earn the commission. "I had no idea the prices would be so high," he told Tapa. "I guess we'll have to forget the whole idea and just write a letter or something."

"Don't you still have those Army vouchers? I thought I saw them in your wallet when I went to rent the van."

"Yes, I completely forgotten about those!" They had used them to charge their hotel rooms and some of their meals, joking about making the Army pay for their expenses. "Do you think the store will accept them for such a high priced purchase?"

The clerk behind the counter had been disappointed when it appeared that the couple was not about to purchase one of the cameras. Ivram motioned for him to come back and he beamed with renewed optimism. "Excuse me," Ivram began, "but I'm actually buying this camera for my job. It is so difficult to procure this type of equipment through the proper channels, I'm sure you can understand that."

"I agree, Colonel. There's just no end to the amount of bureaucratic inefficiency these days."

"Yes, well I was wondering if your store would accept a military payment voucher for this camera over here?" Ivram made a point of designating one of the more expensive models, knowing that the salesman would be even more anxious to complete the sale. "Of course I have my identification right here and if you'd like, I could dial my office."

The clerk quickly studied the identification documents. "No, Colonel Romanov, this will be just fine!"

Tapa burst out laughing when they got back into the van. "If I knew it could be that easy I'd have bought out the store!"

They drove to the train terminal and she was about to pull up in front of the baggage service area when he told her, "No, keep going! Something isn't right, there are still far too many police and other security people in the area."

"Do you think they've found the device?" She looked over at him with growing concern that their mission may have all been in vain.

"I don't think so. If they had, there would be all sorts of military vehicles and bomb units here or else they'd all be gone. No, they haven't found whatever they think they're looking for yet. The question is why are they looking for it here?"

She turned back in the direction of the guest house where she supposed they would have to regroup. He startled again her by calling out, "STOP, over there!" She couldn't figure out what he had in mind this time, then she saw the small discreet sign that read:

FILIMENKOV & SONS
FUNERAL DIRECTORS
CREMATIONS AND MORTUARY SERVICES

They both assumed somber expressions as they entered the small office of Fredrikey Filimenkov. A tall, bony gentleman in his mid to late fifties greeted them and showed them into a small office crammed with papers, supplies and assorted funerary equipment. He had raked long dark strands of hair across his head from right to left in a meager attempt at masking the overall lack of hair on top. Ivram, or rather Anatoli Romanov, explained, "I've just returned from the east with the remains of my dear sister. She died very suddenly while we were touring the southern republics. Here is the death certificate."

"Colonel, you have my most sincere sympathy. Be assured you have come to the right place. We will certainly give your sister a tasteful funeral." Filimenkov smiled thinly and nodded his head in a respectful manner that befit his profession.

"Well, you see, except for my niece here, she had no other family. We have not lived in this city for many years, but it was her dying wish that she be returned to St. Petersburg for burial. All we really require is for you to pick up her remains at the train terminal and deliver them to Saint Isaac's Cathedral tomorrow morning for a requiem and interment. We will meet you there."

Certainly, Colonel, if that is all you wish, I can arrange for it. You may, of course, want to consider a nicer coffin for her final repose than what may have been available in Qyzylorda. They have no sense of formality down there. We can also prepare her properly, if you like."

"Thank you, that is very kind of you. However, it has been several days since her death. I'm really not sure exactly what it was that caused her death or just how good those Kazakhi morticians may have been. We were forced to travel during some very hot weather. I'm sure that you are use to such things, but perhaps it would be better..."

Mr. Filimenkov understood exactly what his bereaved client was trying to convey. "Yes, yes I understand. Rest assured, sir, the coffin will not be disturbed."

They returned to the guest house and informed the owner that they had decided to stay on an extra day. Back in the room, Ivram busied himself with setting up the video camera and deciding what would be the best angle to shoot from. He wound up disassembling the bed and moving the desk and chair in front of the long wall. Streaks of sweat appeared across his shirt. Tapa said, "I knew we should have gotten you some new clothes this morning."

"Yes, I agree. It wouldn't be right to do this wearing a Russian officer's uniform. Can you run across the street and pick out a simple tee shirt or something?" While she was out he jotted down a few notes and prepared himself to make his address to the world. She came back with a dark green polo shirt and a pair of chinos. "I thought I asked for something simple," he chided her.

"Honestly, Ivram, you're about to make a statement to the entire world as a representative of the Chechen people. You don't think I'd let you do that looking like a vagabond gypsy, do you?"

He changed and took a seat behind the desk, facing the camera. Tapa had to stand in the small bathroom to hold the camera. He felt awkward and stumbled over the words. After two false starts Tapa laid down the camera and filled a glass with water. "Here, drink this slowly and we'll start all over." Ivram set the glass down and began:

"MY NAME IS GARYK IVRAMOVICH GADAYEV. I AM NOKHCHII, A CITIZEN OF THE CHECHEN REPUBLIC. MY PEOPLE HAVE BEEN CRUELLY VICTIMIZED BY THE OPPRESSIVE REGIME OF BORIS YELTSIN. WE ASKED ONLY TO LIVE AS AN INDEPENDENT NATION, BUT WE HAVE RECEIVED ONLY DEATH AND DESTRUCTION IN RESPONSE. GROZNYY, OUR CAPITAL, LIES IN RUINS. RUSSIAN TANKS AND ARTILLERY FIRE HAVE DESTROYED ITS SCHOOLS, MOSQUES AND EVEN ITS HOSPITALS. OUR CHILDREN HAVE BEEN MAIMED AND OUR WOMEN FORCED INTO UNSPEAKABLE ACTS OF VIOLENCE.

AND THIS IS NOT THE FIRST TIME THAT THE CHECHEN PEOPLE HAVE BEEN SO WANTONLY ILL-TREATED BY OUR RUSSIAN COMRADES. THERE IS A LONG HISTORY OF THE BLOOD OF OUR PEOPLE BEING SHED BY THE CLAWS OF THE BEAR. THE INFAMOUS BUTCHER, STALIN, EXILED NEARLY ALL OF OUR PEOPLE TO FORCED LABOR CAMPS. THOSE WHO SURVIVED WERE ALLOWED TO RETURN ONLY BECAUSE THE RUSSIAN INDUSTRIAL COMPLEX WAS THIRSTY FOR OUR PETROLEUM RESOURCES. THAT WAS JUST ONE OF MANY ATROCITIES THAT WE HAVE BEEN FORCED TO ENDURE FOR MORE THAN TWO CENTURIES.

BUT THE GREY WOLF IS NOT AFRAID OF THE BEAR. WE HAVE

NEVER BOWED TO RUSSIAN OPPRESSION IN THE PAST AND WE HAVE NO INTENTION OF DOING SO NOW. THAT IS WHY IT IS TIME FOR THE RUSSIAN PEOPLE TO FEEL THE SAME PAIN THAT MY PEOPLE ARE FORCED TO ENDURE. IT IS TIME THAT RUSSIAN BLOOD IS SPILLED ON RUSSIAN SOIL. IT IS TIME FOR THE WHOLE WORLD TO DEMAND THAT THE OPPRESSION OF THE CHECHEN PEOPLE AND OF ALL OTHER ETHNIC MINORITIES BE BROUGHT TO AN END.

SOME WILL SAY THAT MANY INNOCENT PEOPLE DIED IN ST. PETERSBURG TODAY. THAT IS TRUE AND IT IS UNFORTUNATE. THERE HAVE BEEN MANY INNOCENT PEOPLE WHO HAVE DIED IN CHECHNYA AS WELL. TODAY'S ACTION IS BEING DONE IN THE HOPE THAT THE DYING MAY STOP HERE.

Ivram had been speaking in Russian. He switched now to his native Nakh dialect and said, "WE SHALL NOT FORGET! WE SHALL NOT FORGIVE!"

He remained silent for a moment and then nodded to Tapa to switch the camera off. He played it back; embarrassed about the way he looked, but satisfied with what he had said. "Well, I guess that should do it," he said to her.

"Now what?" she asked. "How do we make sure that this gets broadcast anywhere?"

"Oh, that's very simple. We just deliver it to the local office of CNN!"

68

As the day stretched on Katryn's emotions were wrenched with each new lead or reported possible sighting. Her hopes would rise, only to be dashed again when the follow-up report came back negative. Borz paced the room like a caged leopard. "I should be out there looking for him. We are so useless staying here."

"I don't know what to tell you," Sergi told them late that afternoon. "Perhaps it would be best for you to get some dinner. Return to the hotel where you can get some sleep."

"You certainly don't think I could sleep tonight, do you?" Borz said it, but those were exactly the same words that were forming in Katryn's mouth as well.

"This may all be a wild goose chase, I'm afraid." Sergi had been sitting on the couch next to Katryn. He reached his arm around her shoulder and gently lifted her up as he stood. Borz followed as he walked her out of the office and down a dimly lit corridor lined with official looking wooden doors with opaque glass windows. "If he were really going to do something I would have expected to receive some advance communication by now. You know, a threat or a political statement of some sort. We've received nothing like that. I'll keep you informed of any new developments. As a matter of fact, I'll let you have this." He pulled a cell phone out of his jacket pocket and handed it to her. "I'll pick up another one."

They were standing in front of the elevator and the door slid back in response to Sergi's summons. "It's been a long day. You both could use some rest." The doors closed. Separating the two of them from Sergi.

"Well, I guess we've been dismissed," Katryn remarked a bit perturbed at having been shown the door.

"Yes, we were only in the way, I'm afraid." They were surprised by how warm it was when they stepped outside of the building. The sun was still brightly shining and a summer breeze barely stirred the leaves on the trees along the avenue. "I don't know about you, but I need to walk around a bit. The exercise will do us both some good and, who knows, we may just run into him out there." Borz turned to his right and started to walk. Katryn just naturally followed.

They roamed the streets of St. Petersburg for several hours, peering into shop after shop in the desperate hope of catching a glimpse of Garyk. They both knew it was an insane gesture in a city this size, but what else was there to do? Their walk took them back past the railroad terminal. Evening crowds hurried past them. Normal people going about the daily routines of life. Katryn wondered what would become of them if Garyk couldn't be stopped.

Across the street, two men in blue coveralls struggled to carry a casket out of the baggage office. A lanky looking gentleman in a black suit kept a watchful eye on their progress and opened the rear door of an old black panel truck to allow them to slide their cargo inside. He rewarded them for their services with a few coins dropped discreetly into the hand of one of the workers. Solemnly he walked around to the front of the vehicle, climbed in to the driver's seat and drove away. The scene barely caught his attention, but for some reason Borz felt a sudden chill as the truck moved past him on its way down the road.

"I'm sorry, Borz, I just can't walk any more. I'm exhausted."

"Yes, you're right. This is really futile, I'm afraid. They were standing in front of a small restaurant that proclaimed to have the world's finest Slavic delights. The aroma emanating from the establishment seemed to confirm the claim. Borz was suddenly very hungry. "Would you care to join me for dinner?"

Their conversation at dinner was subdued. Under different circumstances Katryn thought she would probably like Borz. In fact, she remembered him from Viktor's wedding as a rough and ready oil field worker with a warm heart and a terrific sense of humor. His presence tonight, however, was a constant reminder of Garyk and the crisis at hand. She listened to his narrative about events down in Chechnya. Reluctantly at first, but as his story evolved she began to empathize more and more with the tragic tales of Chechnya.

"I'm beginning to understand the passion of your people," she told him. "But that still doesn't justify Garyk's senseless desire to wipe out an entire city."

"Yes, I agree. That is why I am here." Borz sounded apologetic, almost embarrassed by the actions of his friend.

"You know there is considerable sentiment in Russia in support of the Chechen people. I'm certain that Garyk's action will only serve to unite the country in opposition to your quest for independence." Borz could only nod in silent agreement.

It was after ten o'clock when she retired to her room. There had been no further word from Sergi. Katryn was in the shower and almost missed hearing the phone when it rang. Still wet, she grabbed for it and it slipped out of her hand. She reached down to get it, hoping that he wouldn't hang up before she could sign on. He didn't.

"Katryn, there's been some major developments! First of all, he's finally made contact. A video cassette was dropped off at CNN's International News Bureau about an hour ago. It's a political manifesto explaining why he is doing this. He used the word 'today' twice, but there were instructions to air it tomorrow morning. Apparently it was a young woman who dropped it off, but no one can remember much about her."

"So it's going to happen tomorrow for sure," she said. Katryn was standing in the middle of her room, wet and naked. She had started to dry herself off, but Sergi's revelation made her lose track of her wetness. Her hand dropped to her side and the towel fell to the floor. She sat down on the edge of the bed. "Is there anything more?"

"Yes, and this is amazing. Apparently there had been a goddamned coffin consigned to the baggage section from that morning train. It was moved directly into a holding area when it arrived. Nobody there thought to tell us about it. Christ, can you believe that! Katryn, the name on the freight bill of lading was Anatoli fucking Romanov!"

"So you've recovered the nuclear device then," she said with a sense of relief.

"Unfortunately, no. The damned thing sat there until nearly seven this evening. Then someone arrived with a hearse and claimed it. There's a scrawled signature nobody can read. We're trying to run down every frigging funeral director in St. Petersburg right now, but most have closed for the day. It's taking us some time."

"Oh my God! Sergi, I just realized. Borz and I watched them load that damned thing as we walked by the station this evening."

"Katryn, are you sure? Can you remember the name on the hearse?"

"It wasn't a hearse, it was a truck, a black truck! There was no writing on it at all. Should I come back over there?"

"No, but this may be helpful. I still don't think anything will happen until tomorrow morning. I'll send a car around for you at 0630."

69

Tapa arrived back in the room after delivering the video cassette. She found Ivram sleeping soundly. Quickly she undressed and climbed into bed next to him. During the night she was awakened by the touch of his arm closing over her. He muttered something inaudible in his sleep and she asked "What?" Then she heard him say, "I love you, Kat." Tears filled her eyes and she cursed this woman whom she had never met.

In the morning she woke before he did and hurried into the bathroom. She was fully dressed and sitting in the chair when Ivram finally rolled over and smiled at her. Nothing was said about his subconscious declaration, but it weighed heavily upon her. "You're very quiet this morning," he remarked as they made their way down to the van.

"I guess it's that kind of day."

The tower of Saint Isaac's Cathedral rose magnificently in front of them. It was circular, splendidly colonnaded and it stood more the twice as tall as any of the surrounding buildings. A massive gold dome, crowned with a golden cupola topped the whole thing off. They found a place to leave the van several blocks away and walked back along the Neva to the cathedral. Ivram related the history of the edifice to Tapa as they approached. "The structure was commissioned by Tsar Alexander I well over 150 years ago. Can you believe this great monument to Russian Orthodoxy actually housed the Museum of Atheism! It's only recently been converted back to a religious institution."

"Okay, I'm impressed. How do you know so much about all of these different places?"

"Thank Ruslan Khasbulatov for that. When I was working for him I was required to travel extensively. I spent a lot of time wandering these cities alone."

They slowly climbed to the top of the tower, stopping along the way for him to rest his weary leg. "I'm sorry, I shouldn't have asked you to do this," she apologized.

"Of course you should have. The views from up there are spectacular!" And they were. Sweeping panoramas of St. Petersburg, the Neva
flowing in from the Southeast and to the west the Gulf of Finland.

"Ivram, it's all so very breathtaking! I've never been this high above
the ground in my entire life." They walked slowly around the upper
promenade, leaning occasionally against the ornate grille work that
protected sightseers from plunging over the brink. This allowed Ivram
a chance to tell her about yet another marvel of the city.

It was nearing ten. From the tower they watched a hearse drive
slowly around to a side chapel doorway. A figure climbed out of the
passenger seat and looked about him in all directions. He was too far
away for them to observe exactly just how nervous the poor man was,
but even from that distance they could tell he was tall and slender. It
must be Filimenko. They made their descent while the casket was
being unloaded and prepared to be carried into the cathedral.

Several pallbearers had been conscripted for this duty. As the procession entered an orthodox priest came up and greeted the funeral
director. He wore a full length black cassock, trimmed with red pip-
ing and had on the traditional black headdress of a minor cleric. A
long curly beard covered most of his face and he held his hands in
front of his chest in piety. He bowed his head politely to greet the
man. "Good morning, Mr. Filimenko I believe. The Romanov family
has requested a private chapel this morning, it will be just the two of
them and, of course, the deceased." A smile broke through the
whiskers when he said that, pleased with his attempt at a little
maudlin humor.

The cleric led them toward a small ancillary chapel, behind the
main altar. "They have specifically asked to be afforded some time
alone. I'm sure you understand. I will be back at ten-thirty to offer mass
for the deceased. Is that all right with you?"

Filimenko fidgeted a bit with a hat he was carrying and seemed ill
at ease with the situation. He looked to one of the pallbearers for guidance in this matter, finally nodding his head and saying that this would
be just fine. Once the funeral entourage had exited the chapel and
moved a discreet distance away, Ivram and Tapa proceeded into the
room.

Ivram offered up a prayer of thanks to the Almighty for seeing them
through to the culmination of this mission. Would the Almighty take
offense that he spoke to him in this strange setting, emblazoned with
statuary and the symbols of Christendom? He moved to the casket, quickly unfastening the many seals that secured the coffin cover and pulled it
open. The device was still there, intact and shielded in the protective

lead lined case they had placed it in several days before. With Tapa standing watch by the entryway, he began the procedure to disengage his security measures, activate and ultimately detonate the bomb.

He just finished keying in the commands that transferred full control of the device over to his laptop computer when Tapa called in a hushed voice, "Someone is coming. A priest, I think." He pulled down the top of the coffin and hurriedly flipped as many of the seals as he could. Then he and Tapa assumed their position as sorrowful mourners in the front pew. The laptop was held tightly at his side.

A man entered the chapel. He wore a priestly cassock, but his face was freshly shaven. Smiling broadly, he said, "Well, Garyk, it seems that fate has brought us together once again."

Tapa gasped and Ivram turned, incredulous, to see a slightly balding man about his own age. "Sergi, this is quite a surprise." Ivram was actually more confused than surprised. "I didn't realize that you'd given up the Army for the priesthood."

"Only for this morning, I'm afraid." Sergi reached into the recesses of the garment and pulled out a nine-millimeter revolver. He pointed it at Ivram. "You've given us a very big scare, my friend. It's time to bring this little game of yours to an end."

Ivram slid his hand down along the laptop and eased open the cover. From experience he ran his fingers lightly across the keyboard and depressed three keys, which triggered the activation mechanism. "It isn't over just yet, Sergi. You see I have my computer here next to me. I only have to press down ever so slightly on the ENTER key and the timing mechanism on the detonator in there will be triggered."

"Please don't do this, Garyk." It was a woman's voice, coming from just beyond the entry of the chapel. He couldn't see her but he would know the sound of that voice anywhere. It was Katryn. She moved into the room and stood behind Sergi. Another person came in with her. Borz!

"Well this is a fitting way to put an end to everything, isn't it. I must say, Katryn, you look delightful. That little outfit suits you much better than your old army uniform. I'd nearly forgotten how attractive those legs were." She was wearing a beige suit; the jacket opened at just enough of the neck to reveal a hint of cleavage and the skirt was cut several inches above her knees. "Borz, I am surprised to see you here. Are you intent on betraying your people?"

"No, not to betray them, but to spare them and to save you, too, I hope. Come, my friend and brother, don't do this thing. It's not right."

"It's the will of the Almighty."

"No, it cannot be the will of the Almighty One. Ivram, this cannot help us. Only this morning I heard that our militia is fighting to retake Groznyy. If we succeed, the Russians may be forced to concede our position. But if you do this, Ivram, the entire Russian nation, the world too, will rise up against us!"

"Please listen to him Garyk," Katryn pleaded. "I've learned a lot over the past two days about the pain and anguish you have endured. I know that I'm responsible for a lot of that. I'm sorry."

"You know nothing of pain and suffering, Katryn. You've always turned your back on it. Did you ever once shed a tear for our precious Alexandra?"

"Of course I did, but you were never home to see it. It's time to put that all behind you, Garyk. I know that if you wanted to, you could be the person to lead Chechnya into the future. Viktor tried to do that. You can complete the job for him, Garyk. You owe that to him and to his family."

"I am leading our people right now. It is time for the Russians to learn the consequences of their brutality and indifference to the plight of all Moslems. They must learn that when you shed the blood of others you must be prepared to have yours shed as well."

"And would you kill your own son for this cause of yours?"

He looked at Katryn, unsure of her meaning. ""Why? What does Georgi have to do with this, Kat?"

"He is here, Garyk. I sent for him last night." Katryn motioned outside of the chapel and the tall young man entered. His hair hung in dark curls and deep, penetrating eyes bore into Garyk. She put her arm around him and held him close to her. "He should be with his father and mother when they meet their deaths. Isn't that what you really want? To bring us all to an end."

"Father, I don't understand what all this is about. What does St. Petersburg have to do with Chechnya?"

Ivram looked at his son. He had grown so much during the past three years. It hurt him to realize how much he had missed. Katryn had denied him the opportunity to be a part of his transformation into manhood. "If Georgi is to die, then that is your doing, Katryn, not mine. What is one more ounce of Chechen blood going to mean in the vast sea of blood that your people have created? Perhaps you're right. It is better that he is here."

"I'm not a Chechen, I'm a Russian, isn't that right, mother?"

"Of course not, Georgi. You are your father's son as much as you are mine. You cannot deny your heritage, but perhaps you can bridge the gulf that has been created, not only between your father and me, but also between our two countries. Look at the future, Garyk. It is your son.

Tapa wanted to hate this woman, but she couldn't. Even though Katryn was shorter, by a good three or four inches, she was a commanding presence in the room. It wasn't just her good looks and smart clothes. She was so self-assured, so strong. Tapa understood now why Katryn had kept such a strong hold on Ivram. Or was it Garyk; she was very confused. Tapa reached for Ivram's hand and squeezed hard on it for strength.

"No, Katryn, this is the future." Garyk made a motion with his arm. Clearly, he was ready to activate the device. The room filled with the ear-piercing sound of a Magnum pistol being fired. The noise reverberated in the tiny chapel and echoed through the cavernous cathedral. It startled all of them. Tapa looked up in shock. Borz was standing in front of her, smoke streaming from the barrel of the pistol in his hand. "Please forgive me, my brother, but I could not let this thing happen." He lowered the gun, dropped to his knees and began to sob deeply.

"Oh my God, Garyk!" It was Katryn. She moved quickly to him once the initial shock had passed. Kneeling beside him, she wrapped her arms around his legs, lay her head in his lap and also began to cry. Tapa could only sit there, staring vacantly at the statue of the Blessed Virgin mounted above the altar in front of her. It seemed to float in the air, extending its arms, as if to enfold all of the participants in the tragedy unfolding in her presence.

Other officers and policemen rushed into the chapel. There was loud shouting and mass confusion echoing through the ancient cathedral. Sirens blared outside. Sergi alone seemed unmoved by all that had just transpired. He walked over to the limp body of Garyk Ivramovich. The laptop was resting on the seat next to Garyk. It had fallen shut on its side when the bullet struck Garyk and was lying in the pool of blood that was forming on the pew. He reached down and picked it up and opened it. The screen contained a digital clock display. The numbers were ticking down.

4:51
4:50
4:49

"Oh God, I think we may have a little problem here."

Katryn raised her head and saw the numbers clicking down. She bolted upright. Crimson stains covered her suit and blood was on her face and in her hair. "Sergi, we have to stop this thing! Can we disarm the device?"

"No," Tapa said softly, almost from a distant place. "Ivram told me that once he activated the timer any attempt to disarm the warhead itself would result in its immediate detonation."

"Then we must try to stop it here!" Katryn grabbed the laptop out of Sergi's hand and sat down next to Tapa. She keyed in some entries. This minimized the clock display into the upper right hand corner of the screen. The remainder of the screen now displayed:

PLEASE ENTER ACCESS CODES

```
┌─────────────────┐
│                 │
└─────────────────┘
┌─────────────────┐
│                 │
└─────────────────┘
```

Katryn looked at the young woman sitting next to her. "Did he tell you what the access codes are?"

Tapa was still dazed and disoriented. "No," she said weakly.

"Oh my God Sergi, there will never be enough time to break this code." The clock display had just clicked past 4:00.

"Try entering his name," Sergi suggested, but that only resulted in an "ACCESS DENIED" message.

Tapa seemed to be coming out of her state of bewilderment. She turned to Katryn and said, "No, try entering your name."

Katryn looked at her, wondering if she was still in shock. "What the hell!" she thought and punched in K-A-T-R-Y-N and hit ENTER. Again the screen flashed, "ACCESS DENIED." On a whim she entered K-A-T. The prompt immediately defaulted to the second access code box. "I'll be a son-of-a-bitch,' she said aloud. She looked at Tapa and asked "Now what?"

Tapa was fully cognizant now, caught up in the urgency of the moment, but unsure what she could possibly do to help. They were the experts, not her. "I have no idea. Your birthday, maybe."

Katryn tried a number of possible dates and names. None seemed to trigger anything other than denials. There was under two minutes left on the clock. No one in the room had taken a breath for some time. All eyes were focused on her, the only hope for their salvation, and she had no more ides left. "Oh what the heck," she muttered and banged out **062977**. It was their anniversary. Abruptly the screen changed from blue to green. The message read

DO YOU WISH TO TERMINATE NOW?
Y/N

She tapped the Y and it read

PROGRAM TERMINATED

The digital clock display disappeared. Around her the seven or eight people crowed into the chapel all exhaled at the same time. Without thinking she reached over and held Tapa in a firm embrace. They remained clasped together like that for some time, crying loudly over their shared loss.

Borz had taken a seat in the pew next to Ivram. Tears still streamed down his face. Sergi extended a hand to him. "Come, you did what you had to do. Don't blame yourself for this."

"Who else is there to blame? I myself introduced him to Shamil."

Katryn stood up and placed her hand on Borz' shoulder. "I think we all had a hand in this, Borz. Perhaps it was just inevitable."

"Yes, maybe this really was the will of the Almighty. Well, at least it's over now."

"This part of it is." Sergi said. "Unfortunately, there are still three nuclear warheads out there unaccounted for!"

70

Borz drove the family car. Seated beside him, his wife was holding the latest addition to their family, a young girl they had named Tatyana in honor of his sister. Their three other children fidgeted in the back seat, as adolescents are wont to do on family excursions, complaining that their siblings were not giving them enough room.

A state of uneasy peace existed in the country. The Chechen militia had in fact retaken Groznyy and the Russian forces were actually compelled to withdraw. There was an agreement with the Russians that granted them quasi-independence until the year 2001, when the whole question of Chechen independence was to be reviewed. People were going about the task of rebuilding. Borz was still required to work long hours restoring the oil fields to their former productive capacity. But now he had his family to come home to each evening, and that was all that really mattered.

The car came over the hillock, revealing the small, rock strewn valley beyond. Borz was always amazed by the serenity that this place accorded the beholder. There was a solitary structure below them. It was a simple one-story cottage surrounded by tall sunflowers in magnificent full bloom. It stood not far from where the old two-story stone house had been. Actually, the fireplace from that old building was still partially intact, surrounded by piles of stone and rubble still. Many of its stones now constituted the new building. Several goats could be seen scampering across the hillside beyond the cottage.

Borz pulled the car into the yard in front of the cottage. Across the valley, nestled against the side of the mountain, he could just make out the form of the old stone tower. He knew that beneath the tower were buried the remains of his dearest friend and true brother, Garyk Ivramovich Gadayev. He knew that because he himself had seen to it that the body had been flown back to Groznyy last year to be interred near his mother, grandmother and two centuries of Gadayev family members. Viktor's body was not there. His body had been recovered and given a state funeral not too long back in the national cemetery, beside those of his wife and children.

For the first time in more than one hundred years, eight generations to be exact, no Gadayev family lived in this valley. Well, at least not one named Gadayev anyway. There was a ninth generation here now, but the young child's name was Zagiev, his mother's name. Katryn had willingly agreed to the transfer of ownership.

Tapa heard the car tires on the loose gravel and came out of the house to greet her guests. Her son clutched at her breast, demanding more attention then she was able to give him at the moment.

Borz gave her a great hug and the two women exchanged kisses on the cheek. "Tapa, you are looking wonderful," Borz exclaimed. "I regret not getting down here sooner. With our little one coming almost at the same time as yours it was just not possible to get away."

"That's okay, Borz. I'm glad you could make it today. I want you to meet Ivram Viktor Garykovich Zagiev." She proudly held her son up for them to see.

Borz laughed and said, "My, such a long name for such a tiny infant."

"Perhaps that's true," she said. "But he will certainly grow into it. Since he could not have his father's last name, I wanted him to have everything else." It was a beautiful day, so she brought his playpen outside and set it up in the shade of the cottage. Both of the babies were placed inside it. A bond was quickly established between them and they conversed in the universal language of infants. Borz' wife had prepared a picnic lunch and they all sat together enjoying the day and the happy sounds of giggling and cooing.

When they finished eating, Tapa took Borz by the hand and led him away from the others "I will never be able to repay you for all you've done for me, Borz."

"What I did was nothing. There is no debt to be repaid. Sergi was the one who convinced the authorities not to press charges against you for the attack on the missile base. Actually I think they didn't want your allegations about those damned soldiers trying to rape you to become public."

"You are far too modest, Borz. What you did was to make me a part of your family and build this home for little Ivram and me. We have a life again, thanks to you." Tapa kissed him on the cheek, then went back to see what was making the baby fuss so much.

"Yes, at least for now, Tapa. At least for the moment. Let's just hope that the Russians are content to stay out of Chechnya so that both our children can grow up here in peace."

A sudden gust of wind moved through the valley. It sent a chill through Tapa, causing her to pull her black shawl up over her shoulders. A sense of foreboding began to well up inside of her, but just as quickly, it was dispelled by a screech of laughter coming from the two occupants of the playpen. "Now what are those two up to?"

Up in the hills beyond the stone tower a grey wolf trotted through the underbrush. She stopped upon hearing the sounds of laughter rolling up the mountainside from below. Cautiously she eyed the scene to insure that this presented no danger. Satisfied that the human activity below in no way affected her or her family, she continued to make her way through the heavy vegetation in search of an evening meal.

Two young pups scampered along behind her. They nipped at each other and bounded over the rocks and tree limbs that were seemingly placed there solely for their own amusement. After all, their kind had always populated the hills and valleys in this region and they were the rightful heirs to all of its bounty.